FOREST GODS

THE FIRE BEARERS:
BOOK TWO

by Ryan Campbell

SOFAWOLF

SAINT PAUL, MN

Forest Gods

Copyright © 2015 Ryan Campbell

Printed in the United States of America

Second Edition • POD Printing: May 2023

ISBN 978-1-936689-49-1

Sofawolf Press, Inc.
PO Box 11868
Saint Paul, MN 55111-0868
www.sofawolf.com

Cover and Interior art Copyright © 2015 by Zhivago

FOREST GODS

THE FIRE BEARERS: BOOK TWO

Ryan Campbell

Kwaee, god of the forest, has turned all his power toward the destruction of the human tribe he accuses of serving the treacherous fire god Ogya. Seeking reasons for the ancient conflict, Clay and Doto embark on a dangeous journey far outside the forest in search of savanna god Sarmu.

Meanwhile, in the human village, the healer Cloud fights new and terrifying threats from the forest and tries to help her people survive. But, at every turn she must battle prince Laughing Dog, who seeks to turn their king down a path that could lead to the end of humanity.

Both their journeys present dangers they never expected, and secrets that may have been better left buried.

CHAPTERS & ILLUSTRATIONS

*This book is for the old stories that have made us who we are
and for the storytellers who told them to us.*

Acknowledgements

Thanks first of all to my wonderful readers, Matthew Charles, Kevin Frane, Watts Martin, and Tim Susman, who very kindly put up with these books getting steadily longer.

Thanks to Sofawolf for their continued support of this series and their hard work putting out such high-quality books.

Thanks to Zhivago, the artist, for bringing this world to life once again and giving such a distinctive and beautiful style to these worlds.

Thanks to all my readers who gave the first book a chance, and especially those who gave it such kind reviews and helpful word of mouth. You're the reason I get to keep doing this.

And thanks above all, of course, to my husband David, who continues to be supportive beyond anything I deserve. The first book was released on the date of our fifth anniversary; this sequel will land just shy of our seventh. Everything that I understand of love is because of him.

—Ryan

When an Old Man Dies

First Claw, King of the People of the Savanna, was dead. As King, he had seen the rains come and pass thirty times. He had led his people through the years of flood, and then the years of drought. When the flames had destroyed their village, angry and red in the night, he had not fled, but had braved their hungry teeth to carry lost children free, dragging them out of crackling homes of mud and wood, through the millet fields that had lit up the darkness as bright as furious day. With implacable patience he had led his displaced people southward, year by year following the rains toward the great forest as the Firelands advanced and spread and buried the savanna in sand and dry stone. When fathers and sisters, aunts and sons had perished from burns, from choking on smoke, or from weariness, thirst, or exhaustion on their long journeys, the King had been by the sides of the mournful to grieve with them, to help carry their sorrow. The People of the Savanna had lost their homes, their crops, their livestock, and the land of their mothers, but yet they had their King to show them where to go, to help them take those first faltering footsteps into strange lands, to help them find food, establish new homes, and learn how to construct light, portable tents of hide and bone. Whatever else they had lost, they had their King. They had loved him, and loved him still. But now King First Claw was dead. And they did not know what to do.

Now they wept around the council fire. Now they beat the mourning on the drums, sending out their wails to the gods, their cry for the dead. They burned the King's body on the fire, sending it to Father Wem, and the smoke went up in thick black clouds. And the Teller spoke in a loud, clear voice, giving the people their final narration of the King's life, proclaiming his victories and losses, his strengths and flaws, so that all would remember their King as he was. He would live on through his people, but his people had little assurance that they would live on without him.

And so, the healer Cloud supposed in some ways it was good that they had Great Ram as their new King. The boy was consciously and deliberately like his father. He stood like him, spoke like him, carefully adopted all the same positions and opinions. In these chaotic days, that would give the people some sense of stability and continuity. But Cloud feared that that same sense of devotion had made Ram incurious and dependent. He lacked King First Claw's cunning and wisdom. And while certainly the people needed someone familiar to root them when all else changed, more than this they needed someone who could adapt and respond to that changing world.

And how that world threatened them now. The forest itself had turned against them, lashing at them with vines, raking at them with the branches of trees. Those who ventured beneath its canopy were never seen again. Many had had to disassemble their tents and dig up parts of the wooden village wall in order to move the closest homes farther away from the menacing trees. Some even wished to leave entirely, to venture out into the savanna and rebuild their lives there, but Cloud suspected they would find small comfort in the open savanna, where there was little game and less water. Here, caught between the wrath of the forest god Kwaee and the steady and unstoppable advance of Ogya, was the only place they could survive. They needed leadership. And blessing or curse, that leader was Great Ram.

The new King sat on his stool, a little ways from the fire. He attempted a serious and regal bearing, but Cloud could tell that he was drunk on palm wine and grief, his typically straightened shoulders slumping, his head nodding with the beat of the drums. She looked around for his wife, Hibiscus, who should have been at his side during this time of mourning, but did not see her anywhere.

Ram had lost a father and his brother. He would need someone by his side now, someone to show him how to be strong, so Cloud pulled her dress tighter around her shoulders and went to stand by him. She put her small hand on his back. He did not look up at her.

"A fine King he was," she offered quietly.

"And a fine father," Great Ram said, slumping toward her. She caught the stink of the wine on his breath; he was drunker than she had thought. In this moment, he was not the proud and confident young man he had become, but the vulnerable little boy she had known many rains ago, the boy who had come to her with scraped limbs or a burning fever, and, once, a dislocated shoulder. That time, his eyes had gone wide with barely-concealed pain and fear. She saw that same fear in his eyes now, and it worried her.

"Your wife is not with you," she observed. "Is she all right?"

Ram looked around the pyre and shook his head. "She was feeling tired. She went to lie down. The baby, you know."

Cloud frowned. She did not much care for Hibiscus, who was frail and wilting under the best of circumstances. While pregnancy gave some women strength and focus, Hibiscus had grown only more idle and indolent, seeming to thrive on the extra attention and special treatment her pregnancy afforded her, though she was less than two moons into it. "If she's unwell, have her come to see me. Your wife should be a comfort to you now."

Great Ram didn't seem to hear her, his gaze still distant. "She is a comfort enough, in her way. When I'm with her, I know what to do. I know how to make her pleased. But out here, in this—this—" He broke off, and when he turned to her, his eyes were liquid with drunken intensity. "I thought it would be so easy. *He* made it look easy. All I had to do was say everything he said. But now he's not here to say it. How am I supposed to know what a King would do? How did my father know?"

Cloud frowned. There were so many answers to that. You listen to those who know. You pay attention. You act carefully and with patience. And you *don't* know, not really. You make mistakes, terrible mistakes that you can't take back, that you bear with you for the rest of your life. You wear them on your shoulders and carry them in your fingers and etch them into your skin.

But what could a boy know of that? How could she explain it to him? What could she say? *You can't know, boy. You can't be a good King. Not now, not at first, no matter how much you may want to. No matter how much everyone may need you to.* That would only make things worse. She searched for the lie to tell him, the one that *would* make him a better King, but she didn't know it. She'd had an easy and comfortable rapport with his father. She'd been not only an adviser; she'd been a friend. Her advice had mingled with his questions as easily as fingers interlacing; he'd scarcely needed it most of the time. She suddenly missed him deeply. His absence from the world hatched a small wasp of pain in her throat.

Ram took her silence for an answer. "I suppose none of us will ever be the King he was."

"No," Cloud said, and listened to the word escaping her lips with a kind of panic. Before the hurt could spread too far across Great Ram's face, she added, "Not the same kind of King. A different one. You mustn't try to imitate him anymore. An imitation is never as true as the thing it mimics, you know. You must be your own kind of King. I know it will be hard."

Ram eased back on his stool. "I thought I was ready. I didn't understand what it would mean to have everyone need me to—"

"It's a hard thing. They shouldn't have to need you." Cloud squeezed at his shoulder. "It shouldn't have to be you."

"But it is. I'm the first son. And if I were gone, it would be Clay. Except that he's—" His voice broke. He stared fixedly into the flames. "There's only me. Why does the son become King anyway? Who made that rule? Why must Kings be born from Kings?"

"It wasn't always so," Cloud mused, half to herself. "My grandmother used to tell me that back in Bogana, where I was born, the eldest women would choose their King. And the People of the Savanna once had a council of elders long ago, and no King at all."

"No King at all. It sounds better to me now. I thought I wanted this before. It was all I thought about. But now…now I don't want to be all alone, having to decide what we do about the forest and food and willful brothers and—and demons."

"Decisions are easier repeated than first spoken," Cloud agreed. "But your people need consistency now. They need someone they're familiar with, someone they can trust. Everything has changed for them, and they need a guiding star to watch while they travel those changes."

Ram chewed on a lip, glowering. Then he straightened, his eyes gone bright, his voice brighter. "Why don't you do it?"

"Do it?" Cloud asked, wary. "Do what?"

"You said it yourself. Once there were councils and not Kings. And you come from a place where the women choose the King. Why don't you be their guiding star? They know you and trust you. And you advised my father."

She stared at him, astonished. He had just offered to hand rule of the People to her as though it were a meal he had no appetite for. "Ram, you don't know what you're saying."

"I do." His jaw bulged as he clenched it in determination, a habit he'd inherited from his father. "I don't want this. I'm going to have a child soon. First Claw was always too busy being King to be a father to me. You know that. Everything he did was a lesson about how to rule. But I'm not going to be that way with my son."

"A son, is it?"

"Or daughter. Whichever. So why should I be King? What have I to gain from it?"

Cloud sighed. She should have known that that question had been lurking behind his ambition. The way he'd paraded around in his finest clothes at any opportunity, the way he'd adopted officious tones when speaking to his brothers or companions, the way he'd always been eager to select the best of everything—he had never truly understood the weight of rule. "Great Ram, you cannot think being King is for *you*."

She pointed one knobbed and callused finger out into the dark, at the bowed heads around the pyre. "It's for them. You understand that, don't you? It's not a privilege. It's a responsibility. You were born to it. The gods chose you for it. And what you have to gain for it is their lives. Their happiness, if you are a good and wise King."

Ram slumped, the light going out of his eyes. "Suppose I can't be a good and wise King. Wouldn't you be better? You already know everything about it. My father listened to you half the time anyway."

Cloud toyed with the idea. Rule the People of the Savanna? Lead them through this time of darkness? Surely she, along with the other elders, had wisdom enough to guide them better than this poor, unready boy. Perhaps they could find old tales that would appease the angry forest gods. They could lay restraining admonitions against the heat and foolishness of young blood. They could ensure that the memories and traditions of the people persisted even in troubled days. But one of those traditions was that the first-born son of the King inherited his rule. People accepted it. If that were challenged now, what else might they be willing to throw out? It was a dangerous step to take.

She looked down. In the firelight, her green dress looked grey, the holes and tatters filled with caught shadows. No. She was no ruler. She was a healer. That was her duty, and to abandon it would be as careless and irresponsible as Great Ram shrugging off his royal robes.

"You know that I will help you however I can," she told him. "But you are King. That is what your people require of you now. Your father will look down on you and guide you, as will your ancestors and all those gone before you."

"All those gone before me," Ram repeated dully. "Father, Mother, uncles and aunts and grandparents. And Clay, of course. He must be dead too, surely. You must think so. Don't you?"

Cloud frowned. It was a question that had at one time or another been raised by everyone in the village, and everyone had an opinion. Most agreed with the trackers' opinions that Clay had wandered into the forest for some reason and been stalked by a leopard that had later killed him, and likely dragged him up into a tree to devour him. But the tracks had been strange. Some believed demons from the forest had lured Clay away. Others

suggested that Clay had been drawn into the darkness by jin-lights, which
were known to appear in areas with standing water.

She looked up over the southern wall of the village at the dark, shaggy
hills of the forest. A low wind stirred the shadows. She shook her head. "I
think the simplest answer is usually the true one. A leopard dragged your
brother off."

Great Ram scowled at her answer. "Dog says that he thinks Clay
might still be alive. That maybe someone kidnapped him. But there were
prints only of the hind feet of a leopard and Clay walking alongside."

"Or before, or after," Cloud reminded him.

Great Ram ignored her. "Laughing Dog says maybe someone was
wearing leopard feet to make the tracks."

"Why would someone do that?" She hadn't heard this theory before.
She knew the tracks had been strange, but tracking people or beasts through
the forest was a tricky business, like looking at shadows to guess the shape
of a thing. "I don't know, Ram. Of course it may be possible he was alive
when he was taken. But if he went into the forest, *that* forest, with how it
has been lately, I don't see how he can be alive now. The hunters we lost in
the first attack were strong and swift, and none escaped. Clay couldn't even
walk. It would be better to let him go—Ram." She caught herself. She had
nearly called him child just then. But he wasn't a child anymore. He was
King. "Focus on the people who are still here and need your help."

King Great Ram leaned toward her. His eyes were watery; the bite
of wined breath stung her nose. "I don't know how to help them, Cloud.
I don't. I've tried to ask myself what Father would have done, but he never
had to face anything like this. And when we lost Clay, even he couldn't bear
it. He shut himself away and shriveled up, and…" He trailed off, seeming
to forget what he was saying for a moment. "I know I could be a good King.
And I want to. But I need to know, Cloud. I need to know that things are
going to be all right, that the forest killing us, the drought, the famine, all
this—I need to know that if we just pray, if we make the right dances, sing
the songs the gods want us to sing, then things will be all right. I need to
hear it, Cloud."

He took her shoulder in a hand that was large and strong, roughened
by years of hunting and work. He pulled her closer. "Just tell me this is going to end," he pleaded. "Tell me Clay will come back. Tell me the gods will
forgive us for whatever we've done."

Cloud's heart ached with pity for him. She longed to console him, to
hold his head against her side as she had when he was a child. She reached
up and took his hand in hers and removed it from her shoulder, then

stepped back. "I can't, Ram. You're King now. You've got to see things for how they are. You don't get to hear that things are going to be all right anymore. Kings don't ever get to hear that."

At that, Ram sat up straighter. His face tightened, eyes narrowing in resentment. Well, fine. Let him resent her. Hate her even, if it blunted his grief. "Where is Laughing Dog?" he asked. His voice was steadier now, angry. "I want to speak with my brother."

"He is eating," Cloud answered carefully. Laughing Dog's habits had become a touchy subject of late about the camp, but so far as she knew, no one had brought their concerns to Great Ram. Hard to lodge accusations against the grieving brother of a grieving King.

"Eating," Great Ram growled. "Of course he is. He is always eating. He eats enough for three men, and this when food has become so scarce. I've tried to tell him that he is the brother of a King, and must set an example for others, but he doesn't seem to hear me."

"It does seem strange," Cloud said. It was relieving to learn that Great Ram too had noticed this. "He devours his meals like a wild beast, and when finished, he stares at people still eating like he means to attack them for their own."

Great Ram took another draught of wine from his calabash. His head would ache tomorrow, and it would only compound his misery and grief. "I caught him in the food stores," he said, his voice low.

Cloud turned toward him in shock. "What?"

"He was in there after all others were sleeping, stuffing his face with as much food as he could. Our children hunger, our hunters bring back less each day, and my brother has been devouring what little we have left."

The news was appalling, and yet, Cloud found, not surprising. She had seen the hunger that burned in Laughing Dog's eyes, the haunted expression on his face, the way that fire seemed to transfix him. "Well," she said, "he was out in the wilderness with no food or water for a very long time."

"That was what he said when I confronted him! That it was only natural that he should be so hungry. But I don't think it's natural at all. You've seen him. Does he look like a man who's been out in the savanna?"

"No," said Cloud. "He doesn't."

"He's not himself," Ram said. "It's like I've lost both brothers. Everything is being taken away from me. Everything I have, a fistful of sand." He was slipping back into his melancholy again.

"You said you wished to speak to him. I will find him for you."

The King gave her a confused, drunken stare, then nodded. He turned back toward the fire where his father's body burned. "Through my fingers," he murmured. "All of it."

〰

Laughing Dog was not eating, nor was he around the council fire. Only when Cloud ventured out of the common areas toward the tents did she find him. She recognized him more by the strangeness of his figure than by familiarity. He had grown larger in both muscle and flesh since his exile, with a breadth to his shoulders and a roundness to his middle that had not been there before. None of the other people were so heavy; scarcity of food and the effort required to find it kept them thin and lanky. Laughing Dog had a fullness to his frame that Cloud had not seen among the people since the times of plenty, when she was a girl.

He was standing a little off the path, his round back turned away from her, staring into the flame of a torch. She was about to call out his name, but then heard him speaking in low, frustrated tones. She halted on the path, scanning the village. No listener stood nearby—none that she could make out, anyway. Laughing Dog muttered as if to another person, but spoke only to himself.

"No," he said. "I've told you it won't work. You are a deceiver. A liar. I've won, and you hate me for it." A pause, as though waiting for someone else to speak. "If you could, you would have done so already. Your threats are empty." Another pause. "Yes, I have tried to convince him, but that has nothing to do with you. It is for my reasons alone. One day my people will bow to no one. Not you, nor any other." His back tightened. "That's a lie too. You do not have him. He's dead. Chew on his corpse all you like, but I know he's gone." He turned at these last words and started when he saw her standing there. "Cloud! I didn't hear you."

"But I heard you," she answered. "Who were you talking to just now?"

Laughing Dog looked afraid for a moment, but then adopted a smooth smile. "Ah," he said. "How embarrassing. I was speaking to no one, as I'm sure you can tell. I was only imagining how a conversation with someone might go, and in my head, it turned into an argument. Surely you've done that before, practiced an argument you imagined having with someone else."

"No," Cloud said. "I don't plan to argue with anyone."

"And yet somehow you always manage to disagree with everyone." The smile never left Laughing Dog's lips.

"What are you doing out here? Your father burns on his pyre as we speak, and you're not there to honor him."

That dropped the smirk from his face. "And how ought I to honor him? By watching his flesh char in the fire? Will his smoke ascend to Wem faster if I am there to witness it? Tell me, Cloud, what good will it do anyone for me to stare at my father's bones while they blacken?"

Cloud strode up to him. She had to tilt her neck to look into his face. "You honor him by being his son," she snapped. She hadn't intended to show her anger, but this was not usual for Laughing Dog. He had always been unmindful of the feelings of others, but never callous. She wanted to seize him by the shoulders and pull him back to the boy he used to be. "You honor him by being present, by showing that you care for his passing, for the traditions that he upheld, for those who grieve for him as well."

Defiance flashed in Laughing Dog's eyes. "Those traditions that you speak of brought us here, to the edge of ruin. And the people that care for him do nothing but coo to me about how beloved by all the gods he was, and the great paradises that await him."

"Which you think untrue?"

He snorted. "I think if he were truly beloved by the gods, they would not have sent a beast to murder him. They would not have ordered the forest to take his son and his hunters, nor stranded us here to starve in the first place. If I must judge honestly, Cloud, then by what I see of this world, the gods hated my father, and his spirit does not rise on the smoke to Wem. It simply fades as his body burns." His eyes brimmed unexpectedly. "I can't be at that fire, Cloud. I can't watch everything that I loved about my father disappear while people attempt to comfort me with their favorite lies."

Cloud could muster no response to this. It was not the usual arrogance she expected from Laughing Dog. His words were instead full of bitterness and despair, the words of a man who had lost his footing in the dark. "I'm sorry," she said. "I'm sorry for what's happened to you." She put her hand on his arm, and he flinched slightly at her touch. "Try not to be alone. It will help."

"I'm never alone," Laughing Dog said, his lip curling in bitterness. "Never."

She frowned at the odd remark and withdrew her hand. "Your brother seeks you."

"Well then, I had better not keep the King waiting, had I? No doubt he will try to make me feel as though Father never left." He stepped past her and headed toward the council fire, and she followed after.

As they circled the fire, several approached Laughing Dog to take his arm and offer him consolation. They told him tales of how the old King had helped them through hard times, offering aid when they were in need, reminding them to keep strong through the journeys south every time the rains skipped a year, every time they had to journey farther and farther from home in search of food and water. Some spoke of how First Claw had given them his own food when they hungered, or carried children when they were too weary to walk. He would never be forgotten. Laughing Dog smiled thin smiles and thanked them for their kind words, excusing himself, as he needed to speak to his brother.

Others wanted to know what Great Ram intended to do about the forest, and these he dismissed with a shrug and said he was certain they would all know as soon as he did.

The King was slouching on his stool when they reached him, his eyes watering. "There you are, Dog," he slurred. "Glad you could bother to show up to say g'bye to Father."

"I said my goodbyes already," Laughing Dog answered stiffly. "I was there beside him when he died."

Great Ram squinted up at him. "Yes, you were there, weren't you? So very strange that you didn't see the beast that killed him. Seeing as how you were right there."

Cloud had to bite her tongue to keep from interjecting. This matter might be between brothers, but Ram's comments were foolish and cruel. Laughing Dog was growing angry, his fingers clenching into fists at his side.

"I curse myself again and again that I did not see it," he said. "But as I said, the animal knocked me to the ground. It seized the back of my head. Were not my hair so thick, it would no doubt have torn open my skull with its jaws. I chew on the events over and over in my mind, trying to understand what happened, why it was I could not see the beast, why I could not save Father. I heard it growl, Ram. I turned to look, and there was nothing there. It had to be a trick of Kwaee. It had to be. I see no other option."

There was the desperate strain of truth in Laughing Dog's voice, Cloud noted. She knew the timbre of his lies from his boyhood, smooth and self-assured. He had not been lying when he had spoken of his time in the savanna, but he had not been telling the whole truth either; she was certain of that. But whatever had happened the night of King First Claw's murder genuinely perplexed and frightened him.

Ram, too, seemed surprised by his brother's conviction, his wet eyes blinking. He looked down at his mostly emptied calabash, and then let the remaining palm wine spill out into the earth. "I'm sorry, Dog. I just. It just. He was just gone, and none of it makes any sense, and I just want to understand. And then, you have been strange since you came back. You know that? Very strange. Everyone's been talking about it. You should know."

"Everyone who?" Laughing Dog asked, his face even.

Ram shook his head. "Everyone. Everyone."

"I was exiled. I experienced epiphany. The gods spoke to me. How could that not make a man strange?" Here again, Cloud observed the impassioned urgency of truth. "And now I come back to find the forest is attacking our people, and our brother kidnapped, our father murdered. Ram, how am I supposed to act? What's the normal way to respond to something like that?"

"No," said Great Ram. "No, you're right. That's why I wanted to see you. Tomorrow. Tomorrow night, there will be council with the elders. We'll decide what to do about the forest."

"I have told you what must be done," Laughing Dog began, his voice raised, but Great Ram held up his hand.

"I know. I know what you think. That's why I want you to come, even though you're not an elder. You have...points." Ram swayed on his stool. "Important points. They should hear them." He made a face. "Too much wine. This is the last time I have this much wine, the very last. Cloud, why did you let me?"

Cloud came forward, stepping between the two brothers. "You are King," she said. "I can't tell you what to do anymore. I can warn you, as I did, but I can't stop you, even if it will make you sorry the next day."

Great Ram rubbed at his eyes with one hand. "Then give me something for tomorrow, so I will not be so sorry."

She wanted to agree. The poor boy suffered, his father dead, his people in jeopardy. But now was not the time for him to learn he could avoid consequences. Soon he would be making decisions about the lives of his people. The pain of a bad decision there would be one she could never alleviate. "I can't," she told him. "The herbs I could give you come from the forest. If we run out of those, I can't get more. I need to carefully conserve them for people who will not be healed by time and rest."

"You see that?" Great Ram said to Laughing Dog. "You become King, and suddenly all you hear from people is what they can't do." He scowled at Cloud. "Fine then. You're dismissed. But you will come to that council meeting. I'm guessing you won't be as stingy with your advice as you are with your medicines. As usual."

She nodded. "I will be there. Rest well, King Great Ram." She looked back as she left. Laughing Dog and Great Ram were talking to each other in low, impassioned tones. Laughing Dog nodded at something and gripped Great Ram's shoulder and arm in fervent, filial affection.

She tried to fight the rising sense of uneasiness in her heart.

There was little shade at the council, and many of the elders grumbled their displeasure. Normally, large fronds and leaves could be propped up on poles to provide shade, but with the forest in revolt, even leaves were in short supply. The morning was still early, but the ground was already so hot from the sun that Cloud elected to wear her slippers: little sleeves of antelope hide that protected her soles from the burning heat of the earth and stone. She settled herself down on a log two seats away from Great Ram's stool, not so close as to seem presumptuous, but close enough that she could look him in the eye when she spoke to him—close enough that all would know she meant to have his ear.

The Teller settled down on a log across from her, shuffling his blue robes and rubbing the sweat from his face and balding head. He gave her a quiet nod, and she returned it. At the very least, he could be counted on not to oppose her position. The Teller seldom spoke at council meetings; instead he listened and observed, and sometimes threads of their discussions and decisions would weave their way into his tales.

Other elders arrived and sat around the circle, a few bringing their own shade, propping up hides on sticks to make a little square of shelter under which they could sit or recline. Cloud noted with satisfaction the assembly of greyed and balding heads. It was good to have so many weathered tempers present. Councils were not intimate business, but neither were they public. Only the oldest and most venerated members of the village were permitted to sit and advise the King. How could it be any other way? Who knew best the turns of the stars across the back of Father Wem, the tug of a weaving thorn, the trace of a thousand tracks across the savanna? Only those who had followed those tracks, pulled those thorns, traced those stars a thousand times beyond counting. Those who had lived through the fat and the lean, the fires and floods, and found truths in each of them—they would provide the King his best counsel.

From beyond Cloud's tent, Laughing Dog strode up, his gait powerful and purposeful. "King Great Ram will be here soon," he said in a loud voice. "He begs your indulgence as he prepares." He looked back and forth among the elders as though expecting praise or thanks for reporting this information, and when no reply came, scowled and planted himself on the log just to the left of the King's stool. Cloud was unsurprised to see him take the presumptive spot, but she could not suppress a small frown at his audacity. He had made even the act of announcing the King a calculation, a move to establish himself as a more intimate confidant than the rest of them. Then again, she'd done the same by choosing her seat.

Some time passed before their new King finally appeared. His gait was unsteady, his dark skin slick with sweat. Ram had been in the habit of wearing his royal finery whenever he had the opportunity, but he was not wearing it today. Cloud wondered whether the events of the last few days had caused kingliness to lose some of its luster. Or perhaps he was merely too hot and unwell to suffer much clothing this morning. He was wearing a hood, at least, to shade his eyes from the sunlight. He sat on his stool, hunching forward, barely acknowledging the council. People remained silent until he spoke. "Welcome, council. Thank you for joining me this morning."

The words were half-groan. Cloud pitied him now. She had never overindulged on palm wine, but her husband had been fond of it, and she had listened to his symptoms and treated his complaints as well as she was able. She wished she could have spared some willow bark for Great Ram.

"It is a hard time to lose a King," Ram said. "Much more a father, a friend, a voice of wisdom in these troubled times. And they are troubled. The land turns against us. The trees try to murder us. We have water, true, but food is scarcer." He leaned his head forward and rubbed at his temples with both hands. "Medicine and leaves, twine and wood are scarcer. On the savanna, these things were not so common as to be easily found, but at least when we found them *there*, we felt safe to take them. Here, anything that comes from tree or bush may be a danger."

Another elder cleared his throat. "The farther from the forest we move, the safer the plants seem to be." That was Bad Water, a man who had seemed old to Cloud when she was a girl. He sucked at his two remaining teeth with smacking sounds. "It's not all plants, but only those of the forest that oppose us. We could move away from the woods. Not back where we came from, but just a little distance. Enough to find new game tracks and more safe plants and trees."

"Retreat is a resolution I must consider," Ram said. Laughing Dog leaned up as if to speak, but the King firmly waved him back down. "A resolution among many. Still, we have no assurance that the curse of the forest will not follow us there. And scouts have been sent in journeys several days, both to morning sun and evening sun. As far as they traveled, the forest struck out against them."

Mosquito spoke; like the humming of her namesake, her voice was high and thin. "Who is to say the forest is behaving strangely? In the home we remember, there were times of great rain, and times of no rain. Here it rains every day. Perhaps here there are times when the forest is angry, and times when it is not. None of us have ever lived near the forest."

Cloud turned to the Teller. "Do you know, or have you heard, of any tales about an angry forest?"

The Teller drummed his fingers against his staff, considering, his forehead creased in a deep frown. "I have not heard such a tale," he said after a long pause. "But there may have been. The savanna has many old stories that were carried away from the lips of their tellers by the breath of Father Wem. We have forgotten much. But if a forest like this has been seen before, no tales of it have come to me. Remember now what we thought and felt when we saw it for the first time, after years on the savanna? We could not believe our eyes, to see so much green. Even the existence of forests had faded from many of our tales, and now, living here, we begin to remember them. But we remember the gods even when we forget the places. Mpo, whose great water few of us have seen. Atekye and Asubonten. And we remember Kwaee, god of the forest."

Across the circle, Cloud saw Laughing Dog bare his teeth like a snarling animal, but the Teller did not seem to notice.

"We remember that Kwaee is a harsh god, and easily displeased, but…" The Teller wavered, his gaze going distant and troubled.

"Tell us, keeper of the people," Bad Water said, and Mosquito and Great Ram echoed him. Cloud did not; when the Teller paused, it was sometimes because he expected this request from his listeners, and all in attendance would urge him to continue with his story. But Cloud saw the worry calling from the squint of his eyes and the shake of his hands.

"No," he said, shaking his head. "It is only an old memory. I don't recall it clearly enough."

Great Ram sat upright, the sour of last night's wine twisting his face into irritation. "If you remember anything at all, you should speak it. Perhaps we can discern meaning in it that you cannot."

The Teller shook his head. "It is a faded memory, lost for not being told. But when I was a very young boy, there were older tales of Kwaee. Nightmare tales, told to frighten. In them, Kwaee was the shadow, the monster. He had done a terrible thing. I don't remember this thing. I should not be telling it; stories unremembered are lies. But I was very frightened of Kwaee for a long time."

"And in the Teller's unremembered tales, we see the truth of it," Laughing Dog shouted, jumping to his feet. "It has been too long. We have lost Kwaee's true nature in the stories. Now we live here, we see he is an angry and murderous god."

"Laughing Dog!" Cloud called out. She could not put quite as much reproach into the name as she intended; by now, she expected these sorts of outbursts.

He ignored her. "I challenge anyone to show me how I am wrong! A forest beast attacked your King, and another has apparently taken our brother, and perhaps killed him too. The wood threatens and punishes us, and for what? Who among you can name an offense? Have we sullied the great Lord Kwaee's name? Have we insulted him? Disrespected his ground or his creatures?" Laughing Dog stared around the circle, meeting each of the elders in the eyes. "Go on, tell us what we have done to earn this retribution."

Cloud spoke quietly. "I recall one young man who would not bless his spears nor anything he took from the forest."

"Yes," Laughing Dog said, fixing his gaze on her. He was shaking with conviction. "One foolish boy makes a small error. For this he will destroy an entire people? Has no boy in the history of our people ever erred before? Should we be grateful that no one fool has brought down the wrath of the gods on all of us by now?"

"Yes, we should," Mosquito chirped. "We all know that the gods are above us in power and thought. They made us, and it is by their grace we survive. If they choose to unmake is, that is within their power and right. Who are we to challenge that? Who are you?"

"I am a man who wants to stay alive," Laughing Dog said. "I am a man who mourns his father and brother, who fears that his people might not survive. Do I not have that right? When we bless our spears and arrows and hunt, the antelope does not die easy. If it is the will of the gods that he die, why does he bellow and kick? Why does he run and struggle to survive? It's his right to try, to fight for life. And that is my right too." He thumped at his chest with one fist. "It's a right that belongs to all of us. We will spit in the face of any foe that tries to destroy us. We will do our best to pierce its heart, be it animal, human, or even god. It is in our nature, the nature the gods gave to us when they made us. How then can it be wrong?"

The council sat in silence, the elders looking back and forth at each other. Laughing Dog stood, broad chest heaving with emotion, his fists clenched at his sides, and then he sat down, frowning intently at the others.

"The boy is right," Bad Water said. He straightened his curved back to meet his fellow elders in the eye. "Everything struggles for survival, and so must we. Perhaps it is a show of strength Kwaee looks for and would respect. The forest's a dangerous place. Maybe it respects danger. Think of a lion. It's stronger than a man, but when we confront it, we don't lie down and show our bellies to it and hope it thinks kindly of us. No, we show it our strength. We shout and shake our spears and show it we're dangerous, and the lion goes away in respect."

"A god is not a lion," Cloud said severely.

"How do you know?" Bad Water smiled. "We have never seen them. Anyway, why shouldn't we try? Back in the savanna, when the droughts came, we prayed and prayed for water, but the gods sent fire instead of rain. Why? Didn't our prayers please them? Why did they ignore us?"

"Because the gods are unknowable," Great Ram said. "You know this. The Teller has told us over and over that we shouldn't presume to know the minds of the gods, that it isn't our place to question them."

"But that's what you're all doing!" Laughing Dog burst out. "Who says the gods want prayer and worship? Who says they listen to us at all? Why do you presume to know their minds about this?"

Cloud shook her head slowly. "The stories guide us, Laughing Dog. Through them, our ancestors show us the way forward when it's dark. Would you forget all their wisdom? Would you just cast aside the knowledge of the ages?" She snorted. "You think you have learned more in the scant few rains you have seen than the memory of all those built up over hundreds?"

Laughing Dog took a deep breath. "Do you know what this vaunted knowledge of the ages has done in my lifetime?" His voice had gone still and quiet. "It took my mother. It let my friends die of drought. It burned our homes. It sent us on a long walk across the savanna in search of water and killed more of us. It dumped us here on the edge of this forest, condemned me to exile, and now has abandoned us to the mercies of a cruel god who seeks to starve and murder us. What else could this knowledge wish us to suffer?"

The council was quiet again. Then, at the side of the circle opposite Great Ram, a figure leaned up, wrapped in a cloak stained black with age. The woman was Two Broken Hands. She was very old, the eldest of all the council, so ancient Bad Water by comparison seemed youthful and vigorous. Her head was round and mostly bald, the hair still clinging to it wispy-white. "Sacrifice." Her voice was the slither of a serpent across the sand.

"What?" Laughing Dog asked, staring at her.

Cloud's skin prickled. She had never liked Two Broken Hands, although like Cloud's parents, she had come from Bogana, the village by the great water. But she was a woman born into violence, and darkness was always in her thoughts. She followed the old ways, true, but not all the old ways were wise. "The people do not sacrifice," Cloud said. "Not blood."

"And where are the people now?" Two Broken Hands leered from beneath her cloak. Her neck shook with the effort of holding her heavy head upright, making the skin shake like the wattles of a guineafowl. "Starving. Dying. We remember what the gods demand. Not prayer alone. Not mere words. Action."

Great Ram put his hands on his knees. "No," he said. "We'll have no more talk of this. I will not hear of those dark times, nor move our people to it."

Two Broken Hands bowed her head. "As you wish," she said. "But remember who committed the offense. Remember who made everything wrong." She lifted her hand, the knuckles swollen with arthritis, and pointed at Laughing Dog. "Him. He will be all our downfall. The forest god craves his blood. You should spill it for him."

"I said that's enough!" Great Ram shouted. "No more talk of sacrifice. We will not consider it."

"You will," Two Broken Hands rasped. "You will."

Great Ram rose to his feet. "This council is ended. There will be no action taken against the forest. We will redouble our devotion to Kwaee. There will be extra prayers and dances done in his name. We must all prove to him that we honor and worship him. That is the will of the King. Is it understood?"

"It is understood," Cloud said, and the council repeated the words with her. She felt relief wash over her, though it was tinged with worry. Two Broken Hands' words were like a little poison seed dropped from her lips. The seed could not be taken back. It would sprout and grow.

She got up to leave and as she did so, caught Laughing Dog's expression. He was staring fixedly at Two Broken Hands, his face puffed and darkened in abject hatred.

Paradise Lost

"How large can the savanna be?" Doto panted between the words. His steps were slow and stumbling, toes dragging against the ground.

Clay looked back at him. They had been traveling for only two days, and already the god was exhausted. Stepping through the wall between the forest and savanna had been uncomfortable and disorienting for Clay, but it had been devastating for Doto. Without the magic of the forest surrounding him and sustaining him, he'd barely known how to walk. He still moved with the feline grace of a leopard, but the supernatural power and swiftness that guided his limbs was gone. Frequently he stumbled and fell, and though this happened less often now, he still cried out in surprise or growled at his disorientation each time.

"We don't know how large it is," Clay said. "If we traveled for perhaps a moon, we might reach the Firelands." He noticed Doto's ears flattening at the mention of the great desert. "But I would die long before we reached it. The closer you get, the less water there is. Much, much farther away, many moons of travel, to the west, the savanna meets the great water. No one I know has ever seen it, but they say it is like a pond that covers the world, and in all directions it has no end."

"I have seen the great water," Doto said, managing to sound scornful even while panting. "It is just very wet. If you are not impressed with being wet, then you will not think much of it. And you can be wet in the forest, you know. It rains, and there are rivers and swamps."

Clay turned away so Doto would not see his smile. The god's little jealousies had once been alarming to him, but lately he found them reassuring. His god didn't want to lose him. "Some tales say there is another great water, far, far to the east, but I don't know if that is true. As far east as you can go, there is nothing but more savanna. Maybe it too has no end."

"It has an end," Doto said. "All the savanna was once forest. If the forest had no end, my father would never have needed fear Ogya. His power would have been ceaseless." He stopped, resting his paws on his knees, and panted, pink tongue bobbing between his fangs. "I think we should stop for a while," he said. "You are no doubt tired."

"All right." Clay came by his side and sat down on the hard earth next to Doto. "I can use this time to work on a spear." He laid the acacia branch he had been carrying across his knees and began stripping the thorns away with a flat-edged rock.

Doto leaned closer in curiosity, then sat next to him, curling his tail behind Clay's back. "What are you doing? Are you making a stone tooth? Why?"

Clay grunted with the effort as he ground the points off of the more stubborn thorns. "So that we can catch food," he said. "I don't know what we'll find out here, but hopefully something. Hares, maybe, though they can be difficult to fell with a spear. But there are many different things to eat on the savanna. Warthog, ostrich, antelope. We just need to be patient and lucky." He sighed at his rough spear. "I'll have to use slate for the spearhead. Flint would be much better, but it's harder to find, and takes a long time to shape."

Doto lifted his head. "I will catch food for you," he announced. "I do not need a tooth stick. I have proper teeth, useful teeth. It is a sad thing to be a meat eater and have flat little teeth like yours."

"If you are able to catch food," Clay said cautiously, not wishing to offend Doto, "then that could help. But it's not right for a god of the forest to go running around in the savanna chasing down prey. I was born here. You should let me try." It would do no good to point out that Doto would be all but useless. Clay didn't think Doto could even creep up on game out here, much less kill it. And the thought of the god injuring himself at the kick of an antelope hoof or the gore of a wildebeest tusk was alarming. Doto said he couldn't die even out here, but Clay was in no haste to learn whether that claim was true or simply more of his boasting.

"Very well then. Even though you are a tiny part god now as well. Still much less god than I am. You may try." Doto settled back down, looking relieved. "But I can still hear and smell the beasts before you can. I'll let you know where they are. And we should ask if they know where Sarmu is before we kill them."

Clay gouged notches in the end of his branch. "Still no luck in finding him, then?" Clay asked.

Doto's shoulders slumped. "In the forest, I could find any god by feeling the power in the ground and air and plants. It was easy, like feeling water flowing under your fingers. Here I can feel nothing except the heat. And there are bad feelings in my legs and back and paws. I don't like them."

"Bad feelings? Like what?"

"I don't know," Doto growled. "Bad feelings. How do you explain a feeling? It…it…"

"Hurts?" Clay suggested.

"Yes," Doto said, surprise straining his voice. "A little. Only Kwaee has ever hurt me before. Why does it hurt?"

"You're tired. And probably hungry. Why don't you rest? I'll try to find food on my own." With a strong, thin vine that he'd gathered from the forest before they'd left, he bound his jagged piece of slate to the branch. It was not a good spear, but he was a good hunter.

He held it out, balanced on both hands, and closed his eyes. "Spear, with your permission I took you from the acacia, and with your permission I carved you into the shape of a spear. Now with your permission—"

"What are you doing?" Doto said in a loud voice.

Clay opened his eyes. The leopard was crouched right before him, brow furrowed in a look of puzzlement. "I'm blessing my spear," he said.

"Why? What do you mean, blessing it?"

"I'm asking it to—"

"You're talking to a piece of wood?" Doto snorted. "That is stupid. Wood does not have ears to listen. It cannot hear you. You must stop doing this stupid thing."

Clay felt a rising panic at this challenge to his people's traditions, but reminded himself that a god would have no reason to bless anything. "I'm praying to the spirit of the wood," he said, "asking it to agree to be used as a spear. If I don't, then I disrespect the tree it came from by taking from it without asking. The spear may not fly true, or it may break. That's how I hurt my foot." He looked down at it, tracing his fingertips over the healed brown flesh that, in the forest, had become a leopard's paw, but was now human once more.

Doto sat back. "You are commanding the wood as I command it," he said. "The words are not important. You send your will into the wood and guide it. Only gods can do this, but now you are part god, so you have learned it. You are clever to have figured out how to do this, but it will not work outside the forest."

"It's not because I'm a god," Clay said. "All my people do this."

Doto looked down the bridge of his muzzle. "Then they are wasting their time," he said coolly. "Only gods speak to the spirits of the world."

"Maybe fire bearers are different," Clay suggested.

"*You* are different. You have god magic in you. When we go back to the forest, I will teach you more. I will show you how to use it to make it obey you as it obeys me. You only have a tiny bit, so it will not work very well, but it will work. But not here, in the savanna. My magic is not here. Talk to your little stick if you wish, but it will not do anything."

Clay smiled. "Sometime I would like to see how well you and Laughing Dog would get along. He's my brother. He talks a little like you sometimes."

"But he is not a god," Doto reminded him.

"No," Clay agreed. "Though sometimes he thinks he is." He sobered then, remembering that Laughing Dog had been exiled, sent to wander the wilderness until he learned humility from the gods. Was Laughing Dog returned yet, safe among his people once more? Clay doubted it. Teaching Laughing Dog to respect the gods would be harder than teaching a mongoose to fly.

"That is a foolish thing to think," Doto said. He sat down once more, tail curling over his toes. "Perhaps some god will come along and teach him a lesson."

"Let's hope so," Clay said. "He needs it." He closed his eyes and finished his blessing of the spear silently. "All right. I'll go find us something to eat." He stood to go.

"Wait!" Softly furred fingers gripped at his ankle, the leathery pads of Doto's fingertips rough against his skin. Doto looked up at him, his ears folded back, his gold-green eyes wide. "Don't leave me here."

Clay ran his fingers through the soft, spotted fur on Doto's head. "There's nothing around that can hurt you. I won't go far."

Doto tilted his head, the tip of his tail switching. He gripped more tightly, his claws pricking at Clay's skin. Then he let go. "Of course nothing here can hurt me," he said with a sniff of indignation. "I am only concerned for your safety. You are my worshiper, after all. I must care for you. It will please me to have you hunt for me. I am hungry." He sounded his usual commanding, assuming self, but notes of frightened desperation strained his voice. "But I could go with you."

"It's better if you wait here," Clay said. "I'll find food. It might take a while." He gently disengaged his leg from Doto's grip and stepped away, waiting for another protest or complaint, but none came. Doto curled his tail over his paws once more and sat still. When Clay looked over one shoulder, he was sitting there still, his spots blending him into the brush and earth of the savanna, though not supernaturally so, as they had in the forest.

Stepping softly, Clay headed out, feeling the hot, baked earth of the savanna under soles that had become accustomed to the cooler and softer ground in the forest. Well, one foot had, at least. The other was new, the brown skin that covered it lighter in color, like a newborn's, and delicate to the touch. He limped a little on it still, the sole not callused and toughened against the harsh soil. He wished he had a pair of bark and leather soles to protect his feet, like his people used sometimes to travel harsh terrain, but he would have to do without. He was grateful just to have a foot once more, to be able to walk without the aid of a stick, to run, even. When he had left the forest, the magic that had given his foot the shape of a leopard's paw had left it, but rather than withering into the stump it had been before, his foot had reformed in human shape. Even Doto did not seem to know why. The magic of the gods seemed unpredictable. Did Kwaee know the effect of his power before he used it? Did Father Wem? Clay considered for the first time that perhaps even the gods did not always know what would happen.

So much of what he had understood had changed. The gods were irascible, even fallible. Some seemed to know of humans and think fondly of them, as had the river god Asubonten, and some, like Kwaee, hated them. And the gods fought with each other, battled. Kwaee and the fire god, Ogya, had apparently been at odds for rains beyond counting, and beyond the memory of all peoples. In no tales that Clay had ever heard had their hatred for each other been recorded. He would have so much to tell his people when he returned.

His people. Again his heart ached for home. It was not a home that he had lived in very long; most rains of his life had been spent in a long migration across the savanna in search of food and water, his people carrying the remnants of their old lives on their backs, building camps and staying for a year, then traveling on again when the rainy season did not come. But though he had not even lived at the edge of the forest for more than six moons, he longed to return. Home was the familiar walls of the camp, the rich, leathery scent of his tent, the stink of Cloud's incense. It was the sound of Broken Calabash's flute, and Great Ram's insufferable severity, and Laughing Dog's wit and mischief. It was the Teller's tales around council fires and the gruff smile of his father. Dances, the sizzle of spiced meat cooking, the continual hammer of spears and arrowheads being shaped.

For the first time in more than a moon, he was away from Doto and all the excitement and adventure the god represented. Clay had developed a deep fondness for him that went beyond worship, but it was nice, for once, not to be pelted with indignant and judgmental questions and observations about everything. For now, just for a time, it was pleasant to walk in the silence of the savanna and think of home.

He wondered, though, what home there would be to return to. Kwaee had turned the forest against humans. It would attack them if they ventured beyond its borders. The thought crawled like a spider up his spine: that part of the camp had been situated inside the forest, including his own tent. Could people have been hurt, even killed? He couldn't let himself think of such things now. There was no way to know and no way to do anything about it if he did know. He and Doto were doing what they needed to do: finding Sarmu. If anyone knew the source of Kwaee's rage against the fire bearers or the events of the conflict with Ogya, it would be the savanna god. He might be able to give them the answers they needed to calm Kwaee. If they could soothe the forest god and quell his fury toward humans, then all would be well, his people would be saved, and he and Doto could be together.

He looked back. Doto was still faintly visible, a small speck sitting alone in the middle of the savanna, barely distinguishable from a scrub of grass. Clay pitied him, suffering out here, away from the rush of life in the forest. He reached up to close his fingers around the leopard-shaped, wooden fetish that hung from his neck, remembering again the way his senses had keened when he wore it, the way the forest had spoken to him, responded to him, and bent around him. Wearing it, he had felt more a part of the forest than he had ever felt part of anything before. The energy of the world had flowed through him, given him life. And then he had stepped through the boundary into the savanna, and it had all gone away. It was stifling, like being smothered under hot cloth, all his senses numbed. If he was feeling this, with the small fraction of a god's power he had been granted, what must it be like for Doto? If Clay missed home, how much more must Doto long for his? But the god had ventured out of the forest, out of safety and power and comfort, and all for him.

A twitch of movement arrested his attention. Careful not to move too quickly, he turned his head. A fat monitor lizard sprawled on a rock, its jaws gaping slightly, its body a yellowish grey that made it blend into the rock almost perfectly. It was unusual to see monitors out in the heat of the day; this one must have scrambled out of its hole in search of a meal. It was a large one, as long as Clay's arm, with thick limbs, and would make good eating. Its forked tongue fanned the air, scenting him. Clay steadily lifted his spear. If there were any sudden movement, or if it spotted a bird of prey overhead, it would disappear in an instant. With a quick thrust, he skewered the lizard in its belly—it hissed and flailed its limbs and tail, flopping off the rock and onto the ground. Then it twitched and was still. He prodded it a few times with the butt of his spear to make sure it was dead. Monitors had a savage, nasty bite, and they did not let go easily.

With the heavy lizard slung over one shoulder, he headed back to Doto, relying on the sun to lead him to the spot, now indistinct from the brush of the savanna, where his leopard god still sat. Perhaps the meal would lift Doto's spirits. He'd been interested in neither dancing nor mating since they left the forest.

Mating. Clay's ears burned hot at the thought of it. How had it come to that? Everything about it should have been wrong: Doto was not only not one of the people, he was a god. To lie with him was sacrilege, to say nothing of lying with another male. The gods themselves opposed it. Clay thought of his nights before meeting Doto, lying in his tent, awake and aching with need and no place to direct it. The girls had not appealed to him; he had never sought their attentions, and they laughed about him and called him frightened and shy and strange. It was thoughts of Left Rabbit, the hunter, thoughts of his strong body and kind smile that had filled Clay's mind and left it burning into the night with energetic and confused arousal.

All said the gods forbade the joining of two males, and above anything else, Clay had wished to obey and please the gods, so he had quietly dismissed the unwanted desires, using his devotion to push them out of the way into the corners of his mind. But then a god had requested—no, demanded—that Clay lie with him, and in an instant all those thoughts that had been crowded away had come rushing back into his mind. Devotion did not prohibit his desires; it insisted upon them. Clay had yielded to Doto so swiftly and eagerly that it left him breathless, and there, in the arms of his private god, he'd found rapture. The mating had been rough and ecstatic, half-animal, half-divine. Was this what all men felt in the grip of passion? Clay thought not. Surely nothing could compare with being clutched and filled and caressed by a god, feeling his magic flow through you and into the world around you, his strength above you, sliding against your back, his breath in your hair, on your cheek, his heat inside you. Clay yearned to feel it again and again. No one else among his people could ever have experienced that.

There had been no mating since they entered the savanna though, nor dancing. Doto was listless and miserable without the connection to his forest to fill and sustain him.

Clay could see him now, sitting where Clay had left him in the grasses, watching him with that steady, patient gaze, ears tilted toward him. Clay waved to him, and unslung the lizard from his shoulder to show Doto his catch. The leopard's pink tongue licked at his jaws.

When Clay reached him and dropped the carcass, Doto fell on it, sinking his fangs into the scaled flank and tearing away a whole leg with a popping and ripping sound. Clay turned away, repulsed at the sight. Doto could seem so human at times, so like Clay. But then he would do savage or unfeeling things that left no question as to his true nature. He was not human. He was beast and god.

The wet and crunching sounds of eating had stopped. Clay turned. Doto sat, lifting the heavy lizard toward him, his ears back, an unusually meek expression on his bloodstained muzzle. He licked his jaws and lifted the carcass a little higher. "I was hungry," he said. "I forgot. It's your kill. You must be hungry too." He lowered his head.

"It's all right," Clay said. "I need to cook my part anyway. You should really cook yours too. What if the forest magic doesn't protect you from getting sick?"

Doto sniffed at the half-gnawed monitor leg. "I don't need magic to protect me. Of all the animals, only fire bearers have to cook their food, and even without my magic, I am not a fire bearer. I will not be sick." He looked around as if confirming he wasn't being watched. "You may make a fire," he decided, "though I don't like Ogya being able to spy on us through it. His power may be greater here on the savanna than in the forest."

Clay nodded and, feeling the weariness in his bones, got up to find something to burn. It wouldn't be too difficult. There was little wood here, but many dry grasses and shrubs. The fire would not last through the night, most likely, but it would be enough to cook food.

"Clay," Doto said. "Thank you for coming back. When you went to find food."

"Of course I came back!" Clay said in surprise. "I couldn't leave you."

"Yes, you could. I took you from your nest. I made you walk across the forest when you were hurt and hungry and tired, and I did not care that it hurt you. I would not let you leave. Now I am weak and tired, and I do not know where I am. You could leave. You could run away and stay out of the forest and I would never find you." His gold-green eyes were earnest. "I thought that you might do that."

"Oh, Doto." Clay reached out and combed his fingers through the fur on Doto's cheek. "You're my god. Nothing will keep me from coming back to you."

〰

The night was dark, and Clay could see nothing but stars. In the forest, the fetish around his neck had enhanced his sight, and there even at night he could see clearly enough to move around, but out here it had no power, so he lay and listened to the insects chirruping in the grasses. He smelled the bitter char of the extinguished fire and the lingering, rich scent of cooked meat.

Not long after lying down to sleep, Doto had nestled up to him from behind, putting one heavy, furred arm around Clay and clamping him close. His body was uncomfortably hot, but his strength unyielding, and Clay could not have pulled away had he wished to. As it was, he enjoyed the solid firmness of Doto's muscled chest against his back, swelling and falling, the slow pant of the great cat's breath in his hair.

Clay shifted, trying to get into a more comfortable position, and Doto growled low in his sleep. His arm squeezed a little tighter, as though Clay might run off in the night. It was surprising to him that Doto feared it so. Did he not understand what they had?

It was possible he did not. And what was that? Clay asked himself. Passion, assuredly, deep and powerful. Pleasure. A growing relationship between god and mortal that transcended any of those in the stories Clay could remember. An abiding, persistently thrumming arousal that rode crescendos into ecstatic copulation. And it was not forbidden by gods; perhaps yet by his people, but which of them could deny a god his claim? So he and Doto had a relationship, male and male, as any male and female of his people might. Only it wasn't the same. Not just male and male, but worshiper and god.

He thought then of his parents, what he could remember of them from the time when his mother lived, and the gentleness between them. He thought of Cloud and her wistfulness when she remembered her long-dead husband. He thought of friends marrying, as their parents had before them, suddenly wrapped up in each other so deeply they forgot the rest of the world for a while. He thought of the look in Great Ram's eyes when he took his bride Hibiscus. None of them would know the embrace of a god as Clay had. But they had love, and that, he realized, was something he and Doto did not have. At least, it was not the same. Doto was affectionate toward him, even fond of him. And he had made great sacrifices for him. But Clay did not think the god loved him, not as Clay's parents had loved each other. Perhaps he was not even capable of it.

Clay was a mortal, and Doto a god. What could he ever be to Doto but a devotee or a prized possession? What future would there be for them? Clay would grow old and one day die. Doto could not live away from the forest for long, so if Clay were to be with him, he would have to live apart from his people. The longing for home came back to him, stronger than before. He closed his eyes and tried to push it out of his mind. He was in the arms of his god. That ought to be enough for anybody.

~~~

The sun was still low in the east, and birds flitted back and forth in the tall grasses, darting after insects. Clay blinked out over the endless horizon. "Can you ask one of them?"

"I will try," Doto said. "But most birds are difficult to talk to. They do not keep thoughts very well. Parrots are smart and will talk, but parrots are—" He paused, rubbing at his chin. "Poots."

Clay couldn't help giggling. "Poots?"

"Yes, the name you call things you don't like because they behave in undesirable ways. So you call them an unappealing word for waste."

"Oh!" Clay tried not to laugh again. "Right. Shits, maybe?"

"No, that does not sound correct. I think it is poots."

"I like poots better anyway," Clay agreed. "So parrots are poots?"

"Yes. If they know what you want they will not do it out of stubbornness. Or as a joke. It is very irritating."

"But these birds might know where we can find Sarmu?"

"They might. If they can pay attention long enough to hear the question. We would be better off finding a furred animal. They are better to talk to. Or a scaled thing. Our dinner last night might have helped us, had you not been such a quick hunter."

Clay smiled. "Next time I'll try to bring the food back alive."

"That is good," Doto said, nodding. "Hot blood is always better for eating, too."

He dropped to a crouch, prowling forward toward the birds fluttering around in the tall grasses. He could not fade into invisibility, the way he did in the forest, but he had a knack for moving along places in the terrain where his spots and golden fur blended naturally with the grasses and the light and shadows. His movements were slow and graceful. When he neared the grasses, he crouched lower and began growling something in a deep voice. There were syllables of some sort, odd hisses and flicks of the tongue, the same language that Doto had spoken to Kwaee when he had brought Clay to the forest temple.

After a moment, he stood, startling the birds, which flew out of the grasses with a rustle of wings, settling down some distance away. "I do not understand," he said, looking puzzled.

"What's wrong?"

"I do not understand," Doto repeated. "Them. Any of the sounds that they make. And they did not seem to comprehend anything I said to them. They did not respond to any of my words, even when I threatened them."

"Maybe they didn't care for being threatened?"

"It is not that. They did not know what I was saying. I spoke the god's tongue to them, and they did not understand it. But all creatures understand the god's tongue."

"I didn't understand it when you spoke it to Kwaee," Clay reminded him.

"That is different. You are not a creature of the forest."

Clay shrugged, wincing at the still-aching pain of the bite in his shoulder where the one of the chasing baboons had sunk its teeth deep. "Neither are they. They're savanna birds."

Doto's eyes widened in alarm. "I have never ventured out of the forest before. I never attempted to speak to the creatures beyond its borders. If they cannot understand me . . ." He sat down on the ground, putting his head in his paws. "If they cannot understand me, then we have no way at all of finding Sarmu. I cannot feel the divine energies in the earth. I cannot speak to the beasts. You said the savanna is large, larger than you have ever traveled."

Clay's heart sank. "Yes, it is. I could spend a lifetime journeying it and never see the same place."

"Then we have no hope," Doto said. "We will never find Sarmu." A hopeful tone crept into his voice, and he lifted his head from his paws. "We may as well return to the forest."

"No. *No.*" To abandon their search so soon? To abandon his people to Kwaee's wrath? The idea was unthinkable. "We have to keep looking. There must be some other way to find him. You told me you knew how to find gods!"

"I do know how to find them. In the forest," Doto said. He looked much cheerier than a moment ago. "But we are not in the forest, and my methods do not work. What would you wish me to do, spend an eternity walking through this terrible place trying to find a god who could be anywhere? It would not work. You must accept that the thing you want cannot be done."

"But—but Doto," Clay stammered. He knelt in front of his god, taking the broad leopard paws in his slender fingers, and looking up to meet his eyes. "Listen, if we can't find Sarmu, then we need to find some other way to appease your father and help my people. If the forest is against them, then they could die. Not just my father and brothers and friends, but all my people. Do you understand?"

"Of course I understand," Doto said, but his gaze was unblinking and perplexed. He squeezed Clay's fingers. "Their deaths will be difficult for you to adjust to. Mortal creatures do not understand it. You will have emotions about this. It will be all right. I am patient. All things die. You will learn to understand with time."

Clay dropped Doto's paws, stumbling back from him. The casual callousness was like a blow, dizzying him with the reminder that Doto was not human, and whatever relationship they shared, it was not one of equals. For the first time in many days, he felt suddenly and terribly alone.

"What is wrong?" Doto asked. "Are you injured?"

"How could you say that? How could you just talk about my family dying—my *people* dying—as though it meant nothing? How would you feel if your father died?"

Doto tilted his head. "I would never live to see that. The only way that my father could ever die is if the entire forest burned. That would destroy my own temple and me with it. So if my father died, I would be nothing and would feel nothing."

"Just imagine it," Clay urged. "Try to think of what it would be like for you if you were still alive, but he weren't around anymore."

Frowning, Doto answered, "I do not know. He is very cruel and unpleasant much of the time. He was not always so, but he has been for a very long time now. If he died, then I suppose I would feel relief. The forest would be mine, and I could stop it from hurting your people, and then you would be glad, and we could return there, and you would worship me and dance with me and mate with me. It would be a good thing."

"Then me," Clay said, exasperated. "What would you feel if I died?"

Doto's eyes widened at that, and then his expression went dark, the fur lifting across his neck and shoulders. "I would never let that happen," he growled. "You are mine. I will never let anything kill you. I would kill anything that tried it. I would stop at nothing."

"Right, but you are here with me now." Clay considered pointing out that here, in the savanna, Doto might have no power to stop something from killing him, but he didn't want to provide any further motivation for Doto to drag him back to the forest. "Suppose you were far away and couldn't stop it? How would you feel?"

The fur on Doto's back bristled even thicker, his tail switching lightly, then faster. "I would—I would—" he growled. The claws at his fingertips slid out, white and wickedly pointed. He panted twice, broad chest swelling, then gathered control of himself, lowering his paws, calming all but the twitching of his tail. "It would not be acceptable," he said. "There is a part of me in you. It cannot be lost. I would be damaged by it."

Clay put his hand on Doto's knee, smoothing the spotted fur there. "There is a part of me in my people too, in my father and brothers, and part of all of them in me. Not in the same way as you and I," he added hurriedly, seeing Doto's objection on his face, "but a part all the same. My people give me strength and meaning. And I care for them. I love them. If something bad happened to them, it wouldn't just be hard for me. There would be a part of me that would never get better. It would be hurt forever. Do you see?"

Doto gave him a considering look. "Your people are your forest. You take strength from them, and if they die, you are diminished. You speak as though you are god of the fire bearers."

Clay tried not to look shocked at the implied blasphemy, but his mouth dropped a little. It was the sort of thing Laughing Dog would say, that they were each their own gods. "No, no, of course not. The fire bearers have no god, not like the other beasts do. There is Adowa, god of antelope, and Okore, god of eagles, but no god of fire bearers. All gods are our gods. We serve all of them."

"But you worship me most of all," Doto reminded him.

"Of course," Clay said, gripping Doto's thigh just above the knee. "You are the only god of Clay." He paused. *All gods are our gods.* "Doto, I think I might be able to find Lord Sarmu."

Doto's ears swiveled forward in interest. "You have a way? And what is that?"

"I can pray to him! If prayer can reach the gods, then maybe he'll hear me and come to us, or at least send a sign that tells us how to reach him."

"I do not know," Doto said. "Your words when you say these prayers are strange, and I do not understand why. But I do not know if I could hear them from far away. And if I were a savanna god, I would not see any reason why I ought to listen to them."

Clay took his paws again. "I have to try. Just let me try. I'll pray to him, and then we'll travel a little while longer, to see if Lord Sarmu will answer. He might listen, if he knows I am traveling with you."

Doto looked uncomfortable, but nodded. "Very well. You may make the attempt. And we will allow Sarmu five days to respond. If he does not, then you will come back with me to the forest."

"All right." Clay agreed. He would go back with Doto to the forest for a time, he decided privately, but he would not be able to stay for very long.

He would have to return to his people, and like it or not, Doto would have to accept that. Home was waiting.

∿

The next day, they came across a streambed that still ran with fresh water from the afternoon rains. Though its current took it south toward the forest, and its flow narrowed and thinned the further they traveled, they would have clean water for a time, and the chances of finding food would be greater. They followed it through the day, tracing its path northeast. In his evening hunt, Clay caught a slow-moving warthog, and took the discovery along with that of the fresh stream as hopeful indication that Sarmu had heard his prayer. Doto had not been as encouraged, and had protested about traveling farther from the forest when they still had had no clear word from the savanna god. Five days, Clay had reminded him. They had five days to travel while awaiting an answer from Sarmu. Then they would turn around.

That night, he roasted up the pig, but Doto once more protested the fire and took his portion raw. The sight of him eating uncooked pig meat and entrails was still stomach-turning to Clay, so he turned his gaze west and watched the red sun dip toward the ground. Somewhere in those burnished grasses were his people, perhaps dancing, lighting a fire, playing music. He sighed and turned his mind from them. At home, he would have slept alone in his tent. Here he would sleep in the strong arms of his god and feel safe and desired.

Even if just now his god was tired, weak, and surly.

"There is no point to traveling farther north," Doto complained the following morning. He waded through the tall reeds and grasses along the stream. They refused to bend and bow out of the way of his divine procession, so he simply kicked and trampled them. He didn't seem to know how to step high to flatten the grasses before him, and so occasionally would stumble, tripped by a low root or tangled stalk, or a bent stem would smack at his legs, making him yowl in annoyance. "The farther we go, the farther we will have to head back when Sarmu doesn't answer."

"He will answer," Clay said. He lifted his feet dramatically, showing Doto how to move through the grass, but the leopard did not seem to notice.

"How do you know?"

"I have faith that he will. We have faith in the gods."

"Faith is stupid," grumbled Doto.

"I have faith in you," Clay said. "We must give Sarmu a chance too. How likely will he be to help us if he sees that we don't believe in him?"

"I do not know. I have not met Sarmu. Perhaps he will be unhelpful, like my father. But I can feel that we should not be going this way."

Clay stopped, turning around. "Can you? Is it a magical feeling?"

"No," Doto said. "Not magic. Just a bad feeling in my stomach. The farther we go this way, the worse it gets. We should not be traveling farther from the forest."

His concern growing, Clay pressed, "What does it feel like? Maybe gods can't leave their territory for very long. Maybe we need to get you back."

"Gods can leave their territory. It is just unpleasant." Doto switched his tail and pressed at his stomach with both paws, leaning forward. "It is just a bad feeling, like my legs when we are walking too far. Only it gets worse and worse, and—"

His ears folded back, his pupils contracting into narrow slits. He wiped drool from the corner of his mouth and then leaned forward. "Clay, I—" he began, but gurgled the last word as his dinner poured from his muzzle into the grass. He looked up with a terrified expression and retched again.

Clay rushed to the leopard's side as he dropped to his knees in the reeds, broad back arching as he heaved out everything he'd eaten and drunk that day.

"Something's…wrong…" Doto managed, fear straining the words between his heaves.

"I think it's the warthog," Clay said, putting his arm around Doto's waist.

Doto gave him a look of horrified disgust and vomited again. "Don't… say…warthog," he groaned, once he could speak again.

Clay crouched near him and stroked the fur on his neck and the back of his head. "Okay," he said.

Doto's stomach clenched and wrenched, trying to propel its contents out, even though it was empty, and at last he slumped to one side, lying in the grass, water streaming from his eyes and nose. "It's a bad food," he said miserably. "A bad food."

Clay tugged him a little distance away from his mess and cleaned him up as well as he could with leaves and water from the stream. "Here, drink a little."

"No," Doto moaned, pushing Clay's cupped hands away from his muzzle.

Clay sat by his side for a while, letting him pant and recover. "It needed to be cooked," he said after a time. "The thing you don't want me to mention. Remember, I told you we can get sick if we eat meat that isn't cooked?"

"That is for fire bearers. Gods do not get sick from eating uncooked meat."

"But maybe your magic doesn't protect you outside the forest," Clay said.

Doto blinked at him and then rolled into a crouch, pushing himself to his feet. "You are right," he said. "I need to get back to the forest." He took a few steps and stumbled, heaving again.

Clay rushed to his side again, pulling Doto's arm across his shoulder. "You won't make it, not like this. You need to rest."

Doto snarled, tugging his arm away. He took a few determined steps south. "I do not need to rest," he declared, his voice loud, but shaking. "I do not need to cook my food and I do not need to rest. I am a *god*." He collapsed to the ground.

∿∿∿

Clay sat with Doto next to the fire and kept him as comfortable as he was able. He'd had to drag the heavy leopard a good distance from the streambed so that he could make a fire without risking it spreading to the dry grasses, and the whole time, Doto had protested, trying to get up and stagger away and falling down again. He'd objected to the fire as well, claiming that if Ogya could see him in this weakened state, he would come and attack them both, but he didn't complain very hard before lapsing into sleep.

He was very ill. Clay had seen people with food poisoning before, and it was always foul and unpleasant, but this seemed worse. Clay wished Cloud were there with advice. He wracked his memory for the ingredients she had used as remedies in the past, but could remember only a few, and none of them were to be found nearby. There was little else he could do but keep Doto drinking water, whenever the cat would accept it, at least. Doto would stubbornly insist that he didn't need anything for long stretches of time before eventually relenting and requesting water.

The next morning, Clay constructed a little shelter of rushes from the stream and tried to keep Doto cool. As the day progressed, the food poisoning only intensified, and Doto weakened. He no longer complained about the discomfort and the heat; nor did he refuse water when Clay urged it on him, but accepted it listlessly. He lay still and limp, and his ears no longer twitched when the flies landed on them. Clay did his best to keep them switched away using a bundle of tasseled grasses.

When the day darkened into evening again, he lit a new fire and sat beside Doto, stroking at the fur on his side. He was hungry, achingly so, but he couldn't leave Doto in this condition. Clay would be fine for a day or two without food.

"You are strong," Doto said. His voice was so quiet it was nearly lost in the crackle of the fire. "I never saw it before."

"I'm used to this place," Clay reminded him. "And I've been sick and weak too, you know. You should have seen me after my foot was injured. I was as helpless as a newborn."

Doto rolled over to look up at him. His eyes looked like the surface of an old pond, long after the rain had left it, thick and filmed. "No, I mean, not just now. I remember when you were sick from your foot, in my forest. I took you from your home, and you were hungry and hurt and sick, but you followed me. You followed me even though you were dying. It must have been very difficult. You are strong."

Clay traced his fingers along the lean swells of muscle across Doto's belly. "You are a god," he said, smiling. "Who are you to call me strong?"

"In the forest I am a god." Doto took Clay's fingers in his paw, brushing at his palm with a leathery thumb. "But without my power, I am weaker than you." His eyes darkened. "Perhaps this is what Kwaee meant when he called me weak. You have no power here, and you shame me."

"Doto, no!" Clay was growing alarmed. He had never heard Doto speak this way before; his god had always concealed any hints of ignorance or failing behind a litany of boasts and conceits. To see him break now made a stone of worry grow in Clay's stomach. Or perhaps that was just the hunger.

Doto squeezed his fingers more tightly. "I am weaker every moment. We must be prepared for this body to die."

"Doto. Doto, you're not that sick." Clay felt tears spring to his eyes.

"Do not worry. I will return to my temple and will be in a new body." He paused. "I do not know if it will hurt, nor how long it will take. My father told me nothing of these things. But I will find you again. You must come back to the edge of the forest, just inside. Be careful that you wear my fetish so the forest does not attack you. Be wary, too, of wild animals that may be hunting fire bearers. If they pursue you, the border of the savanna will not slow them as it does Kwaee's magic. It may take some time, but I will find you again. I will stay a little ways inside the forest and run very, very fast until we are together again."

"It's just bad food, Doto," Clay said, rubbing at the leopard's ears with his free hand, feeling them flatten backward under his touch. "It won't kill you. You'll get better. Maybe by tomorrow."

"I have been in the minds of creatures when they died. Many, many times I have done this. This is what it feels like. They slide away from their bodies into nothing. It is like walking through the border of the forest, and losing your power, but behind that border is another border, and behind that another still, and each time you lose more. I am walking through those borders now. But you must not worry. I am only returning to my temple. I will come to find you again."

Doto looked toward the fire, squinting at it as though he could barely see it, then turned his gaze back to Clay. "Worshiper. You will . . . you will dance for me again. It will please me."

"Of course, Doto." Clay rubbed the wet from his cheeks. It was silly to cry. Doto wasn't dying; he was only sick, and even if he did die, he wasn't gone. At worst, going back to the forest would be a minor inconvenience, a journey of a few days. There was no reason to be upset. But seeing Doto lying weak and helpless, going through the motions of death, making a last request—it all felt like the real thing. At the camp, they danced dances of praise and worship, but also story dances, led by the Teller, and these could be stories of great victories or great losses. Just as the dances of triumph could make you feel big and bold and happy with a victory you never achieved, or only remembered from many years ago, so too could the dances of loss and grieving settle in your heart and drag you to the ground and make you feel as though your world had gone. Now Doto danced his own death—not real, surely, but affecting all the same.

Clay squeezed his eyes closed and reminded himself that a god could not die. He had seen his mother placed on the acacia pyre, her body turned to round and spindly shapes hidden among the bright and dark of flame. The drums had beat her mourning, and the people had danced it. But there would never be a pyre for Doto, and Clay would never dance his death. The thought was both strange and comforting.

"Clay?" Doto said, gripping his hand more firmly.

"Yes, Doto." Clay stood, letting Doto's paw fall to one side. He moved to the fire, breathing deep, smelling the smoke of burned rushes and the wet of the stream nearby. Frogs, nestled into the mud banks, chirped loudly over the sound of the fire. All around was black and starlight. He drew in the words of his prayer to Doto, the rhythmic twist of hip and thump of foot, and danced.

For the first time, he danced for Doto on his own, human feet. Before, in the forest, his one foot had been wounded, and after it had been healed, he had danced on one leopard's paw. And since they left the forest, Doto had been too tired and unhappy to care much for dances. But now Clay danced the prayer to him on his own two feet. One was yet tender and sensitive with new skin, and it took him a moment to find his rhythm, but when it came, it came like new rain after a long drought.

He sang.

> *The forest has come to greet the savanna*
> *and spill into it the blessings of Doto the mighty.*
> *You are the god who dares to stand before the flame.*
> *You are the god who can bend the forest*
> *with the movements of your fingers*
> *and before you the oldest of trees must bow.*

The world was alive around him as he spun and leaped, and his voice sang clearer and louder. The sounds of the frogs in the stream grew distinct: he could hear each frog individually, this one subtly but unmistakably deeper; that one crying out faster and more urgently; all of them signaling to their mates, *Here, here, I am strong and beautiful. Here!* Beneath their cries—the peeps and chirrups of grasshoppers, the whine of mosquitos keening above the rushing surface of the stream. He could smell that more strongly too, soaking into the wet earth on the banks, stilling among the reeds, where algae bubbled and clung.

A rush of wine-like giddiness rose into his mind. The fire burned more brightly in his vision, so he fixed his gaze on the darkened savanna, which no longer hid in the utter blackness of night, but in the dim murk of late twilight—not clear, but no longer unseeable. It must be lit by the stars, he thought. They were brighter than he could ever recall seeing them, uncountable, whirling points of light.

"Clay!" Doto's voice called him out of the dance. It was not the weak whisper of moments before, but strong and urgent.

Panting, he stopped dancing and noticed the surface of the ground beneath his feet. It was soft and cool and matted. He curled his toes and felt the claws on his left foot tear through some yielding material. He looked down.

The ground in a wide circle around the fire was thick with grass and vines. They were lush, verdant, fat with nourishment, sprawled around his toes. Thorns grew among broad leaves, and sprigs of young trees sprouted up all over. He stepped toward them and they bent before his path, bowing out of the way of the divine power held within his fetish and the clawed leopard's paw that had reformed at the end of his left leg. All around, for several paces in every direction, the forest had formed where savanna once was.

A strong paw gripped his shoulder. "Clay." He turned around. Doto stood before him, tall, eyes shining, his fur no longer clumped and matted, but thick and lush and shining. "You healed me." He clasped Clay to his chest in a roughly affectionate embrace.

"I think you healed yourself," Clay croaked through the pressure of the hug. "I just—I just…"

"You brought the forest to me," Doto said. "Truly, you fire bearers are a wondrous species. How did you do it?" He leaned back, holding Clay at arm's length and gazing at him as though he were an orchid found in the middle of the Firelands.

"I didn't do anything different," Clay confessed, bewildered. "I danced. I've danced like that many times in the camp, with my people, and nothing like this happened. It must need both of us. It must be like in the forest, when I danced for you there, and the flowers grew."

"But here, outside the forest!" Doto looked around, marveling. "Truly the blessings of Doto the mighty have come to greet the savanna!" He boomed the words through a proud grin. "Look."

He crouched to the floor of vines and matted leaves and held his paw just above the earth. Beneath his fingers, the plants rustled, a curling white shoot rising up, twisting and spreading. Its stalk thickened, and tender, pale leaves unfolded, jittering at the unnatural pace of their development. They lengthened, slowly at first, and then spread and broadened all at once, like the opening of butterfly wings. The sprout matured into a sapling, and then a small tree, delicate branches gracefully extending and fanning into twigs and leaves. Between the leaves, small buds clustered, swelled, and then burst open into cupped pink flowers that stretched and yawned at the night sky, clouding the air with an aromatic mist of sweetest nectar. They dropped to the ground in a shower of petals. Their stems bulged and engorged and rounded, filling out into fat green fruits that grew so large and heavy, the slender branches of the tree dipped nearly to the earth. The globes streaked with red and gold, and ripened into the familiar fruits that Doto had invented for Clay back in the temple. Impossibly sweet they had been, refreshing as cool rain, and yet as satisfying as a meal of meat and sorghum. Clayfruit, Doto had named it with a smile.

"Eat," Doto urged him, plucking a fruit so large it half-filled both paws and proffering it.

Clay took it and sank his teeth into it, and the crisp sweetness of its flesh expelled all other thoughts from his mind. It was still living from the branch, and the cool juices burst from its skin and flooded his mouth and throat.

Doto beamed at him. "Is it good?"

"Of course it is!" Clay rubbed juice from his chin with the back of his arm. "I'm so glad you're better."

"I am too," Doto said, his brow lowering. "Having this body die would have been of great inconvenience to me. And it was very uncomfortable. But you danced for me, and I am myself again." He cupped Clay's cheek, smiling fondly at him. "You danced for me. You saved me." He took a deep breath.

Clay stepped closer, putting his hand on Doto's chest. He dropped the fruit.

Together, they tumbled into the vines. Their mating was passionate and hungry, the magic of the forest invigorating Clay. Doto was voracious, as though the torpor of the past few days had been a wall damming back a torrent of passion. Clay sprawled atop him, his arousal buried in the soft fur of Doto's belly, and the god curled about and entered him with the sweet, familiar ache of divinity and filled him with his spirit.

Clay nestled into Doto's arms, rested his head on the broad, firm chest, and could not remember anything that had been troubling him. He slept long, deep into the morning, and Doto did not wake him.

∿

When at last his eyes opened, they met Doto's gold-greens staring intently back into them. "It is time to go," Doto said. "You are rested."

Clay yawned and stretched stiff limbs. The grasses bent and curled around him reverently. Their lovemaking had sprouted a field of flowers in the circle of forest and dusted that field with a fuzzy coat of pollen. "Do you know how to find Sarmu?" he asked. His voice was deep with sleep, still. He felt relaxed, and did not want to rise, but the sun was already growing hot on his bare skin.

"Certainly I know how to find him," Doto said. "I told you I would be able to."

"Yes, you did." Clay smiled.

"I can feel the energies in the ground, but they are faint, very faint. They are stronger toward the north, it seems. North and east. But now that you are awake, I can speak to the animals."

Doto gently disengaged Clay's head from his arms and stood, turning toward the stream.

"Frogs!" he called. Clay could understand him, but the words were not the language of his people. If he considered any of them, they turned strange and meaningless in his mind. "I am Doto the mighty, god of the forest, god of Clay. I visit the land of Sarmu on urgent matters. Tell me, frogs, where is your savanna god? Where might I find Brother Sarmu?"

He waited. There was silence from the stream; the frogs had ceased their croaking with the sunrise. After a time with no reply, he called again. "Do you hear and understand me, frogs? Where is Sarmu? It is a god who addresses you. You must answer!"

Again, silence. The wind rustled in the rushes. Clay sat up in the grass, about to suggest that perhaps the frogs had all left, or were sleeping deep in the mud during the day. But then a low, mournful answer creaked from the stream. "*Loooooost.*"

It was joined by another voice, croaking in agreement. "*Looooost.*"

The cry was taken up by another frog, and then three more, and then ten, and then a hundred, and then the air was loud with them, each loudly groaning his bewilderment in a guttural, discordant chorus. *Lost. Lost. Lost.*

They followed the stream northeast as far as they could in the remaining hours of the day, journeying toward the faint presence Doto had insisted he could feel. Clay had not wanted to leave their small oasis of forest, and Doto had been even more reluctant, but they forced themselves to go on. When it grew too dark to see, with only a rind of moon in the western sky to light their path, they stopped for the night, and this time, they lit no fire. Again Clay danced for Doto, and again the world leapt into vivid clarity, the blackness of the night lessening, the moon swelling into the dazzling grin of Mother Fam. They dined on the red and gold clayfruit, mated, and lay on the soft carpet of flowers that sprouted in their ecstasy. Doto dozed off quickly, but Clay lay awake, energized by the magic around him and the brightness of the nodding stars.

Questions whirled in his mind, unknowable but impossible to dismiss. How could Sarmu be lost? Who could lose a god? Doto had had no answers. Animals did not always know where their god was, he claimed, but to say Sarmu was lost suggested that no one had seen him in a long time. It worried Clay. First Kwaee boiling in hatred of the people and vowing their destruction, and now Sarmu, missing. Were the gods in turmoil? Had something terrible happened? These were questions too great for him. He could only follow Doto and hope that they found answers.

He turned his head, pressing his nose into the swell of Doto's arm, strong and softly furred and comforting. His eyes closed, the warm scent of his god surrounding him, he tried to sleep.

A persistent pressure in his bladder grew more uncomfortable. He tried to ignore it for a time; he wanted to leave neither the circle of forest nor the security of Doto's arms. But he had drunk deeply from the stream, and eaten nothing but fruits filled with sweet juice. He would have to get up.

He slid himself from Doto's arms with slow, careful movements, not wishing to wake the slumbering god. He padded to the edge of the dance circle, hesitated, and stepped through. The night drowned his vision as the magic left him, his nose and ears feeling plugged, their heightened senses gone. As his left foot traveled through the edge of the forest circle, it felt as though it were withering, the fur on it thinning into nothingness, the toes shrinking, claws flattening into stubby toenails. Grace fled his stride, and he stumbled in the dark for a few steps. He looked back, hoping he could find the forest circle again in the dark. At first, he could see nothing at all, but then, as his eyes became accustomed to the absence of magic, he could make out the silvery outlines of Doto and the forest circle in the dim moonlight. He sighed, reassured, and made his way through the brush, untying his breech leathers. He stopped at a distance great enough where he hoped the smell would not be offensive.

There was the swish of grasses against legs. "Doto?" he said, turning, but then a pair of rough arms seized him from behind. Human arms. A hand clamped over his mouth.

"Now, now, don't struggle, boy." The man's voice was low and thickly accented, the words spoken right into his ear. A roughly stubbled chin rasped against Clay's shoulder. "You sure and been traveling with a demon, and I trust nay. Best and don't danger me. You understand?"

Clay could scarcely breathe, the man's hand was sealed so tightly over his mouth. A man in the dark was never good. In the savanna, you approached another in light of day, or not at all. Darkness was for dark business. He twisted in the man's arms, kicking, and managed to wrench himself to one side.

The man swore under his breath and snatched at him, catching his arm and yanking it painfully, make the baboon bite in his shoulder roar in agony.

"Doto!" Clay called in desperation. "Help me!"

The man pulled him back, his hand across Clay's mouth again, clamping his head against a dense, bare chest. A hot point of stone pressed up against his throat.

"You know sharps, yea, boy?"

Clay stilled himself, trembling.

The man nudged the point deeper. "Now you've dangered yourself."

The silhouette of a feline rose from the forest circle, ears perked toward them. Then they flattened back, and Clay could hear a low, threatening growl. The dark figure bounded toward the edge of the forest circle and stepped through.

The knife dug more firmly into Clay's skin; it was well-sharpened and painful, the waxy flint pressed flat against his neck below the line of pain. Clay held as still as he could, not even daring to breathe.

Doto stumbled toward them, staggered by the loss of his magic, his paws outstretched. In the moonlight, Clay caught a glimpse of his bared fangs. The cat's tail switched as he neared them.

Clay's breath came in short pants through his nose. Why didn't the man back away? Or run?

Doto was almost upon them now, and his fur was bristling in fury. His eyes flashed green in the moonlight. "Let him go," he growled, "and I will not tear out your entrails and leave you for the vultures and ants."

The man holding Clay was shaking in naked fear, but kept his grip on the knife firm.

"Let him go *now*," Doto roared.

A shape rose up behind him, that of another man who had been hiding in the bush. In his hands he held a long, sturdy club.

Clay shouted a muffled cry into the fingers across his mouth.

Doto whirled just as the other man swung; the club arced wide and connected solidly with the leopard's skull. There was a dull thud. Doto dropped to the ground. He did not move again.

Clay wailed into the man's hand.

The other man came up. He was taller, his shape burly. "You saw it true, Jai. A demon sure." He nudged Doto with a foot and then crouched down, pressing his knee into the cat's back. "And what now?"

"We bind them both," the man holding Clay said. "This boy was captive nay. A witch, sure or like. Wait for sunup, and then maybe we cut this demon's magic out of its heart."

Shadows From the Forest

Cloud stepped into the shade of her tent and found Red Moth sitting on one of the straw and hide beds, waiting for her. The woman's arms were bound in splints made of bamboo and twine, resting at angles that looked stiff and uncomfortable. She blinked up at Cloud, her round face shining with sweat.

Cloud hurried to her side, kneeling and laying her back on the thick bed of skins, taking care not to twist or jar the setting bones. "What are you doing here?" The worry she felt over the council put a scold in her voice. "You should be resting. You move those arms around and they'll heal wrong."

"Had to," Red Moth said through closed teeth. She groaned as she allowed Cloud to recline her. "It's worse. So much worse. Can't eat—"

"The pain is that bad?" Reason for concern. Broken bones were not enjoyable, but they shouldn't cause agony. That could mean something else was wrong, maybe something deep in the wound that she wouldn't be able to identify or heal. Maybe infection. She examined the long splints that she had fashioned for Red Moth. "Did these get hit or turned? Are you being careful?"

"No—yes, I'm being careful. It's not the bones. My stomach—" She gritted her teeth. "Cloud. I don't want this. I cannot bear it. To be like this while he is not here... Please. You must have something. Something that will...send me after Bramble."

Cloud's fingers twitched away from the splints. "I don't have that kind of medicine." Her voice was hard and stony. It was the wrong voice to use. More softly, she added, "We all miss Bramble. He was a good man."

Red Moth tilted her head away, facing the darkness of the tent. "I wish I could miss him. I know that I loved him. When they told me he had gone into the forest and not returned, I thought I would die. And I thought when I ran after him that I didn't care what happened to me next."

Tears streaked dark across her cheeks, washing away the dust of the day. She shook at the next words. "I was wrong. When the forest moved like an animal around me and the trees grabbed my arms, the pain was so great that all I could think was that it could have him. It could take my husband and tear him into a hundred pieces if only the pain would stop."

Cloud rubbed a worn spot of her dress between her fingers. "You don't blame yourself. You don't, you understand? It was the pain speaking. Not you."

"I pulled free of the forest and ran back here. And it was better, for a while. You helped me. The pain went away. I grieved for Bramble. I missed him. But now it is a new pain, worse than ever."

"A new pain?" Cloud asked with rising alarm.

"Yes. In my stomach, my gut…" Red Moth writhed on the bed, clawed at her stomach with curled fingers as though she could rake the pain out of herself. "It hurts so much. I can't eat. I can't sleep. I can't mourn my dead husband. All I can do is think about the pain." She turned wet eyes up to Cloud. "Why should I suffer this? Why should I be expected to live when my body does this to me?"

Cloud put her fingers to Red Moth's forehead. The skin was warm, but slick. Sweat should mean a fever had gone. It was a troubling sign. "I will give you more medicine," she said. This would be risky; supplies were so limited. If she ran out, she was not sure when or where she would be able to get more. She would have to scout the savanna to the north and hope she found something. "But you are not to die. Just as the pain spoke to you in the forest, it's speaking to you now. It tells you that you would rather lose what is most precious to you than suffer longer."

Red Moth gave her a desperate look. "The pain will go away?"

"I hope so," Cloud said.

She made a gagging sound. "Up. I need to get up!"

As quickly as Cloud was able, she slid her arms beneath Red Moth and helped her to sit upright, careful not to jar the splints too much. No sooner was Red Moth sitting than she leaned forward and vomited.

Cloud turned her face away as the woman heaved. The stuff was foul-smelling, black in the dim light of the tent. She had never seen anything like it before. This was not merely pain or injury. This was sickness, some terrible affliction that Cloud did not recognize. "Is that all of it?" she asked.

Red Moth nodded. Her eyes were streaming, her nose was running. There were strings of dark in that, too. "Will you wipe my face clean?" she asked.

"Of course." Cloud leaned Red Moth back once more and then fetched wool and water to dab her face clean. "You had better stay here for now. I'll make a potion for you."

Red Moth nodded and closed her eyes. "Thank you," she said. "It hurts so much. I just want it to stop hurting."

The spatter of bile on the ground next to her stank. It would need to be scraped up with dust and wood to clear it out; otherwise the stench would fill the tent and make it unlivable, no matter how many incenses Cloud burned. She cast another worried look at Red Moth. The woman could not remain unattended. With her arms unusable, she would have trouble sitting up, and if she vomited again, she could choke. No. Someone would need to sit by her night and day. Cloud was going to need help.

She stepped out of the tent to fetch tools to clean away the mess, squinting her eyes in the bright afternoon sun.

A little boy stood there—what was his name again? Whistling Thorn, she thought. Son of No Rocks and Firefly. He had come to her several days ago, swollen from the stings of many wasps. Now his light brown skin was covered with pinkish pocks, some of them darkened black from his scratching. He swayed back and forth as though drunk.

"Little Thorn," Cloud said. "What are you doing here?"

He looked up at her with wide, white eyes. "My stomach hurts," he groaned. Then he leaned over and poured red-black liquid from his throat into the sand.

∧∧∧

"So what if they are sick?" Great Ram demanded. His voice was loud, and they stood not too far from the common tents, where others might hear. "You're a healer, aren't you? Give them medicine. What's it got to do with me?"

"Discretion, Ram," Cloud cautioned him. "It wouldn't be wise to let others overhear you."

Ram scowled at being chastised. He straightened, pulling his purple robes about his shoulders. "I'll decide what others need to know, not you. I'm not the child you used to silence, you know."

Cloud ignored his petulance. "No, I know you are not. But at least hear what I have to say before you decide who should hear it." She cast a pointed look at Laughing Dog, who stood just to the right of the King, large and imposing, fleshy arms folded across his chest, above a belly that had grown wide from feasting. "Not all will share your discretion."

Ram sighed as though being asked to perform an unwanted chore, made a show of looking around for any who might have overheard, and asked again in a low tone, "Good? All right. So why have you come to me? Is it bad food?"

"I do not think so," Cloud said. "More would be sick, and the sickness would be something I'd seen before. There are only four that I've seen so far. Red Moth, Whistling Thorn, Dancing Spider, and Mongoose. And this illness…it's strange and worrisome."

"Mongoose?" Laughing Dog asked, his eyes widening in alarm. "But that is my promised's father. I don't understand. How could he have taken ill?"

Great Ram ignored him. "Was it some kind of venom? A snakebite perhaps. There are strange creatures about."

Cloud shook her head. "A snakebite would leave a mark we could find. No, this is nothing I have ever seen before. I fear it may be a plague."

"Plague, what is this?" Great Ram frowned. "Another forgotten tale?"

"It was something my grandmother told me about," Cloud said. "A kind of spreading sickness that would sometimes afflict her people."

"The people by the great water," Laughing Dog reminded her. "Not our people. A strange, foreign people. Why should we care about what happened to them?"

"Because." Cloud put stone into her voice. She needed to frighten them as she was frightened. "That is the reason my family came here to live among the People of the Savanna. This sickness, usually it will come and then be gone, and it's not too bad. Some die, but most are ill and get well. But sometimes a greater sickness comes, one that kills. Those who are sick have to be kept away from those who are not, or the sickness spreads to the healthy, to anyone who touches them or feels their breath, and it kills them too. It was a sickness like that that came to Bogana, when I was only a baby. It was terrible, my grandmother said. Old men, young, women and children, faithful and wise, foolish and cruel, it touched them all. Many died. It spread fast and far. And though my grandmother was wealthy and had a fine home, we fled. It would have killed us all."

"And you think this plague could be happening here?" Ram asked. He shrank backward. He was afraid, then. Good.

"I don't know," Cloud said. "I have never seen this before—all these people getting sick the same way at the same time. But if it is plague, then why are Thorn's parents not sick, nor the children he plays with? If Mongoose is sick, then why not Ant With a Leaf nor High Grass? And where did their sickness come from? I can't make sense of it yet."

"Perhaps the gods have struck them down," suggested Laughing Dog. An offensive smile curled across his wide face.

Cloud stared at him in surprise. "You make jokes when the father of your promised is afflicted? Laughing Dog, how could you?"

He dropped his eyes, but anger flashed in them. "I—I'm sorry. You're right. It's a poor time to try to make a point."

Cloud shook her head. To Great Ram, she said, "I want a new tent built next to my own. I'll be able to keep the sick in there and look after them, apart from the others. If this is truly a spreading sickness, we may be able to stop it before any others fall ill."

The King took a knife from his side—his father's knife, Cloud noticed, flint and ivory. He turned it over and over in his hands, running the blade across his thumb. "Why now?" he asked. "Why must this happen now, when we are already so weakened? Sometimes I think you must be right, little brother. Perhaps the gods do hate us."

"Or maybe they simply don't respect us, as Bad Water said," Laughing Dog said. "He was a good friend of Father's, you know."

"Bad Water is a good man, and wise," agreed Cloud. "But your father also knew that friendship does not determine the wisdom of counsel. Experience does. Great Ram, trust my experience with tending the sick. It's a burden I can carry, and you have enough of your own."

The King nodded, staring at the knife in his hands. "Go, then. Get a few people to help you construct this new tent. I'm laying this in your hands, Cloud. I am trusting you. Keep our people well."

"I will do everything I can," she answered. "Thank you, Ram."

She turned and headed back toward the crafting area of the village. The carpenters and leatherworkers would have little to do right now, what with diminishing supplies for their handiwork. With a little luck and hard work, they could have her new tent built by the next evening.

Laughing Dog caught her arm in one hand, startling her. She had not even heard him approach. He loomed over her, his eyes glittering with anger. "You think you can talk to me in front of my brother like that?"

"Yes, I do," Cloud snapped. She had no time for his nonsense now. There was work to be done. "You're too close to your brother. You're not an elder. You're not an adviser. He needs the counsel of people with experience and wisdom, not a headstrong boy filling his ears with arrogance. These are dangerous times."

Laughing Dog bared his teeth. "You're right. And you shouldn't go making enemies, Cloud. Not in these dangerous times." He squeezed at her arm, and his grip was painfully strong.

She held herself upright, keeping the wince from her face. "I'm not your enemy, Laughing Dog. Do you think you have enemies here?"

He released her arm, flushing darker. "I was exiled."

"By your father," she pointed out. "Who loved you. He didn't do it to hurt you. He was trying to protect you and the people."

"And that's all I want, too—to protect our people and help them to be strong, to lead them to a better path."

"It is your brother's place to lead, not yours," Cloud said. "He was born to the kingship."

"Yes, lucky for him that the gods chose him to be born first and not me, isn't it? But I don't care if he's King, if that's what you're thinking. I just need him to see what's right!" His fists clenched.

"And you know what's right?"

"I do!" He fixed her with a wild and certain gaze. "I know things, Cloud. I spoke to the gods out in the savanna. I know better than anyone what they think of us."

She gathered folds of her dress between her fingers. "And what is that?"

He opened his mouth as if to speak, but then paused, his eyes widening. His brow furrowed. His jaw went slack. "No!" he said loudly. "No!" The words were not spoken to her, nor to anyone else that she could see.

"Laughing Dog?" She took a step toward him.

Ignoring her, the boy lifted his water skin from his belt and poured its contents down his throat, gulping as though he had not had a drink in days. He drank what would have been a day's ration or more out on the savanna and still kept swallowing more, his eyes bulging. He tilted the skin up above his head, splashing it into his mouth, gasping between swallows.

Not until he squeezed the last few drops from the skin did he seem to remember she was there. He wiped water from his fat-rounded chin with the back of one arm and scowled at her. "Just keep away from my brother. He doesn't need your advice, not if you're going to make sly comments about me and dig the earth out from beneath my words."

Sometimes it was better to say nothing. She stood silent and still as he ranted, but it seemed only to make him angrier.

"If you oppose me, you're not helping my brother, and you're not helping our people. I won't let you do it. Do you understand, Cloud? I won't let you. You keep your mouth shut, or things are going to go very bad for you. Very bad."

He was shaking with anger now. She stood silently, her hands clasped at the front of her dress, and when she made no reply, he turned on his heel and stalked away.

When he was gone, the tightness flowed out of her back and legs, and the ground moved beneath her. Her fears were confirmed. Laughing Dog had come back from the wilderness alive, but he had come back mad.

~~~

Rain fell hard and heavy, shading the forest in a dark grey mist. Cloud pressed up against the village wall, standing in the thin boundary between their home and the angry forest. The sound of rain in the leaves whispered its threats at her. It would kill her in an instant, if she set foot near it.

Through the rain, she could make out the line of destruction that marked the edge of the forest's wrath. She thanked the gods for keeping her vision keen into old age. She didn't think the angry magic could reach her beyond the edge of that destruction, but neither was she eager to move away from the wall. She had seen the marks the vines and branches had left on Red Moth's arms and legs—dark, bloodied bruises that hinted at wrath and violence. Moth had managed to escape, but only barely, and she was young and strong. Cloud had no such advantage. Still, the risk had to be taken.

Ahead, the splintered remains of the destroyed wall jutted up against the forest like broken teeth. Amid the thick snapped and splintered timbers were the hide and bone remains of several tents, discarded treasures scattered among them: a bead necklace, a straw doll, a hunting horn. The greyed carcass of a goat that had panicked and dashed into the forest now stared with hollow eyes at the canopy. Flies crawled on it still.

The damage was not limited to the fence and tents. In its fury, the living forest had lashed against itself, scarring the tree roots with yellow gashes. The branches that had smashed at the fence had swung so violently they had snapped, and now hung down toward the ground, the broken ends of their limbs jutting outward like splintered fingernails. All the damage formed a plainly visible border between the forest and the savanna, between wrath and peace.

Why here? Cloud wondered. What made one side of the line safe, and the other deadly? She scanned the wreckage, and then saw what she came for, nestled just inside the undamaged brush: a thick, green bush with bright orange flowers and star-shaped leaves. It was a bosu plant—dewroot. It was almost impossible to find in the savanna, so rare that she'd not recognized it at first, but invaluable in bringing down fever and helping the sick to hold their water. Her patients could die of dehydration if they could not keep water inside them. She needed the plant.

Her eyes on the dark and rainy forest, she crept forward. Her arms and legs trembled, and she was not certain whether they did so from age or fear. Her dress, heavy with water, dragged behind her and caught on a branch or root. She gave it a little tug and cringed when she heard the rip.

A gnarl of branch had hooked at the edge and torn a ragged hole. It was foolish to try to go forward wearing it, so she unwrapped the garment from her thin shoulders. It was not a true dress—more of a robe. Supposedly, the people in the west had the skill of stitching and joining fabrics to create garments that naturally hung from their hips and shoulders in flattering ways, but the People of the Savanna had never learned this art. Fabrics were rare to them, purchased from traders who journeyed across the savanna. Usually only the very wealthy wore clothing made of fabric, but this had been a gift from her husband, and so she wore it. She had had to experiment with different ways to wrap and pin the fabric until she found something that worked, but it took so long to put on or remove that she generally left it as it was unless she needed to wash it.

Now, stretching out the fabric, she could see the damage that time and wear had done to it. Everyone called it green, and green it once had been, as deep and beautifully green as the leaves of an oasis after a long journey. But the sun had kissed its whiter hues into the material, leaving it faded and stiff, no longer the soft, luxurious material her husband had given her. The paler color only made its many stains show more plainly: dirt and grass and berry juice, and the yellow-brown residue of life that waxed over any clothes worn for very long. Any place not stained was torn, ragged holes gaping all throughout the cloth. It had been a lovely thing once. Now Cloud did not care to look at it. She folded it carefully and set it atop a fallen tree.

Without the dress around her, she felt vulnerable and exposed. Her limbs were thin, her flesh unpleasantly pale where the dress usually covered it. When she stepped through the grass, she saw her bones through loose skin. Her knees looked wide and knobbly. Warm rain fell down her bare shoulders and hunched back and down her narrow thighs.

The sound of something moving came from the forest—something large. She hugged her arms across her chest and looked hard into the rain. Maybe it had just been a gust of wind and rain. But maybe not. Hurriedly, she moved forward and dug at the plant with her fingers. She needed the root, not the leaves. The crashing sound came again—there was definitely something moving in there.

She didn't dare look up. She clawed at the earth. The water had made the ground soft, but its brown, finger-thick roots went deep. Dirt crammed under her fingernails. She wished she had thought to bring a tool for digging. She couldn't be more than half an arm's length from the edge of the angry forest. Risking a glance toward the border of devastation, she saw the forest moving, not just nodding in the rain, but reaching toward her, blades of grass bending in her direction, tendrils of vines lifted like fingers, clutching toward her. She couldn't help herself; she let out a low groan of terror.

Something in the forest answered it in a low growl, deep as a lion's, but different. Not the cough of a leopard either. Something else. Fighting back her fear, she grabbed the dewroot with both hands and pulled hard. It would not come free. She yanked at it again, leaning back with all her weight, and the root tore free of the ground, sending her falling backward, just as the growl from the forest came again, louder, almost a roar.

She cried out, lifting her hands before her face.

There was nothing there. The forest swayed before her in the rain, grass and branches still bending toward her as though beckoning her toward them, but she could see no animal beyond them.

Again something moved, a bush shifting as though shaking rainwater from its leaves. Behind it, dark eyes glittered.

Cloud grabbed up her dress and ran for the village gate as fast as she could, ignoring the protests and pains in her joints. She did not look back.

~~~

"How is my father?" Ant With a Leaf asked. The tall woman had to crouch low as she entered the tent. She wrinkled her nose at the stench of sickness and bile that underlay the heady scent of incense filling the space.

Mongoose's already wrinkled, brown face creased in a smile. "Ant, it's good to see you." He reached his thin arms out to her, and she moved toward him.

Cloud stepped between them. "He's doing all right for now," she said, "but you shouldn't get too close. If it is a spreading sickness, then you risk falling ill too, and the people can't afford the loss of another hunter."

Ant frowned. With her proud, sculpted features, the expression looked more like regal disdain. She would have made a fine bride for a King. Cloud wondered what Ant thought of Laughing Dog's changes. She couldn't have failed to notice the great amount of weight the prince had put on, and if Cloud, speaking only occasionally to Laughing Dog, could see his madness, surely it must be evident to his promised as well.

"It is my decision whether to visit my father," Ant With a Leaf said. "And are you not just as vulnerable? Who will be our healer if you're gone?"

Cloud took Ant's arm and guided her back toward the entrance. The woman resisted at first, but followed. The new tent that had been built for the sick was impressively large, with enough hides for many people to rest, though the supplies had been spread thin, and the small piles were scarcely more comfortable than lying on hard earth. She looked over her shoulder at the four occupied beds. "Listen. I may not have much say in this village anymore, but the sick still belong to me. If I say you stay back, you stay back. Don't be afraid for me. I've taken precautions. I know how this is done."

Ant bit her lip, scowling. "All right," she said finally. "I know you're doing your best. But it's hard not to see him, to go about wondering and worrying. May I speak to him from here?"

Cloud nodded.

The woman crouched, resting her arms on her knees. "How are you feeling, Father?" she called.

Mongoose leaned up on one elbow. He tried to disguise his wince of pain, but it was easy to make out even through the dimness and the incense smoke. "I'm feeling much better, my dear," he said. "Cloud is taking good care of me. How is the hunt?"

Ant With a Leaf rolled her shoulders back, making popping sounds in her spine. "I wasn't asked on the hunt today. Not everyone thinks I'm as important as Cloud does, it seems."

"Not asked on the hunt?" Cloud asked. "Why not?"

The tall woman shrugged. "You would have to ask my promised that. He took a band of only twelve hunters and went off on his own."

Cloud chewed at her thumb. Laughing Dog was out of the camp. "And the King? He stayed behind?"

"Of course he did! Kings don't hunt."

"I need to speak to the King. Ant, please, stay with the patients. Come find me if anything goes badly wrong, but don't go near them. You understand?"

"I suppose so. But what's wrong?"

It would be better not to say anything, Cloud thought. But no. Ant ought to be warned. Cloud stepped closer and lowered her voice so that the patients wouldn't hear. "Laughing Dog, he's been different, yes? Since he came back?"

Ant's face went smooth and expressionless. "Yes. Very different. I don't like it."

"What?" Mongoose shouted. "What's that?"

Cloud waved him down. "I don't like it either. Listen. I think something happened to him in the savanna. I've seen it before. Heat and thirst over a long period, they can—they can hurt a person. Make them...not right anymore. You understand? You've seen an egg cooked in its shell."

Ant's careful expression collapsed into one of dismay. "You are not saying this to me."

"Ant, he's not well. I'm afraid he's gone mad."

The woman pushed her away. "How can you—how dare you say such a thing to me?" She huddled back like a cornered antelope.

Cloud put a hand on her arm to soothe her. "I pray to the gods it's not so. But look at him, how large he's grown, how much he eats. I've seen him talking to someone not there. He's angry. He threatens people. Ant, he wants to burn the forest, to punish Kwaee for taking his father. And his behavior is so erratic. You've seen it, I know you have. We need to help him. You understand?"

Ant stared past her and didn't answer.

"But he won't listen to me," Cloud pressed. "And he has the King's ear. I don't think Great Ram understands how sick his brother is. But he has to know. He has to listen, and not while Laughing Dog is hovering over his shoulder." She gave Ant a moment to consider this before adding, "You are his bride to be. If you spoke with me, he might listen more readily. I could get Yellow Bug to watch the patients."

Ant With a Leaf kneaded her fingers, twisting her rings. Cloud could watch the thoughts and emotions flicker through her mind like storm clouds across the sun. Then they cleared. Ant straightened, her head pressing into the roof of the tent. "No," she declared. "I won't accept this. Not without proof. Of course he's behaving strangely. He's young, younger than I by several rains, and in the last few months, he's been exiled, and then, when he came back, his brother was dead. He saw his father torn apart by a wild animal, right in front of him." Her lips tightened and she turned an accusatory gaze toward Cloud. "He's not sick. He's *suffering*. He doesn't need you making things worse for him, not now."

Cloud reached out to take Ant's hand, but the woman twitched her fingers away. Well, all right. The woman had a right to be angry. "Listen, I understand that he's suffering, but the King needs to understand what's happening, and I have to tell him. I understand that the boy is your promised, but Ant, be careful. I'm afraid for him. And I wouldn't see you hurt."

"What are you two talking about over there?" Mongoose asked loudly. "You need to speak up. Is it something about Laughing Dog?"

"Do what you have to," Ant With a Leaf said. Her voice was cold and carefully controlled. "I won't stop you." She moved toward Mongoose's side.

"Then stay with your father," Cloud said. "Just don't get too close. Neither love nor strength of will can stop disease."

⌒⌒⌒

When she called out at the King's tent, she was answered by Hibiscus. The King's wife did not invite her into the shade, as was polite, but instead swayed out of the tent and leaned up against the side, bobbing her head from side to side to wag her earrings ostentatiously. "The King isn't here," she said, gazing out at Cloud from lowered lashes, "so you can't bother him right now."

Cloud folded her fingers together and resisted the urge to snap at Hibiscus. It would accomplish nothing. "Can you tell me where he is?"

"Don't you want to see me?" Hibiscus trailed her delicate fingers across the gentle swell of her belly as though it were already rounded and heavy. "I'm with child, you know. And I've been feeling so tired lately."

"If you're ill, you should come and see me," Cloud said. Pain flared in her fingers as she tightened them in annoyance. "But a little tiredness is normal. The best thing is to get up and do something. Keep yourself busy"

"You should be the one coming to check on me," Hibiscus said. "I'm not supposed to over-exert myself. You're the healer. It's your job to take care of me."

Cloud took a deep breath and let her hands fall to her sides. "I'll try to come check on you more often," she promised. "But for now, it's urgent that I speak to the King. Can you tell me where he is?"

The king's wife pouted like a small child. "He's over by Clay's old tent. But I don't think he'll want to see you. You're mean to him." Hibiscus rubbed her belly again and retreated back into the coolness of the tent. "You should be nicer to people," she said from inside. "They talk, you know."

Well they might, Cloud thought to herself. She didn't care much if people talked, so long as they still listened. She pushed her irritation with Hibiscus out of her mind and went toward Clay's tent. It had been moved, of course, along with many of the other tents, when the forest had come alive. It was farther from the wall now and still empty. She wondered if anyone still expected the boy to return. How long would they leave one of the nicer tents vacant? Well, there were too many empty tents these days, though some had been dismantled to construct her large dwelling for the sick.

Now that she knew where to look, it didn't take long to find the King: he was sitting by the entrance to Clay's tent, sipping something from a gourd. The sweet aroma of palm wine was faint in the air. He gave her a wary stare when he saw her approaching, and only then did she realize how she must appear, marching up, her green cloth lifted above her knees, her lips clamped together. She tried to force herself to relax. "King Great Ram, I need to speak with you urgently."

"Look, if this is about the wine, I've hardly had any. I learned my lesson the other day." He cleared his throat. "Anyhow, it's none of your concern how much wine I drink."

"No, Ram, it's not about the wine. It's about your brother. You have to know. He's—"

She was interrupted by the sound of a buffalo horn rising high and jubilant above the camp.

"He's back!" Great Ram said, standing up.

Cursing the timing, Cloud put her hand on his arm. "Wait a moment, Great Ram. Just one moment." She wished he had remained seated for this. Standing, he towered chest and shoulders over her, and she would have preferred to meet his eyes.

"Yes, what is it?" He didn't even look down at her; he stared off in the direction of the camp's entrance with the impatience of a bored child.

She tightened her grip. "Listen to me. With everything that has happened, it's possible that you haven't seen it, but you must see it now. Laughing Dog is not the brother you remember. Whether in grief or illness or because of the heat he suffered in the desert, something has gone wrong. He doesn't sound like himself. He doesn't talk like a sane man anymore."

The King turned to her now, his gaze gone cool and cautious. "Oh yes? And what would your advice be, then?"

"I strongly advise that you remove him from your counsel. His words won't help you rule now. He can only lead you astray. Send him to me, let me help him, and—"

"And keep him from telling me things you don't agree with, is that it?"

"It has nothing to do with that." She snapped a bit to hide the partial lie. Of course she was concerned with Laughing Dog's state, but that was a small worry compared with that for the people. In times of great hardship, madness too could be a kind of spreading sickness. "I'm a healer, Ram," she said more gently. "And he's not well, that's all."

"He's grieving!" The words sprang from Ram's mouth like they'd escaped him, and he crumpled forward with emotion. "He's lost a father and a brother. We both have. Can't you know what that's like? You had a father too, didn't you?"

"Of course, long ago."

"No, but that's your problem, isn't it?" Ram said bitterly. "You don't understand grief."

Cloud was so astonished at this accusation, she had no words.

"It isn't your fault, I suppose. You see people die all the time. You're there with them so much you've grown used to it."

She shook herself out of her amazement. "You're right that I see it all the time. And I see their families and friends, too. I know what grief looks like. I'm telling you the truth, Ram—I feel deeply for you and Laughing Dog. But what I have seen in your brother is not grief. It's something darker, and maybe dangerous. You must be careful with him."

"He told me you'd say something like that, you know," Great Ram said. "He knows you've never liked him. Everyone knows it. They know it was you who got my father to send him out into the savanna. If the heat addled his mind, it's because you sent him out into it. And why? You don't like the things he says. You want him gone. Admit it."

"Ram!" She used her sharp voice, the one that still made him flinch instinctively when he heard it. "You know better than that. All that I've done, I did for your family, for our people. I never wanted this for you."

There were words she didn't say then. She didn't tell him how she had urged King First Claw not to exile Laughing Dog, how she had begged him. Take him in, instead, she had told him. Keep him by your side, as you do your eldest. You won't help him by removing him from communion with his people. Don't isolate the boy. She had urged him in the strongest tones one could use to urge a King. But what good would it do to tell Great Ram this now? How would it help the boy to know his father's grim determination, to know his disappointment in all his sons?

The King had thought Great Ram thick-witted and inflexible. Clay he had dismissed as too weak and yielding to lead. And he'd seen Laughing Dog's vain and compassionless pride, his refusal to accept that others might possess wisdom and strength he did not, and even in the face of Cloud's counsel, exiled him for it.

No. Cloud would not poison his sons' memories of him with these secrets. So instead she simply said, "I have always loved you boys. If I am ever harsh, it's only because I hope my harshness will spare you greater pain. I don't want Laughing Dog to suffer. But I'm afraid he's going to hurt you, Ram. I'm afraid he will do something—"

A great cheer rose up from the camp, near the entrance gate.

Great Ram put his heavy, callused hand on her shoulder. "Come. Let's go see just what my brother has done."

They went down from the little rise on which the finer tents were settled, past the tents of the people, past the sick tents and the circle for the council fire, past the rubbish heap and the stone and wood piles, down into the craft areas. There the people were gathered, shading their eyes from the bright afternoon sun. Children shouted and ran about. Men laughed and clapped each other on the back. Women embraced in joy. In their midst stood twelve of the strongest and fastest hunters in the camp, their arms folded across their chests, their skin smeared with charcoal and ash in striped patterns. Laughing Dog stood before them, his massive, fleshy body swollen with evident pride, his bright teeth gleaming in a triumphant grin.

"Look at what my new fire hunters have brought for our people, my King," he announced. He dipped his head low, spreading his thick arms wide. "Look at what the strength of men can bring."

At the feet of the hunters was a catch that made even Cloud's stomach growl with hunger: four huge eland carcasses, their throats slit, their flanks scorched black in places. It was meat. Life-sustaining, mouth-watering meat.

The King stepped forward, lifting his hands high. "Laughing Dog, my brother, you will be well remembered for this. After nearly a moon of little food, you and your hunters deliver us a feast for three days! Your people owe you their thanks and praise." With these last words, he gave Cloud a steady look over one shoulder.

She shook her head in defeated acknowledgement. When she looked back, she saw Laughing Dog staring up at her, with a knowing smile below those mad, dangerous eyes.

/\/\/\

Cloud woke in the night. Her tent was dark, the open roof showing only stars. She didn't sleep as much as she used to these days, but she could tell that this was earlier even than the dark hours she normally rose for work. The night was still deep. She wondered what had roused her and lay silent, listening.

For a moment, there was nothing, and then from outside, the sound of a man shouting, and then another. A crunching sound, like splintering wood, and a woman's scream. It could be only one thing. The camp was being attacked.

The confusion of sleep rushed away from her mind, leaving only keen alertness. She rolled to her feet and found her knife in the dim red light of the embers from her fire. No peoples had ever attacked another in her memory, but there were tales of raids in times of desperation and great need. Times like now. The sick would need protecting.

She ducked the opening in her tent and blinked in the darkness. The bright orange lights of torches starred her vision, and opposite her tent, along the southern wall of the camp that bordered the forest, the lights bobbed and danced, leaving glossy, blurred trails as their bearers darted back and forth. No way to tell from here if those were her people or the raiders. She could see, though, as the torchlight cast shadows across the high row of logs that formed the camp's fence, a place of darkness, a gap, with splintered wood jutting up from the bottom like broken teeth. The fence had been smashed in by something. She had no idea what could have wielded such a powerful force as to fell the fence.

A man's shadow darted across the fence, and then the shadow of something else, something *huge*, loomed above it. Two great arms pummeled down, and the man's shadow fell. She heard his cry as he dropped. Then the shadow of the large beast sprouted long, thin arms—spears—from its back and belly. It bellowed a deep, groaning roar and fell forward.

Cloud ran toward the sick tent's entrance, the pains and stiffness of old age forgotten, urgency giving her limbs and joints the readiness they needed to survive, to protect her people. She risked a quick glance inside the tent to ensure all were safe and accounted for. Mongoose shouted in alarm when he saw her appear, but she whispered her assurances and told everyone to keep quiet.

She positioned herself before the entrance, standing in a half-crouch, her little knife held at the ready. It would do little to stop a beast like the one whose shadow she'd seen, but it was all she had. Her patients needed her. She waited, her toes curling into the packed earth, her heart pounding so loudly that the cries and chuffing animal grunts were barely audible.

Animals, not raiders. A torch would fend off an animal better than a knife. She darted forward and snatched up the torch near the path, holding it with both arms, waving it slowly to make it burn more brightly as she backed toward the opening of the sick tent again. She scanned the darkness for threats, but it was only darkness.

Then she saw something, a great, black shape looming up out of the darkness, as tall as a man, but much more massive. It made a low, rumbling sound and came forward. In the torchlight, she could see that it resembled a monkey, but it was far larger, covered with dark black hair. Its shoulders and arms were humped with powerful muscle, its head domed high.

She was seized with the impulse to turn and run away as fast as she could, but instead she waved the torch at it with both hands. "Get back!" she shouted. "Get out of here!"

The beast lumbered toward her sideways, on all fours, and then reared up on its hind legs, towering over her at almost twice her height, each of its arms as long and thick as her whole body, and roared. Its eyes were beady and angry, its teeth as long as a lion's, flashing white in the firelight.

"Get back!" she shouted again, but terror stole the words away and left her with only a squeaking whisper. She held the torch up as high as she could with both arms, jabbing it at the monster's face as it loomed over her.

It roared again and lifted one arm to slap at her. She flinched back from the impending blow, holding her feeble spark before her as though it could burn away all the darkness in the world.

The beast made a *whuff* sound, dropping to all fours again. It stumbled to one side, pawing at its neck. The thin shaft of an arrow jutted from it, dripping with dark blood. The great beast turned around, emitting a low cry, eerily like that of a man.

Behind the creature stood Ant With a Leaf, tall and proud, her bow drawn with another arrow ready.

Unsteadily, the beast ran at her on all fours, its powerful legs propelling it forward at startling speed. Ant loosed her arrow, and the beast's limbs collapsed beneath it. It tumbled and fell at her feet. Its sides swelled with a deep breath, sank, swelled again, and sank. It did not take another breath.

Cloud dropped to her knees, her arms shaking as she held the torch. "Ant. Thank the gods."

Ant came forward and took Cloud's arm, pulling her gently to her feet again. "Are you all right?"

"Yes," Cloud said. "I'm all right."

To her surprise, the taller woman pulled her into an embrace, arms closing tightly around her. "You stood in that beast's path with only a little fire," she whispered into Cloud's ear. "You saved my father's life. I will never forget it. Never." Then she released Cloud and, bracing her foot against the fallen black beast, wrenched her arrows free and ran back into the night.

Cloud sat at the entrance to the sick tent, too shaken and exhausted to stand, her torch still held at the ready. She shivered as she watched the darkness, but no more of the beasts emerged to trouble her.

When the shouts and grunts finally quieted, and the frenetic movements of torches and shadows at the far side of camp stilled, she calmed her patients and went to find out what had happened.

Three were injured and would require aid: a weaver; a carpenter; and Scorpion, one of Laughing Dog's twelve fire hunters. Each of these had broken bones and bruises. Of the remaining injured, none had anything more serious than a few cuts and scrapes.

From them, she learned the story of what had happened as she bound their cuts and set bones. Sometime in the night, the beasts had crashed through the fence, waking those who slept near it. The creatures had been maddened, attacking anyone they saw, slapping the torches aside. With powerful arms, they had pounded down the nearby tents as though they had known that people were sleeping inside, snapping wood and tearing hide as easily as twigs and grass. Hunters had felled four of the beasts, including the one Ant With a Leaf had killed, and if there were any remaining, they had fled back into the forest they came from. The King was safe and had not been roused by the attack until it was too late.

Cloud treated the wounded, thanked the gods that none had been killed by the monsters from the forest, and then returned to her tent to prepare poultices for the next morning. She was certain she would get no more sleep that night even though guards had been assigned to stand by the gap in the fence and watch the forest. But soon, despite her certainty, fatigue sapped at her mind, the energy and fear from the attack ebbing away and leaving only a drowsy exhaustion.

"Cloud! Cloud! You have to come now!"

She opened her eyes, not remembering closing them. She was sitting near her little fire for brewing medicines, her head nodded forward. "What is it?" she asked, looking up.

A little girl stood outside her tent. Baobab, the Teller's daughter. "She's dead," the girl said. "A monster killed her. It's really awful and everyone's upset. They say it's just like the King died."

"What?" Cloud got to her feet. The alarm that had vitalized her earlier did not avail her now. "Who's dead?"

"Come see," Baobab said.

Cloud followed her out into the camp. The morning light tinged the eastern sky, already bright enough that torches were no longer needed. Baobab led her up through the tents toward the area of the camp where the King and elders lived, and Cloud felt a creeping dread. "Who is it?" she asked.

"There," Baobab said, pointing toward a crowd of people clustered behind one of the tents.

Cloud moved toward them, and when they saw her, their muttering quieted. They parted to let her come forward. In their midst lay a body. As Baobab had reported, the victim had been badly mutilated, very much like King First Claw had been. It lay supine on the ground, arms splayed, face covered by fallen cloth. The stomach and heart had been torn out and partially devoured, the skin shredded by carnivorous fangs. The victim's neck was thin, the skin loose with age, the fingers long and knobbed, knuckles swollen. Cloud did not need to move the cloth to know whose body lay before her.

It was Two Broken Hands. The forest had claimed its sacrifice after all.

Demons

Doto's thoughts were thick and slow. His head pulsed with pain, and something gripped his wrists and ankles, crushing them together. His eyes cracked open to the morning light. He could see nothing but sky and the bobbing heads of grasses, but he could hear Clay breathing and the sound of a crackling fire.

The pungent reek of char and sizzling blood and bird flesh stung at his nose, but he sniffed at the air, picking through the scents for other odors. Clay he could smell, musky and a little acrid, and beyond that the ripe, black smell of ashes. There were feathers, the scent of a bird he did not recognize. And through the smoke and grass, the odors of two fire bearers. Men. One of them large, both with the sickly-sweet stink of hunger about them.

The memories of the night before bloomed in Doto's mind, though focusing on them was unpleasant with his head pounding so. He had woken to Clay's cry and seen him held by another fire bearer. There had been a knife to Clay's throat. The sharp tang of Clay's terror had filled Doto's nose, and he'd leapt to his feet, intent on killing this insignificant, foolish creature for daring to threaten a god's possession. But then something had struck him from behind—that must have been the second fire bearer, who he'd been too careless to notice. In the forest, either of them would have been insignificant, their menace laughable. But out here, with his power gone, they had snared him, and his shame and fury seethed through him and coiled in his chest like a viper. He would break free of his bonds and tear out their bellies for what they had done.

He tugged at his wrists firmly, but the twine binding them behind his back did not yield. If he had fallen in Clay's dance circle, he would have his strength. He wondered how close it was. He could not smell the forest from here. He pulled harder, growling quietly, his shoulders straining, but his efforts only made the twine bite deeply into his wrists.

A voice near the fire spoke. "It moved. Woke, it did."

Doto lay still. Would they bludgeon him again? He did not care for the thought.

A deeper voice answered. "It looks still to me."

"Sure and sure I saw it move. Go and look."

"Look I will, but keep you your longsharp. Your knots may hold a demon nay."

Footsteps rustled through the grasses toward Doto, and then thickly callused fire bearer toes nudged at his side. "Demon. Are you waked?"

Doto remained still until it nudged again, and then snarled and lunged at its fleshy brown calf, his fangs bared.

The fire bearer shouted wordlessly and leapt back, out of Doto's reach.

Well. At least he had taught it that he was not safe. He rolled to his side to peer up at it. It was large, taller than he, with broad shoulders. He could tell that at one time, it had been thick with muscle, but hunger had withered it. It was not so mighty now as it once had been, but it still appeared strong. It was larger than the bearer he'd seen last night, the one holding a knife to Clay's throat, so this must be the one that had struck him from behind. Its face was lumpy and unpleasant, thick brows squeezing its eyes into a squint, and it had scars across its chest and arm from a large beast that must have clawed at it long ago. Whatever the beast had been, it had had bigger paws than Doto.

Doto gave the fire bearer a low, menacing growl.

"Like and he tried to bite me before!" the bearer said. It bared its pathetic, square little teeth and gave an imitation of a growl in return, then swung its foot and kicked Doto in the ribs.

Thorns of pain sprouted and tightened in Doto's chest, nearly dizzying him with their sharpness, but he made no outcry.

"Doto?" Clay's voice came from a little distance behind him. "Doto, did they hurt you? Are you okay?"

"Quiet," said the other fire bearer, the one still near the fire. "Lest you want to meet my sharp again."

"I am unhurt," Doto said through his teeth. "No fire bearer can harm me."

"Fire bearer?" said the one near the fire. "What is that? Rise him, Ulo." So, the big claw-scarred one was Ulo. Doto would remember his name.

Ulo stepped over him, warily keeping his toes away from Doto's muzzle, and grabbed him by his arms, hefting him up with a strong tug that wrenched Doto's shoulders in their sockets.

Doto balanced precariously on his bound feet, his tail jagging left and right to keep him from tilting. From here he could see that they were camped some distance from the forest circle and stream. Clay lay bound to his right, and the sight of his worshipper lying helpless and frightened on the ground made his fury rise again. He would make these pitiful fire bearers suffer for what they had done.

By the low fire sat a thin, short bearer, the one Doto had seen with its knife to Clay's throat last night. Its head was smooth and bald, its smile twisted and cruel. It was turning meat, spitted on a stick, above the flames. Behind it was the carcass of the slaughtered bird Doto had smelled, but it was unlike any bird Doto had ever seen. It was huge: standing, it would be taller than he. Its body was a bedraggled clump of thick black feathers, and, like its legs, its neck was long and naked in the grass.

"We cut out its magic now, Jai?" Ulo asked. His thick fingers clasped around Doto's scruff, tugging in a way that made him still. It had been long since anyone had held him in that way; Kwaee had done it, roughly, to tug him around, and before that…Doto struggled to recall. A gentler touch.

"Now cut it nay, Ulo," said the smaller bearer, rolling to his feet. He came closer. His eyes were close-set and focused, like an eagle's, darting swiftly from place to place. "You want its magic, yea?" He jerked his head toward the forest circle behind him.

"Sure." Doto heard the sticky sound of the fire bearer licking his lips.

With his teeth, Jai slid a greasy hunk of meat from the stick and snapped it between his jaws, drippings of fat drizzling into his thin beard. He chewed with his lips drawn as he sauntered over to Doto. "Grew yourself a patch of forest there, yea? Fine with fruits and flowers it is. Tell me true now, and I'll share with you ostrich meat."

His breath was foul; up close, the reek of hunger was stronger, but there was rot on it as well. The fool creature did not know to chew grass to clean his teeth. Doto wrinkled his nose in disgust. "I care nothing for your tainted bird flesh. You will release me immediately, and my worshiper."

Jai chewed gristle between his teeth slowly. "Your worshiper, he is? Your witch, you mean, yea?"

It would be a mistake to let them realize he had never heard of this witch thing. Denial was safest. "He is not my witch. He is my subject, and under my protection."

"Your protection?" Jai grinned. "He can't be thinking that's worth much now. Tied up, you are. Tied up, he is. Dead you'll be soon—"

"I cannot die," Doto interrupted him. This foolish creature thought to challenge him, to threaten him? Even the lowest beasts knew never to threaten a god. He tested his bonds again, shoulders straining.

"Die you can nay?" asked Jai. "Sure and you can grow pretty circles of flowers, and fruit that calls the tongue, but I've nay heard of a demon that were proof to the sharp."

"Demon!" Doto scoffed. "Why do all you fire bearers call me demon when first you see me? What do you think demons are? They are you. It was fire bearers who burned the world long ago. They slaughtered the forest and spat in the faces of their gods. You are the demons." His old, remembered hatred of the fire bearers from the tales rose up unbidden, and the last words he spoke as a growl. He did not like these bearers; they were nothing like his Clay. They were insolent and filthy and vile. Had he captured one of *these* long ago, he would have had no hesitation in dragging it screaming to his father and slaughtering it in front of him.

Jai looked puzzled at this response and chewed another hunk of meat from his stick before responding. "Demon, you call me? But sure and I am demon nay. A man, I am. And if you are demon nay as well, then tell me, what manner of creature wears the face and fang of a beast but like a man walks?"

Straightening his back, Doto declared, "I am Doto, god of the forest."

Jai stared at him stupidly for a moment, then looked over Doto's shoulder at the fire bearer behind him. His eyes widened. But then he responded neither in reverence nor in terror, but in laughter, his stinking breath puffing into Doto's face, spittle flecking the fine fur there. He bellowed his infuriating guffaws, and a moment later, Ulo hesitantly joined in with a deep, rolling chuckle.

"A god are you?" Jai said between laughs. "Doto, god of the forest? Sure and gone and deposed Kwaee and taken over! Now decided to take a sojourn into the savanna, adoring stripling at his side?"

"I am a god!" Doto roared into his face in fury. He was satisfied to see Jai shrink back in shock, his laughter silenced, though Ulo still chuckled on behind him.

Jai pressed his lips into a thin line. "If a god you are, then tell me: a god I found, felled him, bound him, and now have him here at my mercy. What would that make me?"

Doto showed all his fangs. "A dead man."

Jai's arm twitched, and a knife sprouted from his hand. He pressed the point to Doto's throat. "You scorn me nay more, demon. Tell us your magic, the magic that grew forest here. Sure, here and a day beyond. Found them both, we did. Full of food. Poison, like or nay."

"It's not poison," came Clay's voice from near the fire. "I swear to you it isn't. Please, take as much as you want, if you're hungry."

"Of course it's nay poison," Jai said, his mouth twisting into a sneer.

"Jai, maybe he tells true," said Ulo. He stepped forward, though he kept his hand firmly on Doto's scruff.

"Sure and he tells true!" Jai worked a lump of gristle from between his rotting teeth and spat it at Doto's feet. "Go and eat all you like. Take bunches home with you, for Kelea and your bab! In their hungry smiles stuff it. Thank their goodman and da they will as they die."

As Jai spoke, Ulo's fingers cinched tighter and tighter on Doto's scruff, until he wanted to cry out at the pain of it. But he would not. He would not let these pathetic creatures see that they could hurt him. "First the demon would die," Ulo said. The scent of anger mixed with that of hungry, smoke-stained fire bearer.

Jai's smile stretched thin. Doto didn't like it. When Clay smiled, it changed his whole face, but when this fire bearer smiled, nothing changed. It was a lie of a smile, showing no teeth. How backward these fire bearers were. When they were pleased, they bared their fangs, and when they were angry, they hid them. "No," Jai said. "First you would die." Still keeping the knife to Doto's throat, he gestured toward the forest circle. "Go and taste some of the fruit, Ulo. We'll see sure whether this demon has poisoned it."

The thick fingers released Doto's scruff, and he was able to relax a bit, to balance on his toes better, putting his body into readiness as the big fire bearer came forward, hands outstretched.

"But Jai, what if it's poisoned yea? Make the witch try it. We care if he dies nay."

"Please, I'll be happy to try it," Clay said. "I'll prove to you it's not poisoned. None of this is needed. We'll give you as much fruit as you want. You don't have to do this to us."

"What proves it if the witch dies nay?" Jai demanded. "Only that his demon serves him true. Ulo, sure and you must try. Memory those of home, on forest edge, hungered and stilled for you while forest wars. Taste for them, for people and king. For your bab squalling at Kelea's dry teat. Man enough to feed him, you are."

Ulo's brow lowered, his jaw bulging as his teeth set. "Man enough true." He stretched out his shoulders and walked toward the circle of grass and flower, sapling and fruit.

Doto ignored the knife at his throat and watched intently. He was outside of the circle now, but could he still affect it? Could he grow and move the vines from here? If so, he would coil them around the big fire bearer and tear him limb from limb. Perhaps the display would frighten Jai so much he would run away. And then Doto could get free, hunt him down, and rip open his belly.

He couldn't feel the energies in the ground, but that didn't mean they weren't there. He sent his will out, out, down through the savanna grasses and into the earth, through the soil and rocks and roots, beneath the fire, and into the forest circle, willing it to rise up through root and stem and leaf. *Bend, leaf,* he commanded. *Grow, stem. Spread, roots.* He could feel nothing. He narrowed his eyes, peering. Did the leaves move, or was it just a breeze?

Jai squinted at him. "What do you, now? Seek to work your demon magics on him, do you?" He jabbed the knife up under Doto's chin. "He dies, you die."

Doto ignored his irrelevant threat. He slowed his breathing, concentrating as Ulo entered the forest circle. He forced the awareness of the circle into his mind, creating within his thoughts the sensation of Ulo's toes, round and clawless, callused to a wooden texture on the bottom, sinking down into the fresh grass of the forest circle. He felt the weight of the bearer's heel, crushing flower petals, grinding pollen into the soft forest earth. Stems snapped beneath feet as Ulo moved into the center of the circle, where he would not be safe, where the saplings whose lean, silvered branches still bowed with heavy fruit. There Doto would kill him.

He tilted back his head, breathed out steadily, and closed his eyes.

Jai must have suspected Doto's intentions—he drew in a sharp breath, his weight shifting against Doto as he turned. "Ulo!" Alarm frightened the snarl from his voice. "Ulo, get out of there!"

Doto sent violent rage into the vines. He shook with the effort, pouring every drop of his wrath into them. *Grow, thorn, ensnare, kill, kill, kill!*

"Ulo!" Jai shouted again.

There was a long silence.

"Fine it is!" Ulo called back, voice bright and hopeful. "There's nay danger!"

Doto opened his eyes. The large bearer stood in the center of the forest circle, holding up one of the clayfruits. Not a leaf had stirred, not a root had crawled deeper into the soil. He was powerless.

The fear emptied from Jai's eyes as Ulo returned, carrying the fruit, which looked small in his big hands. "Well, go on then," Jai said, sounding surly, as though ashamed at his cry of alarm now that it had proven unwarranted. "Bite it and see if it's safe true."

Ulo stared at the clayfruit, chewing at his bottom lip. With a slow reluctance, he lifted it in his fingers and sank his teeth into it. The juice ran down his lip and into his beard. He shivered, and his eyes went wide. "Wonderful it is!" he exclaimed. "Any other fruit I've had is good as nay! Try some, Jai!" He held out his big hands with the pulpy remainder of the fruit oozing juice over his fingers.

Jai jumped back as though Ulo had handed him an angry serpent. "Try some I will, when you've lived half a day and are healthy as now." He steadied himself and then gave Doto's shoulder a firm shove.

Doto lashed his tail as he tried to steady himself on bound feet. He toppled over, unable even to put his paws out to brace the impact against the ground. His shoulder and the side of his muzzle thudded hard against the earth, and he let out a short yowl. The pain was unexpected and intense, but he barely felt it beneath his seething hatred for the bearer.

"Lie still," Jai ordered him. "Or my friend will hurt you."

He gave a long, threatening growl in response.

"Doto?" Clay called. "Doto, are you okay? What happened?"

Jai ambled across the grass, his lean frame blurred against the glare of the mid-morning sun behind him. "Fine your pet demon is," he sneered. "For now. And if my fast friend Ulo lives to see the midday sun, so may he."

"Please," Clay's voice begged in a high groan. "Please just let us go. We've done nothing to you."

"Like and sure," Jai said. "You should have done when you could. Waiting for us are our people, many of them, more than a witch like you could number, had you ten times finger and toe. And they hunger. Wars them, the forest does. Kills them all if they enter. No forest scarces the meat, but scarces more the fruit and root and nut and seed, sure? Scouts travel far to feed the hungering, and here we two find you. Now we have witch and demon magic to fill the round bellies of our strips. Nay, witch. We'll nay let you go. Even if our families were full of belly, we'd nay free you. Demons in our savanna meet the sharp and go back to Fam."

"I'm not a witch." Clay's voice was full of despair now. "I swear by all the gods that I am not. I'm just trying to help my people and get back home, just like you. It's all I want."

"Think nay of home and freedom now," Jai said. "Think better of how much pain you want before you die."

〜

The sun crawled its path across the sky and Doto lay helpless in the dirt. Ants and gnats crept across his hide, and biting flies lit on his face where the fur grew shorter, giving him experimental nips. He could do nothing but squirm, and these efforts soon exhausted him. Several times he tried calling to Clay, but was rewarded with only a heavy kick to the side from Ulo. These men were as different from Clay as bird from fish. He was beginning to understand why his father hated the fire bearers so.

Every now and then, Jai would ask Ulo how he was feeling, and Ulo would profess great wellness of being and satisfaction. Doto wished he could make the fruit sour in his belly and sicken him, but he had not even that power. No, all that Doto, god of the forest, could do was lie in the dirt and try not to drool it into mud.

A hope crept into his mind. At night, these men would go to sleep. Doto could not walk, but he could crawl. Like a snake, he would wriggle his way through the grasses until he reached his forest circle. There, his power would be restored, and the men would be sorry indeed if they ventured in after him. He had only to wait until nightfall.

When the sun was high above, Jai enquired as to Ulo's condition, and the larger fire bearer again claimed to feel fit and well, and even expressed an interest in having another of the fruits.

The grasses rustled with Jai's footsteps as he returned to Doto. Narrow fingers gripped his scruff and tugged his head up. He blinked blearily at Jai's lean smile.

"Good news for you, demon. Ulo dies nay, so you die nay, at least for now."

Doto licked his jaws; his tongue and throat were dry, and his voice rasped when he spoke. "Then what? Take the fruits back to your miserable people and leave us alone, beast."

Jai laughed loudly at that. "Hear you, Ulo? The cat calls a man a beast! Has it comedy, or is it stupid?"

"I don't think either," Ulo said, coming closer. He scratched the back of his neck.

Jai's black eyes glittered like coal. "Stupid, I think it is," he said, his close-lipped smile widening. "Else already we'd know its magic, yea. Know, and nay wish injury it. Rise it standing, Ulo."

Doto stiffened as the big man's arms went around him and yanked him upright again. His tail twitched angrily between the fire bearer's calves.

"There we are," said Jai, standing from his crouch. He still had his knife in his hand, and gestured with it toward the forest circle. "You will tell us how the growing was done. Your magics will aid our people. With it we'll feed them sure."

"You cannot use my magic," Doto said, filling his voice with all the scorn he could muster. "You are not a god. You have no power. Only I can use it."

"Then use it now," Jai said. "Show us."

Doto's ears perked upright in sudden hope. "Take me over to the forest circle, and I will."

"Right." Ulo gripped him from behind with both arms. "I'll carry you over there." His grip was painfully tight around Doto's waist and bound arms as he carried him a few steps.

Doto's heart raced. The fools were actually going to bring him, of their own volition, into the patch of forest where his powers would emerge. In a moment, he would be free. He readied his will to flow into the plants.

"Wait a minute." Jai's voice was sharp and urgent. "Wait. Put him down."

A surge of disappointment coursed through Doto as the big fire bearer lowered him to the ground again. "Don't you want to see how my magic works?" he asked. "That is the only way I can show you."

Jai slithered up him, insinuating the point of his knife under Doto's chin. "A pitiful lie," he sneered. "If only in the green you can work your power true, then whence the green, demon? How did it come to be there?" The line of his mouth tightened, his lips whitening. "Then why should you wish to be put there? A trap, it is, sure and sure." His dark eyes darted back and forth. "Sure, a trap and more. You enter the green, and there call your poisons or your fellow demons to destroy us."

He looked over at Clay. Sweat slid down his bald head. "Then why the witch? What use is he?" He scratched at his chest with short, chewed nails. "To call the demon, sure."

Jai turned and went to Clay, roughly yanking him his knees. "You, boy. Witched the demon here, you did. Tell it true. Teach us how you called it."

The sight of Clay's face sent a deep pang through Doto. His worshiper was frightened and miserable, and there were patches of blood where his skin had scraped against the ground. Clay met his gaze and held it, his eyes the color of jeweled mahogany in the sunlight.

"I didn't call him," Clay said quietly. His voice was unsteady. "He's a god. He goes where he pleases."

Jai spat at Clay's feet. "A god? Never. A demon, sure. Which god could be bound and threatened? A god I'd nay worship. Think me fool, to be deceived so quick?"

"What if you're wrong?" Clay asked. He turned his gaze from Doto to Jai's slitted eyes. "What do you think will happen to you?"

Jai's narrow line of a mouth finally split to bare his square teeth. "What do you think will happen to you if you talk nay?" he snarled, and he lifted his knife to Clay's cheek, sliding it up under one earlobe. "Only one ear you need to hear my questions, witch!"

The voice of Doto's sole worshiper and mate cried out in terror.

What would you feel if I died? The terrible question sounded and echoed in his head. *What would you feel?* The question rose louder and louder, drowning every other thought and feeling, filling him with dreadful necessity. He roared, wrenching his feet against the coarse cords that bound around his ankles. They dug and scraped into his skin, cutting deep, but he barely noticed the pain. Ulo cried out for him to stay still, but he ignored the fire bearer, twisting right and left, trying to yank his arms free of the bearer's grip. He ground his ankles together, twisting his leg until he felt an angle at which the cords loosened. He wrenched one foot free. There was a burning pain and a tearing sensation as the rough twine, sunken into his skin, pulled and tore a strip of his flesh down his heel, but now he could walk. With a powerful twist, he pulled himself free of Ulo and lunged toward Jai, his claws flexing out of his still-bound paws, his fangs bared. In a few steps, he would be able to rip out the man's throat with his teeth.

Without even a pause of surprise, Jai grabbed Clay by one shoulder and stepped behind him, putting Clay in between Doto and himself. His knife went to Clay's throat. "Step more and he dies."

Doto stopped mid-stride and, without free arms to balance, nearly tumbled forward. "Let him go or *you* die," he growled, but the last word was knocked from his lungs by the great bulk of Ulo slamming into him from behind. Thick arms wrapped around him and squeezed tightly

"Once I killed a lion, true," the large fire bearer said into his ear. The pressure around Doto's chest increased; his breaths came shorter and shallower. "Sharp nay, neither longsharp nor close. Only my hands. I crushed it until its ribs broke and its breath came nay, and it died. And a lion is larger and stronger far than you, sure and sure. Know you what it did? It threatened my friend Jai. For that I killed it true."

"I...cannot...die..." Doto gasped.

"But go to sleep you can," Jai said. "And then who will protect your precious little witch?" He smiled again, and then his smile faded.

"Tell us your magic," Ulo said. "And maybe I'll want to hurt you less."

Doto tried to answer, but his breath was too small for the words. Bright lights flickered across his vision.

"Tell us," Ulo said again, but Jai interrupted him.

"Ulo. Look." He pointed with his free hand at the ground.

Doto took a deep, desperate breath as the pressure around his chest eased, and his head pounded with the sudden flow of air and blood in his veins. Panting, he turned to look where Jai was pointing.

He had left a few bloody footprints on the ground; his skin had torn down the back of his paw, and he could feel the warm blood, sticky and clumping in his fur, and could smell its tang in the air. What was surprising was not the injury or the blood, but the magic it had awakened. From each drop and smear of blood, plants had grown thick and wild: berry-laden vines, fruit-bearing saplings, seeded pods, twining lianas, and high grasses.

"In his blood, the magic dwells," Jai said, his voice wondering. "True and that is what we need. The demon's blood." He stared at the freshly sprouted plants, then back up at Doto. "We take him back to the village and spill his blood to grow a whole field of forest, one that bears fruit true and attacks us nay. Two fields, ten, our own forest filled with food."

Doto gaped at him. The fire bearer was mad. "How much blood do you think I have?" he asked.

"That hardly matters," Jai said, shrugging. "We have your witch. We can drain you of all you have to grow food. And then we will make your witch call you back again. And again. And again. Bleed you dead for moon after endless moon we can, sure and true."

⌄⌄⌄

Doto shifted on his knees; the ground was beginning to dig into them. He was supremely uncomfortable. The fire bearers had put his back to a small tree and bound his wrists and ankles behind it. He could neither stand nor lie down, but was forced to kneel against the tree. He could straighten or relax a little, but no position was tolerable for long. He was exhausted and starving and his foot hurt.

Once the fire bearers had seen that his blood carried the forest inside it, they had quickly gathered their belongings and untied Clay's feet. Then they had marched both Doto and Clay south, each with vines noosed around their neck that were tied so as to give a choking yank if either of them tried to run. Jai kept his knife at Doto's back the whole time. The bearers had taken them southeast, away from Clay's village and away from Sarmu. The situation was inconceivable to Doto. He had thought his father cruel, but these fire bearers were worse. They had forced him onward, without food or rest, on a wounded foot, with no regard for how he felt about the matter, and worse, when they arrived, they planned to bleed him into the savanna ground, over and over. Doto had no expectation that this would go as planned. Sometime they would forget to pay attention, or to bind him tightly. Or when he died, he would return to the forest and be safe.

But Clay... He had no idea how to save Clay. If he died, they would try to get Clay to bring him back, and that was beyond his abilities. These monsters would surely kill Clay if he failed to bring Doto back. So they would have to escape before arriving at the bearers' village, however far away that was. Jai and Ulo wouldn't say; in fact, they would answer no questions at all, and rewarded any queries or attempts to speak with a kick, a knock on the back of the head, or a prod from the knife point.

Doto looked up at Clay. His worshiper was bound, as he was, to another tree, some distance away, too far for them to talk without alerting Jai and Ulo, who now slept around the cooling embers of a fire. He ached to hold Clay again. Up until the day Doto had left the safety of the forest, he had never truly suffered. He had been lonely, of course, and punished by Kwaee at times, but he had never felt the hunger, exhaustion, and pain that mortal creatures felt. He marveled that they could go through their lives withstanding it, that they could bear to continue at all. But as unpleasant as his pain and fatigue had been, witnessing Clay's was all the worse. Doto had felt each of Clay's exhausted steps, every brutal clap on the back of the head from Ulo, as though they were his own. And he was helpless to stop it, helpless. All the powers of a god, and he could not save one frail little follower.

Clay was slumped forward against the tree, no doubt trying uselessly to get some sleep, and Doto longed to provide it for him, to hold Clay against his chest and feel him drift into peaceful stillness. Instead he had to watch Clay bob against his bonds, uneasy breathing preventing any real rest. So he gazed, eyelids drooping with weariness, listening to the cicadas as he waited for whatever terrible suffering the next day would bring.

Then Clay pitched forward. Doto's heart stilled—for a moment he thought his fire bearer had collapsed, but no, he caught himself on his hands.

His hands.

Clay had broken free of his bonds. Again they had a chance for escape. Doto watched with rising eagerness as Clay twisted around the tree, picking at the twine that bound his feet. Whatever he was doing to free himself, it was taking a long time. The moon crawled across the sky as if eager to bring the morning sooner.

Doto peered toward Jai and Ulo, his ears swiveling. He could hear only the cicadas and the slow, rhythmic breathing of the men. Occasionally one of them would groan and roll onto their side, and Doto's heart would forget to beat for moment.

Finally, Clay leaned forward and stood. He stretched upward, craning his neck toward Ulo and Jai, and when apparently satisfied that they were not moving, took careful steps toward Doto. The grasses rustled beneath his toes.

Now Doto wished that Clay still had his leopard's foot, or better yet, four of them. The bearer was always more graceful when walking on cat toes. Were Doto the freed one, he could have slunk through the brush on all fours, carefully lifting each limb to step up and over the grasses in stealthy, soundless movements. He could have crept right up under Jai's nose without waking him. As it was, the fire bearer seemed to make as much noise as an elephant blundering through the underbrush. Surely their captors would awaken. Doto kept his ears anxiously trained toward the sleeping pair, but they did not stir.

Then Clay reached him. He looked tired and frightened, and his wrists were chafed and bleeding. He crouched and stroked Doto's cheek. Initially this annoyed Doto. Why waste time when at any moment they might be caught? But just the touch of his worshiper's fingertips—lightly brushing his skin through the fur, combing his whiskers back—and the tension melted out of him. He had not realized how much he had longed for closeness.

He lost himself in the touch, his eyes closing, and then it ended. Clay's fingers pressed against his muzzle in a plain signal to be silent, a silly one at that. Of course he would not make a sound! He would be far more silent than any clumsy fire bearer.

Sidling like a river crab, Clay moved around to the other side of the tree, loose rocks and dirt crunching under his soles. His fingers brushed lightly against Doto's wrists and paws as he worked at the knots in the twine. Why didn't he just chew through the cords? Those flat little teeth had to be good for something, didn't they? But Clay insisted on attempting to untie the knots, and while Doto wanted to whisper back and suggest that he try chewing, he didn't trust his voice to be low enough not to wake the bearers. Clay was making too much noise as it was, giving little grunts of frustration as he tugged and pulled at the twine. Doto tried pressing himself closer to the tree to give Clay a little slack to work with, his knees digging into the hard roots and pebbles at its base.

A sound, the pop of a stiff joint. Doto paused, his ears flicking toward the fire bearer's camp again. He could still hear the two breathing, but something was different. One was breathing faster. Steadily he turned his head toward the camp, hoping his eyes would not flash in the dim orange light still cast by the fire.

One of them was standing. Ulo, large, shoulders slumped with sleepiness. The silhouette of his bearded head turned left and right, and then fixed on the tree where Clay had been tied, where the moonlight plainly outlined an empty trunk.

Doto's fur lifted, prickling his skin. He curled his tail about and frantically slapped its soft tip against Clay's face, trying to alert him.

The shadowed bearer turned to stare at him. "Hey," he said, voice still slow and thick with sleep. Then, louder, "Hey! Hey Jai, they're trying to escape!" He ran toward the tree where they both crouched.

Doto felt Clay's fingers tug desperately at his knots; it was foolish; he would never undo them in time. "Run, Clay," Doto hissed back at him. "Don't worry about me! Run!"

Clay gave a shuddering gasp, turned, and bolted, his toes scrabbling for a moment in the gravel as he struggled to get to his feet. He ran out, away from the camp, but Doto knew his knees and feet would be stiff and chafed from hours of bondage.

Ulo was galloping after him like a maddened ape, and he had a head start. He bounded past Doto's tree, his feet kicking up dirt that caught the moonlight in little puffs, then took several furious lunges forward. His fingers raked through the air as he leapt, a primal, predatory silhouette in the night. One groping mitt caught Clay's shoulder.

Clay cried out wordlessly as he was seized, his body twisting in Ulo's grip and buckling to the ground. He struggled face down in the dry grass, trying to get up.

Ulo stood over him, one foot planted in the small of his back. He was panting, hands on his knees; the big man was unused to running. "Thought you'd catch your demon free and escape, did you, true? Planning to gash us both in our sleep, like as nay."

He drew back his foot and kicked Clay hard, so forcefully that the little bearer was lifted into the air with a pained yelp, knocked onto his back. Doto flinched back against the tree as though he had been kicked himself.

"Try and run now, strip." The big man growled the words through his teeth, and they dripped with bloodthirsty satisfaction. He kicked Clay again. Doto could not see from his position where Ulo had struck Clay, nor how hard, but there was another cry, this one longer and more despairing.

Never before had he heard a sound like it from Clay, nor any other fire bearer, but he recognized it all the same. He had heard similar cries from forest creatures, prey caught in the teeth and claws of their predators. It was the sound of a creature that was in pain and helpless, that knew it was going to die and could do nothing to stop it.

The sound of his mate's cry sent Doto's blood pounding, and the heat of it drowned thought from his head. He tugged furiously at his bonds, the twine biting deep into his wrists and ankles. He had broken free before, and he could break free again. He shook the tree he was tied to. He roared and snarled in god-tongue, forgetting the fire bearer's language, thinking of nothing but rescuing his precious bearer any way possible. If he could have, he would have pulled off his paws and crawled his way to Clay on bleeding limbs.

But he could do nothing. Ulo had tied him much tighter this time, using thicker cord, winding it around his wrists and ankles many more times, and the tree pressing against his back made much squirming or movement impossible.

Ulo kicked Clay again, a solid thump. Clay gasped for breath and croaked Doto's name. Again and again the man struck him, each blow sending Doto reeling, and now Clay was barely crying out at all. He only wheezed and gasped between the blows.

Jai sauntered past Doto, his thin mouth smiling tighter than ever. He paused by the tree, and Doto snapped at him with fangs that couldn't quite reach the thin bearer's vulnerable belly. "What troubles you, eh? Lashed to a tree, are you? A strange prison for a forest god, isn't it?"

"Jai, trying to escape, he was!" Ulo said. He aimed another savage kick at Clay's ribs.

"Easy, easy, Ulo. The witch must walk the morrow. Still a wide journey back to the village, yea? Let's nay make you carry him."

Jai crouched down, his face beyond Doto's reach. The stink of his rotting gums wrinkled Doto's nose. "So then, forest god, command the tree. Free yourself. Strike us down and save your precious little pet."

Choked with fury and fear for Clay, Doto could make no response. He trembled with bridled rage. Every muscle strained against his bonds.

"Nay then," Jai said, standing. "As I knew." He walked over to the wheezing shadow that was Clay and stared down. "Once and once again you and your demon broke free. You must be taught nay to run from us a third time. Need we to sleep without training woken eyes on the two of you all dark. A wide journey we have, and walk you must."

Jai looked back toward Doto, and his smile broke again, little round teeth bared, glittering in the moonlight. "But sure and true, you need your legs only to walk. Ulo. Break the witch's arms."

Untold Stories

As Cloud came around the side of the village fence, she saw a figure standing a little ways away, watching the forest. She recognized him: the hunter, Mirage. He was standing tall and watching the forest as if in challenge. He canted from side to side like a lion judging a strike. His bow was in one hand; in the other, he carried a torch, its flame popping in the humid morning air.

"A little early for a fire, isn't it?" Cloud asked, walking up behind him. She nodded toward the midmorning sun when the boy turned.

His youthful features soured into a scowl. "This isn't your concern."

She stopped next to him. He was one of Laughing Dog's fire hunters, chosen because he was young, strong, and a capable hunter. In Cloud's experience, young, strong, and capable hunters were accustomed to confronting large, charging animals, but not so comfortable facing down old women half their size. So she stood near him and let the hot savanna air brush her dress against his calves and bump the wispy mass of her hair against his shoulder. "Suppose it depends on what you're going to do," she said. "The forest is my concern as well as yours. Don't you think?"

He stepped past her again, lifting the torch toward the darkened woods as though he could light all their shadowed secrets. "It doesn't depend. My decisions are mine alone. Two Broken Hands was my grandmother, not yours."

"I had a grandmother too," Cloud reminded him. "And she died too."

"Not like that." Mirage's voice twisted in disgust.

"No." Cloud didn't think she would ever forget the way that body had looked, all dark red flesh and white bone, the insides gone. "That was a bad death."

"And what about King First Claw?" He shook his head. "This is what I don't understand. Why isn't *everyone* shouting to burn the forest and punish

Kwaee for what he's done? How can people just sit back and shrug and just—just take it?"

Cloud sighed. "We're all sad that the King is dead. And we mourn Two Broken Hands."

"And Flint," Mirage added, his words shaking with remembered anger. "And Mighty Ant, and Six Star, and Bramble. The forest took them too, though no one seems to care."

"Do you think their families mourn less than you?"

Mirage hesitated. "Yes," he answered. Then, more confidently, "If they really cared, they'd want to fight back. They'd want vengeance."

"Are you so certain?" Cloud looked up at him, and he evaded her gaze. She suspected his shame. Two Broken Hands had never been a kind woman, and most people avoided her, her children and grandchildren included. She had been alone when she died. "Many have lost fathers and brothers. I don't know how you felt about Two Broken Hands, but I sat with Great Ram after his father's passing. He grieved more than many children for their fathers, but even he has decreed that we respond with reverence and patience."

"Then he's weak," Mirage said. Fear lit his eyes as soon as the treasonous words left his lips.

In Cloud's earlier days, she would have felt the urge to slap him for this insult, to scold him until his ears wilted. But time and recent events had softened her. Her world was running out of room for more harshness. Instead she patted his arm. Grey ash from his hunting stripes rubbed off on her fingers and made little puffs in the air. "Love's private. Between your spirit and hers. It doesn't need proving. No one judges it."

"Some people do." Mirage looked back toward the walled village. "They say that if we really cared for our people, we'd fight back."

"And what do you think? Why does what those people say matter so much to you?"

"I just—" He turned away, exasperated. "I just want to do something. I want this to stop. I want people to stop getting killed. No one will tell us what we did to deserve this. I'm tired of not knowing, not doing anything."

"I know," she said. She looked down at his bow. With it he held an arrow, a coarse tow of lovegrass tied just below the flint head. She didn't need to touch or smell the bundle to know it was soaked with palm oil. "But doing nothing is still better than doing the wrong thing, isn't it?"

"Maybe doing nothing *is* doing the wrong thing."

"Maybe." She looked into the forest. Its calm was dark and deceptively alluring, full of game and fruit, and above all, medicine. It was medicine she had come out here to find: barks and roots and herbs that strayed beyond whatever mystical wall made up the edge of the forest. Scouts from the village had been busy marking it, carefully testing just how far they could walk before the trees twitched toward them. They had laid down a trail of yellow stone to delineate the border between savanna and forest, between unthreatening want and malevolent feast. Cloud could see no clear logic in what made one side dangerous and the other not. Herbal plants and fruiting trees grew on one side as well as the other, but on the one side they were safe to touch, and had been picked clean, and on the other side, they would try to kill you.

"Maybe we should just surrender to it. Or fight it," she said. "But in there, the forest, that's our hope, isn't it? We've come all this way. The savanna's dying. Our old home has burned." She felt very tired, a weary exhaustion that went deeper than muscle, deeper even than bone. She thought that if she were to die now, her spirit would be too tired even to return to Father Wem. Her legs felt weak, so she leaned against Mirage and was comforted by his solid presence. "The forest is all we have. You don't understand why everyone doesn't wish to burn it? I don't understand how anyone *could* want to. If the forest burns, then where do we go? What do we do? Then we have no hope at all."

"You sound like my mother," Mirage said bitterly.

Cloud did not answer that. All in the village knew of Mirage's family affairs; they could hardly be kept quiet. Mirage had not complimented his mother.

Nor did he wait for a reply. "I told her and told her that she should bring my father before the King and ask to be declared unwed. But she was afraid. She told me he was all she had, and that without him, she would be alone. And so she let him beat her and beat her, and she would cry and beg him for forgiveness and grovel until the King finally stepped in and unwed her himself. It shamed our family."

Cloud remembered. It had been an ugly time. Familial violence in the village was rare, but it ran like a venom through Mirage's line, down from grandmother through father.

He set his teeth. "Now the forest hurts us and kills us. Over and over it beats us. And everyone says, 'Oh, we're sorry forest, please forgive us, don't hurt us.' They're just afraid."

He lifted his bow. "Well, I am not afraid."

"Mirage, no! It's not the same." Cloud reached up to grasp his arm. She saw into his face. She saw him, striped with white ash, and beyond him into the cruelty of a father twisted by Two Broken Hands, a miserable old woman molded by the barbaric traditions of blood sacrifice to the high gods. Two Broken Hands herself had spoken of her grandfather, a priest who had soaked the ground with the blood of tributes to Kwaee and Ogya. And Cloud saw, too, a mother who had named her son after the first thing she had seen when he was born: the lie of water on the horizon, a false hope of relief. She saw a young man who had known privation and misery much of his life, and who, when he looked to the future, saw nothing but more of the same.

She had nothing to offer him. "Mirage, I understand. But this decision, it's not yours to make. It affects everyone. You can't burn only one life. You hear me? You will burn them all. This is something a King must decide."

Mirage shrugged her hand from his arm and lit the tied bundle at the end of his arrow. He dropped his torch into the dirt. The palm oil made the tow burn slow, blue and dim. "It's not just my decision. A lot of us feel that way. Someday the King may have to decide if he wants to lead or be left behind."

He drew back his bow, tilting it toward a large tree, shaggy with dried moss. It would burn easily if it were not too wet from yesterday's rains.

She made one last, desperate attempt. "Mirage, the King has decreed against this. It could be seen as treason."

He smiled mirthlessly over his shoulder at her. "Cloud, you know the main difference between treason and loyalty?" He focused on the tree before him. "Time."

He let his arrow fly.

~~~

"You set fire to the forest. Without my consent. Against my direct orders." The King rubbed at his temples with one hand. "What burned and how much? Is it out?" He swayed slightly on his feet, squinting at Mirage as though finding it difficult to see the hunter prostrated on hands and knees before him. The ashes striping Mirage's back and shoulders had smeared away, leaving only dark streaks down his sides.

"We hope it's out. We couldn't follow it into the forest to be sure." Cloud looked past Ram toward the southwestern wall of the village. Beyond it, even though a light rain fell, thin trails of white smoke still rose.

"At least five trees burned beyond recovery, King Great Ram." The hunter, Beetle, stood with his spear to the ready, as though expecting Mirage to spring up and attack the King at any moment. He had not been chosen to be one of Laughing Dog's fire hunters, and Cloud suspected he was somewhat resentful of them. "One of them a sycamore fig. Underbrush burned all throughout before the rains came and drowned the fire. The barks smolder still, but the fire will likely not spread farther."

"A sycamore." Ram shook his head in disgust. "Good food and good wood wasted."

Mirage looked up, though he didn't lift his hands from the ground. "It was only a few trees. Not like we could get at them anyway."

"Ah, well, that's fine then," Ram said, curling his lip. "Only a few trees. We're lucky. And what if a hundred had burned? What if the entire forest had gone up, and set fire to our own village? What would you be saying to me then?" He put his foot on Mirage's shoulder, shoving him back to the ground again.

Mirage's hands slipped in the mud and he sprawled face down with a splash.

"Ram." That was Laughing Dog's voice, calm and dangerous. He had come up to stand behind Beetle, thick arms folded above his sagging belly. "He's still my fire hunter."

"Your fire hunter?" Ram looked up, his face darkening with anger. "Yours? He's my subject, Dog. Maybe you've forgotten that. And unless I'm very mistaken, I thought I made it clear that no one was to lay torch to the forest. Well? How about it, Mirage? Was I vague in some way?"

Mirage pushed himself up again, mud running down his face, the rain leaving dots and streaks down his cheeks and forehead. "No, King Great Ram."

"Did you misunderstand my decree? Did you forget?"

"No, King Great Ram." Mirage shivered with emotion, though whether fear or anger, Cloud couldn't tell.

"So." Great Ram swayed where he stood. "You defied me, then."

Laughing Dog came forward and stood close to Ram, speaking in low tones, as though in confidence, though his words were plain to Cloud, and no doubt Beetle as well. "Ram, consider. Only two days before, his grandmother was killed by a terrible beast from the forest. As a loving, devoted grandson, how could he not be moved to vengeance against it? Do not his ancestors look down on him?"

Great Ram's eyes watered as he glared at him. "Don't think I don't hear you, Laughing Dog. You're not half so sly as you think you are."

"All I mean," Laughing Dog continued smoothly, "is that the man is grieving and irrational. Some clemency might be afforded, given circumstances. Our father never blamed a man for loving too deeply. And he is a good hunter. We need those more than ever right now."

"Then you would have me ignore his crime." Ram spoke the words as though disgusted, but Cloud had seen a flicker of uncertainty on his face when Laughing Dog mentioned their father. "Just let everyone know that the King's decrees mean nothing, is that it? Anyone can disobey any law they like, as long as they feel strongly about it?"

Laughing Dog smiled as if the notion had been proposed by a silly child. "I'm not talking about every case. Only this one. Let me deal with him. He will be run last among my hunters. It is a position of shame."

"It's a position of honor to be included among your hunters to begin with!" Great Ram snapped. He turned to Cloud. "Well? I know you're dying to give me your advice. What do you think?"

She ignored the insult as she ignored the reek of palm wine in his words. "I agree with Laughing Dog that mercy is called for," she said. And, as the smile of surprised satisfaction crawled across the prince's face, added, "But I do not think this was a crime of grief or anger. Why wait two days? He had time to think about what he wanted to do. I fear Mirage may have been listening to poisonous influences."

She caught a glimpse of Laughing Dog's eyes, staring at her like two dark arrows aimed at her head. She quickly looked back at the King. "Tell the people you understand that grief makes men foolish, but that the law must be obeyed. Mirage should be removed from the ranks of the fire hunters, and not permitted to eat anything they kill for seven days."

"Without a skilled hunter like Mirage, those kills will not happen as often," Laughing Dog said. "There will be less food for everyone. Don't punish the whole village for the error of one hunter, brother. Let me take him in hand. I will ensure that he never violates another of your laws again."

As Cloud had feared, Ram softened at his brother's words. "Will you? You will take it upon yourself to get him to obey? Him and all your fire hunters?"

"As always, brother," Laughing Dog said. He crouched and put his hand on Mirage's shoulder, pulling him upright. "You are loyal to your King, aren't you?"

"Yes, Laughing Dog," Mirage said, looking up at him.

"And you'll obey his laws without question from this day forward?"

"Yes, Laughing Dog." The hunter's voice was sure and certain.

"Well." Great Ram frowned, stepping back. He drew himself up with magnanimity. "All right then. But Cloud is right too. No more eating from any of his kills for seven days."

"Brother," Laughing Dog said, pouring honey into the word. "After seven days he will be too weak to hunt well. And how eager will he be to kill when he knows he can't taste of it?"

"What, then? Would you have me not punish him at all?" Great Ram roared at him. "Three days, then. Three days with no meat. And don't say another word about it."

Laughing Dog spread his hands. "You are just as always, brother."

"Ram," Cloud said, stepping forward, "this is a mistake. He deliberately worked against you. You can't let that go unanswered."

The King jabbed an index finger under her chin. "That's *King* Great Ram," he said. "Not Ram, not Great Ram. King Great Ram! My father's not here anymore. Do you understand that? He's up there now, watching me—watching us with our ancestors." He turned his eyes upward, staring toward the rainclouds, as though he expected to see First Claw's head staring down from him with a stern expression. "If I have to carry all his burdens and serve as he did, then I'll damned well have the respect and obedience that comes with them. I've made my decision here, and I don't want to hear any more about it."

Cloud dipped her head. "Yes, my King."

King Great Ram glared at her. She'd emphasized the word, drawing unspoken compare between the office and his outburst. For a moment they hovered in that silent space between action and regret. Then Ram closed his eyes, turned and walked away, nearly slipping in a puddle as he went.

Once he was gone, Laughing Dog reached down for Mirage's hand, helping him up from the ground. "Come on, you," he said. "It's going to be very hard for you for the next several days. Shame on you for disobeying the King." He spoke the words severely, but concealed plain laughter behind them, and Mirage grinned back at him as they headed off.

Cloud reached up and squeezed the water out of her hair, which had become heavy and sodden in the rain. Things were getting worse, not better. What were they supposed to do with a drunken, foolish King and a mad prince working against him? What *could* be done?

Beetle came and stood next to her, watching Laughing Dog go. "Some days," he said, "I think we were better off before we came to the forest. We were hungry and thirsty and sick and miserable. But on days like this, I miss it. What has happened to us?"

"It's just a hard time," Cloud said. "It's always a hard time with a new King. He has to learn how to be a good King, and it's never easy at first."

All the same, she remembered long ago, when King First Claw had ascended to King after his father had died. It had been a difficult change, but his mistakes were honest, and he never repeated them. Time turns all bitter meals to nectar, of course, but she remembered those troublesome days with a certain fondness. First Claw had been her friend, and had come to her often for advice. He had seen learning to govern as a challenge and a grave responsibility, one to be embraced, not resented.

"I'm loyal," Beetle said gravely. "You know I am. But our people need leadership. They're angry and afraid. We need a King with wisdom and experience, someone who can guide and reassure us."

"Well," Cloud said, "we've got the King we've got."

The next morning, Cloud tended her patients and then went up the hill to visit Hibiscus. It had been several days now since she'd moved those suffering from the strange illness into the new sick tent, and none of those stricken had recovered. In fact, far from improving, their condition seemed to be worsening with time. Red Moth and Whistling Thorn were the first afflicted, and they moaned and clutched their bellies, evacuating water and food so rapidly that it was all Cloud could do to keep them from dying of thirst. None of the usual medicines seemed to help.

Her new patients were those people who had been injured in the attack by the forest monsters. Why they had fallen victim to the disease was a mystery to her; she had allowed no one near the afflicted for fear of contagion. Perhaps the beasts had carried the illness with them from the forest, but then why had those who had cut up or disposed of the carcasses not become ill? Why only those injured, and not those who had merely encountered the creatures? There was no sense behind it.

She was equally at a loss as to how to help them. As time had passed and their suffering increased, they had begun to resent her failure, begging her for succor she had no means to grant and moaning curses and imprecations against her when she could not. She was used to this; suffering put people into an ill temper, but normally she was able to offer her patients some relief and ease them back to health. Now, all she was able to do was to give the suffering a shady place to lie down. She kept them clean, at least, and away from those who had not succumbed to the illness.

And so, although usually she found the King's wife gratingly indolent and demanding, today she welcomed this opportunity: a chance to put her suffering patients out of her thoughts for a short time and lend her healing talents to someone they could do some good. She brought with her a calabash of amaranthine tea for health, as well as shea butter to smooth over Hibiscus's joints, where it would ease her soreness. It would also be good on the belly, to relax the stretching of skin.

Halfway up the steady rise to the wealthier part of the village, she noticed two large figures standing before the entrance to the King's tent. They both held spears, one leaning on his as though tired, the other propping his at the ready. They were not speaking to each other, nor did they appear to be awaiting entry. At closer range, they proved to be two of Laughing Dog's fire hunters: Broken Stump and Grenadier.

The fire hunters seldom ventured outside of their group of twelve of late; even when not hunting, they banded together, moving through the village or surroundings in a pack. They spoke primarily with each other, sharing private jokes or sparring, and they engaged with other members of the village with diminishing frequency, even going so far as to actively shun and mock the hunters that had not been selected to join them. Now two of them stood outside the King's tent as though assigned to be there. Cloud felt uneasy at their presence.

They exchanged glances as she approached, and squared their ash-striped shoulders.

"Good morning, Grenadier, Broken Stump," she said, doing her best to sound pleasant and unworried. "Do you know if the King is about?"

"He's not here right now," Broken Stump said, holding up a hand. He was a short man, though still taller than her, his frame thin and angular. Though he had not yet seen thirty rains, his hair was already greying, but he was renowned for his wiry strength. He could throw a spear so fast and so far that it might have been an arrow and his body the bow.

"Only Hibiscus," Grenadier added.

"That's fine. It's her I want to see." Cloud made to enter the tent, but the two men stepped together, blocking her way. They stood stiff-backed, gripping their spears more tightly. What did they expect, that she would lunge at them like a lion?

Grenadier cleared his throat. "Sorry, Cloud, but you're not to enter the King's tent. And you're not to see Hibiscus."

She stared up at him. He stood head and shoulders above Broken Stump, but unlike the other man, was thick-fleshed and rounded in a way that befit his typically soft, gentle demeanor. "What do you mean?" she asked, puzzled. "I'm an elder of the people. I'm an advisor to the King, and the healer besides. You boys have no place to stop me."

He rubbed at the back of his neck with a mitt that was more paw than hand. "Sorry, Cloud. Prince Laughing Dog says to stand guard and not let anyone in."

So. It was *Prince* Laughing Dog now. She pressed her lips together. "Does he. Perhaps we should ask the King what he thinks."

Broken Stump thumped the end of his spear in the dirt. "King Great Ram said we should obey the prince. Anyway, it was him who first said not to let you visit his wife."

This last piece of information greatly startled her. "The King said this? But why? A pregnant woman needs the attention of a healer. Hibiscus herself requested that I come and tend to her."

Broken Stump shook his head. "She don't want to see you now. Not my business why not."

"It's on account of all the sick people," Grenadier explained, looking embarrassed. "People are saying things."

"Saying things? Things like what?" She knew people were disquieted by the strange illness, but she had heard no unusual gossip.

"It's…well, they're saying that—that if people go to you, they get sick. And they don't get better. People say you're giving them the disease."

She nearly dropped her calabash of tea. "Giving them what? That's absurd. How could I?"

"Look, it's no secret," Broken Stump said curtly. "None of those people you got in that sick tent were sick before they saw you. They were all banged up, maybe, but not sick. Then they go to you, to that big smoky tent of yours. And they never come out. You see how it looks? So the King and his wife don't want you around their baby."

The suggestion was beyond unbelievable—it was insolent. "How it looks? You curse your own tongue, Broken Stump. Whose hands were first in the world to hold your newborn body? Mine. And you too, Grenadier. The King as well. Every man and woman here for the past thirty-five rains was caught by these fingers before they ever touched the ground. And now you think suddenly I don't know my work?"

Fidgeting with his spear, Grenadier half-mumbled something to one side.

She fixed him with her severest gaze. "What was that? Say it to me, boy, not the ground."

He met her eyes guiltily. "I said, but then you weren't using forest medicines."

"And what's that got to do with anything?"

He looked down again. "Prince Laughing Dog…well…some people are saying that Kwaee can poison us through the forest. That you won't stop using forest medicines, and that's why everyone's getting sick."

"But that's nonsense. I'm using the same medicines I've used for years. It makes no difference whether I picked the plants in the forest or not."

Grenadier shrugged. "It's just what people are saying."

"Well, it's foolish," Cloud snapped.

But was it? Something was making people sick. And now that she considered it, they had all been people she'd treated before. Red Moth, who was the sickest, had first come to see her after the forest had broken her arms. And Whistling Thorn she'd treated for wasp stings. The thought grew heavier and solider in her mind the more she chewed on it. Could she somehow be causing this terrible affliction?

No. She was doing nothing different. Most of the remedies she used were taken either from the savanna or from the forest before it turned. She administered them with prayers and blessings just as she always had. But still, the suggestion was troubling.

"Anyway, I am not bringing any medicines today," she said. "Only shea butter for the skin, and amaranthine tea. Hibiscus will have no objection to that."

Grenadier and Broken Stump exchanged another look, but before they could reply, Hibiscus thrust her face through the tent opening. "Get away from our home, you old witch," she shouted, her face pinched as though she had a taken mouthful of bitter melon. "You won't make the King's wife sick today. Not her baby either. Go back to your horrible tent full of disease and stay there!" Before Cloud could respond, Hibiscus pulled the flaps of the tent closed and disappeared.

Cloud stared in shock, trying to collect herself after what had happened. She opened her mouth and closed it again.

"Go on," Broken Stump said, gesturing with his spear. "You heard the King's wife. You're not wanted here."

"Sorry, Cloud," Grenadier added, looking uncomfortable. "I guess you should probably go."

Cloud looked down at her hands, feeling strangely lost. "Well, take the tea and butter anyway," she said, holding them out. "Maybe Hibiscus will change her mind after she's had some rest."

"All right." Grenadine took the gourds. They looked small in his thick fingers. "I'll give them to her later."

"Thank you." Cloud turned and descended back to her tent full of the stench and moans of the sick and suffering. For a while, she held a faint hope that Hibiscus would recant and accept her offerings, but later that day she found the calabashes outside her tent wall, their contents spilled into the dirt, the gourds smashed.

⁓

Laughing Dog's tent was unguarded. Cloud hadn't really expected otherwise, but neither would she have been surprised to find a couple of fire hunters standing outside. For a man suffering from madness, the prince's control over the camp was thorough and effective. Paranoia could do that to a person though. It could make him spend every moment imagining dangers from unexpected corners, trying to guard and prepare for them. If Laughing Dog truly believed that Lord Kwaee was bent against the people's destruction of their people, then he would likely see such plans and schemes everywhere.

Cloud had seen paranoia like that before; it had touched her own family, long ago. But this didn't seem like paranoia to her. Rather, Laughing Dog's actions seemed cunning and deliberate, born not of fear, but of some desire or hunger she couldn't discern. It troubled her deeply.

She paused outside his tent, about to announce herself. A foul odor hovered about it, thick and miasmic in the air. What did he do in there when no one was watching? Sometimes it was smart to be a little nosy. With her stick, she pushed the heavy zebra hide aside. There was only darkness beyond. She stepped in.

The sight of the place Laughing Dog called home so appalled her that she drew in a great breath of disbelief—and immediately regretted it, as the wretched stench nearly caused her to choke. She pulled one strip of her dress to her mouth and squinted in the dim light.

Garbage was strewn on the ground, all along the tent walls, and piled up in heaps to one side. There were melon rinds scraped almost down to the husk; spat seeds with gobbets of rotting fruit still clinging to their hulls; clusters of discarded nut husks; assorted crumbs and drops of unidentifiable dark fluids congealing in the dirt; stacks of empty gourds; and scattered everywhere, piles and piles of bones, black with fetid clumps of meat still clinging to any spots not scraped clean by teeth. She pressed her dress more tightly over her nose and mouth—the mass of garbage was pungent with the sickly-sweet reek of rot and fermentation, and clicking beetles teemed over the mess, winding their ways around swarming clumps of black flies.

It was the sight of these last that she couldn't bear. Her chest seemed to sink in and constrict, her breaths coming shorter. She backed toward the entrance, and as she did so, she saw Laughing Dog skulking in the rubbish and gloom. He was crouched, hunched over, his great, flabby bulk folding over his thighs. With both hands he held a hank of some meat, probably antelope. He had been gnawing on it when she entered, but now he looked up at her, and his eyes flashed, twin points glinting in the light from the opening. She stepped back out of the tent in horror, trying to find a breath of unfouled air.

"Come out of there," she called, when she felt steadier. "We need to talk, you and me."

Something rustled inside. Bones clattered, and then Laughing Dog crept out of the low tent opening and stood upright. In the sunlight, he looked like his normal self—or what passed for his normal self these days. He was still ash-striped, broad-shouldered, powerful-looking, and fat as the chiefs of old, but not the hunched monster she'd imagined in the tent.

"Cloud." He sounded unconcerned to have been caught in such squalor.

"Just what is going on in there?" she demanded. "It's filthy. How much have you been eating, that you make such a terrible mess?"

He shrugged his round shoulders, and his belly shook. "I and my hunters feed this whole village. As long as all have enough, who cares how much I eat? And the inside of my tent is none of your concern."

"It is if it spreads disease," Cloud snapped. She remembered the flies buzzing around inside and shuddered. Where there were flies, there would be maggots. "Many people are sick. How do you know this mess and the flies aren't the cause?"

"Old bones and a few bugs don't make people sick."

"There's a lot you don't know. There's sickness, and then there's plague. You've never seen that. If you want to spread plague, you've got a good start in there."

Laughing Dog reached to his hip and withdrew his knife, a shiny black thing that was reputed to be harder than any other stone. He turned it over and over in his fingers. "I heard it's you making people sick, Cloud. I heard anyone who goes to your tent never comes out again. That's why I ordered Scorpion not to come to you when the creatures wounded him."

She wasn't surprised to hear that line of attack, not after her encounter with Hibiscus. "I go in and out of the sick tent all the time. If I weren't caring for those people properly, I'd be sick, too. And as you can see, I'm quite healthy. You should tell Scorpion to come see me, if you don't want his wounds to fester."

"I think you didn't understand me," Laughing Dog said. He scraped at his fingernails with the edge of his knife. "I said you're *making* them sick. Of course you wouldn't harm yourself."

That, she hadn't expected. She tried to remind herself that the boy was mad. She'd seen it, seen him talking to himself, seen him try to drown himself, or drown some voice only he could hear. But this…this was not madness. This was calm, deliberate manipulation. "Why would I ever do such a thing?" she asked haltingly.

Laughing Dog turned his gaze back to her, and false pity shone in his eyes. "None of us know, Cloud. We only know that you haven't been the same since my father died. We're all worried about you." He shook his head. "Poor Cloud. Maybe you don't even know what you're doing. Sometimes old people get…confused. Maybe you're accidentally mixing up your treatments? One plant can look a lot like another if you're feeling emotional. Even poisons and medicines."

"I don't keep poisons," she said firmly. "Nor am I confused. About anything. I see more than you think, Laughing Dog."

"*Prince* Laughing Dog."

She ignored that. "I know you and your hunters are getting pretty popular lately, what with all the food you've provided. I'm as grateful as anyone else. But don't go thinking that just because you know how to throw a spear you're fit to care for the sick, or lead a people. You have a long life to live before you're an elder."

Laughing Dog snorted.

Cloud thumped the end of her stick in the dirt. "Go ahead and puff like that around the other elders, see if they don't crack you across the back of the head, prince or no. It wasn't so long ago you were sent out into the wilderness for failing to respect the advice of your elders and the traditions of the people. If you think folks have forgotten that already, you're going to get real disappointed, boy."

"Do you know what else people haven't forgotten?" Laughing Dog asked. She'd finally gotten to him. Puffy anger had creased the bored expression from his bloated face. "They haven't forgotten how all the elders' so-called wisdom and experience left us starving and parched in the savanna for years. They haven't forgotten the people who died tired and hungry while people like you and Father sat around being wise. They'll remember that." He spat the words. His wide body loomed over her, three times her size. He gripped his dark knife in his hand. "And they'll remember how Prince Laughing Dog and his fire hunters fed them and protected them from the evil forest god while their simpering elders pled for appeasement and sacrifice."

He looked about to fall on top of her. Despite herself, she took a frightened step back. "I will call a council of the elders," she stammered. "We will convince the King. Your fire hunters will be disbanded, and you will be exiled again."

Laughing Dog's sneer twisted into a smug half-smile as he straightened up. "No one's going to listen to you. You're a confused old widow who can't keep her patients from dying. No one's going to let you get rid of the only people keeping them fed. Your time is over, Cloud. You may have been respected once, but now you're just a sad, nutty old crone in a stinking dress full of holes. You know what old people do? They forget the time they're living in. They hold us back. And then they die."

He turned to reenter his tent, but paused on the way in. "If you've forgotten, ask Two Broken Hands."

The Teller stood atop Gamewatch Rise, in the shade of the broad-limbed acacia tree that crowned it. He leaned on his staff and chewed jugo beans. The sweet, nutty beans had always been his favorite snack, and Cloud kept her eye out for them whenever she went searching for herbs, but they were harder to find so close to the forest.

From Gamewatch Rise, a hill so tall that the younger children liked to pretend it was one of the high places, you could see the forest sprawling across the south, a thick green curtain that extended from sunrise to sunset. To the north, the savanna rippled off into the distance, speckled with trees that grew sparser the farther from the forest one traveled.

Cloud had hoped she might find the Teller here. He liked spending time in the village, watching children play and the adults work, listening to their chatter, gathering the beads of their lives together into long, colorful story chains. But he also would come out to the hill in the heat of the day, when others sought the shade and shelter of their tents, and he would look across the horizons and tell himself the stories of the land. It was said he wanted to find the tale for each tree, an origin for every little hill or mound, and when he had finished with those, he would name the grass and narrate the ants that climbed it.

"Ah, Cloud," he said without turning. "How are the patients?"

She thought of Red Moth, who had stopped complaining about her stomach, and no longer spit up the water she drank, but who was now so weak that she could lift neither arms nor head. "Not well," she answered. "I fear for them. How is the savanna?"

He turned to her, and smiled. "A rabbit birthed seven kittens. Jackals found and ate five. The other two are hidden."

She considered whether he might be joking. The Teller had a sense of humor. "You can see that from here?"

"No," he said. "But do you doubt that it happened? Somewhere, it happened."

"If you only guess that it happened, true or not, that's not a very important story, is it?"

"Isn't it?" He leaned heavier onto his staff and turned out to the savanna again. "It's an important story to the two that lived. It's an important story to the five that died. It's an important story to the jackals who have full bellies."

Cloud sat next to him on the hill, crossing her skinny legs and straightening her dress over them. The grass was comfortable. "I don't think we have much care for stories these days," she confessed. "People are too frightened. The stories are old and don't tell us what to do."

"No care for stories?" the Teller asked, amusement in his voice. "It is caring for stories so much that has us troubled!"

She knew he was waiting for her to ask what he meant, so she didn't. The Teller was accustomed to the call and response of his tales around the fire, and despite his age, he still enjoyed an audience far too much for his own good. It was a game to see who could keep patient the longest: she, in refusing to ask for an explanation, or he, in his eagerness to explain his meaning. She won.

"Each of us has a story that we tell of ourselves," the Teller said. "The story is made of many parts. Some parts, like our names, are given to us by our parents. Some parts are given to us by our people, by our elders and heroes, kings and Tellers. Some parts of the story we find in our spirits. And we tell the story of ourselves through our lives. It grows and changes in the telling. We tell the story of ourselves to others. We tell the story of ourselves to ourselves. We ask ourselves questions: Will I marry? Will I fight? Will I play music? Will I obey? We look to the stories of those around us and the stories of our ancestors to decide what we should do and to decide what we *will* do. The story of ourselves is always a lie and always true. Only when we know both the truth and the lie can we be happy."

"The truth and the lie?" she asked, and then scowled, annoyed with herself for asking the question he expected.

"Let me tell you a story," he said. "Once there was a King who had three sons. One son told the story of himself and could see nothing but the truth, and he grew arrogant and could not see his own weakness. One son told the story of himself and could see nothing but the lie, and he grew meek and could not see his own strength. One son took his father's story for himself, and saw neither the truth of his story nor the lie. He became nothing, and could not see himself at all."

Cloud snorted. "Your stories are usually harder to understand than that one, Basket," she said. Not too many people knew the Teller's old name. She knew he didn't like it, so she teased him with it when others weren't around. "But I fear the one son may be mad, or worse. It's a pity either of them have to be King. I miss First Claw."

"The sons must be King. Another story. Who told it first, I wonder? There were other stories, before that one became the story." The Teller sighed and sat down next to Cloud, laying his staff across his knees. He held out a handful of the little round nuts. "Jugo bean?"

When Cloud declined, he popped two more into his mouth and chewed on them with a thoughtful expression. "Not so many of them left. We should try planting some. We had crops in the old village. Maybe if we grow some here, we won't need the forest so much."

"Lost Knee and Big Storm have been trying to plant sorghum and jugo beans," Cloud said. "But the rain washes out the seeds before they root."

"That is a story," the Teller said. "How many of our own seeds will it wash away, I wonder? You could be a Teller too, Cloud."

She smiled. "I'm better at keeping limbs whole. You're better at keeping the soul of the people whole."

The Teller chewed silently. Then he said, "Lately I wonder how well I am doing at that. I don't seem to know the stories we need. There are so many stories I don't know. We have our tales of Kwaee and Sarmu, of Wem and Fam, and the making of the people. And there are lies and truths within all of them. But there are other stories we have forgotten. I heard them when I was a boy."

It was unlike him to speak so frankly. At least, it was unlike him to do it lately. When they had both been much younger, Basket had confided in her often, but these days he kept his opinions guarded, speaking them only in the guises of games and tales. "You said something about dark stories of Kwaee when we were at the council, back before…" She decided to let it go at that. "Before."

"Yes. They tug at the edges of my mind. They were important stories. The Sarmu Legends, I think they were called. But they were from another people, from another time, and they are lost now. Maybe forever."

Cloud shook her head. "I don't know how they could help us with the forest or with the plague we're facing. People are dying, and I don't know what to do."

He turned to look at her, his eyes soft and kind. She thought he saw the story of who she was, before her hair had grown wild and matted, before her skin had creased and drooped, before any of her teeth had fallen out. She had been fierce and beautiful. He had seen it then. Perhaps he did still.

"I have a story of myself," he said. "All truths and lies, as tangled and troublesome as grey hairs amid the dark. I don't always know which is which. But when I'm troubled, I ask myself the story of myself, all that I know. I try to see the truth of it, and I try to see the lie of it." He put a callused hand on her shoulder. "Who do you tell yourself you are? What is your story?"

Cloud thought back. She had many stories. Her husband. Her grandmother. Her aunt. And *him*… So many stories that had made her who she was. The wind made the savanna grasses bow and rise before her; it bounded up the hill and caught her dress, tugging it away from her as though it would strip it from her body and carry it away forever. She almost lost her balance.

She caught the hems of the faded green fabric, pulling it tightly around herself again. There was only one story that was meaningful right now. "I'm just the healer. I make the sick and injured well again. All I want to do is help our people."

Basket smiled at her again, as he had smiled at her in those fierce and beautiful days. "All true," he said. "All a lie."

〰

Sometime during the night, Red Moth died. She did not cry out, and no one was at her side. Cloud found her in the morning, her yellowed eyes staring beyond the tent roof, her jaw slack, a foul-smelling crust gritting the corners of her mouth. She had no relatives remaining. Her husband was dead, killed by the forest, and she had no surviving children. But she had been kind-hearted, and she had known how to spice and cook food that took people to their childhoods when they tasted it. She had many friends, most of whom had not dared visit her because they feared the plague. They would come to her pyre and mourn her. They would demand to know why Cloud had failed to make her well, and Cloud would have no answers for them. They would want to know if the others would die, too.

She looked out over the beds and wondered the same. Whistling Thorn, Mongoose, Dancing Spider, Fiveroot, Twig—would she be able to save any of them?

Mongoose stirred in his bed. "Red Moth?" he called. "Is everything all right?"

Cloud came over and took his hand. "Red Moth is dead," she told him quietly. In all her time as healer, she had never found a kinder way to say it. The finality of it permitted no gentleness, no comforting lead-in. Better to say it and let people confront it on their own.

Mongoose closed his filmy eyes. "It's better. Her pain was terrible. We will send her back to Wem."

"Yes. And your pain? How is that?" Cloud winced as soon as the question had left her lips—what good reminding him how closely he hovered near Red Moth's fate?

Mongoose showed no distress at the question. He closed his eyes, breathing slowly, feeling out the aches and complaints of his body, taking assessment of its condition. Cloud did the same thing every morning when she woke, checking to see what was sore, what was stiff, what felt wrong, before getting up and facing the day. "I think it's going away," he said. "My stomach doesn't clench so badly anymore. I think I could keep down some water, if you have any."

"That's good to hear." That was a lie. Red Moth's pains had eased before she had slipped into a waking sleep. Mongoose might well be entering the same stage of the sickness. "I'll get some water."

She stood and moved to the door, but as she did, Twig lifted his head. He was the carpenter who had been injured in the attack of the monsters, and shortly after had fallen to the plague. The same had happened with Fiveroot, the weaver. "Cloud," he called to her, his voice strained with pain and exhaustion.

"Yes, Twig. What is it? Do you need to get up?" She hurried to his side and crouched next to him, taking his hand in hers.

He shook his head. "I heard what you said. Red Moth. She's dead."

She nodded and squeezed his hand.

"It was the sickness. It killed her." He looked her steadily in the eyes. "You can't do anything to stop it, can you?"

She had trouble looking back. "I'm doing what I can."

"It's going to kill us all. We're all going to die." The words were spoken flatly, numbed of any anger or fear.

She couldn't keep her fingers from shaking against his, so twitched them away. "I'm doing everything I can. I'll pray. I'll try new remedies. I won't give up, and you mustn't either."

He looked into her eyes a little longer, gaze shifting as if he searched for something. Then he turned his head away and did not speak again.

It was a bad thing when the spirit despaired of living. The body would not keep going without it. She would have to find a way to encourage them all. But for now, Mongoose needed water, and there was a body to prepare. She would strip away the splints and bandages that bound Red Moth's arms; they would not be needed now. She would clean the body, rub it with oil and incense, and bind the wrists and ankles. There would be a pyre tonight.

When she stood, she saw Whistling Thorn, who was the son of Firefly and No Rocks, who had seen seven rains, who was already fascinated with seeds and how, when pushed into the fertile belly of Mother Fam, they sprouted green and tall. Whistling Thorn, who would one day be a farmer, who would see rains come and go, come and go, who would grow like his plants and have thin but strong limbs and wide, rangy shoulders like his father, who would find a girl he adored, and who adored him, and in her plant his own seeds and so bring life and joy to the people. Whistling Thorn stared at the tent wall with vacant eyes, and though his narrow chest still rose and fell, it did so shallowly, so faintly that his breaths did not rustle the hairs of the eland pelt on which he lay.

There was not enough incense and oil; Cloud would have to visit the stores and request more, for there would be a pyre tomorrow as well as today. She feared then that Twig was right. The sickness would kill them all.

Intercessions

Doto raged against the tree for not freeing him, but it remained unyielding, scraping against his back and his arms, which were crooked painfully and bound behind it.

Clay lay on the ground, unmistakable pain wheezing in every breath. He clutched at his stomach, fingers making a frail cradle around the fresh bruises and blood welling there, curled up as though he could protect himself from any more of Ulo's swift, brutal kicks.

Doto had been helpless to stop the violence. His throat was raw with his roaring, and yet he could not stop. His worshiper, his mate, his *Clay* was in pain and he could do nothing. He felt mad. Now the big, ugly fire bearer was going to break Clay's arms, and Doto could only bellow and thrash against his bonds. His useless struggles against the knotted twin had cut gashes into his wrists, and hot blood ran down his fingers.

Ulo crouched to the ground and grabbed Clay's forearm, his huge hand nearly encircling it. With easy strength, he hoisted Clay upright.

Clay moaned in fear and agony. Blood ran from the corner of his mouth.

"I'll murder you all!" Doto snarled. "You let us go now, or there is no place on earth my wrath will not follow you. I'll visit such terrible pains on you before I allow you to die."

Ulo hesitated at the threat. The air stung with the sharp scent of his fear, a keen edge that cut through the cloud of Clay's terror. The big fire bearer turned to look at the smaller one.

"Please," Clay begged him, not looking up.

Jai tilted his head. "Could he have hurt us aye, he'd have hurt us sooner than now. He threats you only at the urging of his witch. Break the arm."

Ulo nodded slowly and gripped Clay's arm in both hands. He would snap it backward. It would be easy for a man his size, like breaking a dry reed. Then what chance would Doto have? His body would eventually die, and when that happened, he would be reborn, unharmed, in his temple. But then he would be far from here, forced to make the trip back through the savanna, alone and without his magic. Finding Clay would be impossible. Doto would lose him forever. Uselessly, he dug his toes into the earth and leaned forward, hoping somehow to tear the tree up by the roots, or break it in half, but without the strength of his forest, he was as weak as any mortal.

Ulo's thick hands tightened.

Clay's arm bent. His slender fingers, sticking out of the curl of Ulo's fist, gave a few last twitches.

Doto closed his eyes, unwilling to look.

"Wait!" Clay shouted. "Wait, you're making a terrible mistake!"

"Wait?" Jai asked, sounding amused. "For what? For morning? For a soothing rain? Nay."

"I don't need my arms to walk." Clay's voice fluttered with fear like a trapped moth. "But I need them for the dance."

"Dance?" Jai came closer and seized Clay's braids in his fist, yanking his head toward his. "What dance?"

Clay's voice still shook, but he spoke more confidently. "The one that controls the demon. Look at him!" He pointed with his free arm toward Doto.

The two fire bearers looked in Doto's direction. Doto snarled his most vicious curses at them in god-tongue, but dismay rose in his heart. Clay thought him a demon now? Was he siding with the fire bearers against him out of fear?

"He's already slipping out of my control," Clay said. "Look at him. He's getting stronger and stronger. I have to dance the magic every day to keep him weak and docile. If I don't…he gets free."

Jai tugged at Clay's hair, tilting his head back. "A spell dance?" His voice was tight and suspicious, his free hand on his knife. "Why did you nay speak of it before?"

Clay's dark eyes narrowed. "Because I knew if the spell began to wear off, he'd kill you first," he said. "Then I could bring him back under control again."

Doto puzzled at this story for a moment—there was no dance of control. No fire bearer could control a god, and if one could, Clay would have done it long ago, back when Doto first captured him. He ceased his struggling for a moment, mystified at this turn, and then he saw the lie of it, as cleverly constructed as a spider's web. He renewed his thrashing against the tree, roaring at them both with a hatred he did not have to feign.

Dropping his gaze as if defeated, Clay murmured, "But if you break my arms, then I can't do the dance. He'll kill me too." He spat into the grass. "I should have run while I had the chance, but I didn't want to lose the demon."

"You're lying," Jai said, but he sounded unsure.

Clay tugged at the arm in Ulo's powerful grip. "Look at him. My magic's about to give out, and he'll break free and kill us all. But if you think I'm lying, just wait until morning. If we're not all dead, you can still break my arms."

Jai stared back toward Doto. "Wait a—" he said, but Ulo cut him off.

"Suppose he tells true, Jai? Suppose the demon looses and eats us?"

Jai shook his head. "He tells true nay, Ulo. Only he wishes to save his arms from breaking. Anything he'd say."

"Yea, but…" Ulo watched Doto with frightened eyes. Doto stopped his struggles and fixed the big fire bearer with a steady, unblinking gaze. He began to growl long and low, an unmistakable and blatant threat. He licked his jaws as though already savoring the big man's flavor.

Ulo swallowed. "But suppose he *does* tell true?"

Jai jabbed his knife against Clay's belly. "This dance. It will calm the demon?"

Clay groaned when the knife touched. "Yes. For a day. A little more."

"And you can work this magic and nay draw near nor touch the demon?"

"How do you think I could have got control of him otherwise? Look at him. He'd tear me to pieces if I got close."

Doto roared and snapped at the air, baring his fangs. Drool slid down the edges of his jaws. He was enjoying frightening the fire bearers, but rage nearly drowned that enjoyment. His blood seethed with fury against the two of them. Every kick, every blow, every insult and threat to him and his worshiper would be answered. He made the branches of the tree shake with the wresting of his arms.

Jai flinched at his roar and looked up at the limbs uneasily, as though he feared Doto were about to wrench the whole tree from the ground. "So you are a witch, true? Him your magic will calm and weaken?"

"Yes, if you let me go soon!" Clay cringed as though he were afraid too, but this Doto easily recognized as subterfuge. He had seen Clay truly frightened before.

Jai looked at him and then back at Ulo.

Ulo shook his head, his eyes bulging so the whites showed around them. "Like and I want to be gashed open by a demon, nay, Jai. We should let him dance."

"And where is our knowledge he will nay work some other magic? Call another demon, like as sure?"

"When I can't even control the one?" Clay demanded. "Keep the vine around my neck. If anything goes wrong, you can pull me over and stop it."

In a swift movement, Jai sprang to his feet. He pulled Clay up by his braids. Clay staggered, yelping at the pain. "A better idea I've had, little witch," the lean fire bearer said. "Dance you your spell. And Ulo will follow true with longsharp at your back. Move false and like a piglet he will skewer you through."

Ulo shifted, his movements skittish as an okapi's. "Jai, my longsharp is back at the flame pit."

"Go then and fetch it," Jai snarled. He cast another worried glance toward Doto's tree, and Doto bellowed fury back at him. "And swift."

The big fire bearer dashed off and came back a little more hesitantly than he'd left, spear clutched in one meaty hand. He turned his anxious gaze between Jai, Clay, and Doto. The tang of his fear touched Doto's nose, and with anticipation Doto breathed in the delicious scent of it.

"Well, go on," Jai shoved Clay forward. "If breaks free the beast due to your dallying, your death will come before ours."

Clay limped back toward Doto, clutching at his side, and Ulo followed uneasily, spear point hovering between his prisoner's shoulder blades.

Starlight glinted in Clay's eyes as he met Doto's gaze. He paused, so close Doto could almost touch him. Together, they hovered in a single breath, full of trust and longing and fear. For a moment, Doto thought he saw something else in his worshiper, something strange and infinite. "Demon," Clay whispered, and it was gone. They had a ruse to maintain. Doto snarled back at him like an animal.

Clay lifted a foot and danced. The movements were faltering and uneasy. Sharp odors of pain and blood clung to him. Doto could smell the salt in Clay's tears of agony, and bared his teeth in fury at Ulo. Clay sang the words.

> *The forest has come to greet the savanna*
> *and spill into it the blessings of Doto the mighty.*
> *You are the god who dares to stand before the flame.*
> *You are the god who can bend the forest*
> *with the movements of your fingers*

and before you the oldest of trees must bow.
If you do not will it, we will never see you.
You stride through darkness and daylight without tiring.
In your land Father Wem smiles and never holds back the rain.

And in his lungs, in his muscles and bones, in the flesh that knitted and healed around his wrists and ankles, in the dampness that soothed his hoarse throat, in the strength that filled his arms and legs, in the sturdiness and yielding bow of the tree against his back, in the roots that burrowed through the dirt, in the tender shoots of grass that sprouted verdant and green around his paws, in the seeds that formed out of nothingness in the soil, thickened into sapling, and erupted and unfolded into the warm and wet air that hung heavy around him and filled his lungs, and in the bare toes of his worshiper that touched and pivoted and sprang across his earth as they sprouted leopardine claws, Doto felt the sweet and sacred embrace of his forest.

He calmed. With a twist of his wrists, he snapped the feeble twisted cord of plant husks that had imprisoned him, careful not to reveal that he was free. The forest had spread around them in a circle, and Clay stopped his dance, leaning and holding his side.

"Something strange happens," Jai said, peering toward them. The fire bearers' eyes were feeble at night, and Doto doubted that in the darkness, they could see the filtering of green forest grass and brush through the taller, dryer savanna grasses. Still, he did not want them to become alarmed too soon and harm Clay.

He focused, sending his mind out into the plants, encouraging them to grow further. It was not easy. He did not have much forest space to work with; the ground became savanna less than a forearm's length below the surface, so he could not grow roots deeply. Even the tree behind him did not easily follow his will; its long roots were still buried in savanna earth. He concentrated, spreading a lattice-like web of roots wide, sprouting vines that snaked through the grass, making a hiss and rustle as they grew and coiled.

"I think it worked, Jai," Ulo said. He kept the tip of his spear at Clay's back. "I think he calmed the demon sure."

Jai walked closer, frowning, his feeble eyes searching through the moonlit grasses. "I know nay. Something is nay right, sure. Quiet. Hear you that sound?"

Doto stilled the forest.

They all stood silent. There was the chirrup of insects and a light breeze that tugged at the tree leaves. "What sound?" Ulo said. "I hear nay thing."

Jai sighed. "Come on, boy, back to your tree you go." He stepped inside the forest circle.

Doto sent his vines into motion immediately. One coiled tight around Jai's foot, and two more snaked up Ulo's legs.

Ulo shrieked, high and terrified. "Something got me!" He made to thrust his spear into Clay, but Doto bent a branch of the tree down and knocked the silly weapon away. Clay fell forward, catching himself on his hands, and dragged himself toward Doto. Now, up close, Doto could hear the wheeze in his voice, smell more intensely the blood and injury where Ulo had dared harm his worshiper.

He let his anger boil. The vines crawled up Ulo's body, sprouting clinging roots that gripped at his flesh, twining around his limbs and middle. Then they grew thorns. Doto bared his teeth in satisfaction as they dug into Ulo's tender, tearable skin.

"Please!" the man screamed. "Please let me go! Sorry I am! We needed to eat! My bab needed to eat!"

Doto enjoyed his pleas. The thorn vines crawled up the man's body, rending his flesh as they went. His hot blood ran down the vines, down his arms and legs to spatter on the ground. He screamed and screamed, desperate, hoarse cries, flailing his arms helplessly as he beat at the gripping, ripping plants. He went toppling to the ground.

Doto wondered that he had never before found pleasure in a creature's suffering. He had seen it endlessly in the forest before, of course. Long ago, he had even yearned to ease it. But beast preyed upon beast. All things lived, and were injured, and suffered, and died. It was the way of everything, a part of life to be endured. But never before had he found it so satisfying. He despised this man, hated him. And he would destroy him.

He curled his vines all around Ulo's chest and arms, lacerating them, then around his neck and face. The thorns punctured his cheeks and throat, one thick vine gagging his screams. Then Doto squeezed, pulled, and tore the man into pieces. Blood sprayed across the ground.

Through the forest, he felt Clay's fingers tighten, gripping the grass where he had fallen. "Doto! Doto, what have you done?"

Doto broke the binding around his ankles and rose. "I've rid us of the stupid little person who dared hurt you. And now I'm setting us free."

He turned his gaze toward Jai. The fire bearer had his knife in one hand and was frantically sawing at the vine wrapped around his foot. "Away, demon!" the man shrieked at him in terror.

"I am no demon," Doto informed him. He strode forward, humming with anger and power, and behind him the plants seethed and twisted. "I am Doto the mighty, god of the forest, and you have angered me."

"Doto, no!" Clay cried behind him.

He flicked an ear backward, irritated. Did his mate honestly fear that Jai could pose a threat to him now? Now, when he had the strength of his godhood flowing and crackling through every limb? He reached the edge of the forest circle and dragged Jai into it. With one paw, he grabbed the fire bearer's hair and yanked him to his feet, just as Jai had pulled Clay upright a moment ago.

"Please," Jai begged him. "Please, just let me go! A demon I thought you were, a god nay! Forgive a foolish mortal! Forgive, and I'll sing your praises always. Learned the dance I did, a little, and dance it I will, in your honor."

Doto inhaled the scent of his terror. "Why should I forgive you? You are a cruel and stupid fire bearer. You would bleed me endlessly and call me back? Nothing in all the forest is so terrible as that. And you think *me* a demon."

The fire bearer thrashed and flailed in his grip, but Doto had the forest's might now, and it could not be broken. "I repent!" Jai screamed. "I repent every offense and injury I gave you, lord! I'll be your humble servant the rest of my life."

"Doto," Clay said, putting a hand on his shoulder.

He turned and saw Clay up close. There was blood in the corners of his mouth, and in one eye, and one lower tooth had been knocked out—a fang, it would have been, were Clay like him. He smelled again the blood and fear on his mate.

"I forgive you," he told Jai. Clay's hand squeezed his shoulder.

The squirming fire bearer sagged in his grip. "Lord—Lord Doto, you are wise and gracious."

"I forgive you every offense and injury against me, as you begged," he continued, his voice going harder. "But you hurt my Clay."

He raised his paw—Jai flinched away from it—and touched the tip of his finger to Jai's cheek. One tiny seed from the spreading forest clung to the tip of his claw, and he pressed that seed to the fire bearer's trembling skin and sent his will into it. It sprouted roots, and these burrowed into Jai's flesh, spreading outward beneath the skin of his cheek, crawling through it as if through soft loam. The man gaped and screamed, but Doto ignored him, curling his lip in bitter satisfaction as he made the little roots thicken and grow, bulge under the man's face like swollen veins. Their tendrils burrowed up toward his eye, poked pale green fingers from beneath his lower eyelid, and then spread across the smooth, white surface, arresting its twitching and rolling movements. The eye went suddenly still even as the other jerked around in terror.

"Doto!" Clay called, tugging at his shoulder with surprising force. "Doto, stop it, please, stop right now!"

"What?" He frowned, looking back at Clay. His mate was frightened and shaking, and tears brimmed in his eyes. There was an expression on his face that Doto neither recognized nor liked. "There is no reason to fear. This fire bearer will never be able to harm me or you again."

"I know he won't! So stop hurting him, please!" Clay gripped Doto's arm and tugged at it desperately.

"But why? This man hurt you. He wanted to hurt me. And I want to hurt him and kill him."

"Listen to the boy," Jai sobbed. A tear of blood ran down from his ruined eye. "Please, Lord Doto."

"Be silent," Doto growled at him.

"You have to stop because it's wrong," Clay said. His voice broke with the words. "Don't you understand that? Don't you understand that it's wrong to hurt someone when you don't have to?"

The claim was bewildering. Doto huffed through his nostrils. "That is foolishness. Who says it is wrong? I am a god. I say what is wrong, not—not worshipers. You are going to challenge me? I am your god, and I say it is not wrong."

Clay looked stricken. "But—" he stammered. "But it still is. It doesn't matter if you say it's not. It's still wrong. You can't do it, Doto. Please. Let him go."

"Let him go?" What possible reason could Clay have to ask such a thing? "No. This is stupid. You are my worshiper, Clay, and you need your god to protect you. I will kill this fire bearer now. You will understand when you are calmed down." He turned back to Jai and sent his will into the roots, making them grow again. He felt them squeeze the eye until it collapsed and dribbled its hot jelly down the fire bearer's cheek. Jai shrieked and clawed at his face with his free hand.

Clay seized Doto's arm again and tugged at it with both hands. "Doto, stop it! Stop it, or…or…"

Doto snarled in frustration, letting go of Jai, who dropped to the ground and rolled back and forth, moaning and clutching at his face with both hands. "Or what?" he growled. "Or what, Clay? What possible reason could you give me not to kill this worthless ash?"

Clay's hands trembled. Tears streaked his cheeks dark. He looked down at his feet, over at Jai, then back up at Doto. "Because if you do, I won't love you anymore," he said.

Doto felt as though he had been struck. He staggered backward in the grass. "What did you say?"

"I won't be able to help it." Clay smiled, but it wasn't a happy one, and that only confused Doto more. "I just know it's wrong, and if you do it, I'll stop loving you. You already—" He shuddered. "Ulo. I don't know if I can take that."

"They are bad men!" Doto protested, incredulous. "They hurt you! I want them to suffer and die for what they did!"

"Like the people at Abansin?"

Doto's retort died in his mouth. Abansin. The city in the middle of the forest, where his mother had been killed, and where his father, in retribution, had slaughtered hundreds, perhaps thousands of fire bearers. He had torn them apart with vines, smashed them against rocks, dragged them into the trees and underground, sent roots crawling through their bodies.

Doto looked down at the torn remains of Ulo on the ground, at Jai lying moaning in the grass, hands gripping a skull bound by crawling roots. His fur lifted.

"Go, then!" he shouted at Jai. "Get out of here. Don't let ever me see you again, or I'll grow those roots down your neck and chest until they crush your heart! And do not ever dare to enter the forest again!"

Jai lurched to his feet, blood streaming down his left cheek, his good eye rolling in terror. "Thank you, Lord Doto! Thank you! You are wise and merciful!"

"Go!" Doto roared at him. Jai snapped his mouth shut, turned, and bolted, tearing off into the savanna as fast as he could run. Doto watched for a time, picking out the figure as it diminished into the south. Jai fell in the darkness several times, but never looked back, scrambling up to his feet and racing off again as though death itself nipped at his heels.

Rolling his shoulders back proudly, Doto turned to Clay. "There. He will not bother us again, I think. And if he does…" He trailed off as he felt the Clay sit down heavily in his grass. He turned to his worshiper, who sat slumped forward, his head in his hands. "What is wrong? You are safe, and I did what you asked. I let him go, even though he had no right to live."

"You killed a man," Clay said into his hands.

"You are still bothered about that? That man hurt you. There was no reason he should have lived." Feeling a little injured, he added, "There was no reason to say that you would stop loving me."

Clay looked up over his fingers. "I was afraid I would. I didn't understand how you could hurt someone like that."

"How could you not want to do it yourself? That fire bearer was cruel. He wounded you over and over again and he threatened your god. Why should you feel afraid that I would hurt him? You should be glad." Doto huffed in frustration. He could not abide this feeling Clay was giving him now. It was as though Clay stood in the savanna, and he in the forest, and between them was the wall that divided the two. Here he was, the forest's power flowing through him, and yet he felt helpless, apart from it.

Then Clay reached out and took his paw, breaking the wall, and the touch warmed and relieved him. "Listen, Doto. I don't know anymore what the gods want. I thought I did, but all my stories weren't true. And all the things we were supposed to do and not supposed to do, they don't make sense anymore. I feel like I'm losing them one by one. But to hurt someone if you don't have to, to kill him? I pray I never lose that. It's evil, Doto, if anything is. And when you do it, it scares me."

Doto sniffed. "That is foolishness. I say it is not evil, and I am a god. Who would you listen to if not a god?"

"I don't know," Clay wiped at his eyes with the back of his hand. "But it doesn't matter what the gods say. There are things more important than the gods." He blinked after saying that, as though the words had surprised him.

"It doesn't matter?" Doto asked, growing more uneasy. This did not sound like the Clay he knew. "Now you are being arrogant. What could be more important than what the gods demand of you?"

"I don't know. I don't understand. I always believed the gods taught against hurting others needlessly. Maybe...maybe Father Wem or Mother Fam oppose it?"

Doto shook his head, but at the mention of Mother Fam, his uneasiness deepened, sinking far into his memory and tugging at forgotten threads there. "The gods enforce the laws of nature, and nature is merciless." They were not his words, but he could not remember when he had heard them. Nor, he thought, were they entirely true. Was not Clay part of nature?

"But it's wrong!" Clay insisted.

Doto scowled. "It can't be wrong if you can't even tell me why it's wrong."

Clay stared down at his hands. He looked over his shoulder at the spot where Ulo's body lay, torn into pieces, staining the grass dark with blood, eyes staring sightlessly in the moonlight. He shuddered. "Look at him, Doto."

Doto peered at the carcass. His stomach growled. He had not had much to eat the past few days. He suspected, however, that Clay would object to his satiating that need with Ulo. "He is dead. He was cruel to you, and now he is dead."

"He's got a wife, a mate. Maybe she'll never know what happened to him. And a baby who will grow up never knowing his father. You hurt them, too."

"And why should I care about that?" Doto asked, but his ears flattened. Clay's words were making him increasingly uncomfortable, and he did not understand why. So what if that man had had a mate and cub? They were none of Doto's concern. He had been right to kill the man. "He was going to kill you. I had to kill him to save your life."

"I know. You had to." Clay gave the dead man another glance and then did not look again.

"Then why are you upset?" Doto protested.

Clay sagged. If he were a leopard, his ears would be down and to the sides, his back hunched, his tail curled over his paws. As it was, he simply wilted like a thirsty shrub. "I don't know. I'm tired. And I've been beaten, and I'm hungry. Let's find someplace away from…from here and go to sleep. In the morning, things will look different."

Looking around, Doto said, "I do not think very much will change."

A sigh. "Doto?"

"What?"

"Let's just go to sleep."

They traveled a little distance away and bedded down in the savanna grass. No matter how Doto tried, he could not persuade Clay to remain in the forest circle. Something about the fire bearer's carcass upset him. Even when Doto offered to drag it away or pull it down into the soil, Clay still refused. And so, stifled and weakened by the absence of his forest and exposed to the dangers of the savanna, including Jai, who Doto was not entirely certain would stay away, they settled down.

Clay fell quickly to sleep, but Doto stayed awake for some time. He kept one eye open, scanning the horizon, his ears pricked for the sound of any fire bearer that might be returning. The thought loomed more and more real as the night went on and Clay slept. His ears would twitch toward rustles in the grass, and his heart would race for a moment before he calmed himself. There were no scents of fire bearers on the wind. None except Clay, at least, but Clay didn't count anymore. He was nothing like those others.

After a while, some animals arrived and began feeding on the carcass. Doto was glad Clay wasn't awake to see or hear that, and settled close behind him. He was fond of lying on his side with one arm around his mate's chest, and normally when he put his arm there, Clay would nestle back against him, never waking, but pressing instinctively into Doto's embrace. It made Doto feel warm and protective. Tonight, though, when his arm slid around Clay's side, his little worshiper shuddered and pulled away, groaning in his sleep, so Doto withdrew and lay on his back, a little distance apart.

The wall between them had returned. It was all so unfair. He had saved his mate, saved him from pain and imprisonment, and maybe worse, and his reward for it was all this uncomfortableness. He sighed and watched the stars crawl. The forest had been so empty, so lonely, and then Clay had come along and filled it with something new and wonderful. It filled Doto, too. He didn't entirely understand it, but everything was better. And now, without even being awake, just by pulling away in his sleep, Clay could take all that new wonder away. He could put Doto back into the emptiness again. And Doto knew he would do anything not to return to that. Anything.

A shiver ran down his tail. He had made himself vulnerable. Vulnerable to a fire bearer, who his father had said had magic that could influence the gods, Kwaee had called him feeble, crippled with sympathies. And wasn't that what he was now? It didn't matter, he realized. He would do whatever Clay wanted, just to make the wall go away again, just to feel his touch and see his smile. He was under the fire bearer's influence. Perhaps Clay was a witch after all, or a minion of Ogya, and had enchanted him. Perhaps the prayer and dance was a spell that had captured him. Wasn't that when he had first warmed to his captive, after that first dance, long ago, in the forest? If so, he didn't want to escape the spell. He didn't want his forest to be lonely again, nor to go slinking back to Kwaee ashamed and repentant. How his father would smirk, or sneer in disgust.

A look had passed over Clay's face when Doto had tormented Jai. Doto had not recognized it at the time, but now he thought he knew it. He had seen the same expression on his father's face before. It was revulsion—not toward the men who had kidnapped and beat him, but toward Doto. But for what? Why?

There are things more important than the gods. He huffed through his nose. He shouldn't be spending all this time trying to decide what Clay meant. Clay was only a fire bearer. He had lived a tiny fraction of Doto's lifetime. What could he know about anything? It was senseless trying to sort out the meaning; there was none to find. He closed his eyes.

In the forest, he had never dreamed, nor did he truly require rest, sleeping only when it was convenient to do so. But out here, without his magic, weariness took hold of his thoughts and pulled them down into a dizzy spiral. The world around him fell away.

~~~

He wandered through the forest paths. There was something he was supposed to be doing, and Kwaee would be angry with him if he didn't do it, but he had forgotten what it was. He pulled at the fur on his arm, worrying. If he wandered, keeping his ears open and smelling the air, perhaps he would remember. But his magic was gone, his senses muted. The forest had rejected him.

He ran down trails he did not recognize. Trees loomed taller than they should. They shifted their great bulks, creaking and cracking as they leaned toward him. He ran faster, frightened now, searching for his lost magic. *Sure and true*, a hard, cruel voice called. *Sure and true.* Jai. The fire bearer had entered the forest. That was what he was to tell his father. The fire bearers were attacking. They had brought witch magic to ensorcel them all, a dread power that could command even gods.

He stepped on something that crunched and screeched beneath his foot. The smell of blood stung his nose as his feet slipped from beneath him and sent him tumbling to the ground. Without his power, he could fall. He tugged at the fur on his arm again, pulling harder to feel the pain.

It was a little genet kit he had stepped on, crushing its legs and tail with his foot. It cried and cried for its mother, its voice thin and tiny.

"Doto, what have you done?" Clay asked him. "How could you?"

"It's the law of nature," Doto answered back. "Nature is merciless."

"But you're nature. You're merciless. I won't love you anymore," Clay said.

Doto pulled at the fur on his arm again and a huge clump came out in his paw. He stared at it in shock; the skin beneath was smooth and brown. He stumbled back and felt himself step on the baby genet again, its little body crunching beneath his toes with a loud squeak.

"Oh, Doto," Clay said, frowning. "You killed it for no reason."

"I didn't mean to!" he protested.

"You can't help it," Clay told him. "You're nature." He turned and began to walk away.

Doto felt small and frightened. He'd been stepped on, crushed. "You're nature too," he called.

"Sure and true," Clay said. The kindness fell away from his face. They were in Kwaee's temple. Clay climbed up into the great moabi throne and sprawled out in it. His eyes were empty and cruel. "Sure and true."

Doto opened his eyes.

He groaned, trying to fight off a hazy, confused fear that followed the dream, as though he lived still half within it, half without. He forced himself upright, curling his tail over his toes. The morning light was grey in the east, and birds called up the sun. So Doto sat by Clay and watched him, playing over in his mind their argument from the day before, the terrible promise Clay had made him.

Doto knew little of dreams. Perhaps they were warnings from Father Wem. Perhaps when Clay woke up, he would be as in the dream: dispassionate and merciless. Doto did not know what he would do if that happened. Use his magic, maybe, and try to heal him. It would be worth the cost.

After a while, Clay finally blinked awake. He looked up at Doto and frowned, but it was not an angry or sad frown.

"Are you all right?" Doto asked. And Clay put his arms around Doto's waist and hugged him tightly, rubbing his cheek into the fur of Doto's belly.

Doto slid his arm down Clay's back, and could not understand for anything why he suddenly felt like weeping. He didn't, of course. No god would do anything so foolish.

∧∧∧

They continued north, following the divine energies that flowed through the earth and grass. The going was slower than before, for the injuries Clay had received at the end of Ulo's foot made breathing unpleasant and difficult. He clutched his side and could not travel quickly; the faster they moved, the more breathing pained him. Doto was not pleased that their pace had slowed so much; the longer it took them to find Sarmu and return, the longer before he could return to his forest.

The savanna still made him uncomfortable, and more so now that the encounter with the two fire bearers had proven his vulnerability. All day he remained alert for any sign of Jai, but the fire bearer never showed himself. Clay said he was sure they would never see him again, but Doto remained uneasy nonetheless. Wounding a predator did not always make it less dangerous.

They made so little progress that day that when they finally stopped for rest and food, Doto looked back and was sure that, far in the distance, he could still see the two trees where he and Clay had been bound the previous night.

"I can't hunt," Clay told him with chagrin, arm holding his tender side. "Not today." He had brought Ulo's spear with him—or, rather, he had requested that Doto go and fetch it from what remained of the carcass. Clay had not only refused to venture into the forest circle; he would not even look at it. The sight of it had caused him to shudder and turn away.

Doto surmised that fire bearers found the sight of their own dead distressing for some reason, and, as he had no such concerns, had gone to fetch the spear himself. But the big man lay in two pieces, face still wracked with terror, his body gripped with crawling vines. His eyes had been picked out by birds in the night, his entrails strewn across the grass and partially consumed by scavengers. His open mouth gaped in a silent, accusatory scream, and Doto found he could not look at the corpse. The sight summoned the memory of the previous night's events into vivid detail. There should have been no reason for Doto to react so strongly, but the thoughts turned his stomach, reminding him of his sickness. He had averted his gaze, groped for the spear and taken it back to Clay.

Clay had proclaimed it a better spear than the one he'd had before. Hunting would be easier. But there was to be no hunting that night.

"Dance for me," Doto said, "And I'll grow us food."

So Clay danced. It was not a very good dance, in Doto's opinion. His worshiper moved slowly, lurching, with stilted movements and listless words. They were rote, mumbled rather than sung with honest jubilation. Doto barely felt the rush and surge of the forest at all. The green grass and bushes and saplings sprouted around his paws, but sparsely, and spread out into a small circle that was barely large enough for both of them to lie down in. Just when he thought no more would appear, a few small, white flowers popped into blossom here and there. One immediately wilted and fell over.

Doto stared at it. "This is not a very good job."

"I'm sorry." Clay looked up at him tiredly. "It's the best I can do today. Honestly."

"Well, all right." Doto twitched his ears in disappointment. He sat down next to Clay. "Tomorrow night you can try again and do better." He grew clayfruit, and they both ate it in silence. The quiet felt strange and uncomfortable. Doto could not say for certain what was wrong, and it bothered him.

"What is different?" he asked. "I have seen you tired before, and even then you were not so quiet. You talk very much."

Clay shook his head. "It's just that I'm tired and sore. And I keep thinking about Ulo."

"Still? That was yesterday that that happened."

He smiled, but his eyes were sad. "I don't get over things that quickly, Doto. It still bothers me. It was horrible what happened."

"But I let Jai go," Doto reminded him. "Like you asked."

"I know you did." Clay reached over and patted Doto's knee. "And I'm glad you did that. But to see a man die like that, torn apart...it's terrible. And worse, to see it done by the one you love."

"So you still love me, then," Doto said.

"Yes."

"But you're still bothered."

"Yes."

Doto nodded. He thought a moment. "And that's why this little forest you made is so terrible."

Clay gave a faint giggle at that. "Maybe a little bit. But I really am tired and hurting."

Doto sighed through his nose, slumping. He munched on his fruit, letting his tail sway slowly through the grass, feeling the tickle of the blades against it. "Well, what do I do to make you not bothered anymore?"

"It doesn't work like that. It happened. You can't make it go away. Not even a god can do that." His fire bearer looked over at him, eyes mahogany in the sunset, sad and hopeful at the same time. "Maybe...maybe if you promised."

"Promised what?" Doto asked suspiciously.

"Promised that you would never kill or hurt someone like that again if you didn't have to."

"That is absurd! Gods do not make such agreements. And anyway, I had to kill that first fire bearer."

Clay nodded, and looked down again. "I know. I just thought... It would have made me feel better."

That uneasiness from before rose again in Doto, the feeling that he was wrong without being able to see how. "It is not a promise I can make. I must uphold the laws of nature. And nature hurts and kills."

"Even when it doesn't have to?"

"Even then, sometimes."

Clay nodded and went silent. So they were back to that again. Nothing had helped.

Doto pondered. Could he make such a promise? He knew what Kwaee would say, and he had little concern for Kwaee's advice. But that advice the only counsel he had. It was his father who had taught him everything he knew about being a god, and Doto hadn't had to travel far to learn that Kwaee, sulky and petulant, prone to cruelty, sitting brooding in his temple for all time while closing his eyes to his own forest, was not an admirable god. If one thing he'd taught Doto had been wrong, why not everything? Who decided what the laws of nature were and how they should be enforced? Doto could have asked Asubonten or Atekye, goddesses of rivers and swamps, but he'd never trusted them, and they had always seemed equally wary of him.

Mother Fam, he thought. She had cared for him when he was a cub, before Kwaee had taken up his tutelage as a godling. There were things she had told him long ago, but he could not remember her lessons. She had left the forest one day and never returned, and after that he had been with Kwaee. He felt an old surge of anger towards her. How could she just leave and not come to see him anymore? He decided he didn't care what she would have had to say, anyway.

He looked over at Clay, who was staring off into the sunset, watching the eye of Wem dip into the great water somewhere far to the west. He curled his tail over quietly and flicked it at Clay's back, and his bearer smiled a little, so he reached over to paw at his side, hoping faintly that they might mate again. It had been a few days.

But Clay flinched away from his touch, nearly falling over in his efforts to avoid Doto's fingers.

Doto drooped his ears. "You do not wish me to touch you anymore?"

"It's not that," Clay said, looking ashamed. "It's just…I'm really sore there. See?" He lifted his arm, and Doto saw, faintly beneath Clay's brown skin, the signs of blood pooling into dark, ugly bruises.

"Lie back," Doto ordered. His wrath towards Ulo rose again, useless, unsatisfied by the man's death. "Let me see how you are injured."

Obediently, Clay lay back in the grass, spreading his arms, and Doto inspected him. The damage was most likely not permanent, but it was ugly. Doto glided his fingers over Clay's smooth skin, finding the places heated from blood collecting just below the surface. All up and down Clay's belly, chest and left side, he was riddled with bruises. From the pain he had reported when breathing, Doto thought ribs might be broken as well. His fire bearer was badly battered. He wished he had another Ulo to punish for this.

But, he realized, that would only make things worse. He had seen Clay hurt before: footless, injured, infected, feverish, starving, exhausted, and bitten by a baboon. All this Clay had suffered with him, and, he realized with a deepening sense of unease, most of it because of him. But through all that, he had never seen his little fire bearer grow as truly dispirited as he was now. Whatever Ulo had done to him, it was not as bad as what Doto had done.

"Your fang is missing," he observed.

Clay poked his tongue through the hole in the row of his square white teeth. He grimaced. "I know."

"Will it grow back?"

"No. It's gone for good. It hurts too. Another reason I wanted fruit instead of meat tonight."

Doto switched his tail. There was an obvious solution, but one he did not like. "You must let me heal you."

Clay sat up in surprise. "Doto, no! You'll lose some of your power if you do that."

"I know," Doto said. "I am not pleased about that. But you have suffered much injury because of me. I am restored to full health in my forest, but you are not. You will not get better for many days, and we cannot afford to lose more time."

Shaking his head, Clay said, "No. I can push harder. We can make it. And anyway, if you heal me, it will make me…make me more…" He splayed the toes of the leopard paw that was his left foot.

"Not very much, I think," Doto said. "I am not making a whole new foot for you. Just mending some bruises. It will not take much magic to heal that. And we can reach Sarmu faster."

He didn't tell Clay how much he feared the healing again. The last time, he had passed out from the intensity of the magic, and when he awoke, he had been changed. His perceptions of the world were different, and he was weaker. For the first time in his life, things were not effortless. He could trip and fall. The forest gave way before him with more reluctance. When he had given Clay his strength, he had received some of Clay's vulnerability in return. The thought of losing more of himself in that way filled him with a rising dread. Every healing would be a sacrifice.

But Clay shook his head. "Just give it another day," he said. "I'll do better tomorrow. You'll see."

That night, as they rested, Doto kept a little space between himself and Clay that night. He feared brushing against Clay's injuries and disturbing his sleep. He had hoped Clay would refuse the offer to heal him, and now he felt both ashamed and relieved for that selfish wish. And that, in turn, confused him. Why should it bother him at all? He was only doing what any would have done. All these frustrating doubts and questions were not very godlike. They must have come from Clay during the healing. He scowled in the dark at the feelings, as though he might frighten them away. Still, he missed seeing Clay cheerful and energetic, and more, missed putting his arms around him, mating with him.

He put his paw against Clay's lean back, feeling it move gently with each breath. Almost, he summoned his magic and sent it into Clay. Almost, the words fell from his lips in god-tongue: *Take what is mine. Out, out, into blood and bone, flesh and scar, take what is mine.* The air swirled around them in expectation of the magic, becoming electric.

Clay stirred in his sleep, drawing in a deep breath and wincing in pain. Doto could do it now. He could heal his little worshiper, and in doing so, make Clay a little more of a god…and himself a little less of one.

He let the magic die down again. The cost was too high. And Clay was unpredictable and became upset over irrational things. He would probably be upset over that, too.

Doto closed his eyes and tried to sleep again, but for the second night in a row, thoughts troubled him. One day the cost would not be too high. One day Clay would be injured far worse than now, and if not, then one day he would grow aged and doddering, Then Doto would have to make an awful choice: lose Clay or lose himself. Fire bearers were frail. They died. It was as inevitable as the sunset.

Doto wished now he had not impressed upon Clay the urgency of their journey. True to his word, Clay was trying harder to keep up his pace, and he was suffering for it. He made an effort to disguise his limp, partly by leaning on his spear for assistance, and walked much faster than the day before. But Doto could smell the pain on him and hear the wheezing in his breath, and no matter how many times he urged Clay to slow down or take a rest, the fire bearer insisted on pressing on, saying that he was fine.

And so, day after day, they continued on, and this time Doto made himself lag a little bit behind so that every now and then, like it or not, Clay would be forced to stop and wait for him, getting rest he might not have wanted, but needed.

"Why are you going so slowly?" Clay asked finally. "I thought you were in a hurry to get back to the forest. And I want to see my people."

"I did want to get back quickly, but now I'm wondering what will happen when we do." It was an evasion of the question, but not a lie. The thought had been worrying him. "If you're going to see your people and I am to go to the forest, what happens then?"

Clay shrugged. "I guess that all depends on what Sarmu says. If he knows a way to appease your father, that's something you'll have to do. We both know I can't go back into the forest while he's angry. Last time, the baboons nearly killed me."

That was true. Only the magic of Doto's fetish, the little wooden leopard around Clay's neck, protected him from being torn apart by the forest. All it would take was one accident for it to be torn from his neck, or fall off. "I know, but after that? If I am able to calm Kwaee and the forest stills again. You will have seen your people, and they will know you are well and living."

"And they'll have some questions about my foot, I guess, which I'm betting they'll remember I didn't have the last time they saw me. I should think of what to tell them about that."

"Not the truth?" Doto asked.

Clay frowned. "Maybe. But I don't know if they'll believe me. My people have their stories about the gods, and if I tell them something different… I don't know what they'll think."

"They will believe you. You can bring them to me, and I will reveal myself. Then if they do not believe you, they will be very, very stupid."

Chuckling, Clay said, "I don't know if my brother, Laughing Dog, would believe you even then. Changing his mind is like trying to make rain fall up into the sky."

"But most people will. And you will tell them to worship me."

"Yes."

"And then you will come to live with me in the forest." Doto watched Clay closely to see his reaction, and Clay looked away, as though distracted by something on the horizon. Doto pressed him. "You will come, yes?"

Clay was quiet. Then he said, "If you command me to come with you, Lord Doto, I will come."

"But you do not wish to come?"

"Leave my family? My people? I couldn't abandon them, Doto. It's where I belong."

"You belong with me now," Doto insisted. "You carry part of me with you. You love me."

"And I love my father," Clay said. "And my brothers. I love the dances and the hunts and the music and seeing the children playing and smelling good food cooking. I miss all of that." He sighed. "I couldn't miss it forever. Why are we talking about this now? It's so far away. We don't know what will happen."

"That is true," Doto said. Clay's words filled him with an anxiety that had been building since they first left his temple. "I cannot live out here, outside my forest. And we do not know what will happen. I have spurned my own father for you. I have given you my magic, in your flesh and bone and around your neck. I have given up much. And now I am afraid that you will not come back with me. It is a bad feeling. I do not care for it at all."

Clay's shoulders hunched. He quickened his pace, walking ahead, so Doto hurried to him and gripped one shoulder, turning him around to look him in the eyes. "Clay, I do not know what will happen. I need to know that I will not be alone. I can't be alone again. You don't know what it was like."

Clay turned his head, and Doto moved to stay in his gaze. "Doto… You know that I'll always pray to you. I'll always dance the dance for you."

"That's not enough!" Doto exclaimed, surprising himself as much as Clay with the urgency in his voice. "It's not enough," he said again, softer. "I need you with me. You are the only good thing in my forest."

"My people aren't leaving, Doto. They will always be by the forest. And if the forest stills, then maybe we can even live in the forest, and then I'll always be near you."

"Not in my temple," Doto said.

"No, but in the forest. I don't want to be apart from you either, you know. You're my god. But I can't choose to abandon my people. I can't, any more than you can choose to live outside the forest."

Doto's budding anxiety began to blossom into fear. "But if I command you to come with me, you will."

Clay sagged in his grip. "Yes, Lord Doto," he said.

Doto now knew the sound of unhappiness in his voice quite well. "But you will be sad if I command you to."

"Yes."

He switched his tail. "Then I will not command you. But I will show you that I will make you happy. I will promise what you asked."

"I asked for something?"

"Yes. And I would not promise it then, but I do now. I promise that I will never kill or hurt another fire bearer. Unless I must." As soon as he said the words, he felt an uncomfortable finality to them. He had willingly chosen to limit his own power, and that, he worried, was something he would regret. But beyond the worry, there was a sense of relief and pride. He had given his worshiper a greater gift than perhaps any mortal creature had ever received from a god. The covenant took his affection for Clay and deepened it in a way he did not understand. There was power, for better or ill, in that promise.

The astonished look on Clay's face was almost reward enough. He blinked as though he didn't understand, wrapped his arms around Doto's chest, and squeezed him roughly. At first, Doto thought that they were about to mate, which seemed an inappropriate response, but after the squeeze Clay let him go.

"And now," he told Clay, "you will promise that if you must choose between your people and me, you will choose me."

The shadow returned to Clay's face. "Doto—" he began, but then he broke off, lifting his head. "Did you hear that?"

Doto *had* heard something: a rapid, rhythmic sound that carried some distance over the savanna. He swiveled his ears, trying to locate its source. "Is it the Cry of the Dead?" he asked with some concern. The *thump-thump-thump-thump-thump* was similar to the sounds he had heard long ago in the fire bearer's village. This noise had come from the north, he thought, but then it sounded again from the southeast. "There is more than one of them, whatever they are."

Clay shook his head. "It doesn't sound like drums. I don't know what it is."

Thump-thump-thump-thump. Again, this time from the west. Doto dropped into a ready crouch. "There must be many of them. They are getting closer." He looked about, peering with his keen eyes. "There," he said, pointing west. "I see something!" Far off, near the horizon, he could make out a tiny figure. It was moving with tremendous speed, raising a cloud of red-orange dust as it did.

"I don't see it." Clay shaded his eyes with one hand.

There was nothing on the horizon now. "It's gone," Doto said, but then the thumping came from behind him, to the east again, and he whirled. Again he saw a figure, speeding along the horizon, the dirt pluming into the air behind it. He tracked it carefully with his eyes, but it turned into a speck and vanished. "It was over there!"

Clay stepped close to his side, worried. "Do you see it? What do you think it is?"

"I don't know," Doto muttered. "Quiet." He focused, turning slowly with Clay, trying to locate the figure again.

A voice, wry and resonant and round with amusement, came from behind them. "Hello, boys."

Doto whirled with a hiss, his claws extending, and he nearly shoved Clay into the dirt as he did so.

Behind him stood a god in the form of a tall, rangy hare, his ears splayed at ease, his eyes twinkling, arms crossed over his lean chest. He twitched his whiskers. "Shouldn't let people sneak up on you like that," he said.

"A god!" Clay's fingers gripped at Doto's side, tugging his fur pain-fully. "Is he Lord Sarmu?"

"He is not," Doto answered stiffly.

"Sarmu?" The hare barked a laugh. "That meandering old lump? He hasn't one tenth the speed I've got in one of my toes. No, come on, boy, you know me. I'm in *all* the best stories."

"Adanko," Clay breathed. "God of hares. He's a trickster in all the tales."

"Trickster?" the hare exclaimed. "I am no trickster! I could never trick anyone half so clever as you boys. No, no, no, what I am is a liar. And a damned fine one. Kidding. I'm awful. An awful liar, that's what I am."

Doto found this god's mannerisms disconcerting. He had not heard of Adanko, but he was plainly a lesser god. "How did you get behind us like that?" he asked. "I am Doto, god of the forest, and I do not care to be deceived."

Adanko grinned. "God of silence, that's me. I live in the quiet when the wind doesn't blow, and in every unspoken word. Damn pity I'm so chatty. My dominion shrinks by the moment." He crouched and beat his foot rapidly against the ground, making a loud, rhythmic thumping sound. And then he was gone. A cloud of reddish dirt hung in the air where he had been standing.

Doto frowned. "That was—"

"Hello boys," said Adanko's voice behind them again. He put his thin arms across their shoulders and leaned his head in between theirs. "I'm also the god of super super fastitude. The secret is changing directions, see? That's why you have to lie. I go left! I go right! I go left! I go right! They're trying to catch me, but they don't know which way I'm going next!"

"Left," Doto said.

"Right!" Adanko shouted jubilantly. "What can I say? You caught me fair. You can ask a question, and I promise not to lie."

Clay dropped down to his knees, spreading his arms before him. "Oh great Adanko," he began.

Doto nudged him with his toes. He was finding Clay's inclination to bow down to any traveling creature with a bit of divinity irritating. "Stop that," he said. "He's only a lesser god. You don't have to worship him."

"Don't have to," Adanko said. "But you certainly can, dear boy. I haven't had a good, hard, worshiping in a hundred rains." He looked right at Doto and winked as he said it.

Doto wasn't sure what the wink was all about, but he was sure he didn't like it. "Why have you come here, hare god? Why are you bothering us?"

"Why?" Adanko twitched his ears as though astonished. "Why? Can't a hare stop by to see the gods when they're passing through his grasses?"

"God," Doto corrected him. "You meet only one god here."

The hare looked suddenly surprised. "Only one? Is that what you think?" He leaned in close, sniffing at Doto. Doto warned him off with a low growl. "What would you say if I told you there were more gods here than you could count?"

Adanko turned to Clay, who at least had bothered to get back to his feet. "Him, I mean," he said to Clay, jerking a clawed thumb in Doto's direction. He poked a finger at Clay's chest. "*You* could count them fine." In a whisper, he added, "I see why you like him, but he's a little dim, isn't he?"

"Look," Doto interrupted, feeling the conversation slipping from beneath his toes, "Stop all this foolish talk about gods. You promised not to lie!"

"Did I?" Adanko asked, rocking back on his heels with a pensive expression. "Hm. Must've been lying about that."

"Then what do you want?" Doto shouted in frustration. "Only to tease and insult us? We have no desire for that."

"What do I want, what do I want?" Adanko rubbed at his chin as though pondering. "Oh! Yes. Sarmu sent me."

Doto's frustration flooded away from him, his ears perking. "Sarmu? Truly, Sarmu sent you?"

"Well, I *might* be lying, but…yes. Pretty sure. Sarmu sent me."

Clay stepped forward, dipping his head. "Please, Lord Adanko, but… Lord Sarmu—where is he?"

"Oh, he's there." Adanko pointed one thin, furred arm to the northeast. "That direction. Exactly. Not lying. Probably."

"The frogs told us Sarmu was lost," Doto said suspiciously.

Adanko snorted. "Frogs. Idiots. And you *listened* to them!" He chuckled in disbelief. "But he is, you know. Very lost."

"Then how do you know where he is?" Doto demanded.

"Oh, everyone knows where he is," Adanko said, nodding. "That way." He pointed to the northeast again. "Locked up in a cage."

Clay frowned. "But who could imprison the great Lord Sarmu?"

"Who indeed?" Adanko asked. "No one, probably. He's not imprisoned."

"You just said he was!" Doto growled.

"I told you I was a liar." Adanko grinned sweetly back at him. "Though that may not have been true, exactly."

Clay frowned. "So he's lost, but everyone knows where he is, and he's locked in a cage, but not imprisoned."

Doto curled his fingers into fists and then relaxed. This was the way this god behaved, that was all. It would not help him to become angry. Kwaee was never patient. Doto would be. "What kind of cage is this, that it could contain a god?" he asked.

"Now you're using your jugo beans!" Adanko said brightly. "What kind of cage, indeed? It's a mountain. A mountain made of fire."

Clay stared at him in wonder. "A mountain made of fire?"

Adanko thumped his foot on the ground. "Made of fire! We call it Ogya-Bepow!" He shouted the last syllable. "It's new. A brand new mountain. A high place, for any tent-dwellers who might be listening. And none of us can get in, and Sarmu can't get out. But he knew guests were coming, so he sent good old Adanko to greet you, and tell you this: give up."

"Give up?" Clay repeated, looking bewildered. Doto was getting annoyed at the fire bearer's habit of repeating everything Adanko said.

"Yes," Adanko said, nodding. "Give up. Because you cannot get in. The walls are sealed with earth and fire, and none shall pass. You will fail, and then it will be all the more tragic that neither of you will hear Sarmu's great and terrible secret that he knows about you, Doto, but has never told anyone, not even me, his curious and annoyingly persistent servant."

"A secret about me?" Doto felt the blood drain from his face. "What kind of secret?"

"Don't know!" Adanko shrugged. "Probably a horrible one. Which you'll never know. Because you can't get in."

Clay narrowed his eyes. "Are you lying about that?"

Adanko gasped. "What blasphemy do you speak now, mortal? I am Adanko, the Unremittingly Trustworthy! I do not lie!"

"Sarmu does not know a secret about me," Doto said. "That is the lie. You are only baiting me, Brother Hare."

"You're right," Adanko said, nodding. "He knows no secrets at all. How could he, trapped inside Ogya-Bepow for hundreds of rains? Well done. You found me out."

Frustration finally broke Doto's patience. "Why do you not speak to us plainly? Why must you lie at all? Do you not understand that Ogya wishes to burn the forest? Do you think he will stop there? The savanna will burn too, and you with it, and your little hare temple, wherever that might be! Why do you not simply tell us the truth?"

The smirk faded from Adanko's face, his expression softening. "Oh, dear boy," he said to Doto, "do you not know why lies exist? It's because they make us strong." Then he looked toward Clay, his brown eyes gentle. "And because learning they are lies makes us stronger."

The hare put one paw on Doto's shoulder. "It's in my nature to run, to lie, to never be caught. And we can't fight our natures, can we? Not us gods. We are who we are, and nothing we do can ever change that."

He stepped back. "That's why I'm never caught, boys. Because when danger comes, I go left! I go right! I go left! I go—" A cloud of dust rose from the ground. He was gone.

Clay and Doto both immediately looked behind themselves. There was no hare to be seen.

"Do you think he's gone?" Clay asked after they had waited a little while, looking around.

"I hope so," Doto muttered, still feeling annoyed at the way the lesser god had toyed with him as though he were a mouse between a civet's paws.

"Do you think he was telling the truth about the high place? Ogya-Bepow?"

"I don't know," Doto said.

"But we're still going, aren't we?"

"We came out here hoping that Sarmu might know something that would help us. Now we *know* that he knows something."

Clay reached out and took Doto's paw. Doto was glad of the comfort, though it reminded him of the question Clay had left unanswered before. "But what if we can't get into the mountain? How can we get in if Sarmu can't get out?"

Doto squeezed Clay's hand. "We'll find a way in. I know it. We'll find a way, find out his secret. Learn what he knows about the war between Kwaee and Ogya. Then we'll go back to your nest."

"Village," Clay reminded him. "And we'll tell them about you and Kwaee and Ogya."

"And then we will go to Kwaee," Doto declared. "We will confront him with the lies that he has told. He will have no choice but to still the forest. The fire bearers will be spared. We will find a way. And then…" He looked at Clay.

Clay looked back at him, and then quickly away.

"And then…" Doto repeated.

Betrayals Old and New

As she cleaned and dressed Whistling Thorn's body, Cloud heard the words of her mother in her head. *Those who choose to be healers must accept that they will fail.* This is how it always ends. Death always wins in the end, and Wem will have his due.

She rubbed incense oils into the boy's smooth skin. His limbs were terribly thin and frail. She bound his wrists and ankles with palm leaves, softened by a night of soaking in scented waters. The oils would help the flames of Ogya to catch quickly and carry Thorn's soul up to Wem.

She had tried to keep Thorn alive, and she had failed, and there was no reason to look at this failure as different than any other. Long past were the days when she might have demanded an explanation from Wem, might have questioned what a small child could have done to warrant so little mercy from the gods. Children died just as adults did, and the role of healer did not belong to those who could not accept that. She had always believed herself strong enough to carry herself through any death. She had survived the deaths of her mother and father and sister, of the King and his wife, and of her own husband. All her losses, all her failures. She could count them through the years.

She brought the child's body outside so that his parents could see him one last time. She had learned not to question death, but that was different than learning to answer it, and those who faced it always wanted answers she couldn't give. That Whistling Thorn had gone silent and staring before learning he would die, Cloud considered a small mercy. She knew that she was brusque and blunt. Suffering asked for a gentleness that had never come easily to her. In the face of it, she knew only direct answers or silence, and so she was glad Whistling Thorn had disappeared into his own mind, with no chance to yearn for a soothing she couldn't grant.

She had stood by as his parents grieved, though. His mother stroked his forehead and sang to him, but his father, Firefly, needed to be angry.

Cloud kept silent as he demanded to know why she hadn't done more. Perhaps she had not said the right prayers. Perhaps she should have been more of a woman. It wasn't natural for a woman to be alone all her life, to skulk about in a tent all day with smoke and seeds, and maybe the gods were offended. He shouted that maybe she had hated Thorn, that she was an idiot, that Thorn had had only wasp stings and now he was dead, and if she had just left him alone, he would be fine. Beneath the angry words, No Rocks sang lullabies her son could not hear.

She did not blame Firefly for railing at her. He was a man caught in a storm of grief, and it blew him from side to side without care for his wishes or civility. She did not blame him because she understood. She rubbed the thin green fabric of her dress between her fingers and waited as he fought the shadow of a loved one's death. It was a fight all made and all lost, and he was no different. He would step out of a world in which he had a son and into a world where he didn't.

Though she had said little and done nothing, when she finally left No Rocks and Firefly, she was exhausted as though she had been up all night. She stepped into her tent and found Ant With a Leaf waiting for her. The weariness settled into her bones and made her joints ache.

Ant sat by the little cooking fire, her shoulders rounded. Her braids, which she normally tied up for hunting, were loose around her neck and back. She still looked strong and determined, Cloud thought. That was something, at least.

"My father is going to die, isn't he?" Ant said, her gaze in the glowing embers.

"I don't know," Cloud murmured. She shuffled across the tent, ducking her head under the hanging roots and dried herbs that would otherwise tangle in the web of her hair, and eased herself gingerly down onto her bed of pelts, sitting and stretching out her stiff knees.

"But you think it. First Red Moth got sick, and then Whistling Thorn. Then Red Moth died, and then Whistling Thorn."

"Two deaths like another don't make a fate," Cloud said. "But yes, I fear for Mongoose's life. I have known him a long time—"

"And you are doing everything you can for him," Ant With a Leaf declared. "I know that. I saw you with Firefly and No Rocks. You shouldn't let them talk to you like that."

"They've got a right."

"No. No they don't. You're an elder. You're owed respect. How could they accuse you of such things?" Ant bristled in anger. "You have done nothing wrong!"

Cloud rubbed at her sore fingers. "We've all done things wrong, Ant. Whatever harshness the world has got for me, I earned it. The things they say in anger... I can't blame them. I've said the same things."

"When would you have ever said things like that?" Ant asked.

"When Wind died."

"Wind. That was your husband?"

"Yes. He stepped on a puff adder. I couldn't save him." Cloud lowered her gaze into her lap, trying to fight away the old memories. Their teeth had worn down, but they still bit.

"That was not your fault," Ant told her, straightening with confidence. "I know you. I saw you stare down a monster with nothing but a torch to save your patients. I know you did all you could to save him."

Cloud gave her a sad smile. "Did I?"

The footsteps of several people approached outside her tent. "Cloud, are you in there?" a voice called. It was Laughing Dog.

This day would not end. Cloud sighed. "Yes," she said. "I'm here."

Laughing Dog pulled the tent flap aside and stuck his head in. "Ant," he said in surprise. "You shouldn't be in here."

"I've come to find out about my father," Ant said. She stiffened when she spoke to him, her voice still and neutral. "He is very ill, you know."

"That's why I'm here," Laughing Dog said. He didn't seem to notice the reproach in her tone. "You don't have to worry about him anymore. We're going to take care of it."

"What do you mean?" Cloud asked sharply. "No one else here is capable of helping these people." It wasn't entirely true. She'd been teaching Yellow Bug what she could about the medicinal arts, but the girl was young, inexperienced and prone to distraction. She was hardly capable of handling patients on her own. And anyway, Cloud had kept her away during the plague, in case the illness afflicted her as well.

"You'll find out soon enough," Laughing Dog said. He wore a smirk that Cloud didn't like at all. "King Great Ram has ordered that you appear before the council."

"The council? What for?" Ant With a Leaf asked.

"I couldn't say," Laughing Dog answered her. "But facing two deaths in so short a time... Someone has to answer for that."

Ant squinted her eyes in disbelief. "You can't mean people think that *Cloud*—it's outrageous!"

"It's all right, Ant With a Leaf," Cloud said, waving a hand to soothe her. "I'll just go and see what they have to say. Visit your father while I'm gone, if you like. Only don't draw too close, understand?"

"Don't worry, Ant," Laughing Dog said. "We're going to make sure your father is well-cared for. Come on, Cloud. You'd better not keep the King waiting."

∧∧∧

The King stood before his stool. His face was grave and severe. Around him, the elders sat, Laughing Dog at his right hand. There was Bad Water, hunched forward like a mushroom, and the Teller. There was Long Neck, the tanner, and Broken Calabash, the musician, and Okra Bush. The elders had left a gap where Two Broken Hands sat usually, and another for Twig, who was lying sick in her tent now.

Joining the elders were two of Laughing Dog's fire hunters: Wasp and Half Moon. Cloud was not pleased to see them there. These were not people who had the wisdom and experience of years; they were young, brash boys, inflated with importance and in thrall to the folly of Laughing Dog. They had no business being in the council, much less seated, as they were, to the left of the King, their skin whitened with stripes of ash, their spears held across their knees as though they awaited a challenge.

"Whistling Thorn is dead," Great Ram said. His voice was thunderous and steady, with no slur of alcohol. Neither did he sway where he stood. In a comforting way, he reminded Cloud of the old King: firm, strong, steady. Perhaps there was hope Ram would yet be a good leader.

"I grieve to hear it," she said. "I'll prepare him for the pyre."

"Two of the sick have died, Elder Cloud," the King said. He had never called her Elder, not even when he was a small boy. The honorific was a remnant of an older time, and his use of it now bore a hint of reprobation. Or mockery, perhaps. "In as many days. This cannot be overlooked."

She spread her hands. "I'm doing all I can for them. This is a sickness I've never seen before. If I were able to try fresh supplies from the forest, perhaps I could find some remedy that could help them, but there is little available."

A murmur went around the circle. She crossed her hands in front of her robe and waited.

Long Neck leaned forward. He looked almost apologetic. "What are the medicines from the forest you are using now?" he asked.

Uneasily, Cloud answered, "I've tried everything I know of. Sweet pear. Acacia sap. Violet root. Oldupai. And willow bark, of course, for the pain."

"You've given these medicines to all your patients?" Okra Bush asked. She was a more recent member of the council, still young by most standards, and still fond of jewelry. The bright hoops in her ears and nose swayed as she spoke.

"No, Okra, not all," Cloud said. "The only medicine I've treated them all with is the willow bark. Their pain can be severe at times, and it's the only thing that eases it."

"And since this illness began," the King said, "you have refused to administer the willow bark to anyone else."

Ah, that was it. Several times, now, the King had requested the medicine for his headaches. King or no, Cloud had not been willing to squander what precious supplies remained to save him the regret of drinking himself into a stupor. It was disappointing that in this troubled time, she was being summoned before the council to answer for that. "No, King Great Ram. I have very little remaining, and what I have must be spared for those in the greatest pain. Can you tell me what this is about?"

Laughing Dog scowled. "What this is about, Cloud, is that you've been willfully sickening and killing our people!"

The blood drained from her face. Words fled her. She gripped her dress so tightly she felt it tear between her fingers.

"Easy, Laughing Dog," Great Ram said. "Let us deal with this."

"How…" she struggled with the words. It was one thing to be berated by grieving parents for her failure, and even to be privately accused by Laughing Dog of sickening her patients, as he had days before. It was another altogether to be dragged in front of the council and accused of murder. "How dare you say such a thing to me?"

Great Ram kept his voice firm and controlled. "Forgive my brother's rash words. He is overwrought due to the illness of his father to-be. He cares very greatly for Mongoose. None of us here think you have been deliberately harming your patients."

"But," Long Neck put in, "no one was sick before they visited you, and you gave them that medicine."

"But it's only willow bark!" she protested. "Healers have used it for generations. You've all had it before, every one of you!"

"It's willow bark from the forest," Laughing Dog said, standing. He strode toward her, across the circle, his thighs shivering under the weight of his bulk. He stopped in front of her, chest and shoulders above her, and crossed his arms over his belly. "Isn't it? Isn't that where you got it?"

She lifted her chin, meeting his gaze squarely. "That *is* where the trees grow."

His cheeks trembled with anger. "So you admit it. You harvested bark from the forest and administered it to your patients, and now they're all dead or dying."

"That's preposterous," she said. "Willow bark never harmed anyone. It eases pain, that's all."

"Did you bless the bark before you took it?" Laughing Dog asked her. She could hear the snare he set on his tongue, but there was no other answer.

"Of course."

"And what did you say?"

"The same prayer as always. I spoke to the spirit of the willow, and asked it permission to take its bark. I asked that it bend its spirit to my purpose, that it dissolve the pain of the suffering, and ease the spirits of the wounded."

The elders around the circle nodded. They all knew the prayers. A variation would be prayed for anything taken from the land. The world was a gift. Without gratitude, it could sour.

"Do us a favor, Cloud," Laughing Dog said, a predatory smile stretching across his face.

"What favor would that be?" she asked. "I've little time for games."

"No game, no game." Laughing Dog held up his hands as if in surrender. "I only wish you to walk into the forest."

She stared at him. "Are you mad?" she asked him in astonishment, and then, an instant later, recalled that indeed he was. "None who go into the forest return alive. You know that."

"Oh, but you'll be all right," he said, and his smile stretched wider as he tightened the snare on his tongue. "You can say a prayer first."

She struggled to keep her expression still and resolute, but there was no standing against that. "We all know the prayers do not save us from entering the forest," she answered reluctantly. "The god Kwaee is angry with us."

"So, you don't trust the prayers to save you from entering the forest, but you trust them fine when feeding the forest to others," he said. He turned his back to her, facing the elders. "I suppose when your own safety isn't at risk, it's not so concerning," he said to them.

"I would never give anyone something that could harm them. The only thing I care about is the safety of my patients!" she cried. Then she saw the Teller, who had remained quiet and stoic through the questioning, turn and gaze at her. *All true. All a lie.*

"Cloud, everyone knows you are a devoted healer," Bad Water said kindly, his missing teeth dampening the words with a lisp. "But you're long used to your ways. Can you see no possibility at all that Kwaee may have turned even the medicine you've harvested against us? All that you've given it to have fallen ill, and those of us who haven't had any are still well. Is it not possible?"

Hibiscus had mentioned the idea before, but she had never really taken it seriously. But why bless the medicine at all, if the blessing could do nothing? If the forest were truly turned against them, could the willow bark be tainted? She looked past Laughing Dog at the eyes of the council, all turned toward her expectantly, some with angry faces, some with apologetic ones. "It…is possible," she admitted. "I don't think it likely, but it's possible."

A movement caught her eye, something strange, a twitch of the braids on the back of Laughing Dog's head, as though something were moving there. She knew her eyesight was poor, but the movement sent prickles down her back nonetheless. She leaned closer, trying to see, but then Laughing Dog turned back to her, his eyes narrowed. "Then the deaths of Red Monk and Whistling Thorn are on your hands," he growled. "If you had listened to me—if you all had—"

"Laughing Dog!" Great Ram's voice boomed above the mutter of the circle. "That's enough. No one here should blame Cloud. Go and sit down."

"But—but you—" he sputtered.

"I said sit down." The King's voice lowered from commanding to angry. "We all know your views."

Laughing Dog scowled in fury, but went back to his place and sat down heavily.

To Cloud, the King said, "It's plain that the willow bark you're administering poses a possible threat to us all."

"But wait," she said, faltering. "It doesn't make sense. Much of what we have now came from the forest. We have food still that came from there. Our tents are built with forest wood and bone, and painted with forest pigments. The animals we eat wander in and out of the forest at ease. Why only the willow bark?"

"We can't know these things," Great Ram said. "Only that this medicine may be a risk. You are hereby forbidden to administer it to any of your patients."

"But the pain!" she protested. "They will suffer!"

"Suffering for a while is better than death," Great Ram said.

"At least let me keep a few on the medicine," she begged him. "Those most recently ill. Then, if the others recover, we'll know for sure, but they don't all have to be in pain."

"No. It's too severe a risk. You are to destroy the willow bark, and any other medicines you have harvested from the forest," he said sternly. He looked around at the council. "And this should be heeded by all of you, the whole village. If we have food or supplies taken from the forest, they must be burned. Anything that might be consumed."

A murmur, louder than the others, went around the circle. "We have little enough food as it is, King Great Ram," Long Neck said. "Meat we have, thanks to our fire hunters, but the people cannot survive on meat alone."

"Would you risk sickening yourselves or your children?" Great Ram asked.

"King Great Ram," Okra Bush said, dipping her head low. "Such a risk has not been proven. None of us have been sickened from eating the food that remains, nor burning incense, nor hunting with spears nor oils taken from the forest. Let us not overcorrect. I suggest that you ban only the use of the medicines for now. If others fall ill, then perhaps we can look to other causes."

"Very well then," King Great Ram said, "though I fear we invite more trouble on our heads. Cloud will destroy her medicines. But all of you keep watchful eyes. If her willow bark is tainted, then anything that came from the forest could be, even the knots in our rope or the wood in our earrings. We must all take caution. Do you agree to this order, Cloud?"

She dipped her head. "Yes," she said, and thought of the cries of pain that would soon come from her sick tent. She would be even more helpless to ease their suffering and cure them than before.

"Then council is ended," the King said.

She lifted her head. As she turned to go, she saw Laughing Dog staring right at her, his fleshy face creased in a satisfied smirk.

⁀⁀⁀

The thin hide walls of her tent did little to muffle the groans of pain next door. She had not yet visited her patients since returning from the council. She didn't know how to tell them that there would be no more relief from the pain, that the death that they all knew was coming would not be all they would have to bear. She hoped the council was right, that the willow bark was the source of the illness, even though that would mean that she herself had been poisoning them. It would mean that she had killed Red Moth and Whistling Thorn. She could live with that, if it meant that

Mongoose, Twig, Dancing Spider, and Fiveroot would recover. It wasn't likely.

From her supplies she took the little basket of willow bark. Of the amount she'd gathered before the forest turned on them, added to what she'd scavenged from savanna trees, a little more than half was left. It would all have to be burned; there was no way to tell forest bark from savanna. She surveyed her medicines, which hung from the tent ceiling in baskets or in bundles tied to drying cords, or had been stacked carefully in calabashes, or tied up in little pouches made of leather. Oldupai—that was gathered on the trip south, and would be safe. But the violet root was from the forest floor and would have go too, as would all the mushrooms. She sorted through the various leaves and roots, oils and powders, separating out all those that could have been tainted by the forest and stripping them from their cords, or pulling down their baskets and piling them up near the cooking fire. Soon she had a reasonably large stack of medicines.

She surveyed the assortment with dismay. Even if the forest were to calm itself tomorrow, the moon would wax and wane many times before she would be able to gather a suitable store again. She opened the flap at the top of the tent. Some medicines could kill if over-ingested, and some turned poisonous when burned. She might consider it a fitting end to die here in her tent from inhaling the smoke of her own medicines. With a last, unhappy look at the medicines, she wondered what would happen when they were needed. For a moment, she considered digging a hole someplace and burying them, perhaps a little ways outside the wall or even here in her tent. But to do so would be to go against the order of the King, and she was not willing to do that.

Reluctantly, she dropped a piece of oldupai on the fire. It was dry, no longer fresh, and the flames caught it quickly, sending clouds of black smoke billowing up to the open ceiling of the tent. She edged away so as not to breathe in any of the smoke, stacking each of the spined, fleshy leaves onto the flames. She burned everything, one ingredient after another: the oils sizzled and burned low and blue; the powders went up in a *whump* and a flash, or coated the kindling and turned black and wet, boiling at the bottom of the fire. Waxy blue honeycomb—that would be hard to replace—crackled and melted over the fire, boiling and spattering in the pit. The mushrooms shriveled up and blackened in the heat; long kalo reeds cracked open, their stored milk seeping from the fissures and hissing as it dripped into the embers. It all went, bit by bit, into the fire and then up through top of her tent. She wondered what would happen if she inhaled that smoke; maybe death, maybe a miracle cure to all injuries. Maybe just a coughing fit. Probably that.

Then, at last, there was only her little basket of willow bark. She grimaced at it; if it had not existed, maybe she would not have been required to burn all of her medicines. Or if she'd only refrained from giving it to one patient. If only she'd considered herself the possibility that the willow bark could be dangerous, or at least not helping. But it was too late. She took a strip of it and held it out to drop it in the fire, but then paused, frowning.

There was something on the bark. She peered closely at it, turning it over and over in the daylight shining in from the opening above. There were little black marks on the willow bark: shiny and liquid-looking, as though something had been dripped onto it. She scratched at it with a fingernail, and it flaked and broke away into her palm. She set the strip of bark aside and took another from the basket. This one too had a spatter of black stuff across it. The marks were tiny and not easily noticed, only a few droplets dotting each piece of bark. Had her tent been closed up and darkened as usual, she would never have noticed, but surely she would have noticed the marks when harvesting the bark from willow trees. Any medicine needed to be inspected when collected; a few insect eggs could pollute an entire batch. She took out piece after piece; each had a few black marks on its surface.

She frowned, pondering. It was impossible that the stuff could have come from something in the forest; it was on every piece of the willow strips, from savanna and forest alike. So whatever it was, it had contaminated the bark after she had gathered it. A type of fungus or mold, maybe? No, she decided. It was solid and dry, and besides, it looked as if it had been dripped or sprayed onto the bark. Even the edges of the basket were speckled with the stuff. Could she have spilled something on it without noticing? She thought not. The basket had been strung high to keep it away from the damp. Which meant that someone else had added it. She sniffed at the black spots and noted a strange scent, like bad eggs and burnt spice.

On a hunch, she checked the ground below the place the basket had hung. She searched the earth there, bit by bit. But if any of the black stuff had spilled there, it had either been turned over in the dust or her eyes were too weak to find it. There was nothing. She got up from her hands and knees, and as she did, she saw on the wall of the tent, higher than her shoulder, a long streak of something pale smudged on the hide: white ash. A fire hunter had been there; she was certain of it. It could have been for any reason, even to steal a bit of the bark for one of their own. But it could have been to poison the bark. Why anyone would wish to do such a thing, she could not imagine, but she remembered Laughing Dog's words to her from days ago. *Things are going to go bad for you. Very bad.* Would he poison injured people just to harm her? Only a madman would do such a thing.

She went back to the fire and dropped in a strip of willow bark, making sure to stay back from the smoke. The flames flared yellow and curled the bark, creeping down it as they changed it to smoke and ash. When the flames reached the black spots on the bark, they turned blue and yellow, hissing and spitting violently.

Cloud fed the remaining strips of bark to the flames one by one as she tried to accept what she now suspected had happened: as the council had suggested, she had been poisoning her own patients, one by one. First Red Moth, given willow bark tea to help her manage the pain of having her broken arms set and splinted, and then Whistling Thorn, covered with welts from dozens of wasps. Then Mongoose, who had come to her with nothing more severe with joint pain, and Dancing Spider, who had struck his head on a tree branch during a hunt. And finally Twig and Fiveroot, both injured in the monster attack.

Two villagers had refused her treatment. One, Hibiscus, had said she was using dangerous forest sources for her medicines. But Hibiscus had complained up until recently that Cloud hadn't been visiting her enough in her pregnancy; her objection to Cloud's visit was a recent thing. Not so recent was Scorpion, who had also been injured on the night of the attack. Why had he not come to her? Laughing Dog had ordered him not to. You're making people sick, he'd said to her. But he'd seemed angry about it, she recalled. And he had led the council in trying to stop her from using it. It was all too confusing. There was no reasoning behind it.

The weariness settled into her again. She tossed the last of the willow bark onto the fire, and the basket on top of it. If someone had been deliberately trying to poison her patients, the poison was gone now.

At least, she thought, the willow bark was gone. She belatedly wished she had saved a piece of the bark. Wherever the poison had come from, there would be more. And whoever had poisoned the bark would still have it. There was no getting around it. She would have to tell the king.

~~~

"You can't go in," Broken Stump said, barring the way with his spear.

Cloud drew herself up as tall as she could. "I am an elder on the council. I have a right to see the King."

The man set his narrow jaw. "He's not seeing anyone. Strict orders."

"That may be, Broken Stump," she said, speaking his name with the same tone she'd used when he was a boy, "but this is an emergency. Great

Ram will understand." And with that, she ducked under his spear and pushed into the tent before he could stop her.

"Ram," she began, but then faltered.

The young man lay sprawled half across his pelts, half in the packed earth of his tent floor, leaning up on one elbow. He wore none of his regal finery at the moment; only the hide around his middle. His eyes were lidded and heavy. He held a calabash gourd in one hand, and there were two empty beside him. The sun flap was closed, and he squinted in the bright daylight streaming in behind Cloud.

"Cloud? What are you—? The guard had instructions."

Broken Stump's rock-strong fingers gripped Cloud's shoulder. "Apologies, King Great Ram. I tried to stop her."

The King tried to push himself upright, and the heel of his hand skidded along the ground. The gourd he was holding sloshed, spilling its contents to the earthen floor, which drank it up thirstily. The air carried the faint sting of urine. Great Ram frowned. "You made me spill my…my… What're you doing here, Cloud?"

She twisted her shoulder free of Stump's grip and sidestepped farther inside. Dismay filled her: the King was so drunk he could barely sit upright, much less understand the gravity of what she was about to tell him. The only thing that would have made things worse was if Laughing Dog were there. But she had already come this far. "I have grave news for you, Great Ram," she said.

"*King* Great Ram," Broken Stump said behind her. "Remember who you're talking to, Cloud."

She glared at him. "And it's news that is best delivered in private, King Great Ram. I would have waited, but it's very urgent."

Great Ram blinked at her. "All right," he said. "Go on, Broken Stump. It's only Cloud. I'll be fine."

The wiry man frowned. "But Laughing Dog said—"

"Laughing Dog isn't the King, is he?" Great Ram snapped peevishly. "Do as you're told."

Broken Stump's expression darkened. "Yes, King Great Ram," he muttered. Scowling, he withdrew from the tent, but Cloud could hear that he didn't go very far.

Cloud looked over the strewn, empty gourds, and back to Great Ram's face. "Ram," she said softly, reaching out to him with one hand.

He pulled back from her touch. "It's not…it's not so much. They weren't all full."

"You can hardly sit up, boy."

Stiffening, he said, "So what if I drink? I'm the King now. Kings can do as they like."

"That's not what King means, and you know it," she told him.

A boyish petulance crossed his face. "What's this big secret you had to tell me, anyway?"

She crouched and stepped closer to him. The sting of wine on his breath made her eyes water. "It's the willow bark," she said in hushed tones. "I think it was poisoned."

He stared at her with a puzzled expression. "That's what we told you. That Kwaee or the forest spirits must have tainted it. That's why we told you to destroy it."

"No. Not by the forest. All of it was poisoned—the bark I took from the savanna as well. There were dark marks on all of it. Ram, I think someone here poisoned it. Someone among our people."

"That's ridiculous," he said, his tongue stumbling over the word. "You saw dark marks on your bark and now you want to blame someone for it." His watery eyes narrowed. "You don't want responsibility for what you did, for…for killing that child. You want to blame someone. All right, Cloud, I bet you have a suspect, don't you? It's…it's my brother, innit?"

She struggled to keep her composure. "Ram, I'm only telling you what I saw. If there's someone in the village poisoning people, the King needs to know of it. And yes, I found a streak of ash along the tent wall, but—"

He sat all the way up, poking a finger under her nose. "He told me you had it in for him," he blurted angrily. "He told me how jealous you are!"

"Jealous? Of what?"

"Of how he's close to the throne and you're not. You've always had it in for him. Whispering in my father's ear every time he got in trouble, getting him punished, getting him banished. You hated him and we all knew it."

"I loved him," she said, so soft she doubted he heard it.

"Well now he's the one with the King's ear. Not you. And you can't stand it. He told me you'd come after him, try to poison me against you. Not Cloud, I said. She's so wise. But then you come to me and try to tell me he's mad, and now here you are, talking about poison, accusing him of—of *murdering children!*" He spat the last words in drunken disgust.

She gripped her fingers tightly in alarm. "Listen to me, I'm not accusing anyone of anything, I just—"

He wasn't listening. "How could you, Cloud? How could you do it to me, after I lost Clay, and then my father died? He's the only family I have left! Why do you think I…I…?" He looked down at his calabash and then took a deep, furious draught from it, yellow runnels of palm wine running down into his beard and dripping onto his chest. When he lowered the gourd, his eyes were squinted in suspicion.

"I can't trust you anymore," he said.

Fear surged in her. "Great Ram, please, listen to me."

"No." He spoke the words as though realizing them. "You have your own agenda here. You always have. Talking against my brother, talking against me. You're supposed to support your King."

"I'm supposed to advise you."

"How can you when you don't even like me? When you don't even—" He lurched to one side, barely catching himself on the palm of his hand. "—don't even think I should be King in the first place?"

"Ram, that isn't true." But it was true, and she knew he saw the lie on her face.

The wine pulsed red in his cheeks. "You think you're so clever. You pretend to be on everyone's side. But I see the way you look at me. You never looked at me like I was a King."

You never acted like a King, she started to say, but before she could, he spit her unspoken words back at her. "I never acted like a King, right?"

She kept her face as neutral as possible.

"That's what you were going to say, isn't it? See, I know you, Cloud. Better than you think I do."

She wondered now if she hadn't made a terrible mistake. She'd fought Ram, been harsh with him from the very beginning. She hadn't treated him like a King; she'd treated him like a spoiled boy who needed a mother to be firm with him. "I could have done things better," she admitted.

He spat a broken laugh at her. "You could have done everything better. You decided before my Father even died that I would make a bad King. Even when his body was turning to ash on the pyre you were cruel to me."

"You needed counsel."

"I needed a friend! Wem's eye, Cloud, I'd lost a father and you decided to be firm with me then, with his smoke stinging my nose? I begged you for comfort and you gave me nothing. Where was I to turn, Cloud? Where?"

She had no answer for him. It had all seemed plain at the time. He had asked her to lie to him, to tell him that the troubles would end, that his brother would return, that the gods would forgive them for unknown sins. And she had denied it to him. She had been willing to let him hate her for denying it. Being truthful is kinder than being gentle, her mother had always told her. The bone hurts when it's set. The flesh screams when the infection is cut out of it. But without those cruelties, there would be no healing, no recovery. She had always lived by that, had always allowed honesty to blunt her words to others. But after someone had been injured, was that the time to demand that they be strong? The wounded needed rest to recover—a person with a twisted ankle did not go out and run on it the next day to help it recover. Only time and care could do that.

Now she saw Great Ram's loss of his father as a deep and terrible wound to his spirit. He did not need an infection cut out, nor his bones set. He had needed time and care, and she had not granted it. She had forced him to confront the loss of Clay, his responsibilities to his people, the madness of Laughing Dog. He had run on that twisted ankle every day, born down by the blows of the monster attacks and the plague and the hunger of his people. He had been trying for so long, and now…now she feared he had broken.

His eyes were wide and wet. "Well?" he demanded.

"Oh, Ram," she said. "You're right. I should have been a better friend."

He squinted at her as though suspecting a trick. "So you were wrong."

It was a test, she knew. She was the elder, he the boy, and that had always been their relationship. She had just never accepted that it was time to let go of it. The words cost her no pride; she wondered whether she truly had any left. "I was wrong."

"And you think I can be a good King."

She didn't dare let herself hesitate. "I think you can be a good King," she answered carefully. It was almost a lie, difficult to find the truth of it when he was lying on the floor smelling of wine and piss, his skin wet with it. But there was still hope for him. There had to be.

"And Laughing Dog. You will give up this vendetta against him."

"I—" The words clung to her tongue. Kindness was one thing, but Laughing Dog was mad. If he had truly poisoned the village, he was a danger she did not dare dismiss. "King Great Ram, I fear for him." *I'm afraid of him,* she thought, but did not say. "His father's death hit him hard."

He drew in a deep breath, and she knew it had been the wrong thing to say. For one, it was a falsehood: the seeds of Laughing Dog's blasphemies had fallen long before First Claw's death.

"As it hit *me* hard?" Great Ram asked in a dangerous tone.

She shook her head emphatically. "Different. You grieve as any son might. Laughing Dog has something else inside him. I fear he is dangerous."

"So. You would have me cut him from my side, is that it?"

She was losing him, and she knew it. She dropped to her knees, holding out her arms to him. "Please consider, King Great Ram. Even your father was concerned about his beliefs."

He drew himself up, unsteady, but sitting straight as a fencepost, staring down at her, his eyes bloodshot. "And then you would be my closest adviser, would you not?"

"That isn't why I'm bringing this to you."

"No? So if I offer to oust Laughing Dog from the council and put you at my right hand, you'll say no?"

The question was a trap. To refuse him would be an obvious lie, one that would fool neither of them. And to accept would make her look covetous, grasping of power. She rested her hands in her lap and was silent.

He persisted. "One step away from rule, isn't it? Almost as good as being King yourself?"

"I don't want to be King!" she would have laughed at the suggestion were she not so frightened. "I just want—I'm only trying to help you. To help everyone."

He grimaced. "Because you don't trust me to make the right decisions on my own. Of course you don't. How can you? I'm just a stupid boy to you."

"You *are* a boy. You're standing up in front of those who have seen more rains than you and your brothers put together and telling them what to do. As is your right," she added hastily, seeing his face redden. "But consider the wealth of knowledge and experience they bring to you. Consider all that they have seen and learned. Would you ignore that?"

His eyebrows knitted. "Of course not. You cannot claim that I have ignored the council's advice in any matter. Cloud, you know that despite everything, I still hold you in the highest regard. Do you think I'm not listening to you?" He swayed, and the anger seemed to drain out of him a little. "I wish things could return to the way they were. It's not like we were ever great friends, but you…shouting at us for fighting too roughly or for joking around while the Teller told his stories, it was…comfortable." His gaze strayed beyond the walls of his tent. "Everything was better then."

Her instincts told her to remain still and quiet, but they had never been reliable when it came to others, so she fought their admonitions and reached down to fold the young King in an embrace, resting her arms around his shoulders and pulling him to her breast. He drew back as if frightened, and then relaxed, resting his forehead against her breasts. Then he wept, his wide shoulders shaking with deep, silent sobs. They came out of him like secrets long held, poured into the shelter of her arms where no one would find them.

For a time he was still, and then he leaned up, his eyes puffy, and reached for his calabash of palm wine. "Ram," she cautioned him.

He wiped his eyes with his fingers, his nose on the back of his arm. "Don't tell me not to drink. If I have to do all this, if I have to be King, then this is one privilege I get."

"As a healer," Cloud began, and then stopped herself. "As a friend, I would warn you that too much wine can trouble the spirit even more. You remember your uncle Six and how often it seemed that the wine was all he cared for."

"Cloud," he said, looking up at her, the calabash gripped in one hand as though it held a last gulp of water. "Please."

She nodded. "All right." It was tempting to leave it at that. She could make certain he was all right and then leave him with fond feelings of her and nothing else. She yearned to give him one final embrace and walk away, leaving him with kind feelings toward her. But there had been little black marks all over her medicine. If she said nothing else, someone else might die. "But Ram, please. Listen to me about your brother. He's not well. And this poison, I've never seen it before, but it—"

"My brother." Great Ram's hands shook as he gazed down into the yellow wine. "You just can't keep silent about it, can you?"

She faltered, standing and stepping back a pace. "Ram, please."

"All this, all your kind words, pretending you cared about me, just you hate him so much. Just because he dares to talk about the gods in ways that you don't like. It's always going to come back to that, isn't it? Just like he said, you won't be happy until he's banished. Or dead!"

"Ram—"

"Great Ram. *King* Great Ram. It's always going to be like this, isn't it? You'll always be needling at me, trying to get me to hurt my own brother, urging me to bare my soul just so you can strike at it unguarded."

"Please listen," she begged him. "Please just calm down. I only want the best for you, for the people. You have to trust me."

"Trust you?" He spat. "I can't trust you. I haven't been able for a long time!" He threw the gourd aside; it struck the wall of the tent, its contents splashing into the dust. "I'm done listening to you, Cloud," he shouted. "The village is done listening to you. No one should have to. You—you're not welcome on the council anymore."

The situation was careening out of control. "Ram," she said, trying to temper her alarm with careful words, "you're very drunk right now. I know you're angry, but you're drunk. People will hear what you're saying."

He lunged forward at her like an angry cat. She fell backward, but he was in her face, his wine-soaked breath damp on her cheeks. "You think I'm afraid they'll hear?" he rasped at her. "You think this is just because I'm

drunk? I think I've been wanting to do this for moons." He scrambled uneasily to his feet and lurched out of the tent.

Shaken, she pushed herself upright and followed after him. He stood,
swaying and squinting in the bright daylight. Broken Stump stood to one
side, his spear at the ready, expression uncertain. Down the hill, she could
see Laughing Dog approaching, his great body striped with ash from a recent hunt.

"People of the Savanna," shouted Great Ram, his voice booming over
the village. "The healer Cloud is no longer to be known as Elder. Her words
are not to be trusted. She is no longer a member of this council. So says your
King, Great Ram, son of First Claw, son of Eleven Shadows."

He turned to her, petulant satisfaction scrawled across his face. "Do
you think they heard that, Cloud?"

She gazed back at him, trying to keep her pity and dismay from welling in her eyes. "Oh, King Great Ram. You wound us both."

His satisfaction melted from his face. "Get out of here," he slurred at
her. "And don't come to my tent again!"

She watched his face, waiting for the fit to pass, for his drunkenness
to somehow evaporate on the hot afternoon breeze.

"Well?" he demanded. "What are you waiting for? Go!"

Broken Stump lifted his spear a little. She went.

On the way down the hill, she passed by Laughing Dog. She looked
away, but when she was near, he spoke to her anyway. "That's why I posted
guards. You should have trusted me, Cloud. I tried to stop you. I tried to
stop this from happening."

Her despair might have twisted her perceptions, but it seemed to
Cloud that even Laughing Dog sounded worried and tense, as though he
had pushed a boulder that would not stop rolling, or started a camp fire that
was spreading toward his own tent.

⁓

Mongoose clutched at his shrunken belly with withered fingers, con-
torting on his bed of hides. The other patients—Twig, Dancing Spider,
and Fiveroot—were moaning too, but either they bore it far better, or their
discomfort was mild by comparison. Cloud took Mongoose's hand in hers
and squeezed it.

"Please," he begged her. "Please."

She didn't ask what he wanted; she feared the answer.

The flap opened and Ant With a Leaf came in, stooping under the low
ceiling. "Father?" When she saw Cloud sitting with Mongoose, she hurried
over, dropping to a crouch next to them. "I'm here, Father." She let her

fingers rest atop the grey curls on his head, plucking at them. "It's very bad, isn't it?" she asked in a low voice.

"Hard to say," Cloud answered. "Pain is never good, but in this case, it may be better than no pain. Those who died lost their pain soon before they went still."

Mongoose reached up as though to brush his fingers against Ant's arm and then contorted, knotting them into his belly. "Please, please!" he cried again.

"You have to do something for him." Ant did not look away from her father as she spoke. Her face was stern. She had always been so. Even as a girl, Cloud had never seen her cry. "You must give him something for the pain."

"I wish I could," Cloud said, shaking her head. "But I have had to destroy most of my medicines."

"Destroy them?" Ant repeated sharply, staring at her. "Why?"

"You didn't hear? The council raised fears that my medicines were tainted by the forest spirits."

"You mean Laughing Dog did," Ant muttered.

Cloud blinked at her in surprise. It was not so long ago Ant had re-proached her for criticizing Laughing Dog. "Yes, he was among those who raised the question. But not the only one. At the council's urging, the King commanded me to burn my supplies."

Ant With a Leaf gave her a disbelieving look, then shook her head. "Foolishness," she said. "That has been the real affliction of late. Foolishness."

Cloud said nothing.

"So you have nothing left that can help him?"

She shook her head.

Ant stood up. "Then tell me what you need. I will go and find it and bring it back here."

"There isn't much," Cloud said. "I have found no willows in the sa-vanna nearby. Nor milkthorn. Lion's tail. That would help him to forget the pain and perhaps find some sleep. Do you know it?"

"I think so. A long, green stalk with thin orange flowers in a bunch."

"Yes. Bring me the leaves and the flowers. I'll sit with him until you return."

Ant nodded stiffly, thanked Cloud, and left.

While Cloud waited for her return, she sat by Mongoose's side and let him clutch at her hand. His fingers squeezed at hers so tightly that her knuckles ground together. Eventually his cries faded into low groans. He began to breathe more steadily as he retreated inside himself to deal with the pain. Cloud wished she could know whether his suffering was a good sign or a bad one. There was no way to know if his pain had increased solely because he no longer had the willow bark tea to mute it, or whether the sickness was being purged from his body. She prayed to Fam it was the latter.

From time to time she returned the squeezes to her fingers. She and Mongoose had not been children together—not quite. Twelve rains had separated them. But she remembered his birth, and the way he had always been a little apart from the other boys: quieter, more reserved and thoughtful. He had grown a juvenile sense of mischief by the time she reached womanhood, and whenever her mother wasn't around, he would tease her about her breasts, or steal off with her preparations when she was in the middle of her healing studies. She had scolded him, had threatened him that someday he would need healing and she wouldn't help. Today her threat had come true.

It took Ant less time than Cloud had expected to come back with an armful of lion's tail stalks. "These are what you wanted?" she asked, looking hopeful, but her face fell when she saw her father curled on his side, not moving. "Is he—?"

"He's still awake. Put a pot on the fire and boil the leaves and flowers."

Cloud talked Ant through the preparation of the tea. Giving Ant a task seemed to calm her. When the tea was finished, they both helped Mongoose and the others drink of it from a gourd shell. The outside sky was dark by the time the patients fell asleep. Even unconscious, Mongoose made faint groans.

Ant stroked at his cheek with the backs of her fingers. "They should have known better than to make you destroy your medicines," she said grimly. "Laughing Dog is going to feel very sorry about it after I catch him."

"You shouldn't speak that way about a prince," Cloud cautioned her. "And especially not your promised."

"Promised?" Ant With a Leaf gave a bitter laugh. "That is a debt I can forgive, I think."

Cloud looked at her curiously. "You no longer intend to marry Laughing Dog?"

Ant leaned down to verify her father was sleeping, then said, "Everyone will think I am stupid, yes? He's a prince. He leads the fire hunters. And he is fat and strong like the richest and most powerful of kings."

Cloud remembered Ant's previous reaction to her warnings of Laughing Dog's instability. It would be unwise to lead this conversation, she decided. "All those things are true."

"You said before that you feared he was mad," Ant said. "And I do not think he is. But there is something wrong with him all the same. He speaks to himself sometimes, in the middle of a conversation. He thinks people work against him, and is always planning things. He talks about it like he forgets I am there sometimes. All those fire hunters he has. What is this special hunting method he uses with them, and why will he not let me come? I am a good hunter. He insults his promised by not bringing me along. He will not even let me come into his tent, not that I would wish to, lately. It reeks like a dying animal. He leaves his kills in there too long, I think."

"He casts a strange shadow," Cloud agreed. "But you don't think he's mad?"

"No. He is too sure of himself. Too careful. I don't know what possesses him. But all those things I said, those are not the worst." She sighed and sidled closer to Cloud, continuing in a lowered voice. "Worst is the way he looks at me now. Once he was all charm and smiles. He wooed me properly, the way a sweet, strong hunter should. Now when he looks at me…" She spoke with a tight jaw. "When he looks at me, all I see is hunger. Like I am an eland he hunts and wishes to devour. He bares his teeth like a jackal. The other night, he came to my tent. He pressed himself upon me."

"Ant!" Cloud was shocked. Such behavior could earn the severest of punishments. Birthright would not protect anyone from that.

"He did not succeed," Ant said scornfully. "I hit him in his stupid nose. You would have thought it was broken from the way he wailed and bled. But the next morning, it was fine. He made that smile I do not like and told me he forgave me. Then I wanted to hit him again, and break his nose for sure."

"It's better to be cautious. He has his brother's ear. The King will brook no criticism of Laughing Dog, it seems."

Ant's eyes flashed with anger. "So we are to take whatever he does and not answer back? There is no justice in that."

Cloud shrugged. "It's surprising how often justice and wisdom part ways."

"If Laughing Dog isn't to be trusted, you should tell the council. They respect you. You can make them listen."

So. Not everyone in the village had heard yet. She took a deep breath. "Ant With a Leaf, I am no longer on the council."

The young woman sat straight up in surprise. "What? Who says you are not?"

"The King. Yesterday. I thought you would know. He proclaimed me no longer an elder and ejected me from the council. I am only healer now."

"But how could he do this? And why? What would make him so foolish? You were his father's most trusted adviser!"

"He was angry. He thought I was accusing Laughing Dog of…a transgression. He took it personally." She considered telling Ant With a Leaf about the dark spots on the willow bark, and her suspicions, but if she had hit the prince in the face for pressing himself on her, what would she do if she thought he had poisoned her father? No, for Ant's own protection, it was better that she not know. "I don't think he'll take it back. For better or worse, my time on the council is over."

"If he would do this," Ant said through set teeth, "then he is not a good king."

Cloud looked over her shoulder. "You should keep such thoughts quiet. Someone may hear you, and good or no, he's the only King we have."

"For now." Ant had a dangerous glint in her eye.

Cloud thought she wouldn't consider actually harming the King, but it was not unthinkable she might pray divine malice down upon him. Once, no one would have imagined such a thing. But times were darker. "Let us pray the gods keep him safe," she said. "If he falls to illness or injury, then Laughing Dog becomes King. And besides, learning to be a good King takes time. You think First Claw ruled wisely when he first took the stool?"

The young woman's expression softened, and a smile came to her lips. "I thought he was always old and serious."

Cloud smiled back. "He was a damned fool is what he was, back then. Always trying to make new rules, bossing people about while hovering over them like a goat in a tree. People would just laugh at him and ignore him at first. It made him so angry. But after a time, he learned and became a great King." She put her hand on Ant's arm. "We must give Great Ram that time, if we hope for him to be a good King."

"That is time we do not have," Ant pointed out. "Things are bad."

"Things have been worse. At least now we have food and water."

Ant threw up her hands. "Why should the King be a son of a King? There are many here with the wisdom and influence to lead the people. Why not you?"

Her? The idea was beyond laughable. It was insolent. "It's not my place. I'm no leader. I'm not even on the council anymore."

"Because some foolish boy-King said you were not. What does he know?"

Cloud cast an anxious glance toward the tent opening. Evening was not the time for a private conversation. People would be venturing out of the shade, no longer sheltering from the heat of the day, and anyone might pass by. "Ant, this is the sort of thing it's better not to discuss."

"Well, why not? People are happy for the meat the fire hunters bring, but everyone knows that Great Ram was not ready. He's a drunk, you know." Ant watched her expression to see if this bit of information was a surprise.

"He's taken his father's death very hard," Cloud said. "And the disappearance of his brother. Leave it alone, Ant."

"Why?" Ant frowned, seeming not to notice the warning in Cloud's voice, or else choosing to ignore it. "If we have a bad leader, then we should replace him with a good one, for the sake of the village."

Cloud clenched her fingers in her lap, tugging at her dress so hard that she heard it begin to rip. In dismay, she forced herself to relax. "You speak of betrayal," she cautioned.

"It's not betrayal," Ant said. "Not if it's for the good of the people." She paused, taking a deep breath. "The Teller says that there were not always Kings and princes. He says the people used to lead themselves. The elders decided for the people."

Cloud hadn't realized that the Teller was so openly spreading dissonance. He had his reservations about their leadership, or so she'd suspected, but to have the keeper of stories openly spreading word of a tradition that did not include royalty could be a dangerous game. First Claw would not have minded, she thought. But if Great Ram felt so insecure in his leadership that he would remove her from the council, what would he do to someone spreading dreams of a world without Kings? "It's true that things were that way once," Cloud said. "But they are not now."

"But they could be."

"And how is that?" Cloud asked, lowering her voice despite the rising frustration she felt. "What do you believe, that I could call the elders to me, tell them we should take over, and the King would be no more?"

"People would follow you," Ant With a Leaf declared. "I know this without question."

"Some might. Some. But would they still follow me," Cloud pressed, "when Laughing Dog's fire hunters no longer brought them meat and their stomachs grew empty? And who would serve as healer then? Who would even follow a healer whose patients may have died from the medicines she gave them? Few here still carry respect for me, Ant. You may not see it, but I surely do. All I am is a loony old healer."

She had hoped this speech would dissuade the young woman, but Ant looked only more resolute, certainty rekindled in her eyes. "You would be an excellent leader. You are wise. You know the people, you know the ways, you know the gods. Who here doesn't owe a life or more to you? And you are strong. I will remind everyone how you stood before the monsters to save the sick. They will remember and respect you."

Cloud wound up her fingers in her robe again. "No, Ant. I am a healer. And that is all. I will not hear any more of this."

"But you could be more!" Ant With a Leaf urged. "We *need* you to be more!"

Cloud looked down. Her fingers had gone white at the knuckles from clenching at her robe. She could see the rip in it, a narrow gap, the little green threads torn. They would never be repaired. She relaxed her hands again and stroked at the material. It tore so easily now, like caterpillar silk. The regular rains here near the forest kept the fabric clean, the color brighter than in the dust of the savanna, but they also revealed how the years had faded the fabric. Where once it had been bright and green as young grass, now it was almost wicker-white in places, as though the sun had wilted it dry. In the places where she had always folded the robe to keep it from falling about her shoulders and hips, it was tearing. Holes pitted it, especially in the shoulders and elbows, and great rents rose behind her heels where she had trodden on it over and over. Her brown, callus-whitened knees jutted through large gaps at the front, and it had gone yellow from sweat around her neck, breasts, and thighs.

"You sound like him." The smell of him returned to Cloud, cool and fresh, not sharp and musky like that of the hunters. He had smelled of wet grass and ground nuts and spice.

"Who?" Ant asked.

Cloud sighed. "I was a young woman, still learning how much lion's tail to give a patient without putting a madness in him. People thought me very beautiful then, or so they told me. I must have been, from the way the men watched me. But early on, my mother promised me to a man. Wind, his name was. He was kind enough, but distracted—full of ideas about how all the places in the world connected. All rivers, he used to say, must find the great water. He would draw pictures of the stars in the sand, and then draw them again and again, and speak of how they moved. It was fascinating to him."

"And you loved him," Ant said, nodding.

"No." Cloud smiled. "I didn't love him at all. He was terribly boring, Ant. You cannot even imagine how boring he was. Do you know what he wanted to do with all his stars and rivers and drawings? He wanted to trade. He would sit with me as I worked and prattle on endlessly about the deals that he could make by traveling from place to place, from the northwest kingdoms to the cow people, from the cow people to Bogana by the great water. He would talk about how all value was not in a thing, but in where that thing was, and because he understood that, one day he would have great wealth, as much as the greatest of Kings. And it would all be mine, he said. I cared nothing for his dreams of wealth or the gifts he promised, but he held my hand so sweetly and smiled at me so adoringly that I could not say no to him. And besides, I had decided that once we married, he would be off on his long journeys for so many days that I would not have to be bored by a lot of chatter about commodities and routes and seasons.

"And so we married. I didn't know then that he would be so devoted to me. I didn't know he would love me so much, and how cruel and empty it would make me feel not to love him back. The more he held me and stroked my skin, the more he cooed to me of my beauty and sweetness, the more I hated him and wished only that he would go away so that I could be alone with my work. I treated him kindly, as a wife should, but I wanted him gone.

"The night before he went on his journey, he held me in his arms so tightly. He wept like a boy while telling me over and over again how long he would be gone and how much he would miss me. What could I do? I lied to him. I told him I would miss him too. And then he left, early in the morning. A day passed, and then a moon, and then three moons, and I found to my surprise that I did miss him. I slept alone in my tent. People treated me with pity at first, but I was not very friendly, and they avoided me. I became lonely."

She closed her eyes, letting the memories return, recalling the tale to herself as much as to Ant With a Leaf. "A full rain came and passed, and still Wind didn't return. I would lie awake and wonder where he was. Was he in the big clay and stone cities of the northwestern kingdoms, sipping honey and milk, surrounded by finery and richness? Had he made his way to the great water, to look out across the belly of Mpo and taste her bounty? Did he even live? Perhaps I was a widow. Perhaps he had been set upon by bandits or lions, or met the fury of Mpo's storms. Perhaps, I thought, I had no husband.

"Another rain passed, and then I began to forget about him, a little. I learned how to bandage cuts and scrapes, how to use poultices to make them heal faster. I learned how to calm fever and set broken bones. I found medicines that could take the fire out of wasp stings. I learned how to draw the poison out of a snakebite and soothe the swelling from scorpions. I brewed teas for calm and for focus, and bit by bit let time take Wind away from me.

"But not all in the village forgot me. There was one young man who started coming to see me. He was no hunter, not a runner. Slight, quiet, but very shrewd. He didn't say much at first, but would linger and watch me work. At first I worried about his intentions, but his eyes were always on my hands and face, and I was glad for company. I began to make him tea when he came to visit, and in turn, he would tell me stories and ask me questions—at first, only about my work. But then he asked about my husband, my childhood. He asked about my mother and father, my grandmother from Bogana, and my Aunt Reeno, who died when I was young. The harder and more uncomfortable my memories, the more questions he asked. He seemed so interested in me, more than Wind ever had. Wind cared about my beauty, my kindness. My new visitor cared about my life, about the things that were important to me. He wanted to know the parts of me that were not always pleasing. Soon I began to look forward to his visits.

"I told you how First Claw was back then. Still young, still learning. Bothering everyone like a biting fly. Many worried that he would not have the leadership and skills to care for the people. And my visitor began to talk of that, speaking of a time when there were no Kings. He said we needed the wise to lead us, not the appointed. He said we needed people who were clever and capable. People like us, he said. I laughed and called him foolish, but he kept insisting." Cloud looked over at Ant. "Wind had called me his queen, but this boy thought I could be one. And he came by day after day and spoke of how we would change the village, make it better, help everyone. It was fanciful nonsense, but I fell in love with him then."

Ant put her hand on Cloud's shoulder. "You should not feel shame for that. Passion makes us strong. And besides, your husband was gone. You had no idea if he was even alive anymore."

"I knew," Cloud said. Admitting it hurt, but she recognized the truth as she said it. "I thought he might be dead, but in my heart I knew he was not. I knew I was betraying him."

"You laid with this man?" Ant asked, her eyebrows lifting. "*You*, Cloud?"

Cloud laughed a little at that. "You think I was born aching and grouchy?"

"No, not that. Just…cautious. You are a cautious woman."

"I am now," Cloud said. She took a breath. "Yes, in the afternoons, when the woman who taught me was out gathering ingredients and I was to be preparing them, the young man would come by, and he would smile at me, and tell me of our plans, and I would lose myself. When I found myself again, we would be off lying in tall grasses, far from scouting eyes, and he would be half-asleep, and I full of light and fire. It was so different than with Wind. Those were the only times I..." She trailed off, losing herself for a moment in the remembered scent of spice and musk and dry grass. "Even now, I cannot wish I'd never had that. Except for what happened."

"Wind came back," Ant said, nodding as though it were a story she'd heard a thousand times.

"Yes."

"He caught you?"

Cloud fought the tears away from her eyes. "How I wish he had. No, he never found out. One afternoon I got back to the village—I knew as long as I returned before dusk, the healer would never know I had been gone, although she complained about how slow my work had been lately. But when I arrived, people ran up to me. They asked where I had been. My husband had returned, they told me, but he was ill. Dying. Why hadn't I been in the healer's tent?

"I ran and found him. He lay on his side in the tent. His leg was swollen up like a baobab. It was purple with blood, bleeding from a weeping sore. He couldn't breathe well. A puff adder had bitten him on the ankle, he said.

"I tried to treat him. I drained his bleeding. Then I killed a guineafowl and pressed its breast to the wound. But it was too late. I knew it was, and he did too. He told me how glad he was to see me, how much he'd missed me. He talked of how far he'd traveled, the things he'd seen. He'd been to the great water, he said, and stared out to the infinite. He'd traveled along the Firelands and seen strange beasts and tasted new spices and heard new tales. He'd been to vast villages of mud and stone, villages the home of ten times the number of the People of the Savanna, where at sunrise you could begin a journey on one side of the village, and the sky would darken before you reached the other. How wondrous were the sights he'd seen, he said, but how much he'd missed our village on the savanna, our people, and me. He told me that on the journey of days and then moons and then rains, he thought of me waiting for him here, and even when he grew so tired that he could not take another step, remembering my beauty gave him strength.

"He had come back with great riches, he said, a wonder of treasures that he carried in a pack on his back, and another on the back of an animal that he had brought with him. But when the adder struck, it had frightened the animal away, and those treasures were lost. He'd been some distance from the village still, and as the snake's venom weakened him, he'd had to leave behind, piece after piece, all the treasures he'd carried: spices and fabrics, shining stones and beads, carved wood and knives, idols of unknown gods. The poison had swelled his leg so much that he couldn't walk, but he'd brought back one thing. My bundle, he kept saying. Where is my bundle? I want you to see it. I want you to see what I brought for you.

"But I could find no bundle, and when I told him this, he wept. He begged me to go find it for him, that it must be here, that he'd brought it back for me. But the venom was already taking him, and I couldn't leave his side again. I made him tea, but he was too weak to drink it. He told me how happy he was to be home, how glad he was to be there with me, that I was more beautiful than ever before. And he died."

Cloud sighed. Very few people knew this story, and most of them were now with Father Wem. It had been a long time since she had last told anyone. Telling it brought the pain back again, fresh in her mind, welling up inside her, but it was a pain that she needed, a comforting hollowness. She sheltered it inside herself again, letting it bite at her heart. "I betrayed him. I betrayed him and he died because of it"

"Desire is a thing no one can resist for forever," Ant's normally hard and confident tone was now gentle and reluctant. "You shouldn't blame yourself for that."

"I don't." Cloud turned away. "I blame myself for not being there. I was the healer. But I forgot my duty to my people. I was with another, sharing dreams of a life that was not mine. I left my responsibilities behind me to dally with another, and because of that, the gods took my husband. If I had been there, I could have treated him in time."

"You don't know that," Ant said.

"I do know it," Cloud said bitterly. "I know how quickly the venom travels and what it takes to stop it. But when Wind came, I wasn't there. I left him alone when he needed me most. For that, I can't forgive myself. It's a mistake I won't make again."

Ant was silent. Cloud found the pain deep inside her and nurtured it, helping it to grow, letting it fill her completely. "I didn't see the young man anymore, of course. He came by every day for a moon, and every day I told him to go away. He tried to comfort me, and I shouted at him until he left. And one day he stopped trying. So that was that. I became the best healer I knew how to be. I never forgot what responsibility was mine. And when people are angry with me, like Firefly and No Rocks when their son was dying, I cannot be angry back. Maybe I couldn't do anything to save little Whistling Thorn. Maybe I am blameless there. But once, I let my husband die. Once, I did not save him. What could anyone ever say to me that I have not earned, that I have never said to myself a thousand times over? If I ever feel angry at them, I just remind myself. Once, I let my husband die. And then, I cannot be angry."

Cloud stood up. "You ought to go," she said. "It's good to remember what your duty is. You're a hunter, and people depend on you for food. I'm a healer, and people depend on me to be here to take care of them when they're sick or injured. It doesn't help anyone when we forget that."

Ant With a Leaf stood. Her face was hard, creased with emotion—perhaps pity, perhaps disappointment. Cloud couldn't tell. "All right," she said. "I understand. But maybe you're wrong, Cloud."

"Wrong about what?" Cloud asked. She hoped that there was not to be an argument. Ant could be stubborn when she wished to.

"About what people are depending on you for," Ant said. "Maybe they need more than a healer."

"Then they will need to look to someone else," Cloud said. "Good night, Ant."

Ant nodded and went to the tent flap. On the way out, she paused. "The bundle," she said. "Did you ever find it?"

"Oh yes. The scout who found Wind had it. We never found any of the other treasures he brought back from his travels—not his pack, nor the animal carrying his other goods—but the bundle, he had."

"What was in it?"

Cloud could not meet her eyes. "A robe," she said. "It was a green robe."

The Fire Mountain

The early morning light stirred Clay, and he pushed himself up on one elbow. Doto still dozed, one ear flicking toward the sound of Clay rising to his feet. Beyond the patch of green that formed the sheltering forest circle stretched the sahil, dusty and yellow in the sunrise. Over that, to the north, Ogya-Bepow, a giant pinnacle scratching the footpaths of Father Wem. Its sides sprawled downward in broad slopes, eerily flat, as though pottery shaped by heavenly hands. Black near the ground, the slopes faded as they rose, disappearing into hazy blue at the mountain's peak. Clay had never seen anything so large in all his life. He had been to the high places on the journey to Doto's temple, and those had been dizzyingly vast, but Ogya-Bepow, reaching from plain to sky, dominated everything around it. Its isolation only emphasized its immensity.

More than a moon had passed since Adanko had pointed them in the correct direction, but finally they spotted it: a strange, triangular bump on the horizon. Clay had been certain they would reach it with only a day or two of travel, but two days passed, and two days more, and still they had not reached it. The little bump had grown and grown until it towered above the horizon, and though yet far away, Clay could make out tiny trees that were still some distance from its slopes. He feared the mountain; it was a thing that should not be, a defiance of nature. From its peak, a hazy, grey plume of smoke rose and spread into the sky, a smudge on Wem's face. When Doto first saw the smoke, he had hissed and named it black cloud. By night, a faint orange glow lit its peak, like the light cast from a far-off torch.

Clay quietly cleared his throat, trying to loosen the sticky dryness in it. The journey had taken them far north of the forest, and the afternoon rains did not fall here, nor had he found any streams to replenish their water. Game was scarcer as well: occasional fowl and lizards were all he had felled on his hunts. Doto had spotted one of the giant, black-feathered birds that Jai and Ulo had been eating that first night—an ostrich, Clay remembered from old tales—but it was a good distance away and running very fast. Clay had never seen a living one before.

In the evenings, he danced for Doto and grew little circles of forest in the sahil. None were ever again as small and sparse as that first he'd summoned after their escape from Jai and Ulo. He'd feared Doto that day and feared him still. There was a pitiless darkness in the forest god, one that didn't understand the cruelty of murder and torment. Doto was his father's son, Clay realized. And now he wondered whether it was foolish to be sharing closeness with someone so alien, a being powerful enough to crush him at a whim. But what choice did he have? Their fates were tied together for now, and even if they were not, Clay was still drawn to Doto, compelled by an attraction that thundered in his head and chest and drowned out all his misgivings. He could no more fight it than he could fight the urge to breathe. Still, he wondered: if he asked, would Doto let him go? Did Clay even have the choice to leave?

They ate game when they could find it, but more commonly the clay-fruit that Doto grew each night and morning. It was a strange and silly name, and eating something named after himself was stranger still. But the fruit was delicious and satiating beyond any description. It quenched thirst—a blessing in the parched lands—and cured hunger. If it could only be encouraged to grow in the savanna on its own, the people might thrive.

"How did you sleep?" Doto asked, his voice a lazy purr.

"Very well," Clay answered. "I feel much better." He stretched his arms up over his head, noting only a stiff tug in his chest where days before there had once been a painful bruise, probably more. Clay was certain that his ribs had been broken. Breathing had been painful, like a knife in the side. Now that pain was gone. He rubbed at his shoulder; the baboon bite had vanished as well, leaving behind only white, splotchy scars, and those were diminishing day by day.

Doto rolled to his feet in an easy motion and stretched out his shoulders, legs, and tail. He yawned, tongue curling between his teeth, and then padded over to inspect Clay, looking him up and down with those wide, gold-green eyes. "Your injuries are nearly gone," he said. "The forest heals you."

Clay had suspected that the rate of his improvement was unnatural. "But I asked you not to. And I'm not more...more like you, am I?"

"I am not doing this to you," Doto said. "But in some ways, you are now like me, and I think that is why you are improving. The forest keeps my body strong and healthy because I am god. In the forest, nothing can truly injure me but another god. But now, a very small part of you is god too, yes?"

Clay blinked back at him. The notion was still impossible to conceive.

"Well then," Doto said, spreading his arms, "the forest heals you too. Only much, much more slowly." He sat down by Clay and leaned into his side, pressing his cheek to Clay's head. His whiskers tickled at Clay's face. "That is why it is best for you to live in the forest now. So you will always be well. Perhaps you will not even grow old," he added in a hopeful tone. "And you can be with me forever."

Clay put his hand on Doto's knee, sliding his fingers through the coarse fur there. He said nothing. Forever. Doto was fond of fanciful guesses, and this one was more fanciful than most. Even if true, it was beyond consideration. To see his brothers grow old and die, to watch his village age—no. It was a silly fancy. This whole journey had seemed more and more like a dream, a shifting between torments and revelations both strange and distant from the reality of his life. His life was home. It was the cool of his tent, and the chatter of people working, the hunger and flush of a hunt. It was talking with his brothers, dancing with his fellow runners at a council fire, and wrinkling his nose in the heat of the day at the stink of a tent or the pile of offal outside the village.

He looked down at his foot and ran his fingers over the spotted fur that covered it, flexing the short toes and making the curved, white claws stretch out. His claws. He was one foot into a dream already. Bit by bit, he was losing himself to it. All he had to do to make it go away was step into his old life once more. He longed to get it back for a while, to return to the world where the gods were distant and invisible, their silent voices demanding only prayer and respect.

But not forever. Not if it meant forgetting new marvels. Not if it meant losing the wild exhilaration that came from pleasing his god.

And Doto had asked him what he would choose. It was a question he couldn't answer; it was like being asked to forever choose between day and night, between song and silence.

"You are quiet whenever I speak of this," Doto observed. "You do not answer. You still give me the bad feeling that you would not come with me. But I made the promise you asked. I told you that I would not hurt or kill anyone else."

"I know," Clay said. That had been surprising and, he feared, blasphemous on his part. What right did he have to request that a god change his behavior or make such a promise? He wondered uneasily if he had altered the world in some fundamental way.

"Well, then?" Doto pressed.

"It's hard for me to think about. Let's just do what we need to do and see what happens."

Doto flattened his ears and looked away. "Then you should tell me something to make the bad feeling go away," he said. "It is very disrespectful of you to allow your god such unpleasantness."

Clay smiled at that and stroked Doto's arm. "You are a mighty and powerful god," he said. "And very handsome. And you've shown me you can be kind. And when I get back home, I'll tell my father and brothers and everyone else about you, and they'll all worship you." Doto was still looking away, but his ears were lifting up. "And you'll probably grow even more feathers on your forehead to match the one you have now. Maybe red ones and blue ones together, or yellow. You'll look magnificent."

Doto looked back at him, his eyes sparkling. "We should hurry to Ogya-Bepow," he said. "So that you can tell your people as soon as possible."

"We will hurry," Clay agreed, getting to his feet. But he looked at the huge peak rising up before them, high as the clouds, and worried. What would be waiting inside it? Would they find Sarmu? Or an angry fire god? And what secrets did Sarmu hold? And how, he wondered despairingly, could any of it help to stop an angry forest god from destroying his people?

⁓⁓⁓

Two more suns rose, yet still Ogya-Bepow guarded its secrets. Reaching the slopes had taken another full day's travel, and Clay and Doto had spent another ascending, traveling in an upward spiral, searching for a way inside. The climb was steep and exhausting, taxing muscles in Clay's legs that he seldom used, and in little time he found himself panting, sweat streaming down his back and chest, wasting water he could ill afford to lose.

Before midday, the vultures discovered them and began following them, sailing down to settle on jutting rocks or on the reddish-black slopes of Ogya-Bepow. No trees grew in that high place, nor grass, nor anything else. The ground, thick with powdery earth that crunched under their feet, collapsed and slid beneath the weight of each footstep, like the great sand dunes of the Firelands, making every step forward a half-step down. Clay could look back and trace the pocked trail of their journey all the way down to the base of the mountain. Occasionally, black scars like dry riverbeds interrupted the smooth slopes, their surfaces glossy and hard, hot enough to burn Clay's toes, with shard-like edges sharp enough to cut through the callus to the tender skin beneath. The flesh of his soles was badly sliced before long, sand clotting the blood. Besides the smooth, black scars, the only other features to break the smooth incline of the terrain were occasional large and irregular red boulders. These were pitted with holes, their surfaces dry and split as though they had been breaking apart for many rains. Crumbled, fire-red fragments lay around them.

It was one of these that Clay picked up to hurl at an insolent vulture. "We're not dying!" he shouted at it. "Leave us alone!"

Doto looked back at him. He was visibly tiring as well, though he had not exhausted himself quite as thoroughly as Clay. "They will not understand your fire bearer language," he informed Clay. "You must use the god-tongue to speak to them."

Clay lifted his eyes to Father Wem.

"Let us stop here for a rest," Doto decided. "It seems unlikely we will reach the top before nightfall."

"The top? We're going to the top?" Clay sat down heavily on the loosely graveled incline. Immediately, the ground gave a little, and fine grains of rock and dust slid down inside his leathers and began itching uncomfortably.

"It is the only way in that I can tell. I have seen no openings or caves along the sides. But there is light coming out the top, so that must be the way in."

"It looks like a fire," Clay said doubtfully. "There's smoke and everything."

Wrinkling his nose, Doto said, "And it stinks. Of fire and something worse. I do not know it. I think it may be the reek of Ogya himself."

"Ogya? Here?" That possibility was worrying. Clay wondered why Doto wasn't more concerned.

Doto's attention was captured by the light at the peak. "It is called Ogya-Bepow, after all. And it is supposed to imprison a god. But do not worry. We are far from the Firelands, and the forest is a safe distance away. If Ogya is in there, the worst he could do is to send me home."

"Which would be bad for me," Clay reminded him. "And if this really is a prison for a god, then couldn't you be imprisoned in it, too?"

Doto's ears went back. "I had not considered that," he said. "We should be cautious, then."

Clay crouched and sprawled back on the dark gravel of the slope, ignoring the heat of it against his skin. "You used to be so fearful of Ogya. Remember, you thought I might be his spy? You wouldn't even let me make fires because you thought Ogya might be watching us from them."

Settling down next to him, Doto said, "Ogya could watch. And I think it very likely that he does. The doings of a forest god are of great interest to him. My father told me many stories of Ogya and the fire bearers, and

I was frightened by them." He looked sidelong at Clay. "Yes, even a god may be frightened. Does that surprise you?"

"Not really."

"Yes, well," Doto said, looking discomfited, "it is true whether it surprises you or not. I still fear Ogya, but not so much. My father's stories were not all true. The fire bearers are not all bad, or at least one of them isn't."

Clay knew he was thinking of Jai and Ulo now. "Many of them aren't. My village is full of good people. You'll see."

"Perhaps Ogya isn't all bad either," Doto suggested. "Or not as scary as in the old stories. I am not as afraid as I once was."

Clay looked at him, remembering the scowling, imperious creature that had captured him from his village, forced him to march exhausting miles through the forest, and treated his every word and action with suspicion and threats. It was hard to see that old Doto in this one. The god might still carry the inclination for great cruelty and even murder inside him, but it was no longer his first reaction. "You've changed," Clay said.

"Yes," Doto agreed. "I have." He reached up to stroke the proud feather that sprouted from his forehead.

"No," Clay said, laughing. "Not what I meant." He looked up at the peak. "So that's where we're going? What if it's just a big hole filled with fire?"

Doto shook his head. "That cannot be it. That would kill Brother Sarmu's body, and he would return to his temple. If he is imprisoned, it must be in some way that keeps his body safe."

"And you're certain that Sarmu is inside this…this high place?"

"In the forest circle last night, the god's energies were very strong. We are so close to him that it makes my teeth buzz." Doto peered at him. "How is your missing fang? Does it grow back with your healing?"

"I don't think so." Clay poked his tongue through the gap in his teeth. "My jaw isn't sore anymore, and the gums have healed over. I think it's gone for good."

"You should let me grow it back for you," Doto said. "I do not care to see you broken. A leopard fang would be very appealing in your mouth, and it would make it easier for you to catch prey without using that spear."

Clay giggled. "I don't think I'm going to be running through the forest catching antelope with my teeth!"

"Well, of course not. That is silly. Antelope are much too large for you. But you are fast enough now to catch maybe a duiker or a tasty bird." Doto licked his jaws. "I miss fresh game."

"Nothing on these slopes but the vultures," Clay said, pointing at one. "I'm guessing you don't like eating those."

"Ugh, no." Doto made a face. "Vultures taste very foul."

"Well, then, it's more fruit tonight." Clay looked up toward the peak again. "How high do you think we'll get today?"

Doto covered his eyes with his paw, peering upward, his pupils slitting in the bright light. "I do not know. I did not think it would take more than a day to climb, but we have not come far at all."

"What if we get to the top and it's just a deep hole all the way down to the bottom again?"

"That would make it a very good prison," Doto admitted. "If that is what it is like, then you will dance for me, and I will grow sturdy vines that we can climb down."

Uneasily, Clay peered back the way they'd come. At the base of Ogya-Bepow, tiny, stunted trees squatted far, far below, so far that it made his stomach wrench and the horizon tilt alarmingly in his peripheral vision. He looked away quickly. "Can you grow vines that long?"

Doto puffed out his chest. "I have heard a very good song," he said. "It says that I am Doto the mighty, and that is true. I can grow vines long enough to tie the whole mountain."

⁓

When they finally decided to stop for the night, however, the peak seemed scarcely closer than when they had rested earlier. Up higher the air was cooler, but the glow of fire at the top of Ogya-Bepow burned brighter and more threatening than ever, and the air stank of bad eggs.

"I don't like it here," Clay told Doto. "Are we really supposed to sleep in this place? What if we go sliding down in the night?"

"I do not care for it either," Doto answered. "But unless you wish to keep climbing, or slide all the way down to the bottom and climb all the way back up tomorrow, we must stop here. You will feel better once you are in the forest circle."

Clay surveyed the shifting, angled slopes doubtfully. "I don't think I can dance here. I can't even walk steadily." At the disappointed droop of Doto's ears, he hastily added, "But I'll give it a try."

Scouting around for a flatter area proved futile; Ogya-Bepow was evenly angled. Clay took a few steps of the dance, but immediately the ground gave way beneath his springing movements, and the whole slope shifted downward in a spreading sandslide. He struggled to right himself, to climb up out of the slide, but every movement only increased the speed of descent.

"Where are you going?" Doto called after him. "I was not serious about sliding down to the bottom!"

"I'm not doing this on purpose!" Clay shouted back. He threw himself backward, spreading his arms and legs wide, bracing against the shifting ground, and finally, his descent slowed, and then stopped. He lay panting, sand and gravel crawling into every crevice in his body.

He heard the rush of more sand sliding downward, and then Doto's paw reached into his vision. "Come on."

He grabbed the paw and held tightly as Doto pulled him back up. "What are you holding onto?" he asked, and then he saw the vine: a long, twisting, sinuous thing that sprouted from the soil above them.

Doto hefted him toward it, curling one powerful arm to lift him upward toward the vine. "Climb up."

Hand over hand, he hoisted himself back up. Pain speared into his palm, blood tickling down his wrist, and only then he noticed the white barbs jutting from the tendril. Moving more carefully, he clambered back up to the place where he'd slipped and managed to stand up again. Doto climbed up behind him, agile as ever, and hopped to his feet.

"How did you grow the vine?" Clay asked, astonished. "Did my dance work so quickly?"

"No, of course not. That was no dance at all." Doto took Clay's wrists in his paws and turned them over inspect the punctured palms. "I needed to retrieve you, so I bled." He lifted Clay's hands, one at a time, to his muzzle, and delicately cleaned sand from the wounds with careful strokes of his pink tongue. He licked his nose. "My blood makes plants grow."

"Yes, I remember," Clay said. He noticed Doto's left arm, the fur black and matted there. The leopard must have slashed it open to bleed into the soil. "Are you going to be all right?"

Doto clutched at his arm with his right paw. "I will be, once you dance us a forest circle."

Clay looked around. The sky was darkening swiftly, and the side of the mountain was between them and the sun. "Well, it's not going to work here. You saw what happened when I tried, and you might not have enough blood in you for another vine."

Looking skeptical at Clay's assessment of how much blood he held, Doto grudgingly nodded. "What do you suggest, then?"

"One of those dark scars," Clay said. "Where the ground is hard and doesn't move." He didn't relish the thought of dancing in one of those. The rock would be cooled off by now, but it would still cut up his feet. "Can forest grow there?"

"I suspect it can grow anyplace you dance for me, worshipper," Doto said. He licked blood from his fingers and then gripped at his injured arm.

The two continued on a little distance, heading steadily around the mountain and upward until they found another of the strange, furrowed beds of rock that etched the sides of Ogya-Bepow. With Doto at his heels, Clay searched the edges of the scar until he found an area that looked relatively smooth, and edged out onto it. The surface was still warm from the sun, but not hot enough to burn his toes.

He called Doto out into the middle, took a deep breath, bracing for the slick hard rock to cut into his feet, and danced. At first, the dance went as usual, a bound, a twirl, a step right, right, and left. Energy filled the air, and the grass spread out under his toes, guarding them from the sharp edges of the stone. Doto stretched out his arms, breathing in ecstasy as the power filled him and healed him. Then the larger plants—shrubs, vines, and saplings—began to sprout, and as they did, the black rock snapped and cracked with loud and startling reports. The sounds jarred Clay out of the rhythm of his dance for a moment, making the memory of his song fall from his lips. He pushed the outer world away, focusing on thoughts of worship, and continued the dance. It must be the roots, he thought, growing deep into the stone, breaking it apart. The snapping sounds grew deeper, both in timbre and into the stone, and jagged cracks opened in the scar, zigzagging away from them like lightning bolts, forking and splitting the rock.

Clay paused in his dance. "Maybe we should stop," he began, but before the words were out of his mouth, a deep rumbling groaned from beneath the earth. Ogya-Bepow shook beneath their feet, a vibration like the thunder of a stampeding herd.

"What is that?" Doto crouched low, his eyes wide, tail switching.

A hissing sound, like rain on the leaves, surrounded them, whispering over the ground for the space of a few breaths, and then faded into silence. "What *was* that?" Doto asked again. His tail bushed thick with fur standing on end.

The air clung to them, oppressively hot and still. Silence hung over it.

Then Ogya-Bepow shuddered again, and the world reeled around Clay. He swung his arms to keep from pitching over backward, and Doto dropped down to all fours, puffy tail lashing. The hissing sound came from all around them once more, rain where there was no rain, wind in the leaves where there was no wind. Clay looked around, puzzled, trying to find the source of it, and then he saw the sides of Ogya-Bepow shimmer and shift before his eyes, like the ripple of heat in the midday sun.

"Look!" he shouted, pointing back. Doto turned to follow his arm. Their footprints in the sand were melting away, erasing from the slopes as though no one had ever traveled there. The sand and gravel hissed as it slid downward, shaken free by the movements of the earth, filling in the divots where they had set their feet as they climbed upward. Clay was grateful now that they had stopped in the bed of rock; otherwise the sliding sand would have carried them rapidly down the slopes and perhaps buried them.

"What is happening?" Doto demanded. The fur down his back and neck stood on end, making him look oddly large and feral.

"I don't know!" Another loud rumble. Ogya-Bepow shuddered again, and this time, it did not stop shaking. The mountain shook as if it wished to shiver them from its hide, fling them back to the savanna. Clay imitated Doto, crouching onto all fours so as not to be thrown from his feet. "I don't think I should have danced!" he cried.

The rumbling and shaking increased in violence and intensity, making Clay's stomach lurch. His bones ached from the vibration, his head shaking around on his neck. Despite his efforts to remain calm, panic rose in his chest; he clutched at the rock with his wounded hands, trying to force it to hold still. Just when he had decided it would never end, it quieted. The hiss of sliding sand diminished into silence once more. The ground steadied beneath his hands and feet.

He looked up. "Is it over?"

Doto lifted his head, ears pricking. "I don't know."

Then came the loudest sound Clay had ever heard. It cracked through the night air, fiercer and sharper than any thunderbolt, so violent that it buzzed in his bones, in the rock beneath him, in the air clapping against his body. His ears rang.

The dim evening sky glowed orange above them.

Hardly daring, his hair standing on end, he looked up. Brilliant yellow fire lit the top of the mountain, rising in a brilliant fountain of light. Streamers of flame shot up around it and arced back down toward the slopes.

"Fire!" he shouted in terror, but he couldn't hear the words over the ringing in his ears.

Doto stared at him, mouthing the word, "What?"

In answer, he pointed toward the top of the mountain.

Doto turned, looked up, and stumbled, his ears going back. The flame spouted higher, spitting a fan of red sparks into the dark sky. It wasn't a fire exactly, Clay saw. It looked, impossibly, as though fire and water had joined together to make some new thing that splashed and flowed like water, but burned with the light of Ogya. Another loud crack echoed across the sky, audible even through his temporary deafness, and an orange and red splash of flame crashed against the top of the peak; brilliant, glowing orange ropes flung outward, darkening to red and then black in the air. The sky around the peak darkened with the shadows of chunks of rock blown out of the top of the mountain and arcing down toward them. The fire splashed again, and then began to creep downward. Clay stared at it in wonder. Never before had he seen anything like it. It was like a river, he thought, a river made of fire.

He curled his toes, feeling the winding bed of strange rock beneath his feet. No. It wasn't *like* a river. It *was* a river. And they were standing in the riverbed. The liquid flame burned bright yellow as it flowed downhill.

"Run!" he shouted to Doto, but again his voice was barely audible over the cracks and rumbles of the explosion above them. Doto shook his head in incomprehension. Clay pointed toward the river of fire, and then beckoned frantically. "Run!" he shouted louder. He turned and bolted, springing out of the forest circle he'd half-completed, stumbling as his senses grew duller and his left foot shrank back into its weak, human shape. The glassy black rock sliced into the balls of his feet, but he barely felt it.

He looked back over his shoulder just as Doto came bounding past him. "Get back into the sand!" the god shouted, veering toward the edge of the stone bed.

Summoning all his speed, Clay leapt after him and grabbed at his tail, yanking him backward. Doto turned with a yowl of anger and confusion. "We can't!" Clay pointed toward the sides of the mountain. "Look! We'll be buried alive!" The sand and earth were moving again, churning and pillowing as they flowed and tumbled down the side of the shuddering mountain. Above them, a massive, pitted boulder tilted in the flowing sand, half-buried one moment, then shivering free the next as it rolled onto its side. The earth furrowed up around the boulder and then sent it tumbling, end over end, down the slopes of Ogya-Bepow.

The river of fire was racing toward them too, however, now so bright that it burned almost white with heat, the soil and dust in its path vaporizing in hissing puffs of air. It was impossibly fast.

Doto grabbed Clay's hand and yanked him forward, tearing down the scar at a speed that Clay could hardly keep up with, his toes slipping on the rock, barely touching it at times. A gust of hot, dry wind slammed into him from behind, half lifting him as he ran. He looked back over his shoulder. The river was vast and bubbling, burning with palpable heat. The coursing fire hit a bend in the scar and crashed upward, a blazing, orange splash of fiery liquid leaping higher than a treetop into the air, fanning and cooling to dark red as it fell back down to the ground in heavy thumps. Clay realized his hearing was returning only because the roar of the approaching fire river pounded in his ears.

There was no escape. Either they would be incinerated by the river or buried alive in the flowing, shifting soil of Ogya-Bepow. The heat of mountain burned at his back and neck. He was already exhausted from running, his sides aching. He felt Doto's paw gripped about his fingers so tightly, they felt about to break, but still his hand was slipping free. He forced himself to run faster, squeezing at Doto's paw, but the god's furred grip slid down just to his fingertips, and then Clay's fingers came loose. He stumbled, grasping after Doto, and fell forward, catching himself on his hands. In a moment there would be a flash of heat. Doto would awaken in his temple, but Clay would go up to Father Wem. He wondered how long it would hurt. He wondered if his ancestors would be waiting for him, if they would be proud of him, if he would see his mother again.

He pushed himself upright and ran. Now he could hear nothing but the roar of the mountain. The heat against his back and legs was unbearably hot. The world around him glowed orange and red. He looked after Doto, racing before him in bounding leaps, choosing his path so he didn't go tumbling down the steep decline, tail lashing for balance. He thought of their last moments in the temple and wished they'd never left that peaceful sanctum. He had thought he would want to return to his people, to help them, but now he regretted not leaving them to their own fates, even as he cursed his own selfishness for thinking it. They could solve their own problems, appease the gods, calm the rage of Kwaee on their own. He just wanted to be back in the temple with Doto once more.

The flesh on the backs of his legs bubbled, blistering from the heat. Well. He had been embraced by a god, and that was more than most people could say. It had not been a poor life, however short.

Then, below them, to the right of the scar, the shape of the mountain itself rippled and twisted like bubbling mud or a clearing mirage, the shadows of sand and rock coalescing into a dark pool. Clay stared, nearly losing his footing as he ran—it was as though the side of Ogya-Bepow had melted. The sliding sand shifted around the darkened spot, small rocks and streaks of black bending around the shadows. Then he realized what it was: an opening. Even as he turned to run toward it, it yawned wider.

"Doto!" he called. "This way!"

The leopard looked back over his shoulder, his eyes wide and terrified, flashing green with the light of the fire behind them. He followed Clay's pointing arm, and his ears lifted when he saw the opening. He leapt toward it, bounding out of the way of the flow, out of the scar and into the flowing sands.

Clay had no opportunity to see what happened next. The fire river thundered behind him. The foul heat of the fire baked his lungs. He dove out of the scar into the soft ground to the side. Immediately his feet were swept out from beneath him; he rolled in the sand and was covered briefly. The earth was heavy and hot, stifling, but then it bore him upward again. He saw the orange sky and the flow of yellow fire going by, painful even in its proximity. He gasped a dry, torrid breath, and then spat dirt before the flowing sand tilted him backward, head over heels. As he fell, he saw the opening close by and twisted his body, rolling to the right. His shoulder thumped against smooth stone, and he grasped at the solid surface with his other hand, trying to hold it close, but then the sand picked him up again. Again he rolled, over and over, trying to keep above the flow of sands, hoping that he had not been turned around in his fall and was still moving toward the opening he'd seen to the side. Hot sand gritted in his eyes, filled his gasping mouth and nose. He spat, trying to keep his throat clear so he could breathe, but more sand only forced its way between his lips as he sucked breath.

Suddenly there was nothing below him. He fell, flailing, and then solid rock struck him in the back and shoulder and hip. His head bounced against stone.

He panted, breathed in sand and choked on it. With rasping coughs, he cleared his throat, spat the grit from his mouth, and panted again.

Doto's face appeared over his. "Are you all right?" the god asked with a concerned expression.

"I think so." Clay tried to lick his lips clean of dirt and ash. "My feet are cut up, and I think I have some blisters." He pushed himself to sitting. The mountain still shook beneath him. The rumble of the fire river and the hiss of the sands still surrounded them. "What happened?"

Doto looked up. "It would seem Ogya was not pleased with your dance," he said. "If this is part of his domain, then you stole a little piece from him. I think he decided to take it back."

"No wonder Kwaee's afraid of him," Clay said. "How could anything stand against such a force?"

Doto gave him a dark stare. "I think nothing can."

This pessimistic assessment of their chances sent them both into a somber quietness. Clay sat on a boulder, trying to rub the sand out of his skin, from his armpits, and between his fingers and toes. The backs of his legs were not blistered as badly as he had feared, but the hair had been scorched from them. His eyes felt raw and scraped with sand and heat. They welled with raw tears. Nearby, Doto crouched, licking the sand from the fur of his arms and shoulders and spitting it to the floor.

Once Clay felt like he could breathe and see again, he stood. "Well, at least we are alive. Where are we now?" The glow of the orange sky and the fire river outside revealed a dark tunnel, its roof a little higher than Doto's ears, extending far into the mountain. The edges of it, facing out into the night air, were ridged with stone, which kept most of the sand from pouring in, though it piled up and poured over the edges here and there in little cataracts.

"A cave," Doto said. "But unlike any cave I have seen. Look at the walls."

Clay stepped closer, wincing at the grit of dirt in the cuts on his feet, and ran his fingers down the surface of the stone. It was perfectly smooth, more so even than the stones of Abansin, the ruined city he and Doto had found in the middle of the forest. The buildings there had been carved and shaped, but were still naturally coarse to the touch as any stone. The surface of the tunnel was smooth as water, so slick that his fingers slid across it. The opening itself was perfectly round, the perfection of the shape unsettling. Nothing like it should exist in nature. "I saw it open up, as we were running," Clay said. "There was just sand and the sides of the mountain, and then suddenly there was a cave. It appeared."

"Only a god could have done such a thing," Doto said.

"Ogya?"

"I do not think so. Why would he spare us from his own fire? And Ogya commands fire and ash. He could not easily shape stone like this, I think."

"Then who?" Clay asked. "Sarmu, maybe? Maybe he's letting us in to save him."

"Maybe," Doto answered, sounding doubtful.

Clay took a few steps down the tunnel, peering into the darkness. "Then we should see where this goes, yes?" When there was no answer, he looked back.

Doto hunched in the entrance. "I do not wish to go down there." He crouched lower, his ears flat.

Clay couldn't blame him for trepidation, god or no. His own heart was still pounding, his knees shaking in the aftermath of terror. "I know. But this is why we came. All there is back there is ash and fire."

"There must be fire down there, too," Doto said. "If it comes after us like the fire out there, we will not escape. Maybe Ogya will hold us prisoner, like Sarmu. Or maybe . . . ."

"Maybe?" Clay asked.

Doto scowled in exasperation. "Why does everything in the world want to kill you, Clay? You are a very unlucky fire bearer. Even the ground assaults you. I do not understand how you are still alive."

Clay smiled. He didn't explain to Doto that nothing much had ever tried to kill him, not until the night a leopard had appeared in his camp and dragged him off into the forest to meet the gods. "It's because I have my very own personal god to protect me. You've saved me many times."

"That is true," Doto agreed. "I am very good at keeping my worshipers alive."

"I'm glad to hear that. Because I'm going down this tunnel now to talk to Sarmu, and I think I'll have a much better chance of staying alive if you come with me." Clay turned and walked down the round hole into the side of Ogya-Bepow. He didn't look back.

After a moment, he heard the pats of soft-padded footsteps approaching. "You are not the god," Doto grumbled behind him. "You should not be deciding where we go all the time."

They traveled for some time into the heart of the mountain, following the path steadily downhill. The light soon dimmed until only Doto could see, and then even his leopard eyes were of no use. It was completely dark. Clay followed the wall, keeping one hand on it, reasoning that no matter how lost they were, he could always turn around and follow the tunnel back out. Doto kept close behind him, one paw on his back. Clay was used to the blackness of moonless nights. Starlight alone was not bright enough to illuminate the darkness, and if it was the rainy season, one could not even see the stars. Doto, however, claimed never to have encountered complete darkness before. He muttered continually to himself about how much he disliked it, and how Ogya could be lying in wait for them, or there could be a sudden pit that would drop Clay to his death. This last concern hadn't occurred to Clay, and he took his steps more carefully.

Doto's grousing echoed hollowly down the tunnel, and for a while, there were few other sounds but their shuffling footsteps, the shaking of the mountain, and the persistent rustle of the wind in the tunnel, which gusted at their backs with a cooler air that alleviated the increasing heat of the tunnel. But soon, they began to hear other things: low, breathy sounds, like a giant considering a difficult problem; or sometimes what sounded like the snarl of a lion. There were different rumbles as well, not like the shaking of the mountain, but more steady and persistent, the sound of a bubbling liquid, as though Cloud were brewing up a particularly thick and viscous concoction. The stench, too, was awful. The reek of Ogya-Bepow, smoke and bad eggs, concentrated and intensified, so heavy and noxious in the shifting air that it unsettled Clay's stomach.

He was beginning to wonder if the foul air would force them to turn back; it was scarcely breathable, even with the fresher wind blowing in behind them. And the darkness was beginning to toy with his mind in odd ways, making him see spots and trails of light where he knew none were. But then Doto said he could see a light ahead, and after a time, Clay saw it too: a faint, orange glow, far down the tunnel.

Encouraged, he picked up the pace a little, still trailing his fingers along the wall, and the light grew brighter and brighter as the air grew warmer, and after a sharper descent in the tunnel, they stepped out into a massive cavern of fire.

The tunnel's floor jutted outward into the center of the cavern on a little spit of rock like the stone tongue at Abansin. It stretched up and over a bubbling lake of orange and red fire, extending toward the center of the cave. Black masses of rock appeared to float in the lake below, drifting lazily in a slow circle, propelled by the entrancing swirl of oozing light. The heat was intense—so terrible that if Clay thought that if he leaned too far over the edge of the spit—not that he was inclined to do so—his skin might blister. Only the comparatively cool draft from the tunnel behind them made breathing possible. It was impossible to tell how high the roof of the cave was; above them, the brightness of the fire dimmed into blackness. The cavern was very broad, and had it not been filled with that liquid fire, a journey across it might have taken an hour or more, but as large as the space was, Clay guessed it was yet only a small portion of the vast mountain, Ogya-Bepow.

But it was neither the size of the cave nor the lake of fire that commanded Clay's attention. In the center of the cavern rose a spire of stone, a platform of rock perched atop it, and above that, placid and massive, floated the god Sarmu. He was a tremendous elephant, ten times as large as any Clay had seen before, round with fat, his great, sagging belly so plump that, were he to try to stand on all fours, his feet would not touch the ground. He hung in the air above the rock as a mote of dust might hang in a beam of light, rolling and twisting, head over feet, shoulder over shoulder, trunk swinging this way and that, the motion seeming not to concern him. If he could stand, Clay saw, he would stand upright, like a man; he had a man's upright back, neck, and shoulders, and his legs, though tremendous and

round, were shaped like a man's as well. Other than that, he was wholly elephant, but for the broad fan of colored feathers that sprouted above his brow.

He gave a great, breathy sigh, and then one wet, brown eye settled upon Clay and Doto. Regarding them with a thoughtful expression, he slowly turned upright to inspect them over the broad bulge of his trunk. "So you two are the ones causing all the fuss."

Clay dropped to his knees in awe. As with the forest god, Kwaee, and as with Asubonten, the massive crocodile who ruled the river, the sight of the savanna god filled him with wonder and fear. Here before him loomed the being that governed the movement of each blade of grass, the migration of all the herds of all the animals that roved the eternal prairie. Nearly every moment of Clay's life had been spent within Sarmu's encompassing arms. When his people had prayed for rain and food, they had prayed to Sarmu;

from him had come every rich meal, every soft bed, the clothes Clay wore, the fires around which he and his people had danced. The savanna was home, and here before him was its maker and caretaker. Nearly all that he had and all that he was he owed to Sarmu. In reverence, he spread himself out on the stone, ignoring the burn of the heated rock at his knees and arms. "Lord Sarmu, I am not worthy to stand before you."

"Ah," Sarmu's voice boomed, rich and gentle. "Little fire bearer. Stand, before the heat of this place burns you. I would not wish it, but neither have I the power to stop it. Rise."

Clay got to his feet to see the giant god gazing kindly at him.

"So you are Clay."

He heard his name spoken by his god's tongue, saw it shaped by his god's lips, and felt it thrum through him, *his* name, made sacred in the speaking. "You—you know me?"

Sarmu's trunk lifted between ivory tusks that could rend the sky. It was a smile. "Of course I know you, Clay. I've watched you and your people all your life. I've seen your travels across the savannas. I've heard your prayers and praise with fondness."

Clay fought back tears. All his encounters with the gods thus far had been disillusioning: Asubonten had been indifferent to him, and Kwaee had hated him. But Sarmu knew his name and spoke it with kindness. Comfort of a kind he had not known since his mother was alive flooded through him. He and his people were not alone in their struggles. Someone was watching. Someone cared.

"And I am Doto," the leopard declared, his back high, tail swaying. "God of the forest."

Sarmu began to drift again, spinning sideways as he watched them, his trunk drooping to one side, over a tusk. "And I know you as well, Doto, though not as well as I know little Clay. I have long been curious to meet you. How surprisingly like your father you are."

"I am not so like him," Doto answered, half to himself.

"No? Well. It has been long since I have spoken to Brother Kwaee. He has not been the most conversant of gods. But then, it has been long since I have spoken to anyone. For more than six hundred rains I have been trapped in Ogya-Bepow. It is a lonely place. I don't get many visitors. But then along you two come, shaking the whole mountain. You must have made Ogya very angry."

"I think that was me, Lord Sarmu," Clay said, dipping his head. "I danced for—for Lord Doto. I'm sorry if we disturbed you."

"Danced for him?" Sarmu looked puzzled, although that might have been just because he was floating upside down. His eyes brightened. "Ah, the divine transfer. A wonderful little trick you fire bearers have. And you don't even know it. None of you know. But then, few of us are privileged enough to know what we are." He frowned. "There were tales. Stories that you were all to know. I never hear you or any of the other peoples of the savanna tell them any longer. It makes me sad for you. We lose ourselves when we forget."

"Forget what?" Doto asked. "What are these stories that were to be told?"

Sarmu sighed. "It doesn't matter now. They were forgotten. And now it is far too late to change what will come."

"But that's why we're here, Lord Sarmu," Clay said. He stared at the great elephant. Something was different. The elephant seemed thinner than before, his belly not so round. But surely he had not changed since they arrived. "Kwaee is angry at my people. He turns the forest against them. He thinks that we have allied with Ogya to oppose him."

"I know," Sarmu said somberly. "I am not like Kwaee, to keep my eyes closed to the world around me. I see all that happens in the savanna, the movement of every blade of grass. I see your people now. How strange that so many different groups call themselves the People of the Savanna. There are seven of them. Do you know that? Seven, all believing themselves alone. How sad. How foolish. If they only would speak to each other…" He shook his head. "You should not have forgotten your stories."

Clay dipped his head low. "Please, Lord Sarmu, it may be important to us. Please tell us of these stories we have forgotten."

A great, deep rumble came from the elephant, but it was half growl. He definitely looked thinner now. His broad thighs had narrowed, his belly retreated to plumpness. And stranger still, his trunk looked shorter. "Why, the betrayal of your people by Ogya," he exclaimed. "How could you all have dismissed it so quickly? Are you fools? Scarcely a thousand rains have passed since that time!" A harder, crueler edge had sharpened his voice.

"I do not know of such stories," Doto said boldly, stepping toward the savanna god. "And I have been alive far longer than any feeble fire bearer."

"Well, of course *you* would not remember," Sarmu said, arching one eyebrow while rolling backward in the air. "You were but a mewling kitten then, and whose stories did you have to teach you? Only Kwaee's."

"Mother Fam taught me too, when I was young," Doto said.

"Oh yes, I heard all about that, little cat." Sarmu waved his ears, which also looked smaller than before. "She told me of all the rules. Never tell him this. Never tell him that."

Doto went still, only the tip of his tail twitching. "Never tell me what?" he asked. He made his voice quiet and dangerous, but how could Doto possibly threaten the immense god? He could not even reach him floating over that lake of fire.

Sarmu grinned, and his teeth had gone curved and sharp. "The stories you heard were chosen for you," he said. "Did you hear of my ascent to power?"

"I heard my father sacrificed his own power to create the savanna *and* you."

"There was savanna still, back then, but it was small. Spots here and there," Sarmu said. "I was only a little god with a tiny realm. Barely worth notice." He grinned widely at Doto, and when he did, his long tusks shrank and withdrew into his mouth as though he were swallowing them. "But when the fire bearers came with Ogya's flames and burned the forest, Kwaee felled his borders in one terrible crash." His gaze went distant. "Can you imagine it? It was wondrous and terrible. Trees falling in every direction, crashing against each other, thundering as they fell, pulling down vines, crushing the underbrush. You could hear it from one end of the earth to the other. Countless animals and birds, crushed under the weight of a downed forest. In a few minutes, Kwaee had shrunk his realm by more than a fifth part. Where once there was deep forest, now for days travel in all directions, there was nothing but wreckage. And then the earth opened and swallowed it down." His tone had gone harder, with a keen, joyful edge to it. A celebration, Clay thought, of the disaster that had felled the forest and created Sarmu's realm.

As if sensing Clay's thoughts, Sarmu turned a stern gaze toward him. "Little fire bearer, this is what you were not to forget. When Ogya saw the wasteland that lay before his minions, the obstacle in his plan to burn the forest, he blamed your people for it. In his rage, he turned on you all, cursed you. Any fire bearer holding a torch or seated by a flame was burned alive that day. Once, your people were numerous. They were as countless as the stars. They filled cities all across the land. But when the sun rose on Ogya's wrath, it found few of you remaining. The cities burned, and the night filled with your screaming. Ogya relished in your destruction. He smashed your homes to shards and splinters. Those fire bearers who survived scattered to the far reaches of the land."

Clay stumbled backward in shock. It could not be true. His people, nearly destroyed by Ogya, the god that they prayed to, the god whose flame they depended on for food and light, whose fires they danced and prayed around? Ogya had nearly destroyed them? He looked with mounting fear over the edge of the rock spit into the lake of fire below them, where the god was surely listening, ready to rise and destroy him as easily as wishing it.

A golden color crawled steadily over Sarmu's hide, brightening the wrinkled grey as it spread across his back and legs. "Do not worry, Clay of the People of the Savanna," Sarmu rumbled. "Ogya needs the fire bearers. Without you, he cannot satiate his hunger again. He needs your people to take up torches and spread his fire. We gods are not very good at taking more power for ourselves. It can be given, but not easily taken. That is why a hungry god needs fire bearers. And Ogya is hungry. He has burned with starvation as he waited for your people to forget his treachery."

Sarmu gazed beyond them, his eyes going distant, their color brightening to gold. "Imagine it: I cowered at the collapse of the forest, a small and insignificant god with little magic to call my own. And suddenly I felt more power than I had ever known. The world awoke beneath my paws, a vast plain that stretched from great water to great water. You cannot know the ecstasy that surged in me." His tongue, pink, slid around his narrowing jaws. "I had ascended. Now I was one of the great gods of the world, Sarmu, god of the savanna, mighty and gentle. For the first time, I heard prayer. I felt the fear and praise of the fire bearers. And then came Kwaee to whisper in my ear. 'This is the price,' he said. 'Guard the world against the hunger of Ogya. Stand between my forest and the Firelands, and never let them meet. And above all, guard the memories of the fire bearers. Never let them forget. Keep the tales.' How could I do aught but agree?"

He yawned wide, and his mouth was full of sharp, predatory teeth. His fat was gone now, his limbs thick and powerful with muscle, his chest taut and lean. "But Ogya tricked me and trapped me here in this mountain, surrounded by fire. There is no escape. So I wait. One day the world will turn."

Clay hung his head at that, but Doto's tail switched impatiently. "How can you say there is no escape?" the leopard demanded. "What efforts have you made? Turn the savanna toward your will and tear this mountain apart! Free yourself from it!"

Drifting horizontally, the god growled low. "You think it so easy, godling? Then summon your forest to free me! Show me how you wield your power here!" His golden eyes, slitted like a cat's, glittered in amusement at Doto's scowl. "No? You cannot wield your magic when out of your realm?

It works only with your paws on forest floor? So I. Could I summon the power of the savanna, I could surely free myself. But when I am in here, imprisoned, it does not hear me. I can govern the savanna, guide it, watch through its eyes. But when I cannot touch my own earth and feel its pulse beneath my paws, I might as well not be a god at all." His gaze went predatory. "Surely you understand this, having traveled through my domains."

Clay stepped forward, wiping sweat from his face. "But Lord Sarmu, was it not you who opened the mountain to admit us?"

Sarmu regarded him with hungry eyes. The flesh of his face seemed shrunken and drawn now, the shadows lengthening beneath his eye sockets and around his jaws. "No, little fire bearer. It was not I who admitted you. I can open no passages in this mountain. It takes all the power I have to hold myself above the ground so that the rock does not scorch my feet. Over hundreds of rains I have learned great weariness, great thirst." He stretched out thick, clawed fingers and toes, and revealed that his massive bulk had indeed shriveled. As Clay watched, Sarmu's gut collapsed, sinking into a hollowness, his ribs spread prominently above them like jutting fingers. "And great hunger." The muscle strapping his limbs had gone wiry and lean and was covered with tawny fur. Nothing of the elephant now remained, Clay saw. Now Sarmu was a lion: gaunt, mangy, ravaged by starvation, his thin lips drawn back from curved, yellow fangs. The only things that remained the same were his titanic size and the plumage that sprouted from his brow. And as he had transformed from a creature of plenty to one of want, so had his kindly demeanor waned into naked resentment.

"Then free yourself another way," Doto growled. "If you are truly so helpless that you cannot use your power to open the mountain, or float out its top, or summon your lesser gods to save you, then why not return to your temple? Step into the fire! Your body will burn, and you will be revived in your temple then."

The emaciated god spun in a slow rightward circle. "So, you bid me murder myself? Will I truly return to my temple? Are you so certain? Or here, in this prison, would Ogya consume my divine essence itself? Would all the savanna be his then? You are very quick to educate your elders, boy!" He whipped his stringy tail back and forth, growling, before finally settling down, even his anger not enough to motivate him from the place he hovered. He scratched at the matted fur on one thin arm. "Even were it true, the fire would be very painful. I should not care for it." He gave the molten cavern floor an uneasy glance.

Clay stepped forward to stand next to Doto, staring at the savanna god in amazement. *This* was Sarmu? This the god of his people's home? "But we are dying!" he said. "And more and more of the savanna dries up every season. How can you do nothing? Are you just going to stay in here until the Firelands cover the whole land? Just tell us what to do! Tell us where we can find help for you!"

Again Sarmu yawned, his tongue curling between his yellowed fangs. "Oh, little Clay of the People of the Savanna. You cannot change anything. It is futile to try. You see only a glimpse of the world in those few fluttering heartbeats you call a life. All things move in cycles. The savanna dries. It starves and thirsts, and then come the rains, and the savanna drinks and fattens. As night follows day, as the moon thins and plumps, so wet follows dry, feast follows famine." He patted at his shriveled stomach. "You see? It is not only my nature. It is the nature of the whole world. There will be times when the rains stop coming, and the forest falls, and the sands spread for seasons past all memory. And then that time of dry will pass too. The rains will come again. They will drown the Firelands. The forest and savanna will spread. We cannot stop this any sooner than we can stop the stars from spinning across the sky."

"But my people will all die!" Clay cried out in disbelief. "Every one of them!"

"Yes," Sarmu said, and his voice trembled with sadness. "They will. It is a great pity. I shall miss their praise."

"And if there was something you could do to save them? If we can find some way you can help?"

"All life is death and rebirth, waning and waxing. Why would I oppose the forces that elevated me from a tiny meadow god to lord of all the savanna?"

"Because Ogya will not stop!" Doto shouted over the roar of the mountain. He clenched his paws into fists and stepped forward on the spit. The hot wind of the fire ruffled his fur. "You say you must respect the cycles of the world, but Ogya wants them to end. His hunger won't be satisfied even when he has consumed every bit of land remaining. You must know this. You must know that he will end all life, including yours."

"Perhaps," Sarmu boomed. "That might be true. But if so, perhaps he is merely part of a larger cycle. Perhaps the whole world will be reborn, gods and beasts alike, shaped anew by the greater gods. All that happens will happen again. Who am I to stand against that? No. I will wait here and watch. Either Ogya's destruction will end or continue. There is nothing that I can do about that."

"You would let all life in the world die?" Clay asked in disbelief. A moment ago he had felt beloved, safe, but now he knew he was more alone than he had ever imagined. What use were the gods? One was greedy and malicious, another selfish and blind, and the third impotent. It was a marvel that his people had ever survived.

"I am sorry, little Clay," Sarmu said. He was plumping up again, his limbs thickening, belly swelling outward, his golden fur thinning. "I don't wish for you, or for any life, to suffer. But I cannot change the world."

Doto stood taller, his face gone stony. "Then help us another way. We came here not only to ask your help in opposing Ogya, but in the hopes that you would know the reason for my father's hatred of the fire bearers. He has told me many false stories. If we knew the source of his wrath, then perhaps we could calm it. Perhaps he would offer the fire bearers some refuge in the forest."

"It would only delay Ogya's destruction," Sarmu said. "It would make no difference."

Clay threw up his hands in exasperation. "It would make a difference to me!" he cried. "In my life! It would make a difference to my father. To my brothers and my friends."

"Your father," Sarmu said slowly. He frowned. "And your brothers."

"Yes!" Clay said, hope rising in him. "Give them a chance for a life. If you can tell us something, then please! Help us!"

The lion was silent for a moment, drifting head over heels as his body plumped out and his fur fell away. "No," he said at last. "All my words can bring you is sorrow. It's better if you both go now. Leave me. I will watch your journeys with fondness from in here."

"What good is your fondness?" Doto snarled, his fur lifting on his back. "Do you think it will matter to anyone when the world is burning? Will they sit among the flames and say, 'Well, at least Sarmu likes us?' You talk of cycles and tell us how we can't stop anything, and you don't even try to change things. Now I see what Adanko meant. All know where you are, but you are lost. I will not be like you. I will not sit by and watch Ogya and Kwaee destroy everything. Perhaps I cannot change the world. But I will try."

Sarmu laughed, a great, rumbling laugh that shook his fattening body. "Oh, little godling," he chuckled around his growing tusks, "how can you stand in the way of the cycles of this world? You are a part of them, and you can't even see it. You cause the cycles. Just as your father did."

"What?" Doto stepped back, bumping into Clay. "I am nothing like him."

"No? I have watched the two of you in my savanna. I have seen you join with your fire bearer. You even begin to love him."

"That is why I am different," Doto said. "My father hates the fire bearers."

"*Now* he hates them," Sarmu said, his trunk lengthening over flattening teeth. "But once he loved them. He was known for it. He loved many of them. Including your mother, half-god."

Clay stared in bewilderment, trying to understand what he had just heard. Doto opened his mouth but no words came out. He worked his jaws soundlessly.

"That is what Kwaee never told you—the great secret of your life he banished Fam from his forest to protect. Your mother was a fire bearer. When she died, Kwaee would not spare his power to save her. But he could not anticipate the terrible pain and rage he would feel at her loss. In his anguish, his forest murdered everyone in her city. Abansin, it was called. Unwittingly, he killed everyone in it. Your aunts and uncles, godling. Your grandparents. Everyone who should have nurtured you."

"It cannot be," Doto whispered.

"Oh, yes. It was your father who drove the fire bearers to side with Ogya against him. *He* sparked the great burning of the forest. That is why he hates you, little half-god. It is why he left you, as a squalling, newborn kitten, alone to die, because when he looks at you, he sees what he cannot bear to see. He has shut his eyes to his whole forest forever to keep that from his memory: his murder of innocents, the terrible pain of a lost love. But it doesn't matter if he doesn't watch his forest. When he looks at you, he sees it. When he looks at you, he sees a fire bearer."

"You lie!" Doto cried, stumbling backward, stammering the words. "You lie just as he did!"

"You see?" Pity shook Sarmu's voice. "Even now you repeat his errors. You love a fire bearer: a weak, frail thing destined to die. What will you do when it happens, little god? You cannot imagine the pain you will feel. You cannot know what you will do. In every way, you are your father's son. The cycle has you too. You are a part of it. You cannot escape."

Doto raised his paws to his muzzle, his eyes wide. He shook his head in wordless shock. Clay reached out to take his paw, but Doto yanked his fingers away. With a horrified stare, he turned and fled down the rock spit, into the tunnel, and was gone.

"Doto!" Clay called after him, running to the tunnel. "Wait! Come back!" He looked back.

Sarmu, rounded and sagging with fat, shook his head, sadness creasing his grey face. "It would be better not to go to him," he said. "He will bring you only sorrow and death. Go home, Clay. Heed the words of the god you have prayed to your whole life. Go home and forget about him. Enjoy what life remains to you."

"I can't," Clay said. He ran into the tunnel after Doto.

Sarmu's voice came after him, heavy with melancholy. "I know."

A Proposal

"As long as you're here, you might as well peel more yams," Buffalo Tail said brusquely. She set down a heavy basket of them on the mat at Cloud's knees.

Cloud nodded her assent up at the young woman, who gave her a tolerant if not exactly friendly smile, and took a yam from the basket. She placed a selection of them on a clay plate and set it near the fire to loosen the skins.

For the past hand or so of days, she had been coming down to the food circle rather than staying in her tent. It wasn't that she was lonely, she had decided. It was just that there wasn't much healer's work to do these days. No reason to stay isolated in her tent—better to be out, find some use for her hands, and hear the news of the day. Most places around the village were visited by the fire hunters though, and she did not have friendly feelings toward them, nor they toward her. But the fire hunters did not visit the food circle; here, Cloud could keep her head down and her ears open. And there was so much work to be done that few objected to her presence.

Any food that was not meat was prepared in the food circle. Villagers, mostly women, sat around her, engaged in the tedious work of cooking. They plucked the legs and wings from grasshoppers and rolled them in palm oil and ground millet for frying. They carved open bitter melon, scooped out the knotty, seeded core, and, to make its flesh more palatable, sprinkled it with fine salt grains gathered from the beds of dry ponds. They boiled young bamboo and peeled the husks back to reveal the tender, white fingers inside, all while laughing, talking, and chewing tooth sticks.

Cloud prodded at one of the yams, deemed it sufficiently softened, and gripped it in one hand, cutting into the bark-like skin with her knife. This wasn't a popular task—difficult work unless you had a good knife, and all the good knives went to the hunters. But Cloud's fingers were tough and strong; she could keep a good grip on the knife and could peel the yams much faster than Buffalo. Cloud had found she almost enjoyed the tedious nature of the work; it left her mind free to ponder, and her ears open to news and gossip.

No one spoke of her, of course. Not while she was there. In fact, she knew that she was the topic of gossip mostly by the way they *stopped* talking when she approached. She was a practically a pariah, an outcast. All knew that she had been stripped of her dignity by the King, that she had been removed from the council. Many believed that she'd poisoned the patients who had suffered from the plague, and for that she couldn't blame them. After all, once she had stopped administering the tainted willow bark, every patient had improved.

That at least was a great blessing. Mongoose, Twig, Dancing Spider, Fiveroot—all had lived. They had suffered great pain during their convalescence, but they had recovered. Now every one of them rested at home with their families and friends, and Cloud had sent her blessings and thanks to the gods many times over. She wished only that she could have discovered the source of the plague in time to save Red Moth and Whistling Thorn.

Their deaths were on her hands, at least in part. How could she have been so careless that she had not noticed the strange black spattering in the willow bark? She would not excuse herself for that failing. But her guilt was miniscule compared to that of the poisoner. That culprit was still among them, and Cloud now kept a vigilant eye for more of those tiny black droplets. She had warned others: all of those in the food circle; and Yellow Bug, her apprentice, who now received most of the patients. Few came to see Cloud with requests for healing anymore.

So now she sat in the fire circle, peeled yams, and sipped alligator pepper tea that she had brewed earlier in her tent. The talk had been interesting enough. Many in the village were split over Great Ram's leadership. Some insisted that their lives were better now, despite the hostile forest and the attacks from within. But others spoke fondly of their nomadic days, following the rains across the desert. No matter the drought and the weariness, they said. Better to be at home among their traditions and wander the savanna than to root themselves down but lose themselves. It gratified Cloud to know that not all, at least, agreed with Ram's decisions, and she allowed herself a small pleasure in hearing others decry them. She placed another set of yams on the plate by the fire and bent her ear toward the chatter of the other cooks.

Then one voice rose above the others, clear and angry, piercing the chatter and chopping, the crackle of the fire. "Go kill something with your fire hunters and stop bothering me!" The murmuring and noise around

Cloud lowered as people began to listen, while still maintaining the pretense of focus on their work. Ant strode into view, followed closely by a scowling Laughing Dog. Cloud hunched down, lowering her head so as not to be seen. She wished the tangled spider's nest of her hair were not so easily noticeable.

"You can't hold onto your answer any longer, Ant," Laughing Dog said. He snatched at her wrist with one meaty hand, yanking her to a halt. She turned toward him, her face a devil's mask. All the cooks suddenly developed a studious interest in their tasks.

"I can keep it for as long as I choose," Ant said. "I am a hunter, not some comfortable, squatting melon husker. What if I get your child? How will I run and hunt then? The people are hungry. They need a skilled hunter to provide food, not a squalling baby to eat it."

There were a few clucks from the workers at the words "squatting melon husker." Heads shook in disapproval, but no one ever looked up nor spoke a word.

"My fire hunters are doing a fine job providing more than enough meat," Laughing Dog said. "Your assistance is not necessary. You do not need to be a hunter anymore."

"Meat that is sometimes charred so much that it makes better paint than food," Ant retorted. "Besides, it is not your decision whether I should be a hunter or not. It is mine. And it is my decision when I marry, too. One I will make when I am ready."

Laughing Dog shook with anger, his mouth creasing the folds of his face. "You have made me wait for five rains for your decision. A woman can make a man wait only so long. She can make a prince wait even less."

Coolly, Ant replied, "I have made this prince wait much longer than most men wait. Perhaps he should not be telling me what I can and cannot do." She tugged her at her arm, but Laughing Dog only gripped it tighter, white around his fingers. Cloud winced in sympathy, but if it hurt, Ant gave no sign.

"Then you admit it," Laughing Dog said, curling his upper lip. "You have made me wait unjustly. I will wait no longer. I want your answer now."

Ant With a Leaf tugged at her arm again, and when Laughing Dog did not release it, gave him a shove in the center of his fleshy chest, forceful enough to send him staggering backward. She jerked her arm free. Head held high and regal, she asked, "You want my answer? Then you will have it. My answer is no. I will not marry you."

Laughing Dog trembled again, holding out his finger. He pulled his lips back over his teeth as though about to roar, or perhaps bite her, but then looked at the workers sitting to one side as if noticing them for the first time. He pressed his lips together, drew himself up into a serene pose. "You are my promised," he said quietly. "You have been promised to me for five rains."

"I was promised to a handsome, smart young man with big ideas," Ant said. "A man who only wanted to make everyone's lives better. Not a greedy man who—who talks to himself and who sleeps in a tent full of garbage and flies. Not a man who bullies old women."

"This…this is about old Cloud?" Laughing Dog asked in an incredulous voice. "Ant, I had nothing to do with what happened to her. That was all my brother. You have to know that. And besides, everyone knows she was poisoning people."

Ant gave him an imperious stare, crossing her arms. "She would never do that. She cared for her patients. She saved my father from the attack by the monsters, standing there with a spear to fight them off even though she had no chance. Why would she do such a thing if she were intending to poison him?"

Sensing a way in, Laughing Dog answered, "Because she's old, Ant. She's confused. Sometimes it happens. Your own grandmother got confused, remember? She was probably mixing medicines without even knowing it."

"She is not confused," Ant said. "Maybe you are the one who is confused. Before, you said it was because she was giving everyone forest medicines, and the forest is dangerous. Now it's a different story."

Cloud hunched lower, but peered keenly beneath her brow at Laughing Dog. Anger flashed in his eyes, and then again he managed to control himself. "Maybe you're right," he said. "Maybe I misjudged her. But if so, it was only because I care about the village and what happens to it. Don't turn me down for one mistake. Don't turn me down for caring too much."

"You think that is the only reason? Do you need me to remind you… how you—" Ant glanced at the circle full of people all busily absorbed in their work. "How you spoke to me the other night?" she concluded, putting the emphasis of meaning into every word. "That is not how a man behaves."

"And I was wrong," Laughing Dog said. "I know it. It will never happen again."

"You are right that it will not."

Laughing Dog clenched his jaw, then bowed his head. "I know that my actions lately have not been acceptable. I know that I have been… strange. I ask only that you consider that it has been a bad season for me. To lose so much of my family, to find myself in a strange place. The exile, the murders, the attacks. Ant, can you not see that I have been trying my best to hold everything together? To support my new King, to help with starvation and the plague. My actions have not been the most admirable at times, but please, take them in light of the hardships you know I have suffered. Forgive them. Forgive me."

To Cloud, the words rang with pretense, but she had never known Laughing Dog to falsely confess to anything. He had always had a firm conviction in his own actions and would fiercely disavow any wrongdoing unless he had been convinced of it. The boy had always despised lies. But he was not the youth he once had been; his tongue had grown more cunning. Cloud had no doubts that Laughing Dog's contrition was feigned, but Ant With a Leaf was young and passionate and had at least once professed to love him. She might be more easily swayed.

The huntress gazed at her promised with eyes that searched as though looking for birds that might be hiding in tall grass. "I do forgive you," she said.

Laughing Dog's remorseful frown lifted into a satisfied smile. "You honor me with your grace, Ant With a Leaf. And I promise you, in the days to come, you will see a different man. I will prove to you that you were right to do me such a honor. I will clean my tent; I know it must be distasteful to such a beauty. You deserve better. I will force myself to move past my grieving for my father and brother, and comport myself better. Regally, as a prince should. And when we are wed—"

"I said I forgave you." Ant With a Leaf held up a hand. "Not that I would change my mind." She looked over toward the cooking circle, and her eyes met Cloud's. "I think we are all pleased that we will see better behavior from you. But my answer is still no. You will have to find a different wife."

Laughing Dog opened and closed his mouth several times. "You—you would not say no to me," he managed. "I am rich. I am powerful. I'm a prince. You would not dare turn me down, not in front of everyone."

"You are the one who started this conversation here," Ant said. "I think maybe you are rich, and powerful, and a prince, but you are not very good at listening. A woman wants a husband who will listen to her. Prove you will make a good husband to another woman by listening to this: I do not want to marry you anymore. Did you hear that?"

Laughing Dog goggled at her. His mouth twitched with words unspoken. He squeezed his hands into his fists at his sides. When he finally replied, his voice was low and dangerous. "You will wish you hadn't said no to me."

"Maybe so," Ant With a Leaf told him, "but that is better than wishing I hadn't said yes." And with that, she turned and stalked away.

The people in the cooking circle lifted their heads to watch her go, then turned their gaze to Laughing Dog.

"No," he said, as if to himself, staring after her. "No she doesn't." He paused. He wore an expression as though he were listening to someone, and when he spoke, it was toward empty air. "Because a King needs a wife, that's why. He needs heirs, and—" He turned to look at all the upturned heads, the eyes staring back at him. He looked surprised to see them. "What are you all looking at?" he roared. "Get back to work!" Then he stomped away in the other direction, muttering to himself.

The chatter around the work area resumed as if nothing had happened. It would be a little while before anyone would begin to talk about it, but talk they would. That Laughing Dog's madness had progressed was worrying, but Cloud was glad that others in the village would finally have to take notice. She wouldn't be the only one to see it. Perhaps the winds were finally changing.

~~~

She opened her eyes. Her tent was dark, and she had been sleeping deeply. She didn't know what had woken her.

"Cloud!" a voice whispered near her.

She leaned up on an elbow, trying to focus on the figure in the darkness. "Ant?"

"Yes, it's me. Can I stay here tonight?"

"Of course," Cloud said, rubbing at her eyes, "but why? Is something wrong?"

"It's Laughing Dog," Ant said in a low whisper. "He was very angry today. I overheard Mirage telling Broken Stump about it, that he was raving to all of the fire hunters. He said he was going to handle me tonight."

"Handle you?" Cloud leaned up on one elbow. "What does that mean? Are you afraid of what he might do?"

"No." Ant held up her knife. "I'm afraid of what *I* might do."

Cloud was very much awake now. "Well, it's no good staying here. You've as much as called us allies in front of him. When he sees you're not in your tent, this is the first place he'll come. We should go."

"Where?" Ant whispered. "His fire hunters will tell him if they see me."

Cloud considered. "Better to leave the village," she said. "Beetle is at the gate tonight, I think."

"He has no love for Laughing Dog. Nor any of the others who were not selected to be one of his fire hunters."

Taking up her robe from its folded spot at the foot of the bed, Cloud rose and dressed. She could wake quickly in emergencies; a prerequisite of any devoted healer.

"What are you doing?" Ant asked. "I should go alone."

"Laughing Dog will be more dangerous to one person than to two," Cloud said. "And if you need a witness, well, I am not the best, but I'm better than none at all." She took up her walking stick. "I'm coming with you."

Ant nodded her assent, looking grateful. Together they crept out of the tent and around the council area and fire circle, toward the village gate, keeping away from the torch-lit paths. There was a large pile of garbage near the food circle, still not cleared away from the work done during the day. The flies buzzing around it made Cloud shudder. She shrank away from the trash heap, flattening herself against the wall. Past the work areas were the tent homes of the workers and the elderly, and beyond those, right up near the gate, were the tents of the hunters, who stayed there to protect the village from incursion, and so that they could leave early in the morning without waking others. If they were going to be spotted by a fire hunter, it would be there. But no one saw them. A couple of hunters stood on the path, chatting idly and leaning on their spear shafts, but they never glanced out into the shadows near the wall.

At the gate, Cloud whispered a quick explanation to Beetle, asking that he not tell anyone he'd seen them come this way. He answered with a furtive glance back into camp and a quiet nod.

Then they were out. Ant With a Leaf had taken a torch from near the gate, so they were able to find their way, following the trails along the edge of the forest, careful to keep outside the stone-marked edge of the forest. This was not the safest place to be at night, but Cloud reasoned that if Laughing Dog hated the forest more than anything, then perhaps he would be less inclined to look for them there.

During the day, the forest appeared shady and peaceful, but at night it looked dark and threatening, seeming to bulge with the unseen dangers it held: rending vines; murderous wood; and huge beasts with beady, strangely human eyes and deadly strength unlimited by the forest borders. Those were not merely creatures of the imagination; they had attacked that one terrible night, and Cloud could think of no reason they might not do so again. No reason to think they were not standing there now, in the shadows, watching them.

She drew closer to Ant With a Leaf. "He wouldn't come out here to look for us, would he?" she asked. She stubbed her toes on a jutting root and swore, envying Ant's long, graceful strides, like the easy but deliberate steps of a deer.

"I don't know," Ant said. "I don't know what kind of man he is anymore. He is greedy and demanding, and he speaks ill of many people in the village. I think he hates the god Kwaee more than anyone has ever hated any god, but once he did not even believe in gods. He has changed so much. I cannot tell whether he would hurt us."

"He was always rebellious."

"Yes," Ant agreed. "I loved that in him. He was always smart, too. He knew his mind and spoke it. He was never afraid of anything."

Cloud looked up. There was a sadness in Ant's voice, behind the anger. "Ant With a Leaf," Cloud said. "How are you?"

Ant turned, the flickering shadows from the torchlight making her face unreadable. "It has been so long since someone asked me that," she said. "I have not even asked myself. I don't know the answer. So much has happened. The forest, my father, the fire hunters, and now my promised. There are so many people I need to be strong for."

"It's tiring," Cloud said.

"Yes," Ant agreed. "Tiring. Not so much for one day, but days become moons, and moons become seasons. My mother and father need me to be strong. My people need me to be strong. Even you need it."

"You don't have to be strong for me," Cloud objected.

"Yes, I do! You don't see it, but I do. You need me to show you who you're supposed to be. And I'm trying, but—" She looked away. "Cloud, I'm exhausted. I don't like this place that we've come to, this forest. The land is full of evil, and I don't know how to fight it. And we are being governed and guided by angry little boys who don't know how to fight it either. It's not right, Cloud. We need leaders. Wise people with experience, who won't send the people to ruin on the backs of some misguided passion or fancy."

Cloud pitied Ant then, pinning her hopes for the people on someone like her. "That's not me, Ant. I'm sorry."

"But it could be!" Ant cried, spreading her arms wide. "Don't you see? All this time that King First Claw governed wisely, he was listening to you. He came to you with every decision to find out what you thought. He trusted you. There is no one better. Anyone sensible would choose someone like you to rule."

"Kings are born, not chosen."

"But they were not always!" Ant said.

"But they are now, and all know it. It's a pity that Great Ram drinks so much, and has only Laughing Dog to listen to. If Clay were still alive…"

"All due honor to those in the arms of Wem, but Clay was a fool," Ant declared.

"Perhaps," Cloud said gently. "But we are all fools in our own way. It may be that Clay was the right kind of fool." She sighed. "My heart weeps at what happened to him. I still half expect that one day he will just appear and say he got horribly lost."

"As if that would solve any of our problems." Ant continued walking, following the trail. "I wish things could be like they were, but then I wonder if 'like they were' was any better. Were we happier moving the village every year, always hungry, always thirsty, always exhausted? It seems like we were."

"The distant lands have no flies," Cloud said, quoting the old story.

"Talking of distant lands, where are we going?" Ant held her torch higher, making shadows dance on the trees. "Are we walking all night, or do you have some place to lie down?"

"There's an old moabi tree a little farther west. Big, with great, thick branches, low to the ground and easy to climb. We can sleep in that and be safe from anything that might come out of the forest."

"You want me to sleep in a tree?" Ant sounded amused. "Do you think me a cheetah?"

"You certainly aren't as quick as one," said a voice behind them.

With a start, Cloud turned to see Laughing Dog standing not far behind. His eyes glinted in the firelight.

"Where are the two of you going so late at night, hmm?" Laughing Dog asked. "Doesn't look good, does it? One a poisoner, and both of you known to harbor ill will against the King's family."

Cloud pressed her knuckles to her breast as though she could slow the painful beating of her heart. How long had he been following them? If he intended no harm, he would have spoken up much sooner. The night was dark, and they were far from anyone who might hear a cry for help. "Get out of here, Laughing Dog. Go home." She tried to say the words clearly and firmly, but her voice shook all the same.

"Or what?" Laughing Dog gave her a genial smile. "I'm here to have a little conversation with my promised. You're just in the way. As usual. A little thing like you getting in the way is likely to be trampled, sooner or later."

"I am not your promised anymore," Ant said, stepping forward to put herself between Cloud and Laughing Dog. She hefted her knife lightly in one hand. "I thought you understood me earlier today."

Laughing Dog put his hand to his belt, as if to take his knife. His hand trembled. He took a deep breath and lowered his arm. "Promises should not be broken lightly, especially not promises made to a King."

Ant lowered her own knife. "It was not my promise. And that King is dead."

"No," Laughing Dog said. "It was not your promise, and none would think to blame you were it broken. It was made by your mother and father, wasn't it?"

"If you hurt them…" Ant snarled, lifting her knife again.

Cloud put her hand on Ant's arm, gripping it firmly enough that Ant's face tensed. Her fingers were tough. "Laughing Dog," she said, "I know you don't like me, but you don't have to like me to think about what you're doing now. You cannot force a woman to marry you."

"That's what you think." He leered, his teeth shining white. "A woman will do much to protect her honor. Or salvage it." His eyes flickered down toward Ant's legs.

Cold despair and fury met inside Cloud then. If he would go that far—if he would even think it—then the boy she knew was gone utterly. She looked at him and saw only a monster, a monster that had eaten the son of her friend. "You cannot want this," she said in disbelief. At her side, Ant was shaking in fury. "You cannot want to take this woman who will hate you as your wife. She will give you no love, no comfort. She will only slit your throat at her first opportunity. What could you possibly want from her that this would grant you?"

Laughing Dog crouched then, as though hearing a sudden sound, although Cloud could discern nothing but the night insects and frogs chirruping. He muttered something unintelligible and furious under his breath, then turned away, clutching at the back of his head and tugging at his braids.

"Get ready to run," Cloud murmured to Ant. She didn't know what drove this madman, nor what he intended. She knew that with her stiff joints and weakened limbs, she had no chance of escaping, not from a skilled and honed hunter, even one who had grown as heavy and fat as Laughing Dog had. But Ant With a Leaf was swift. She could escape. Not into the forest, perhaps, but there would be many places to hide out in the tall grass.

Before they could move, Laughing Dog turned back toward them, his eyes wild and mad. "What I want—*all* that I want," he shouted, "is to save our people. We have to stop the forest, don't you understand that? How can you all not see it? It's murderous. It hates us. And I'm the only one around here with the sense to understand it, with the courage to stand up to it. We *must* do that if we're to survive, we have to fight Kwaee, even—even kill him if possible."

Every time Cloud thought she'd heard the pinnacle of madness, Laughing Dog summoned some terrible new derangement. "You intend to destroy a god," she repeated slowly.

"Yes! There are ways. I know there must be. But how can I do this if the people won't listen, and they won't listen if they don't respect me, if they don't love me! Why will no one understand?" He walked toward them, his heavy body shifting from side to side, his eyes wide. "I need them to listen. If they don't listen, we'll never burn it down. Never."

"Laughing Dog," Ant began. She sounded more frightened than angry now.

"How are they going to respect me? How are they going to listen?" he shrieked. He waved his arms as though swiping at invisible hornets. "When my own promised turns me down? You humiliated me in front of everyone. Well, you'll take it back now. You'll tell them how wrong you were. That you'll marry me after all. I'll be lead hunter. Prince next in line to the throne. And I'll have an obedient woman of my own who has decided that there is none among all the people in the world more worthy of her devotion than me."

He turned as if talking to the forest. "He says it's not important. He says she's a waste of time. But he doesn't know! He's not right about everything! I can drink him into silence any time I want! They have to love me and respect me. Then they'll listen, and then we'll burn these woods into nothing but ash!"

As he turned away, Ant With a Leaf dropped into a crouch, sneaking up behind him, her knife at the ready. Cloud almost stopped her. Hurting the King's brother would not make things better. But this man was unpredictable and dangerous. They had to get away. And Ant knew that Cloud would not be able to run fast enough. She was doing this for Cloud. Had they not been in such terrible danger, Cloud might have collapsed in sudden relief. Here in all the village was one person who still would stand by her, no matter what. She was not alone. She had at least one ally.

Ant stood up behind Laughing Dog, her knife raised, but then the hair on the back of his head moved. A deep growl, like that of a hyena, came from it. She gaped in fear, only for a moment, but it was enough time for Laughing Dog to whirl on her.

"You dare to lift a knife to me?" he roared.

"No," Ant said, and she planted the blazing torch under his chin, engulfing his head in the flames.

Laughing Dog screamed a high howling scream, his head surrounded by fire.

"Oh, Ant, what have you done?" Cloud murmured. The fire roared around Laughing Dog's skull, licking up and down the dry braids of his hair, his features invisible. He screamed and screamed, and then Cloud realized that it wasn't a scream at all. It was laughter—insane, cackling laughter.

He stepped back, and, impossibly, his face was whole, unscarred, his eyes bright and shining. Wisps of smoke drifted upward from his braids. "Now do you see?" he crowed. "I can't be hurt by fire. I have ascended. I am stronger! I've taken the strength of the gods for myself."

"By all the gods," Cloud shouted. "Ant, he isn't insane at all. He's possessed!"

"Possessed?" Laughing Dog shouted. "No! I am not possessed! I am the possessor! The power of the gods flows through me! I will use it to save us, to save our people!" He turned to Ant With a Leaf. "But you," he said, his voice going low and sinister. "You tried to kill me. Just as he said you would. It will be the last time you try that, I promise you." He made a swiping grab for her, and she darted back, tripped, and sprawled in the grass. The torch crackled as it caught the nearby shrubs and spread yellow light across the ground.

"I'll show him," Laughing Dog growled. "Telling me I can't handle my own affairs." He dropped to all fours in the grass and lunged toward Ant With a Leaf, grabbing her ankle. She cursed and kicked him in the head with the flat of her heel, sending him recoiling to one side.

"You traitor!" he howled. He shook his head, rubbing it with one hand, Ant's ankle still gripped firmly in his other. "You untrustworthy snake!" His fingers curled around a stone, and as Ant kicked her leg free, he smashed it down against her shin. Her startled cry of pain cut through the night.

He was too intent on her to hear Cloud running up behind him, her walking stick held in both hands. She couldn't run fast, and her hips complained with the stress, but she barely felt it. She lifted her stick over her shoulder and with all her strength swung it at his head. It struck his skull with a crack.

Laughing Dog slumped to one side, pawing clumsily at the back of his head as though trying to knock something away. Then he fell forward onto the ground, half sprawled across Ant's legs. He twitched and lay still.

Ant shuddered and tugged her legs free, kicking at his shoulders. His body shifted limply, and she shuddered again. "Is he dead?"

"No," Cloud answered, panting. She was surprised at herself, both at what she'd done, and at how little the vigorous act had pained or exhausted her. She felt energized and strong. It was as though she were twenty rains younger. "He's breathing." She kicked dirt over the spreading grass fire, snuffing it out.

"I can't believe it. I can't believe what he did. The fire was all around him. It didn't hurt him at all." Ant looked at Cloud in wonder. "You knocked him right out. What made you think that would work?"

Cloud hefted her walking stick in both hands. "He said that he wanted to burn the forest. I'm guessing he really doesn't like trees." She poked at Laughing Dog's side with her stick, and he groaned softly. "We had better get out of here."

"Wait a minute," Ant said, gripping Cloud's shoulder. "We're just going to leave him there?"

"I'm not particularly inclined to help him," Cloud said dryly. "And we don't know when he'll wake up."

"No, I mean—" Ant hefted her knife. "Supposing he didn't wake up."

"Ant!" Cloud could hardly believe what she had heard. Once in a great while, it was necessary to kill an outsider who threatened the village, but the People did not kill each other. To do so meant permanent exile, wandering the savanna alone with the brand of a murderer on your skin, forever cut off from family and friends and all that was at the heart of you. It was said that even the ancestors would not welcome a murderer in the afterlife.

Ant With a Leaf's face was hard and defiant. "You saw what happened. He is not a man, not anymore. No person could do what he did. You want to let this demon back into our homes where he can hurt us again? Better he dies now."

And if he had been the one poisoning the village, Cloud thought, then maybe Ant was right. Maybe Laughing Dog was a risk they ought to remove from the village. She sighed. "And when we are discovered? We will both be exiled. Are you ready for that? What if this demon takes some new form and comes back? If it took Laughing Dog, who is to say it could not take others? No one will know of it, and you and I will be banished, unable to help anyone or save them."

"Better to fight the lion you see than the shadows you don't," Ant said.

Cloud didn't agree, but saw Ant would be intractable on that point. She tried a new approach. "Are we ruling already? Should not this be the decision a King should make, rather than a healer and a hunter."

"The King will never banish or kill his only living blood. Besides, Laughing Dog is crafty with his words. We will never win that way. He is here before us now. Only now he cannot fight back. I will say you were not here. I am not afraid of being banished if it will save us."

"And if we are wrong?" Cloud asked helplessly. "If it was just a trick of the light, and the poor boy is just sick and deranged? Will you blacken your spirit with that? And face your ancestors with blood on your hands?"

"A trick of the light!" Ant spat. "You saw as well as I. He burned and then did not. And there was something in his hair. Something terrible. He is—he is taken by something terrible. I am sure of it." She frowned though, looking back toward the faint glow of the village.

"Do what you must then," Cloud said. "I could not stop you." She didn't feel that way; after clubbing Laughing Dog in the back of the head, she felt as though she could take down an elephant. But she was sure Ant

With a Leaf would not do this thing. She remained certain as Ant flattened her lips in grim determination and crept toward Laughing Dog, who still lay unmoving and silent. She was certain as Ant lifted her flint knife and pressed the point to the back of Laughing Dog's head, poking into his hair and searching for something. For a moment only, she doubted—when Ant With a Leaf pressed the edge of her knife to Laughing Dog's throat.

Then Ant stood. "I cannot," she said. She sounded disappointed in herself.

"I know. It's all right," Cloud said. "It's good. Come on. We should get out of here before he wakes up."

Ant sheathed her knife and limped over, favoring her injured leg. Cloud would have to look at it later, but not now, not here. "Where do we go?"

"Into the savanna somewhere. He can't find us if we're not following any trail."

Cloud took the torch from where it lay and snuffed it out in the dirt. "And this time, I think, no fire."

The decision to return to the village in the morning had been an easy one. Both Cloud and Ant With a Leaf worried about what they would find, but even though most of Cloud's patients went to Yellow Bug for treatment, Cloud could not abandon those who still needed her. Ant worried about her parents, and whether they would face reprisal from Laughing Dog or the King. Besides, they couldn't stay away forever, and the sooner they approached King First Claw with the terrible events of the night before, the better.

Left Rabbit looked surprised to see them when they approached the gate. "Elder Cloud, Ant With a Leaf, when did you go out? I never saw you leave."

"We've been out all night." Cloud felt the fatigue as soon as she said it. They had bedded down in a thicket some distance from the village, but she had barely slept, and she knew from Ant's muttering and tossing that the hunter was equally restless. Rest had been chased away by visions of the possessed prince shrieking with laughter, his head engulfed in flames.

"All night? You should go see the King," Left Rabbit said, looking concerned. "People have been trying to find both of you all morning, ever since prince Laughing Dog—well, maybe it's best if you see the King."

Ant gave Cloud a look. Well, they'd known last night wouldn't be the end of it. Together, they made their way through the village. People already busied themselves outside their tents and in the work areas: talking, preparing their tasks for the day, eating; and they paid Cloud and Ant little mind. Cloud had been half-expecting sympathetic or curious stares, especially if others had been searching for her, so the people's disregard was reassuring. Or were they being pointedly ignored? Were people afraid to meet their gaze? No, that was paranoia. Cloud pushed it down.

The fire hunters, however, did not ignore them. Scorpion, his body freshly painted with white ash, looked up from the knife he was sharpening, and pointed them out to Hill in High Wind and Burning Star. He said something Cloud couldn't make out. The other two nodded. All three came up behind them, following them in silent escort as they made their way up the incline toward the King's tent. Two fire hunters guarded the entrance. It gave Cloud a shiver; never before Great Ram had a King posted guards. It made him look weak and afraid.

Ant greeted the fire hunters at the tent; she'd hunted with them before, but if the fire hunters felt any familiarity or warmth toward her, they did not show it. They kept their faces impassive, and only stepped aside to admit them after Cloud surrendered her walking stick and Ant her knife. She stooped through the open flap, Ant behind her.

Laughing Dog was seated on a pelt at Great Ram's right hand. "I was wondering if you'd dare to show up again."

"I was wondering the same of you." Cloud fought to keep the dismay from her face. It had been too much to hope that they might speak to the King alone, she supposed. The King himself wore a grave expression, the effect of which was diminished somewhat by the calabash in one hand. So early. Surely he had not yet had time to get drunk.

Ant crouched next to her. "King Great Ram," she began, but the King cut her off.

"What happened to the two of you?" he asked. "Cloud, you were my father's most trusted advisor, and Ant With a Leaf, you have always been so…so serious and noble. And now I learn that you attacked my brother, out in the savanna? How could you? Why?"

"King Great Ram, you have been misinformed," Ant said, dipping her head.

"Have I." The King did not look pleased at this response.

"Most assuredly. I regret that I must tell you that it was Laughing Dog who attacked us."

Laughing Dog leaned in. "You see, brother? I told you that's what they'd say. They laughed about it, said that no one would ever believe two women, one of them aged, could down me."

Scowling, Great Ram asked Ant, "If my brother attacked you, where are your injuries? Did he cut you with his knife? Did he hit you? I see no bruises. Perhaps he only wounded your pride."

"My leg," Ant said, gesturing toward her ankle, where a dark, purple bruise welled under the skin.

"Probably got it running in the dark," Laughing Dog suggested. "Had I attempted to attack them—and what reason could I have to do so?—I would prove a poor hunter indeed to begin with her ankle."

The King scowled at him. So at least he wasn't wholly on Laughing Dog's side. "And there are no other injuries?"

"No," Cloud said. "We were fortunate. He made his intentions very clear."

Great Ram gestured toward Laughing Dog, who Cloud now noticed wore a shoddy binding of leaves gummed up with a sticky poultice. Yellow Bug's handiwork was not improving with her responsibilities, she noted. "No other injuries, you mean, except the one on the back of my own brother's head, swollen and crusted with blood. Did you even think to see if he was mortally wounded? Or did you simply leave him face down in the mud to die?"

"Ram, *think*." Cloud tried not to raise her voice. "What reason would we have to attack him? How would we even have done it? Do you suppose the two of us somehow lured him out of the village simply so we could hit him with a stick? It makes no sense."

Great Ram's face puffed with anger. "Do you think I'm stupid?" he shouted. "I know what the two of you were doing. You were conspiring against me! Laughing Dog has told me everything!" He motioned to his brother.

Laughing Dog's smile was confident and predatory. "Yes," he said. "I first noticed the two of you colluding together after the poisoning began."

Cloud could not help but stiffen at that. Laughing Dog—or rather, the thing that possessed him—was behind the poisoning. She was all but certain of it. Ant put a hand on her shoulder.

"So many quiet meetings late at night, hushed whispers over the fire," Laughing Dog said to Ant. "What are those two up to, I wondered. At first, I thought you simply worried about your father. But then we all learned that Cloud had been making him sicker, not healing him at all. And still you came to visit her. Still those quiet conversations. It gave me worry. Cloud's disdain for my brother is well-known. So when I saw the two of you sneaking out of the village together, I thought it best to investigate. I followed the two you along the trails by the forest. What could they wish to discuss, I wondered, that would make them brave the dangers of the forest at night? I feared something sinister, but I never could have expected what I heard. You, Ant, urging Cloud to usurp my brother's reign!"

"What?" Ant With a Leaf's fingers dug into Cloud's shoulder.

"Oh, it's far too late to feign innocence," Laughing Dog scoffed. "You were both there. What was it you said? Something about being governed by angry little boys. We need leaders, you said. Don't bother denying it."

Ant was silent. Great Ram looked back and forth between her face and Cloud's. He shook his head in blinking disbelief. "So it's true. You thought to replace me. With who? Her?" He pointed a finger at Cloud.

"It's not like that," Ant said. "You have to listen to us."

Laughing Dog leaned back and rubbed the back of his head, giving an exaggerated wince. "Naturally, when the two found they had been over-heard, they were frightened. That one came at me with her knife, and while I was trying to save myself, Cloud hit me from behind. When I woke up they were gone."

Cloud listened with a growing sense of despair. How could this have gotten away from them? How could Laughing Dog have so completely de-ceived everyone? "Ram, listen. You've known your brother your whole life. Does this really sound like him? Is this who you grew up with?"

"People change as they grow older, Cloud," Laughing Dog said. "You should know that. Wasn't that why my father exiled me? In the hopes that I would change?"

Great Ram frowned. He rubbed at his forehead with one hand, and Cloud knew that her words rang true to him. "He came back from the sahil different, yes," she said. "But *too* different. Ram, something came back with him. Inside him. Ant and I have seen it. When he attacked us last night, he was raving like a madman. Ant defended herself with her torch, but it didn't burn him. You understand?"

"It's true!" Ant said, nodding her head. "The fire was all around him, and he didn't burn."

Ram barked a disbelieving laugh. "What are you saying? That Laugh-ing Dog—that *my brother*—is possessed?"

"Is it so impossible?" Cloud asked. "Think of how he's been behaving and talking. Have you seen him talking to himself as if someone else is there? Drinking water abruptly? Look at how fat he has grown, so quickly. And how do he and his fire hunters catch all that meat, where none could before? He's wrong, Ram. Wrong, and you know it. He's behaving like—like—"

"Like someone who's lost his family," Laughing Dog interjected smoothly. "My father, half-eaten by a wild animal, and my brother dragged off into the forest by another. Grief makes us strange, Cloud. You know that."

"Strange?" Cloud repeated. "You call what you've been doing strange? By all the gods, Laughing Dog, you've spat bile and venom at anyone who dares to question you. You've accused me of treachery and betrayal, you've urged the King to remove me from the council, you've turned on Ant With a Leaf, and you expect us to believe that it's all from grief?" She gripped at her robes in anger.

Half-rising, Laughing Dog shouted at her, "My father was murdered! Murdered by the forest! By Kwaee!"

"Nearly six moons ago!" Cloud didn't want to shout, *knew* she shouldn't be shouting, but she couldn't help herself. "How long do you think you can get away with blaming one man's death for the way you live your life?" She caught herself and looked down. In her frustration, she'd pulled a long tear in the green cloth. She let it drop away from her fingers. *How long?*

"That's enough!" Great Ram bellowed. "Am I expected to sit here and listen to you squabble like children? Laughing Dog, Cloud is right. You have been distinctly unpleasant since you returned. We're all grateful for the meat your fire hunters provide, but it's time to start acting like a prince. You will make an effort to be pleasant and gracious to all from now on."

Laughing Dog dipped his head. "You shame me, my King. It will be as you say."

"And Cloud," Great Ram said, "I have no further quarrel with you. No one has given me any indication that you seriously entertained these treasonous proposals. Since the plague has subsided and you obeyed my order to dispose of your forest medicines, you have been an obedient and helpful subject. But I will hear no more of this nonsense about my brother being a demon, and you will not speak of it to anyone else. I understand that the elderly can become… confused…sometimes. I hope that you will understand that, too. Still, I cannot have you spreading these rumors around the village, frightening the people, stirring up dissent. So I will make you a bargain. If you let this drop now, if you do not breathe a further word of it to the others in the village, I am disposed to restore you to the council."

He smiled. "To tell the truth, I miss you in the circles. Of all the things that have changed around here, for better or worse, you are just the same." He glanced at Laughing Dog. "It reassures me, I suppose. Reminds me of the way things used to be, before…before. Besides, it's better I listen to your nagging personally than have to hear it second-hand from others."

Restore her to the council? She clutched at the hope even as she realized with despair it would make no difference. He wanted her on the council only as long as she agreed to be silent on the things he most needed to hear.

Laughing Dog liked the idea less than she. "But Ram, she poisoned our people!"

"And you poison the King's mind," Cloud snapped.

"I said that's enough!" Ram shouted, his face darkening with anger—or was it the wine? "Don't make me change my mind on this, Cloud, or I will change it very harshly."

She sagged. "Yes, my King."

"And as for you, Ant With a Leaf. I cannot ignore this treason, which you make not even a pretense of denying. By all rights, I should banish you."

Tears glimmered in the corners of her eyes, but she kept her head held high.

Great Ram drank deeply from his calabash and gave a deep sigh as though it were water and he had crossed the long desert. "But I am not a cruel King. These are hard times, and hard times make people behave poorly. And as well, we need all the strong hunters we have. My brother assures me he is still quite fond of you. So you will give me a sign that you intend to be faithful to my rule. You will marry Laughing Dog."

"What?" Ant With a Leaf roared her fury and disbelief.

"As soon as possible. I have discussed this with my brother, and we believe that this is the best course of action. You will marry him, and be faithful to him, and make him happy. If you do not," Ram said quickly, before she could interrupt, "then I will exile not only you, but your parents as well. So think about their safety and well-being before you respond."

"The savanna is a harsh place." Laughing Dog's voice dripped with mock sympathy. "The last thing I would want is to see your sweet old mother and father struggling to survive out there. But my brother quite rightly pointed out that a daughter must get her treasonous notions from someone. I do hope we can put all this unpleasantness behind us."

"There, you see?" Great Ram said. "Already he's making an effort of it. And Ant, think—you were promised to him once. You were happy with him once. It can be like that again. Everything can—can be like it was. You'll all see." He lifted the calabash to his lips and then frowned at it. "That will be all then. Dismissed."

Cloud's thoughts whirled like a storm as she turned with Ant and exited the tent. She'd been waiting for Great Ram to see the truth, but he wasn't going to. He was going to drink and drink until there was nothing left of him. And then Laughing Dog would rule everything. She couldn't let that happen. She would have to do something. But why did it have to be her? Why? If only Clay were still alive, she thought. Then it would be out of her hands.

"Marry that monster?" Ant spat into the dirt once they were out of earshot. "He has no right to make me. No King does."

"I'm almost surprised we weren't exiled," Cloud said. "Or killed. I think we happened upon the King at the right moment in his drink. Council member again, eh? Laughing Dog looked none too pleased." She sighed. "But you're right, Ant. What you said last night, about what I should do? You were right. I have been afraid too long. I have let my mistakes cripple me instead of making me stronger. But this is too much. The village needs more than a healer now. We will have to try. There is no one else who will do it."

Ant smiled. "Good. You make me proud to call you friend. Let us plan what to do. And quick, before they throw us out," Ant said. "I will never marry that thing, not ever. Let the boy-King make his threats."

They were interrupted by a commotion at the bottom of the hill. Guards, four of them, and Fistful, the scout, were approaching the King's tent. They had someone with them: a short, thin man. His hands were bound behind his back, and the men kept him close between them. The prisoner, as he drew closer, proved to be hideously disfigured. Thick, ugly scars spider-webbed half his face, crawling over his nose, jaw, and forehead, and even into his ear. Where once an eye sheltered, nothing remained but a mass of black and red tissue. He was stumbling and weak, half-starved, his belly sunken, ribs wrapped only by a grass-thin layer of skin.

"King Great Ram!" called one of the guards. "We've caught a prisoner!"

After a moment, Ram exited his tent, closely followed by Laughing Dog. "A prisoner? Where? How?"

Fistful stepped in front of the group. She was a beauty: wide-eyed, full-figured, and nicely plump; but she could be swift and silent when she wished, one of the best scouts in the village. "To the east, King Great Ram. He was following the forest. He tried to attack me for my food, but he was too weak to put up much of a fight. He—he said he had met someone else who talks like us, King Great Ram." She looked down at the ground. "King, I hardly dare believe it, but he claims that he met Clay."

Cloud looked up sharply. Clay? Impossible.

Ram hurried forward, his eyes wide with hope. "You say you saw this man? Truly? Tell me what you saw and tell the truth. If you are lying to me about this, I will deal harshly with you."

The thin man shuffled forward, squinting with his good eye. "Saw your witch boy, I did, yea, him and the demon he traveled with." His eye turned waveringly to Great Ram's face, searching it. "But surely he was witch boy nay. How like this King he was. How very like. Surely kin he was to you, aye, kin, like as true. I tell you on the spirits of my ancestors, great King, he lives. The boy is alive."

Homecoming

Clay found Doto in the tunnel entrance, sitting in the curve of the wall, head turned toward the sky, tip of his tail twitching like a heartbeat. There was nothing to say, so Clay came and sat next to him and looked out at the stars. Their familiarity glittered his long absence back at him: so many moons since he had last seen his people. They would certainly think him dead. His name would be in the counting of the ancestors. Doto, however, was here. He was frightened and alone. For the first time, it occurred to Clay that perhaps Doto needed him more.

"I called him a liar," Doto said quietly, "but he is not. Everything he said is true. I know it. I have never been truly a god. Always I wondered why my domain was but a little cluster of trees. It made no sense. There are not two gods of swamps, one for high water and one for little bogs. There is only Atekye. So, there is only one god of the forest, and that is Kwaee." He snorted. "Copse god, godling they called me. I did not understand how truthfully they mocked me."

Clay put his hand on Doto's side, combing his fingers through the fur, and this time, Doto did not flinch away. His fur was warm and soft. "Of course you are a god," he said. "You're mighty and powerful."

"Am I?" Doto asked bitterly. "My father did not think so. He saw in me what I could never see: the blood of a fire bearer. He told me over and over in words I didn't hear. He told me that I was weak, like my mother."

"No."

"You *heard* Sarmu. That's why my father hated me. When he told me all the stories of the demons, of the terrible creatures that fire bearers were, he was talking about me." He buried his face in his paws. "The whole time, he was talking about me."

Clay moved around and took Doto's paws in his hands, pulling them down. "Doto," he said, and halted, staring in surprise at the wet, matted fur around Doto's eyes.

Doto turned his head away. "You see? Weak."

"Doto, listen to me. Since the night you came to my tent and took me away, I have met Asubonten, who wouldn't lift her tail to help us cross the river. I met Kwaee, who was blind and cruel. And I met Sarmu, who, as far as I can see, has just been sitting in that mountain for hundreds of rains because he doesn't feel like getting out. All that power, and the gods do nothing with it, except Ogya, who I guess wants to destroy everything. Something is wrong with the gods, Doto. Badly wrong. And I don't know what it is. But you are Doto the mighty." He smiled. "You're braver than all of them. You left your forest. You listen when people tell you things you don't want to hear. You made a promise to me not to hurt people, even though you didn't understand. You healed my foot, and even knowing what it would cost you, you offered to heal me again. I don't know what you got from your mother, but I know that every single thing you've done proves you're better than Kwaee."

Doto flicked an ear back, but only one, as he did when he was pleased and trying not to show it. "According to fire bearers."

"Yes, according to fire bearers," Clay said. "We're the ones who worship the gods."

Doto rubbed at his eyes with his fingers. "Yes, you are. What makes you fire bearers so different, I wonder? No other animal can do what you do."

"We're not animals," Clay said. "I tried to tell you that long ago in the forest, but you already knew all about us fire bearers, remember?" He grinned.

Doto didn't hear the humor in Clay's tone. "I knew nothing then," he said, lowering his ears.

"Neither did I. We were learning, I guess."

"Well, I do not care for learning. It is unpleasant." Doto looked into Clay's eyes. "You had heard of all these things. I thought that if you saw that I did not know of them, you would not fear me. And then I thought you would not worship me. And then when Sarmu said that I was only half a god, I knew that you would leave. You would not choose a mere half-god to be your personal god. You would choose a different god, a true one, a powerful one. You would go home to your people, and I would have to watch you from the edges of the forest forever. But you didn't go." He hesitated. "Are you going to go? Or will you still choose me?"

"Oh, Doto," Clay said. He heard the words come out of his mouth before he could stop them. "I will always choose you." Over all other gods, he meant. To worship, to adore. Not necessarily to run off into the forest with, to live life away from his people, not that. He wasn't ready for that choice.

But it was too late to amend. Joy lit Doto's eyes, and then the god moved toward him. Doto kissed him.

Clay had never been kissed before, not by anyone, much less a god, though they had lain with each other over and over. He hadn't even believed Doto knew how, nor knew what a kiss was. And how could he? Clay himself had not known. It was something more than mating. It was wild and fierce and deep, and it flooded away all of Clay's doubts and questions as if on a river of fire. The god's lips and tongue were soft against his own, but crackled with energy like the air on the day he had healed Clay's foot. It pulled the breath from his lungs and the weariness from his bones. He sank into his god's arms.

It was only later, when they rose from the stone floor of the tunnel to look out over the savanna and the path home, that Clay remembered the promise he had made, the seed of joy that was even now growing its roots around Doto's heart.

Instead of heading toward Clay's village, Doto chose a path directly south, reasoning to Clay that once they were inside the forest borders, they could travel far more swiftly, following the edge west, back to the town of tents and wooden walls that Clay had left so long ago. Home. He was finally going home again. He could hardly believe it. He found new energy in the promise of it.

Doto, however, was moody much of the time. He traveled in brooding contemplation, his brow lowered, ears back. Clay could easily guess what troubled him and knew that talking about it would only make the god bitter. Even when Clay danced, Doto did not look as happy as before. He breathed in and shivered with the flow of his power returning to him, but he often stared into the distance and stroked at the feather on his forehead. It was only when Clay lay in Doto's arms that his god seemed to completely forget his worries, to relax and smile, recalling his joy at Clay's inadvertent promise. "You will always choose me," he would whisper, and he would squeeze Clay tightly, as though afraid his worshiper might try to escape.

The farther south they traveled, the more Clay worried that they would run into Jai or another person from Jai's village. When dancing the forest circles, he chose broad, open spaces where none could hide in waiting for them during the night, and insisted that Doto grow the grass tall enough to hide them. During the night, he kept well within the circles and would not venture out, not even to make water, until sunrise, when he would scan the horizon with divinity-sharpened eyes for any who might have crept up on them in the night.

After more than twenty days of traveling, they noticed the trees grew thicker, the grasses and brush denser and taller. On the thirtieth day, the afternoon rains fell on them again, and on the thirty-second, the edge of the forest was in sight. Doto twitched his tail in excitement at the sight of it and quickened his pace, but his paws squeezed into fists over and over, and his troubled expression deepened. He stopped at the border of the forest, the invisible wall that separated one god's domain from another. Clay could not sense it as Doto could, at least not at first. One side looked no different from the other. But as he stood watching, he could feel something after all: a natural boundary, like the difference between standing in shade or sunlight.

"The forest," Doto said, and traced his fingers down the invisible curtain in the air, his claws extended as though they would tear rents in it. He stared into his realm, his ears twitching toward the sounds of the birds and insects that lived within it. But he made no move to step beyond that border.

"You don't want to go in?" Clay asked. "When we first left, you couldn't wait to get back."

Doto hesitated, the fur lifting across his shoulders. "I want to go in. But outside the forest, I could pretend everything was not true, like the pictures in your head when you sleep. Everything out here is so different, it might be a story I am telling. Once I go in, then everything turns real. When I go in, I will be only Doto, half-god of the forest. I will have to think about my father and what he did. I will have to think about what I am, and the life I will have. I will never inherit the forest from my father. He will never look kindly upon me. So it will be time to decide what happens next."

"And what's that?" Clay asked.

Doto gave him a puzzled stare. "I do not know. I have not stepped inside the forest and decided yet."

Clay smiled at that and waited.

Doto pressed his fingers to the wall between forest and savanna as though it were tangible, a surface that might ripple under his fingertips. Then he stepped through.

He let out a long breath as though he had been holding it forever and then sprang forward, his movement so quick that he might have been a flicker of sunlight. He caught himself on all fours and roared like a wild thing, his tail switching, and then crouched still and faded into the scenery.

Clay could not see him at all. "Doto?" he called, suddenly frightened that the god had disappeared completely, that he had been swallowed up by the forest or simply run off in the ecstasy of his returned power and forgotten about his worshiper. He stumbled into the forest after Doto.

Instantly, the magic flowed through him as though he were a dry riverbed meeting a storm. Far more intense than any forest circle he had slept in over the past few moons, the forest assailed him with smells, vivid colors, sounds, a world of wonder blossoming around him. He felt his toes contract into a leopard's paw, the fur sprouting from his skin, power filling his limbs. He wanted to imitate Doto, drop to all fours and roar. And now he saw his god, lying still on the forest floor, invisible to all but Clay, bliss written across his face.

Clay felt a part of the world again; he could feel the pulse of its life. He had not realized how much he had missed it until now, and his fingers curled around the small, shaped wooden leopard that hung from the band around his neck. It was Doto's power that he felt, a fraction of the god's connection with the forest. He knew if he removed the fetish from about his neck, the trees and grasses, quickened with Kwaee's hatred, would kill him instantly. He could sense its hostility toward fire bearers, a tension in the air, like held breath and a taut bowstring. But with Doto's magic, he was safe.

He bounded toward Doto, momentarily taken aback by the power and grace in his limbs, but he landed easily and pounced atop the leopard. Doto coughed in surprise beneath him. "I did not think you would be so happy to be in the forest again," Doto commented, rolling over to paw at Clay's chest.

"It feels good," Clay admitted. He patted at the wooden cat around his neck. "This lets me feel a little of what you do. Doto, you can't think you're anything less than a god. It's wonderful."

"Is it?" Doto sounded pleased.

"What it's like out there for you, the way it feels outside the forest? That's what it's like for a fire bearer all the time."

"Then you should stay in the forest," Doto decided.

Clay smiled ruefully. "But you know I can't do that. If I lost your gift, or if the baboons found me again…"

Doto frowned and wriggled beneath Clay, his paws finding Clay's rump. "Do not talk of if. We will mate now."

"Doto," Clay began, but he trailed off as his god slid velvet fingers up his sides, pulled Clay down atop him, and kissed him again for the first time since they left Ogya-Bepow.

Clay's objections dissolved; the forest wanted him, and he had to answer it. He clutched at the fur on Doto's chest as his god slid into him. His own arousal jutted, nudging his leathers aside. His feline toes slid along the forest floor, and he felt them splay on their own, his claws catching at stray roots. Together they moved with the trees in the wind—or did the trees move with them? He couldn't tell. With Doto's mating, the plants around them grew and flowered, broad petals spreading, heavy yellow-dusted stamens dripping with nectar.

It was better in the forest. He had forgotten how easily he had risen to Doto's touch here beneath the canopy. The savanna was open, tough, and harsh. The barren and unforgiving plains made intimacy difficult, but here, in the embracing and nurturing forest, surrounded by life, it was as natural as breathing or eating.

But that was not all, he admitted to himself. It was the magic flowing through him; it was Doto responding beneath him; it was that a small part of him was part of the forest now. Doto was right. The savanna had been like a dream. He had been able to forget this part of him, but it *was* a part of him now, a part that would never go away. He belonged here now, and he accepted it as he accepted the movements of his god inside him. He tilted his head back and groaned his submission. He rode his leopard, and cried out as he fertilized the forest floor, as Doto planted seeds inside him, and the flowers around them burst in ecstasy, dusting them both with golden pollen.

He slumped across Doto's chest, and the god licked fondly at his cheek. He closed his eyes, and for the first time in moons, he felt truly happy. He felt safe.

But he was not safe, of course, and neither were his people. He rolled off of Doto and lay on his side next to him. "So what do we do now?" he asked. "Is it real?"

He expected the leopard to scowl and turn recalcitrant again, but Doto rolled onto one side and put an arm across Clay's waist. "It is real," he said with a serious expression. "You remind me why it is real. I will return to Kwaee. I will tell him what I have learned. I will ask him for the truth about my mother. He will no longer be able to hide from what he has done. If it was my father who first roused the fire bearers to burn the forest, as Sarmu claims, then he is making the same error again. He must be convinced."

Surprised at the calmness of Doto's answer, Clay searched the leopard's face for any hint of the distress that had troubled him on the journey back from Ogya-Bepow, but if it was there, he could not see it. "And me?" he asked.

Doto did not look away. "Until my father relents in his hatred of your people, the forest will not be safe for you. And you miss your home. You must return to your village. Tell them what happened long ago with Ogya, what they were not to forget. Tell them to pray to Kwaee." He puffed out his chest. "And me, of course. I would very much like to hear their prayers. Though they will certainly not be as good as yours."

Clay nodded. He was relieved that Doto wasn't going to resist his return home again, but now that his village was so close, he realized that he was going to miss Doto terribly. And the thought of Doto confronting Kwaee alone, without any support, was worrying. Clay had met the forest god once, but those short moments were among the most terrifying of his life. Kwaee had proved to be cruel, pitiless, and manipulative. And Doto, for all his power and his long life, seemed young and guileless by comparison, his passions easily sparked.

But the People of the Savanna needed Clay, and he needed them. And besides, Kwaee would certainly kill him if they met again. He brushed at Doto's chest. "How long do you think you'll be gone?"

"It is hard to say. For a thousand rains, Kwaee has kept his eyes shut to the world, and nothing could convince him to open them. He is stubborn." Doto looked up into the canopy, his ears lowering. "But he loved your people once, and I am proof of that. I will have to remind him. I will have to show him that he was not wrong. It may be a day, or it may be more."

"I'll miss you," Clay said.

"And I you, worshiper," Doto said. "But you will have my fetish to keep part of me with you. And I will return to you. Nothing will keep me away. Nothing."

Their journey through the forest was much swifter. With his leopard's paw, Clay was able to travel with a strength and speed he lacked in the savanna. Doto was tireless, of course, and brimming with elation at finding himself back in the forest again. As Clay ran along the forest floor, Doto scrambled up into the trees and followed above, effortlessly bounding from limb to limb. He fell once, misjudging the jump to another branch, and dropped to the forest floor on all fours, but he only shook his head in confusion, laughed, and scurried back up into the treetops again. Clay continued on at an easy pace, marveling both at his own stamina and at the sensory world of the forest that nearly overwhelmed him, the calls of birds that he could once again understand. At nights, they settled down together on the forest floor, or in the crook of a large tree. Here, there was no need for fire, and Clay was reluctant to light one anyway. Sarmu's story had given him nearly as great a fear of the fire god as Doto's. He did not care to have Ogya's malevolent eye watching him from the embers.

Six days after they had first reached the forest, Doto announced that he had spied the walls of Clay's village. They crept forward together, and once closer, Clay saw the wall too: the high barriers of felled trees and branches. He was surprised to see that the wall had been moved—or more precisely, rebuilt, as the remains of the old wall lay smashed within the forest boundary, great timbers lying across whole segments, the poles splintered by trunks or snapped in two by vines that were still bound around them. A few destroyed tents lay half-buried under leaves and brush, but Clay did not see his among them, nor his father's nor brothers'. The forest's turn against his people must have been a gradual enough thing that they had time to escape its wrath and pull homes out of reach of the destruction. He hoped no one had been caught or killed by it.

He and Doto picked their way through the overgrown paths leading to the village, watching for scouts or hunters. It would not be good, he decided, for them to catch sight of Doto too early. Clay would have a hard enough time explaining his healed foot without having to quell fears and worries over a leopard that walked as a man. The reactions of Jai and Ulo came all too readily to mind.

How small the village looked, and how strange, with its neat row of branches circling it. It didn't quite seem to belong there—an interruption in the savanna, something out of place and unnatural. Then he realized what it reminded him of: the forest circles he had danced for Doto. The village was like a larger forest circle, someone else's territory grown in the middle of this one, brown and dirty and unusual. And had his people not danced that new territory there? Was it not shaped from the pounding of their feet and the singing of their tales? It stank too, he realized. On the wind, he could smell the sour, animal scent of the fire bearers inside. He could smell their garbage rotting in the piles outside the village, and their feces, and the odor of their food scorched by flame. He wrinkled his nose at it.

"So now you are home," Doto said. He pointed. "Look. There, just inside the wall of the forest. That is where your little shelter was planted. I took your—your spear, and I threw it over there."

"My stone tooth," Clay said, smiling.

"That is not what it is called." Doto frowned, missing the fondness in Clay's tone. "Your spear. And then we went that way." He pointed to the south. "I was taking you to my father. And now I have brought you back. And I leave again for Kwaee, but without you." His tail curled over his toes. "You will always choose me," he reminded Clay. "That is what you said."

"That's what I said," Clay agreed. There was no way to explain now that that was not what he had meant. He couldn't take Doto's hope away from him now, not when Doto had the task of facing his father ahead of him. He would need all his focus and patience. It was no time for him to be distracted by worry over Clay's devotion to him. There would be time enough for that talk later, when things were settled.

Doto held Clay close, and Clay breathed in the scent of him: a wild, musky scent, full of earth and bark and rain, that filtered away the acrid smell of the village nearby. "I do not want to let go," the god whispered.

"I know," Clay said.

The leopard pushed his nose under Clay's chin. "One more dance?"

And so, at the edge of his village, Clay danced for Doto. And this time he danced not a circle, but a spiral, just inside the border of the forest. His song called the grass and trees, vines and bushes, to his own personal god. His toes lifted up from Kwaee's forest and set down in Doto's. Pink flowers and white mushrooms speckled the ground where he danced. This land would be safe for fire bearers to wander into. Kwaee's forest might be hostile toward Clay's people, but Doto's bore them no ill will. It would nurture them, too, for Doto grew great clusters of clayfruit there, and infused the trees and plants with his desire to protect Clay and all fire bearers against the malice of the forest beyond.

Doto stood in the center of their little copse and slid his arms around Clay, resting his heavy head on Clay's shoulder. His whiskers tickled Clay's neck. "Come here wearing my gift," he said, "and I will sense you. As long as I have this land, I will be able to see and hear you."

"I'll come every day," Clay promised. He nestled into Doto's arms and kissed his chin. Doto did not move away. He flicked his ears as though about to step back, tensed, and then relaxed again, still holding Clay. After a little while, Clay looked up. "Are you staying, then?" he asked with a smile.

"I do not know if I can let you go," Doto admitted. "It seems a harder thing than leaving the forest itself."

"But you have to," Clay reminded him. "If only for a while."

"Only for a while," Doto agreed reluctantly. He opened his arms. He stepped back, stared at Clay, and then turned and bounded off into the forest.

Clay sighed. He lifted his feline foot and brushed the pads of his wide toes against the delicate pink flowers of his god's forest. He took a deep breath, smelling wet bark, and mice, and the lingering scent of male leopard. Then he went home.

⁓

Beetle was waiting at the gate when Clay returned, and did not see him at first. Clay found that odd; a lookout was supposed to keep keen eyes and ears. Beetle should have noticed anyone approaching from much further away. But then, Clay came following the south wall bordering the forest. No one would expect a fire bearer to come from that direction, so near to the malevolent forest.

"Hello, Beetle," Clay said, smiling.

Beetle turned toward him. "Oh, hello—" His eyes widened. He took a staggering step backward, fumbling for the spear he'd leaned up against the wall. "You—you—" he stammered.

"Beetle, it's me, Clay. I'm alive! Look, I know that I—"

He didn't get a chance to finish. Beetle stared down at Clay's feet, his mouth pulled back from his teeth in a gape of dread.

Instinctively, Clay stepped back, hiding his leopard's paw behind his other foot. But of course, he had no leopard's paw. He was standing outside the forest now; and the stifling suppression of his senses was an ever-present reminder. For a moment, he could not understand what frightened Beetle.

"Your foot," the older hunter murmured. "A spirit!" Stumbling over his own spear shaft, he scrambled backward through the village entrance.

"Wait!" Clay called. "Beetle, wait, I can explain!" But the man was gone. Clay could hear him running through the village, shouting something unintelligible. Well, it couldn't be helped. Surely others would have calmer reactions. He walked through the gate.

Inside, he was met with stares from his fellow villagers, stares that quickly transformed from curiosity to alarm. People dropped calabashes, food, and tools and began backing away, retreating quickly into their tents.

"Wait," he called out again. "Everyone, it's me. I'm all right. I'm so happy to see all of you again." He reached out toward them as he walked through the village.

They didn't listen. Mothers called in alarm for their children, hustling them away into tents. Men dropped their work and backed away, groping with shaking hands for their knives or spears. This moment wasn't going as he'd expected. He'd thought to be welcomed with amazement, certainly, but with joy, not fear. He called them by name, but it seemed only to frighten them more.

From beyond the fire circle, a woman came running: tall, muscled, her hair in long braids, a spear in her hand. Ant With a Leaf. Clay tensed uneasily. She had never been friendly to him, even before he was a ghost. She halted when she saw him, her eyes going wide. "Clay?" she said in disbelief. She approached slowly, gazing up and down at him with wonder. "Is it truly you?" Her fingers tightened on her spear when she saw his undamaged foot.

"It's me," he said.

"Prove it."

He felt unbalanced a little by the question. He still remembered one of his last conversations with her, when she'd privately confessed that she had pursued him as a husband before turning her intentions toward Laughing Dog. She'd called him… "How could a foolish boy like me prove anything to you?" he asked with a rueful smile.

She relaxed, but only for a moment, before hurrying forward and grasping his shoulder. She leaned down to mutter in his ear, "You must come with me at once. No time to explain."

Without even giving him time to respond, she took him by the wrist and hurried him further into the village, moving around the council fire circle. Up the rise toward the finer tents in the village, people scurried about. Clay had assumed that Ant was hurrying him up to see his father, but instead, she pulled him left, past the fire circle, and then pushed him through the entrance to Cloud's tent, following in after him. He blinked in the smoky, dim shelter. The incense stung his eyes and nose.

"Clay." Cloud's wondering voice came from beyond the little fire. "Clay? How can this be? Did you just wander off from us, boy? Were you kidnapped?"

He peered through the gloom as his eyes adjusted, and the little woman shuffled up to him from around her fire. "I have so many stories to tell all of you," he said.

"No time for stories now," Cloud said, and then she gasped, looking down. "Your foot. Impossible! How can it be?"

"A god healed me," he told her. "I was dying from a blood fever, but a god restored me and grew back my toes."

She was quiet. "Gods don't do that," she said finally, her voice quiet and careful.

"They do in the stories!" he protested.

"But not anymore."

"I swear by all the gods that one of them healed me," Clay said.

Cloud narrowed her eyes and pressed her lips together. "You sons of First Claw, every one of you—" she began.

"Where is he?" a voice called from outside. "Who saw where he went?"

Cloud seemed to make up her mind. "Listen to me," she said. "We don't have a lot of time. I don't know where you've been or what happened to you, but things are bad here."

"I know," Clay said. "It's the forest, right? It's attacking people? I need to talk to my father right away."

He knew immediately from her stricken expression that something was wrong. She put a shaking hand on his arm. "Clay. Your father…" She looked as though she'd forgotten how to speak.

"He is with your ancestors," Ant With a Leaf said.

He blinked at her, not understanding. "What?" The ground slid around under his feet like mud during the high rains.

Cloud's grip tightened on his arm. "Something killed him. Something bad. Something with teeth. Nearly half a rain ago now. Whatever it was, we think that it killed Two Broken Hands too."

"That's—that can't be true. I saw him just—" Clay played back the journey in his head. How long had he been gone?

"I know it's hard, but we haven't time for that now. Listen to me. A man was brought here as prisoner about ten days ago. He had a ruined eye and an odd way of speaking. This man claimed he knew you, Clay. He told your brothers he saw you in the savanna, and that you were traveling with a demon called Doto. He said you and this demon attacked him and killed his friend. He said you used witchcraft."

Clay could barely hear anything she was saying. "My father's dead?" he asked. The words were stones in his mouth.

"Clay!" a voice shouted from outside. It sounded like Great Ram, and it was closer.

Cloud reached up and gripped the band around his neck and pulled him down. She bared her teeth, and in a hushed whisper said, "I know it's not right, boy, but you have to get past that for now. Your brother Laughing Dog came back from the savanna and he came back wrong. There is a demon in him. He has attacked us. We think he may have killed others. You understand me? There's something evil in him. I can only pray to Wem it's not in you, too. But you listen. They think this demon killed your father. If you give them any reason to believe that you have something to do with this, your brothers will execute you. They will kill you. Do you understand? Say yes if you understand."

"Yes," Clay said. His tongue and lips were heavy. He heard himself say it from far away. The tent spun. He stumbled to one side, and then Ant With a Leaf's strong arms caught him around his chest. She eased him down onto one of Cloud's hide beds.

The tent flap flew open, revealing Great Ram silhouetted in the bright light from outside. He stared down at Clay. "It cannot be," he breathed. "What is he doing in here? Why do you have my brother, Cloud?"

"Why do you think?" Cloud snapped. "Look at him. He's not well."

"Not well, maybe, but it's a damned sight better than dead!"

"Ram?" Clay blinked up at him. His brother wore their father's necklace of lion teeth and claws. Only the King was permitted to wear it. "Is it true? Is Father…dead?"

Cloud crouched next to him poured cool water over his forehead. "Don't alarm him," she instructed Great Ram. "We don't know what he's been through."

"We don't know what he is," Ram answered, his voice hard. He crouched down and took his knife from his belt.

"Ram!" Cloud cried.

He put his knife against Clay's chest. "You really want him here in the tent with you if he's a demon?"

"I'm not a demon!" Clay protested weakly.

Cloud furrowed her brow. She didn't look entirely comfortable at Ram's question. "He says the gods healed him."

"It's true," Clay said.

Ram glanced back at Clay's foot. He pressed down on the knife. "I would call your story foolishness, but no medicine could have healed that foot of yours. How did this happen? Which gods healed you?"

Clay nearly gave Doto's name before remembering Cloud's warning about the story they had been told. Thinking quickly, he answered, "I'm not sure." He hated lying to his brother. "The forest gods. One came and stole me from my tent in the middle of the night. He took me into the forest and healed my foot so that I could follow."

"This is a fantastic tale indeed," Great Ram said. "And one not easy to believe. Perhaps you're unaware that the forest has turned against us and kills any man who trespasses its borders."

"I know it," Clay said. He looked back and forth between Great Ram and Cloud. "And I know why the forest is attacking."

Great Ram sat back in surprise, lifting his knife. "That would be welcome news indeed, if it is true."

Breathing a little easier without a point pressed against his neck, Clay nodded and pushed himself up onto one elbow. "The forest gods told me that they believe we're allied with Ogya, who they hate, and that we've come here to burn the forest down. They said that we did it long ago. They even call us fire bearers. They sent the forest to attack all the humans in the hopes that it will drive us off."

"They will not succeed." Great Ram frowned. "But it would seem our prayers and offerings have been in vain."

"Not in vain!" Clay assured him. "Not all of the gods believe us to be allied with Ogya. One listened to me, and even now he may be pleading our case. He is trying to convince them that we would never burn the forest, and that we worship all the gods."

"If this is true, it's lucky I never listened to Laughing Dog and his perpetual wheedling," Great Ram said, as if to himself. "Damn Mirage and his willfulness." He looked back at Clay. "You say you don't know which gods they were? What did they look like? How did they speak to you?"

"A—a movement in the trees," Clay said. He knew the lie was making him stammer, but he couldn't help it. "Their voices came on the wind, but they were clear. I know it sounds like imagination, but—"

"But your foot is healed," Great Ram said. "Forest gods, you say. I thought Kwaee was the only god of the forest."

"But there are all the lesser gods, too," Cloud reminded him. "Osebo, Oforote, Batafo, Akoo, Adowa…"

"Were any of these gods you met?" Ram asked.

Clay shook his head. "I don't know," he said. "It's possible." It's possible he could have met them in the forest, he told himself. A god could make itself invisible. But no, it was a lie, it was just a lie. He had not been back enough time for the shadows to crawl across the ground and already he was lying to his brother, breaking his promises to Doto. But what choice did he have? Things had gone very wrong here. Everyone had changed into a darker, more dangerous shade of themselves. His father—he pushed the thought away before it could make him weep. "They kept me for some time before allowing me to return to all of you."

Sitting back, Great Ram regarded him for a moment, his gaze searching and thoughtful. "Come with me," he said finally.

"Ram, he is weak, and he's come home to terrible news." Cloud crouched again and gave Clay more water to drink.

"Can you stand?" Great Ram asked Clay. The firmness of his tone suggested that he expected Clay to do so.

"I think so, yes." Clay quickly drained the water and got to his feet. He still felt a little unsteady, but could stand.

"Then come." His knife still in his hand, Great Ram exited the tent.

Clay followed after, stepping into the sunlight and finding the tent surrounded by two large hunters, their dark skin streaked with light stripes of grey ash—Mother's Tree and Caterpillar, though he hardly recognized them. Beyond them, some of the people of the village had gathered and were watching curiously, though they gave Cloud's tent a considerably safe distance.

Great Ram ignored them, heading up the hill toward the tents of the wealthy. Clay followed close behind, and at his heels were the guards, their spears held at the ready, their eyes intent on him. At first, Clay thought Ram meant to lead him to his own tent, but at the top of the incline, Ram turned, heading for the wall—the very portion that Clay had spent so long repairing with Laughing Dog, back in another life. As they drew closer, Clay saw that there was a man held prisoner there, his arms bound in twine and leather cords that looped back behind posts Clay himself had set into the earth. He was painfully thin, his ribs jutting like fingers spreading from his chest. He sat slumped against the wall, his head hanging down.

When the group approached, he looked up, and Clay's heart began to pound. He saw once again the visage that had been etched into his memory: the bald head; the thin beard; the thin and cruel mouth; and the claw of scars that spread across a cheek, nose, and jaw, that darkened the crimson socket of one eye. Jai.

When the man saw Clay, his good eye bulged, his lower teeth jutting in dread. He shrieked like a bird, kicking with his heels in the dirt. He pushed himself to his feet and flung himself against his bonds with such tremendous wrenches to his shoulders, he looked about to twist them from their sockets.

Clay drew back in horror and fear and felt spear points in his back.

"You know this man?" Great Ram asked him. His voice was angry and dangerous.

"I wish I didn't," Clay said truthfully. "When I found my way out of the forest, this man and his companion waylaid me. They tied me, beat me, and tormented me."

"Lies!" Jai shrieked at the top of his lungs. "Lies he tells you! Let him near me nay! Let him dance nay!"

"Why would they do this?" Ram asked. "What did they want from you."

"Food," Clay answered. "They said their people were starving. I am certain if I had led them here, they would have raided our village."

"Listen to him nay, great King," Jai pleaded. "Know you his demon? It is terrible."

"And the demon he claims you had with you?" Ram asked.

Clay sighed, trying to find a balance between lie and truth. "Brother, he was mad when he captured me. His companion less so, I think. I can only tell you that there was no demon. One night I managed to tear free of the cords they'd tied me with. Unfortunately, I woke them when I did so. I ran as quickly as I could. You remember how fast I could run."

A smile returned to Ram's lips at that. "Yes, and you were none too humble about it either. How fortunate that the gods returned your foot."

Skepticism skulked in that last comment, but there was fondness too—a hopeful sign.

"So I ran back into the forest, hoping that the protection of the gods from its evil would still be on me. It was. I didn't count on the two of them running after me. I suppose they believed that since the forest wasn't attacking me, it must be safe. As you can see, it wasn't." He grimaced, remembering the vines that wrapped around Ulo's arms and legs, the man's screams as he was torn apart. "The forest killed his companion immediately. Seeing him die is probably what saved this man's life. He got away, though not before I saw roots crawling under his skin."

"Lies, all lies," moaned Jai. "The demon it was."

Clay shook his head. "I don't suppose seeing the forest kill a friend and then having it crush your own eye makes a man *less* mad. But look at those scars. Roots did that. You can tell by the shape of them. What kind of demon does that?"

Great Ram nodded. "Your story makes sense, I confess. More sense than his, certainly, with a leopard-demon and a dancing spell." He nodded to the guards behind Clay, and they stepped back. "Brother. I believe it truly must be you. Maybe my own joy deceives me, but I have longed to see you again. It is a miracle. We all thought you dead. Today I have twice the brothers I had yesterday." He opened his arms wide.

"Nay," Jai screamed hoarsely, flinging himself against his bonds. "You must trust him nay, great King! Murder us, that's what he intends! Murder us all, like as true!"

Clay stepped into his brother's embrace, squeezing tightly. He saw Jai's eyes widen, and then the man hung his head in despair, slumping in his bonds. Clay almost pitied him.

Ram straightened and held Clay at arm's length, a grin of happy disbelief on his face. "Well, my long-lost brother is returned. We must have a feast! There will be meat, once Laughing Dog returns with his hunters! Won't he be amazed to see you!"

"King Great Ram," Mother's Tree said loudly. He gestured with his spear toward the bottom of the incline. The largest man that Clay had ever seen was approaching with a hurried gait. Every part of him was round and fleshy, like in the stories of the greatest of kings. His wide belly swayed from side to side as he walked, and his thick thighs shook with every step. Even his round cheeks and wattled neck jiggled with his movements. But he did not appear weak or indolent; beneath the softness of his flesh and the rotundity of his girth was evident strength. His shoulders were broad and lobed, his chest and arms thick and powerful-looking, and his legs carried him with a power and agility that his stoutness belied. Like the guards, his skin was striped with light grey ash, from his forehead to his feet, though the markings were streaked and ran with sweat. When he glanced up and saw them, he quickened his pace.

"Ram," he said as he neared. "What is he doing here? Why have you let him in? He should be tied up immediately!" It was only when he spoke that Clay recognized him. This was Laughing Dog, this giant of a man?

"It's all right, Laughing Dog," Great Ram said, smiling widely. "I've talked to him. The man Jai is only raving. This is our brother."

"Brother?" Laughing Dog stared Clay up and down. "But he has a foot again! How do you explain that?"

"The gods healed me," Clay answered. "It is good to see you, Laughing Dog. I've missed you all so much." Now that the shock had passed, he easily recognized his brother's features in the wide, jowly face that glared back at him in suspicion. Cloud had claimed that there was something evil in Laughing Dog, but Clay couldn't see any strange presence within him. Anyway, hadn't they accused Clay himself of the same? What strangeness had the world come to, that people saw demons everywhere? There were none; he knew that now. There were only the beasts, the gods, and the fire bearers, and each of those had room enough for demons on their own.

"The gods healed you," Laughing Dog repeated, raising a questioning eyebrow.

"I believe he's telling the truth," Great Ram said, and he briefly recanted the story Clay had related before, conspicuously omitting, Clay noticed, the bits about Ogya and the burning of the forest.

As he spoke, the creases in Laughing Dog's face deepened from mere doubt into a frown. When Ram was done, he took a deep breath, and said, "If this story is indeed true, then I will rejoice to have my brother back. But Ram, we have no way of knowing for certain. These are dark times. We have had plague and beast attacks and famine. And now, the forest that has been opposed to us all this time, sends our brother back to us, many moons later, safe and unharmed—better even than unharmed: made whole again? Are we really to expect he won't murder us all in our sleep? It's a ploy so obvious as to be insulting!"

"Or so obvious as not to be a ploy at all," Ram said.

Clay listened in dismay. How could his own brother speak of him as though he were a monster? "Laughing Dog, I don't know why you would say this. I don't know what has happened to everyone while I've been gone, but please, I'm your brother. I would never hurt you."

Laughing Dog's eyes narrowed. In his widened face, they looked close-set and mean. "That's what you would say if you were a trick of the enemy. What evidence can you give us that your story is true? Do you have any proof at all?"

"No," Clay answered, his shoulders slumping. "I guess I don't."

A triumphant smile spread across his brother's face, and then Clay began to fear that Cloud's words were true. Someone who loved him as a brother would have wanted to believe. He would not have been pleased that there was no proof. Could it be that Laughing Dog didn't want Clay to have returned?

"Then, King Great Ram," Laughing Dog said, "I see no choice but to arrest this person until we can verify his claims. Whether he is Clay or some trick of the forest, we should learn it in time. Until then, it's not safe to let him wander around the village."

"Wait!" Clay said excitedly. "I can prove it. Or at least part of it. Come on, follow me!"

His brothers exchanged curious glances, but followed after him, along with the two ash-smeared guards. They asked where he was taking them, but he just told them to wait and see, leading them down through the village and out the gate, where a twitchy Beetle had resumed his post. None of the men enjoyed following him along the southern wall of the village, so close to the forest, but they stopped in amazement when he led them to the little area of the forest where he had danced for Doto.

"You see?" he said, spreading his arms before the field of flowers and fresh saplings and the large bushes whose branches bent nearly to the ground with the heavy clayfruit. "A sign from one of the forest gods. You have an ally in the forest."

"And we are supposed to trust you that this land is safe?" Laughing Dog demanded. "Perhaps you would like the King to take the first step into this supposedly protected little area the gods have created for us?"

"No, of course not," Clay said, stepping forward. "I—" He paused just before stepping into the forest, realizing that his foot would transform. They would see it. He couldn't refuse to enter now, or they would suspect him nearly as much as if he did. He looked back at his brothers, his heart pounding.

"Well, Clay?" Laughing Dog asked breezily. "Do you not trust your own gods?"

Clay struggled for an answer and could think of nothing.

But Great Ram came to his rescue. "Don't be silly, Dog. Clay already told us he had the protection of the forest gods. So if he enters safely, it proves nothing." He took a deep breath. "Well, I am King. That comes with responsibilities. I will enter."

"My King, no!" Alarmed, Laughing Dog reached for him, but Great Ram was already stepping forward into the forest. He set his bare feet among the pink flowers.

"It's so soft!" he exclaimed. "Like the new grass after a first rain." He walked several steps further. "Behold your King," he said, smiling. "The first person to enter the forest since the forest turned! Well, besides you, Clay," he added. "Perhaps the forest gods are not so opposed to us as we thought, eh, Laughing Dog? Perhaps our long-lost brother has brought us the key to the gods' favor."

Laughing Dog's face darkened. He marched up to Clay in heavy, powerful strides. "Listen to me," he growled, his features contorted in anger. He jabbed his finger at Clay's chest. "I don't know what you've done here, or how you managed this, but I—" He faltered, staring down. "What is *that?*"

Clay looked down and saw the wooden leopard lying against his chest. As if it were not too late to hide it, he reached up and closed his fingers around it. "Nothing," he squeaked. "Nothing. I made it when I was in the forest."

Laughing Dog's expression was that of a hunter who knew he had cornered his game. "Did you. A little leopard, is it, perhaps? Well. What a strange coincidence."

"Look at these!" Great Ram called over to them, crouching to pluck one of the clayfruit from the branches. "What are these? A gift from the gods?" He lifted one to his mouth as if to take a bite.

In alarm, Laughing Dog turned and bounded toward him. "Ram, no!" With a swift jab, he struck Ram's hand and sent the fruit flying into the bushes.

"Curse you, Laughing Dog, what in Wem's name was that for?" Great Ram scowled.

"Don't you see?" Laughing Dog said. "The forest has attacked us in three ways: by plant, by beast…"

"And by poison," Great Ram finished for him, his eyes widening.

"Yes."

Ram shuddered and wiped his hand on his robe.

"No!" Clay cried in frustration. "It's not poison. It's food. The gods knew you would be hungry, so sent you their finest food as a gift!"

"Of course they did." Laughing Dog spat into the grass. "Was that the trick?" he demanded of Clay. "Keep the forest calm to lull us into soft-mindedness and then feed the whole village poisoned fruit?"

"Well, we don't know that it's poisoned," Ram said in a reasonable tone.

"We don't know that it's not," Laughing Dog answered. "Suppose one of the children ventures into the grove and tries some? No, King, to protect us, these bushes must be destroyed. Burn them."

"No!" Clay shouted in horror. It was Doto's domain. Burning it would consign it to Ogya; their special grove would fall under the dominion of the fire god. "No, you can't!"

Great Ram glanced in Clay's direction. "You want to burn everything," he said to Laughing Dog. "No, I think simply rooting them up will be sufficient. Have the plants thrown back into the forest."

Clay shook his head in disbelief.

Laughing Dog scowled. "And him, King?" he asked, gesturing toward Clay. "We cannot trust him. You must know that. Look, even now he wears around his neck a symbol of the demon he summoned."

"Does he?" Great Ram came over and peered at Clay's fetish, frowning. "Oh, it's only a cat, Laughing Dog."

"It's a plainly a leopard!"

"I don't know how you can say that. It just looks like a cat to me. Could be any kind of cat. Lion, civet, cheetah."

"It's a leopard!" Laughing Dog shouted in fury. "Are you so stupid that you can't see that? He's brought the vengeance of the forest gods to you! A man came to you and warned you he was coming, that he'd killed another, and here he is, with his foot miraculously healed! Why would you trust him? Why would any of you? Arrest him! You must arrest him immediately!" He left off his raging to breathe, panting and looking wildly about him. His expression fell when he saw Great Ram frowning at him. Even the two ash-striped hunters looked at each other uneasily, their spears dipping.

"Stupid or not," Great Ram said stonily, "I am still your King. I think you may have forgotten that. Have you?"

Laughing Dog took a step backward and held his head low. "Of—of course, King Great Ram. I must have...the heat..." He fumbled for the water skin at his belt and drank from it thirstily, spilling water down his chest. "My humblest apologies."

Ram looked over at Clay. "There is no need to arrest him. I have the utmost confidence that this is indeed our brother returned to us. Clay, it overjoys me to have you back with us again. It grieves me that this was your welcome home. I promise you, we will give you a feast such as I daresay you have not tasted in many moons."

He looked about, squared his shoulders, and nodded to his guards. "See that a man stays with my brother at all times. He is not to leave the village again without my consent."

Clay gaped. "But...but..."

The King smiled at him. "For your own protection. It's good to have you home."

The Silence of the Trees

Kwaee was not in his temple. This was strange to Doto; seldom in the past several hundred rains had he entered his father's inner sanctum and not found him sprawled, brooding, in the great, gnarled moabi tree that served as his throne. Not only was the forest god not here, but the thrum and flow of energies throughout the forest told him nothing of Kwaee's whereabouts. All in the forest coursed to and from Kwaee and could be followed back to him, just as how, in the great pool that stagnated at the foot of Kwaee's moabi, Doto could follow the ripples on its surface back to the willow branch that dipped into it, or the fish that lipped at its surface. This was how he had found Sarmu in the savanna.

But now there were no ripples. It was as though his father did not exist, and this was worrying. He could only guess that Kwaee was guarding his power in some way, hiding himself from the entire forest, but why? Doto had no answers, and no apparent way to find his father, so he sat on the forest floor near his father's moabi and waited.

The forest was quieter than Doto remembered. It was not that it was still; the plants grew and wilted. Rain fell and washed leaves and earth to Asubonten. Predators preyed, prey fled, everything grew and mated and scratched and shuddered and died, but it was quiet. There was no one to ask questions. No one to make irritating and irrelevant observations, no one to put a hand on Doto's side, no one to grow food for, no one to watch over while he slept. Doto had felt real hunger in the savanna, but this was different. That hunger was only in his stomach. But this... He hungered for Clay with every joint and muscle, every breath, every strand of fur. Two days had passed since he had left Clay by the side of the fire bearer's village. Clay had promised to visit their little patch of forest every day, but he had not come, and Doto could not understand why.

He had sensed two fire bearers enter on that first day, not long after he had left Clay, but they had only shouted things about poison and left.

Then other men had come and destroyed all the clayfruit Doto had grown for them. That had been both puzzling and angering. Perhaps, out of all the fire bearers in the world, the only one of any value was Clay. Perhaps all the rest were like Jai and Ulo, too stupid and cruel to be of any worth.

Doto got up and paced around the algae-green pool. Why had Clay not come back into the forest? The more Doto considered it, the more anxious he grew. Clay had said he would tell his people to dance for Doto and praise him, but Doto had felt no prayers. Maybe it didn't work from far away, he considered. Or perhaps something else was wrong. Perhaps Ogya worked against them in some unexpected manner. Or, he thought with a sudden pang of fear, perhaps Clay had ventured into another part of the forest and been attacked by baboons, or worse. That thought sent the plants of Kwaee's temple writhing in sympathetic worry. Doto forced himself to calm. No. If something had happened to Clay, Doto would have felt it. The fire bearer carried a little of Doto within him, didn't he?

Another terrible thought: suppose Clay had simply chosen not to return? *I can't choose to abandon my people*, the fire bearer had said, *any more than you can choose to live outside the forest*. What if now, back with his family and his village, Clay had decided that he was happier there? What if he had decided he didn't want Doto anymore? Doto's breath tried to escape him; he bit at it, forcing himself to manage it. Fears clamored in his mind, too elusive for him to hold onto any one of them for more than an anxious moment or two.

Stop it. Calm yourself. Be the god, not the half-mortal in your blood, he told himself. Clay would be faithful. He had promised he would always choose Doto, hadn't he? But he hadn't looked happy about it either. If he was glad to choose his god, why had he looked so sad and confused afterward?

And it had been two days now. Doto sat again, clenching and unclenching his fists. He slowed his breath down. The sun measured its lazy flight across the sky. The wind swayed the branches of the trees, annoying the birds that sat there. All was well. Clay would not abandon him. Clay loved him. Clay would always choose him.

But maybe Clay needed to be reminded.

Doto got to his feet and was about to leave, when suddenly he felt Kwaee's presence in the forest. The ripples simply appeared, centering around the god's presence somewhere far to the northeast, as though he had never been missing. With great speed, Kwaee approached his temple; traveling that quickly, the forest would shudder at the swiftness of Kwaee's passing; even the air would warm with his movement through the forest. Doto waited, looking northeast.

Then Kwaee stood at the edge of his temple. He looked the same as ever: tall, powerful, a wide crown of feathers sprouting from his forehead, disdainful cold in his eyes.

"Great Kwaee," Doto greeted him, crouching down on all fours as his father stepped down the incline into the valley of his temple.

"So it's still 'Great Kwaee,' is it?" his father sneered. "Not 'Foolish Kwaee,' perhaps? Not 'Simple Kwaee?'"

Doto steeled himself for the argument, forcing his claws to stay sheathed as he stood. "No, Father."

"But you think you got away with it, didn't you? Your little ruse?" Kwaee strode past him and toward his throne. "I ordered you to kill that fire bearer, and you purposefully tried to deceive me. Where is it now? Did you take it back to its nest? Or did you grow bored with it and leave it on its own?"

The words were sharper somehow, crueler than before. It was Clay that Kwaee spoke of. Not some *thing*, not a beast. This was the person who had brought joy into Doto's life. And Doto now knew that Kwaee himself had tasted that joy. How dare he deny it of his own son? What justification for that sneer? The hypocrisy curdled in Doto's throat. "I don't think you have the right to ask. You never told me what you did with yours."

Kwaee looked puzzled.

"Your fire bearer."

"Speak sense, whelp."

"My mother," Doto said.

The great leopard gave Doto a searching gaze. Then his jaws parted, drawing in a startled breath, his pupils slitting. Doto had never, to his memory, seen his father taken aback before. The power and authority he had feared his whole life faltered. He could not have been more amazed if the moon had blushed.

Collecting himself, Kwaee scowled and looked away, his tail switching. "So," he growled, "you know. Who was it that told you? Fam? I warned her—"

"Sarmu," Doto said. "I went and found Sarmu. He told me."

His father looked startled again. "You left the forest? You went into the savanna? Impossible! You wouldn't have survived."

"I had help." Doto shook his head. "Why didn't you tell me?"

"Tell you what?"

"The truth about my mother! Who she was. What you—what you did to her."

"And what would I have confessed to you? That you were born out of weakness? That I killed your mother's father and mother and siblings and all her people? What good would it have done? Would it have made you listen to me more closely? Would you have heeded my lessons if you had known the truth?"

So he admitted it. It was one thing to hear it from Sarmu, but another from his father's own treacherous mouth. "What lessons? You never taught me anything."

"You forget yourself, boy. Who instructed you all these centuries? Who showed you how to be a god?"

"You only told me what you needed me to know. You never taught me about the worship of the fire bearers, about what they can do. You never taught me about how gods gain and lose power, or how to—how to not kill or hurt things for no reason. All you ever taught me was how to be cruel."

"It was what you most needed to know!" Kwaee snapped. He settled down into his throne, putting his head in his paws and rubbing at his temples. "You will never understand how hard I tried with you. How I worked and sacrificed to protect you."

"You abandoned me!" Doto bristled with anger and despair. He had never shouted at his father like this before, and he didn't know what to expect: whether Kwaee would punish him brutally or be surprised, but there was too much passion behind his words to hide. The passion was new to him, something that had been passed to him when he healed Clay, and now it was like a strong current inside him, carrying him down toward some terrible new sea of fury. "Sarmu told me. You left me alone as a newborn. What protection is that?"

Kwaee's brows lowered. "It is true. But can you fault me, after what you had just done?"

"What I had done? And what is that supposed to be?"

Kwaee hesitated. "But you said Sarmu told you. How you killed your mother."

The words hung in the air of a forest gone quiet. Doto could hear gnats humming over the surface of the pond, the whispered fizz of the algae breathing beneath the surface, the wind in the leaves above. "You said that a monster killed my mother," he said, his voice barely louder than the wind. "You said her own weakness killed her. You even told me the fire bearers did it."

Kwaee slumped back into his throne. "So he did not tell you that."

"Tell me what?" Doto asked numbly. "Tell me what?"

Kwaee sighed. He stared up into the treetops. "All I told you was true. It was your birth that killed your mother, boy. The fire bearers are weak. Their bodies are not meant to contain gods. You clawed your way out of her while she screamed, and I could not stop it. Her weakness, the weakness of all the fire bearers. You, the half-bearer within her."

"And the monster?" Doto heard himself ask. He was a long distance away now. His mind was going out, out, into tree and root and branch, into the twitching minds of insects and the patient hopes of frogs and the loud chatter of birds. He was sending himself out, anywhere but here, anywhere he did not have to hear this, but it was no use. His father was the whole forest, and the whole forest hummed with his damning words.

"The monster, me," Kwaee said. "Who put you inside her to tear her away from me. How I lament that act. How I wish, every day, that I had not given her to you, that you would never be born and destroy her. Such pain. I could not imagine such pain. I had known other fire bearers before. I had been fond of them. But she…" He reached up almost absently to stroke at the feathers sprouting from his forehead. "She danced for me. She stole a part of me. She showed me the world as I had not seen it. She made me love it through her. And then you killed her."

The fondness faded from his voice, leaving only a cruel edge. "It was all I could do not to destroy you where you lay, keening and helpless after your first murder." He spat the word. "I had not understood how terrible pain could be until that day. I hated the fire bearers for their weakness, for taking my love away from me. My forest felt it. It killed all the fire bearers. Every one. It turned them against me. You. She. Love turned them against me."

Then Kwaee sent his will into the forest and pushed Doto out, squeezing him out of the minds of birds and lizards, out of the silence of the trees. His power was a wall that Doto could not breach, and it shoved against Doto's being, pressing him smaller and smaller until there was no place left for Doto's mind but in his own, tiny leopard body, no place to run from the terrible words, no ears to hear them but his own.

"It was Mother Fam who found you and raised you. And it was she who brought you to me and convinced me to be a father to you. I tried." He shook his head. "Tried to keep you from your mother's weakness and my mistakes. Never feel compassion. Never show gentleness. That is how all love starts."

Dizziness washed over Doto. The ground rose up and struck him. He sprawled in the roots and grass. He was a half-god. He had killed his own mother. His father had always hated him. The words were heavier than they had been from Sarmu. They pounded him into the floor of his father's temple.

Kwaee stared down at him dispassionately. "But, of course, the lessons could do no good. Not against *them*. You were too much like her. Too much like me. How I hoped you would not be. What a disappointment you turned out to be."

"You were supposed to love me," Doto said, and for a moment, he didn't know where the words came from. But they were Clay's words. The gods were intended to care for all creatures, protect them, love them. But they did not. And now Doto understood that he was just another fire bearer like Clay, abandoned by his own god for unfathomable reasons, alone in a cruel world.

"Love you?" Kwaee exclaimed in surprise. "And then what? Feel that pain again? How foolish do you think me, boy? Would I risk that agony a second time? The last time I felt it, without even meaning it, I killed *thousands*. In one moment, I turned an entire species against me, sent them running to our enemy, Ogya. They burned my domain, and I was greatly diminished before I confounded them. What reason could there be to chance that again?" He peered at Doto. "You do not understand that either, do you, son? I warned you of the fire bearers. I warned you of their magic."

"What magic?" Doto asked. He didn't even truly care to hear the answer.

Kwaee spread his paws. "You must understand that I did nothing. I didn't bring their curse down on me. All I did was watch and listen. I spent time with them. They danced for me and praised me. They cursed me with love. I didn't accept it willingly; it seized me."

Doto's fur prickled. He had loathed Clay at first, had he not? He had been insistent on driving him toward Kwaee. He hadn't given a thought toward Clay's feelings, nor cared about his irritating nattering. When had it changed? What had happened? He searched his memory, but could think of no reason why he should ever have felt differently. And yet now, two days without Clay was a torment, a deep longing that he could not quell. Had it happened when Clay had danced for him, when his feather had grown? Before? He didn't know.

Understanding shone in his father's eyes. "You have felt it too," he said. "I feared it when you brought him to me, and I saw the plumage on your brow."

"But it's not bad," Doto protested. "It makes me better! It makes me happy!"

"That's how it starts, yes," Kwaee said sympathetically. "I remember, son. I remember so well. And you must not blame yourself. You did nothing to cause it. It is their magic working on you, as it worked on me. Why do you think I keep my eyes shut? Do you think I have turned away from the care of my forest all these years out idleness or apathy? I do not choose not to open my eyes to my domain. I *dare* not. Suppose I came across the fire bearers once more? Suppose they entranced me again? Suppose that once again, their magic made me love one. What would I do when it died? Suffer that pain, kill them again, start another war, this time one that the fire bearers might never forget? No."

The passion had gone from Doto's senses, heightened to some intensity he could no longer feel nor understand. He pushed himself to his feet. "That is why you never look past your temple?"

"I cannot risk it," Kwaee said.

"But then why send me to bring back a fire bearer in the first place, if they are so dangerous?"

Kwaee sighed. "Another mistake. Does it surprise you to learn that even gods can make them? So we can. But I needed to know their plans. And I needed to know if I…if I were still weak to their charms. I needed to know you shared that weakness."

His slitted eyes drifted up to focus on Doto's feather. "Plainly you did. So much so that you defied me and would not kill it. Already it had you in its thrall.

"You saw what happened once that creature stood within my temple. Even I could not kill the thing. I held it in my own claws, and felt…pity." His voice twisted in disgust. "But you forget how easily they betrayed us. How quickly they turned to Ogya." His eyes widened in a crazed anger. "They burned my body. A thousand thousand paces in every direction they burned. They are betrayers. They promise worship, and they take it away."

I will stop loving you, Clay had said. Doto remembered the fear at the threat. Promise not to hurt another fire bearer, or lose Clay's affection.

Kwaee shook his head. "When you brought that fire bearer to me, with that feather on your brow, I knew. I saw myself in you. I thought if I told you of their deceptions, told you how treacherous they were, told you that your mother died because of them, it might be enough. You feared me, once. I thought you feared me then. But not enough to kill your prize."

"I love him," Doto agreed miserably. "I can't help it. I could never hurt him. Even the thought of him being harmed frightens me."

"You see?" Kwaee said. "Already it is almost too late. I wanted to spare you. You cannot know the pain you will feel when it dies. It is terrible, far

more terrible than a father pulling out a feather. And when it happens, son, when that pain seizes you—and it will—what will you do?"

"I…" Doto began, but faltered. He thought of the bushes filled with poison berries growing in his temple, bushes that grew fuller and deadlier every time his heart filled with fear of losing Clay. He thought of the fire bearer Ulo, his blood and entrails spilled in an instant across the little forest circle in the savanna. He thought of Jai, the roots burrowing under his face, crushing his eye, and the thrill, the surge of dark joy Doto had felt at causing him pain, a righteous vengeance for the sin of hurting his dear Clay.

Kwaee gave a knowing nod. "You have seen it already, haven't you? Your mother may have been a fire bearer, but you are your father's son after all. There is great power inside you. If you open yourself to that pain, you will kill. It is a part of you. And your fire bearer *will* die, as all fire bearers must. It is in their natures. What will you do? Will you take apart their nest? Will you kill your love's parents or friends? Will you drive them back to Ogya? You cannot know."

Kwaee was right. There was no way to know what Doto would do. Kwaee had always been right. The fire bearers might no longer be the minions of Ogya, but they were dangerous all the same. Even now, Doto longed for Clay, longed for him with every cell of his being. What would he do when that longing was beyond answer? What happened when the power of a god was directed by the agony of loss? He looked up at his father. "It's not they that are dangerous," he said. "It's us."

His father looked surprised. "Perhaps. But we are not to blame. They are the ones that do this to us, son. Never forget that."

Doto looked down at his toes. "What can I do? I love him."

Kwaee smiled, and it was the first time since Doto was a cub that he could remember his father smiling without cruelty or malice. "Look away from it, Doto. It cannot find you here, in the forest. I have ensured that our world will stop the fire bearers from entering. Forget about them. Shut your eyes, as I have. It is not too late. You cannot feel its death if you never see it. Stay here with me."

He lifted a paw, and to his right, a moabi sapling sprouted from the soil, rising and twisting. It rose, forming gnarled bark and spreading branches that twined around his own moabi. Higher and higher it reached, the ground trembling and shifting beneath it, its limbs grasping up toward the sunlight far beyond the canopy. It rolled and contorted as it grew, its roots spreading out, dipping into the pond below, burrowing into the earth. At its face, the bark and branches coiled and shaped, forming a seat.

It was a throne, Doto realized, like his father's—not so magnificent and huge, but a throne nonetheless, perfectly sized and contoured for him.

"Sit at my side," Kwaee said, beckoning to Doto. "Rule the forest with me. You have discovered the secrets I hoped to spare you from, but they need not hurt you. Sit with me, and in time, your passion will fade. In time, you will forget that your fire bearer ever existed."

Doto stared at his father in amazement. At one time, this was all he would ever have dared hope for: his father's acceptance, a seat at his side, a share of the power of the forest. Now it was within his grasp, but it would cost him Clay.

But Clay was among his own people now, and had failed in his promise to bring them to Doto. Clay would grow old one day, or be injured, and would die, and that death would surely send Doto into the madness that had seized Kwaee. And then…and then the darkness would take hold of him. Doto had the power of the forest behind him. In anguish over the loss of Clay, he would break his promise. He would kill fire bearers. His father was right. Of course he was. How could a simple animal like a fire bearer know more of the world than an all-powerful, ageless god? How could Doto have let himself be so deceived? How could he have trusted a mortal over his own father?

He could taste the promised agony already. It ached within him. It burned and tore. It seized at something deep within his chest, tugged, and would not relent. In the moment he had healed Clay he had taken something from the fire bearer and made it part of himself. And he had felt new things, seen the world in new ways. He had hungered and yearned and rejoiced as never before. Now, he felt it begin to wither and shrivel inside him as he climbed the moabi in front of him. His paws felt as heavy as stones as he seated himself in the throne at his father's side.

No Place Like Home

For moons, Clay had been yearning for home. In a life of uncertainty, of moving from place to place, following the rains south across the savanna, home had never been a location, but comfort. Comfort was people working and resting, dancing and eating and telling stories. People feasted when there was plenty and gave each other what they could when there was little. There was worry, at times, when droughts came and they all had to pack up and leave for some new place, but they told each other their stories to ease the worry, reminding themselves that all old places were once new, and that their ancestors had braved these places and had survived and had had many children. The people united in those concerns and reassurances just as they united in joys and sorrows, hope and prayer. That was comfort.

Comfort was the people Clay loved at his side: his father and brothers, aunts and uncles and friends.

He crouched low in the grass and listened to the wind beating the tassels together, the buzz of insect wings. The grey ash that Laughing Dog's fire hunters had rubbed into Clay's skin itched persistently. He put up his head to peek over the grass at the man lying a few paces away: the hunter Burning Star, whose own heavily muscled frame was smeared with stripes that made him blend him into the ground, easy to miss in the shadows of grass and trees. With his head lifted, Clay could hear a faint chatter of voices carried by the breeze, and the high note of a flute, the striking of stone against stone. The village was far off, but, he reassured himself, not entirely out of earshot. He could return any time he wished.

But the village was not home. The people who lived in this otherwise familiar place looked tense and frightened; they laughed less frequently and squabbled more. The village itself, within its hewn walls, felt smaller, dirtier, more crowded, more hostile. Few had spoken to Clay since he arrived, and if any approached him, they did so with apprehensive faces, casting frequent glances toward his left foot. Whenever he explained to them that a god had healed him, they responded with wonder and reverence, and sometimes fear.

He was the same as he had ever been—surely he was the same—but to the people he had once known, he was different: an outsider, a curiosity. Even Cloud and Ant With a Leaf gave him a wary regard.

Could his time with Doto have altered him so greatly? But no, it was not he who had changed. For proof of that, he had only to watch the grave-faced, ash-striped hunters who stalked about the village as though they were its only occupants, speaking only to each other. Or further evidence: the officious drunkard that his brother had turned into. That was an even surer reminder of how lost Clay was. He had returned to find his father no longer King, no longer even alive. First Claw had been sent up to Father Wem, and nothing would ever bring him back.

Accepting the truth of his father's death felt impossible. Clay wanted to grieve properly, as a son should, but could not. He had seen no body, no funeral. He had been away for no more than a season and returned to a place that was not his home. Why should his father be here? This village was a dim shadow of the one Clay had left. It was wracked by plague and animal attacks and angry gods. It was something to wake up from. Why would he hope to find his father in this awful place?

He remembered the last time he had seen his father: Clay had been suspended high in a tree, bound to a branch by vines, Doto's strong body pressed against his own, shielding him from his people's searching eyes. His father had seemed so old then, so alone and desperate. His voice had aged. It quavered as he prayed to the gods for his son's return. *Restore what is lost, keepers of the earth. Restore what is lost.*

The gods had, at last, returned Clay, but not before they had taken his father. It seemed a bitter joke.

"There," muttered Burning Star, his deep voice carrying along the ground below the grass. "Lift up your head, Prince Clay, if you want to see how it's done."

Prince Clay. That was different too. Nobody had ever addressed him or any of his brothers as prince before. They had all been sons of the King, but they were just people, and everyone had treated them as such. Now he might have thought his name was Prince Clay, as often as he was called by it. He didn't like it. It was uncomfortable. It kept him on the outside. He rose to a crouch, looking across the plains to the northwest, where his brother had ventured.

There, beyond a small herd of grazing antelope, stood the final proof that Clay had not come home. The man who called himself Laughing

Dog—no, *Prince* Laughing Dog—stood tall and broad, his body grown so massive with muscle and fat that he was almost round. He too was streaked with ash, his sun-dark skin hidden behind light grey patches and whorls, so that he almost did not seem a fire bearer at all, but some strange beast of the savanna. Up close, Clay had to search his features for hints of the brother he had once known, and those were scarce, not only because of the new breadth and fleshiness of his face. Laughing Dog had always been arrogant and callous, but there was something else behind his eyes now, something ugly and twisted. His lids were continually narrowed in suspicion, his mouth caught in a perpetual sneer. He jerked his head from side to side occasionally, as though hearing someone over his shoulder. Clay recognized little about him anymore. And then, for Laughing Dog to have launched such suspicion and accusations against him, to have howled for his arrest, to have shouted at him with such cruelty and hatred…how could *that* be his brother? And if that was not his brother, and his father was not here, and everything was different, how could he be home?

He dug his toes into the dry earth and hoped for the familiarity of the hunt to bring him back home again.

Laughing Dog lifted his arms above his head. The antelope turned their long necks toward him with mild concern. They flicked their tails, their alert ears cupped toward him.

What could Clay's brother possibly be planning? At the first sign of movement, the antelope would spring away at high speed. There would be little hope of slaying any of them before they were out of range. Clay had not wanted to venture out with the hunters this morning, feeling anxious about leaving the village again. Although his old home felt foreign and tense to him, some secret part within him feared that departing again so soon would be tempting fate; that he would never find his way back again.

Laughing Dog had not wanted to bring him either, and had done so only at Great Ram's order, after complaining that he couldn't spare one of his fire hunters to stand watch over Clay. "Very well then," Ram had slurred through his wine stupor, "you can just take him along with." And at Laughing Dog's further protest, Great Ram had pointed out that Clay was one of their best runners, and there was no reason why he ought not to be a fire hunter too.

So, scowling, Laughing Dog had made Clay smudge sooty stripes across his skin. He had brought Clay out into the savanna with the other hunters, positioned him in the grass, and told him, with a smirk, to keep his eyes keen if he wanted to see real power.

Now he held his thick arms up above his head. His lips moved, but Clay couldn't hear the words. Then Laughing Dog swept his hands downward, and orange light rained from them. No. Not light. Fire. It was fire like the liquid fire that had poured from the summit of Ogya-Bepow, and it sprayed outward in wide arcs, spattering into the grass. Wherever it lit, the grass ignited and went up in a bright blaze. The wind rustled the flames and blew them higher.

The antelope started in alarm, bounding a few uncertain steps away from the spreading fire. At first Clay had thought the sudden fire might be a trick, as Tellers sometimes used to make a tale more dramatic—but he had never seen flames like these: they were stretching higher, blending into a lattice, like the woven leaf-wall used when hunting eland herds. This wall of fire reached higher and higher, moving to encircle the antelope. Twice the height of a man the flames rose. The antelope scattered and bolted in all

directions, some bounding toward the flames, but most scrambling for the broken edge of the circle, where the converging walls of fire had not yet met.

All around the circle, the fire hunters rose from the grass. Like hunting lions creeping on their bellies, they had slunk up upon their prey, and now they sprang upright outside the walls of fire, spears and bows at the ready. Clay, too, stood. He thought to run closer and assist in the hunt, but when the antelope stampeded toward the opening in the flames, he stopped. In his memory, he stood before a thundering herd of eland, the blinding sun in their eyes, racing toward him. He felt caught in that moment. And now the antelope were bearing down on him. His toes curled in frightened anticipation.

But the flames met, the circle closed, and the antelope were cut off. They bleated in terror, wheeling and racing from flame to flame. If they darted near any of the hunters, they risked the lance of a spear or the bite of an arrow. They were trapped. One antelope caught spears in both withers and belly and went down. Another leapt along the edge of the flame and took an arrow through the throat; it collapsed to the grass in a limp pile. Burning Star pulled back one powerful arm and hurled his own spear, catching a third antelope just behind one foreleg. The shaft sunk in deep. It was a heart strike, and the creature was dead before it fell.

The remaining two, in panic, charged the flames and leapt through. Though the walls of fire were thick and painfully hot even from this distance, Clay expected the two would survive it and escape; many times in dances, hunters would leap through a small council fire to prove their bravery, and none to his memory had ever been injured doing so, even when they made a game of piling on fuel to intensify the blaze before leaping. But this fire clung like burning oil; when the antelope landed outside the walls of flame, both carried orange tongues along their backs and flanks. The smoke rising from their burning pelts was thick and black. They screamed high, shrill shrieks of pain and terror, chaotically bounding from side to side, but the fire on their backs only spread until they were engulfed. They screamed again and again. First one, then the other, fell to the ground, lying on their sides. Their legs kicked a few times and then they were still. Their bodies burned in greedy red flames, and thick, greasy clouds of black smoke billowed up into the sky. Clay stared at them in revulsion, his stomach knotting.

"Tonight," Laughing Dog's voice rose above the roar of flame, "we feast on antelope!"

All around the flames, the fire hunters cheered, raising their bows and spears above their heads and clattering them together.

Clay tore his eyes away from the burning carcasses to see his brother striding toward him, gait confident and powerful.

"Well, big brother," Laughing Dog said when he was close, "What do you think of that?"

"How did you do that?" Clay asked, trying to hide his amazement. "Fire came from your hands like magic."

"It is magic." Laughing Dog put one of those hands on Clay's shoulder. It was heavy, gritty with ash, and stunk of burning stone, the same smell of the fire river on Ogya-Bepow. He smiled. "I have the power of a god inside me, Clay. I told you we could best them. I've taken his power for my own, and I'm using it to save our people from starvation. Just as I promised I would do long ago. Remember?" For a moment, he sounded almost like the boy Clay had once known: eager, hopeful, and full of surety.

"Laughing Dog," Clay said in a low voice, looking about to make sure no one else was close enough to hear. "This fire… This is the power of Ogya. You can't control him. You must know that. I've learned things about him since I—since I left. Ogya betrayed our people long ago, and he'll do it again. He's using you."

His brother's eyes narrowed in anger. "Using me? Clay, your time away hasn't changed you at all. You still think I'm weak. Foolish. Things have to be done your way or they're wrong. But I'm the one in control now. I'm the one with the power. Ogya' s power is used only for what I want!"

"What about those?" Clay asked, pointing to the fallen bodies of the antelope, already little more than charred husks licked by low, blue flame. "I've never known you to be wasteful. Did you mean to catch them on fire like that?"

Uncertainly passed over Laughing Dog's face, but it quickly vanished. He shrugged. "I control the direction of the fire. I can't control the antelope. The power is still mine." He turned to walk away.

Clay grabbed at his arm. "Please, brother, listen to me. This power isn't really yours. It's dangerous. The gods themselves have told me this."

Laughing Dog looked back, his face back in that nasty smile. He reached out suddenly, making Clay flinch, but he only tapped Clay's wooden leopard with one finger. "Oh yes, I know all about the gods you've been talking to, Clay. You see, my god talks to me, too. He tells me things. And he's been watching you, out of every flame you've lit to cook your meals, out of a river of fire, out of a lake of it. He's seen you. I know who you've been making friends with. Get rid of them, brother. Swear them off. Never pray to them again. Or I promise you, they will get you killed."

With that he walked off, his round, ashen shoulders swaying in a confident swagger as his fire hunters followed behind, dragging their kills.

Clay stared after him in disbelief. No, he was not home. Home was gone.

⁓

The inside of Clay's tent felt small and lonely. For two nights, suspicions around the village had kept him from returning to his own, situated as it was just near the King's, so he had been made to sleep outside, under the watch of the guard. But then Great Ram, in a drunkenly jovial moment, had announced that Clay posed no great threat and ought to be allowed back into his own tent.

But even though Clay now had permission, he didn't feel inclined to sleep there. It had been a long time now since he had slept beneath a roof of stretched hide, branch, and bone. He was used to the moving air, the calls of birds. He was used to being rained on while he slept. It would be strange to sleep under this stuffy, dead construction, hidden away from the open sky and the watch of the stars. He sat near one wall, the one from which his hunting trophies, sad glimpses into his past, still hung. He put his chin in his hands and tried to remember where he was. Who he was.

"Hello hello," called Cloud from outside his door. He relaxed a little on hearing her voice. She, at least, seemed the same as always. A little older perhaps. A little wearier.

"Yes," he called back, "please come in."

It was not Cloud who stepped through the opening, however, but Left Rabbit, with a heavy stack of pelts—antelope, eland, and even zebra—draped over one sturdy shoulder. "Hello, Clay. *Prince* Clay," he amended, looking bashful. "Where should I put these?"

"Left Rabbit, it's good to see you. Over there is fine." Clay pointed to the far wall, where he used to sleep.

Left Rabbit nodded and set the pelts down, spreading them out. The troubles of the village seemed to have left him mostly unscarred, his smile still open and unassuming. He looked as strong and smooth-skinned as Clay remembered, and reminded Clay of lying awake at night, imagining Left Rabbit's touch, yearning for it, his skin burning with the need for it. Back then, he had dismissed intimacy with another male as a forbidden impossibility, something not even to be dreamt of. Now, such thoughts only sent his mind to Doto, who broke all rules and spoke new commandments. The thought of lying with Left Rabbit now seemed almost conventional, even dull. Who could find interest in mortals after mating with a god?

Cloud interrupted his thoughts as she stepped into the tent, barely having to duck her head beneath the opening. "Yes, thank you, Left Rabbit. That's fine. You can go now."

She waved him out, and once he was gone, seated herself on the pile of pelts, letting out a long, comfortable sigh. "There now. I thought you might not have anything to sleep on, so I brought these over. They were in the sick tent before, but with the plague passed, there's no need for them." Catching Clay's concerned expression, she added, "There's no need to worry. They're clean enough."

She looked around. "Such an empty tent. It must not feel much like home."

"No," Clay admitted. "My spear and knives are gone. My other clothes, my bracelets and beads. Everything. Even the tent's not in the same place as before. I was told they dragged it over here after the forest attacked. I'm glad they had time."

"It didn't attack all at once," Cloud said. "But it wasn't slow, either. Frightening. It happened about midday. First it was little things. Thorny vines that seemed to grab at our legs. Grass that cut our skin. Then the trees started moving, stiff, like old men, bending branches toward us. It was when the roots unearthed and tried to swallow up your brother Ram's leg that we realized something had gone wrong. We saved what we could, but by the time we had gotten most of the tents moved, there were tree limbs smashing apart the fences and grabbing at any who ventured too near."

"It must have been terrifying."

"It was. Worse for Mighty Ant, Six Star, Bramble, and Flint. They were hunting in the forest. We never saw them again."

Clay remembered Kwaee's wrath, the trees that had picked him up, tried to tear him apart, and for the first time, he felt not awed or frightened by the forest god, but angry. Kwaee had killed his friends, and for no reason other than that they reminded him of a long-ago people he still hated. It didn't matter whether he was a god or not. It was wicked. Their bodies were probably still there in the forest, half-buried or swallowed by trees, like the skeletons of the poor people in Abansin.

"And then poor little Whistling Thorn and Red Moth in the plague," Cloud said. "But enough of sad times. I knew your tent would be empty, and so I brought hides. You'll need something to sleep on, after all. I'll make sure someone brings by some spare leathers and things to wear. A spear and knife. And something to make a fire."

"No!" The sharpness of his tone surprised him. "I mean, no thank you. No fire."

Cloud leaned forward, blinking, and Clay found himself wanting to turn away from her gaze, as though she could see the truth stalking behind all the lies he'd told. "What happened to you out there?" she asked him gently. "You are not the meek, quiet boy who left us. Nor the one who threw a tantrum and broke his crutch against a tree, wailing that the gods had no plans for him."

"I'm still the same." Clay became aware he was sitting on a rather hard bump and shifted uncomfortably.

"No. You aren't. There's something different about you. The way you look at all of us. It's like you've never seen us before. Like you don't know us."

"I *don't* know you!" Clay exclaimed. He looked toward the door where his guard was surely standing nearby and lowered his voice. "I know *you*, Cloud, and I've missed you. But everything else here is different. Everyone's frightened. I know things have been hard lately, but things have been hard before, and people didn't behave like this. Now everyone's all close-mouthed and frightened. The whole village is more crowded. It's dirty. It smells bad. I don't mean to offend. But it's not the home I left."

"It's true, things aren't the same." Cloud worked her dress between her fingers. "But you forget that I've known you your whole life, Clay. I know you better than you do. And you're different. You told us you've been in the forest, that you'd spoken to gods. They healed your foot. No one goes through that without being changed. There would be no point to it if it *didn't* change you."

"I feel the same," Clay said.

"Do you?" Cloud asked the question lightly, but she watched him with close attention. He thought of how uncomfortable his tent felt. How he missed the wildness of the forest and the vibrancy of its smells and colors. How he missed Doto's arms. He didn't answer.

Cloud's jawline hardened beneath her wrinkled cheeks. "You must know why I'm asking. Your brother, too, went out into the wilderness. He came back different, saying that he spoke to the gods. But he came back wrong. There is something terrible in that boy. You must see it."

"I do," Clay answered. He shuddered, thinking of Laughing Dog's threat, his nasty smile, the god-fire that had poured from his hands. "But I'm not—whatever happened to him I can't imagine. My experience was different."

"Then tell me." Cloud pressed. "Something happened to you out there. You can't just keep it inside you, Clay." She frowned. "And if you won't tell anyone, then that gives us all the more reason to worry."

He looked into her eyes, full of kindness and concern. She was right. Doto was not a secret he could keep. And Cloud had always been the wisest and most faithful friend of his father. If there were anyone here he could still trust, he could trust her. "Many of the things that I say will be surprising," he warned her.

"I'm old," she said. "I like surprises."

And so he told her everything that had happened to him since the night Doto had appeared outside his tent and declared him a captive. She listened with growing interest, expressing amazement when he told her about the giant crocodile goddess of the river, horror when he described the unnatural scene at the lost city Abansin, and dismay when he told her of their meeting with Kwaee.

But when his tale reached Doto's temple and the events that had taken place there, he faltered. How could he tell her of the bond he had formed with the forest god, of the things that they had done together? The acts they had committed, though sanctioned by at least one god, were forbidden by the people. Cloud would not understand—none of his people would. So he explained only that he had rested and recuperated there before leaving for the savanna.

When he told her about entering the savanna, and the effect this had on Doto's power, Cloud interrupted. "You say that this Lord Doto did not know or care for our people. Why would he accompany you to the savanna, where he was weak? Why did he follow you at all?"

Clay had expected the question, but the lie didn't come easily to him. "He—he wanted to know the secrets Lord Kwaee wasn't telling him. He was interested in what had happened with our people in the war between Ogya and Kwaee."

"But why bring you along at all? You said that you were his captive, but then he protected you and healed you?"

Clay's face went hot. "I...interested him, I guess." He looked away from her searching gaze, then looked back only to see her eyes narrow.

She studied him for a moment, then raised her eyebrows in surprise. She settled back onto the pelts, pulling her ankles close. "You interested him, you say. And this god of the forest, did he interest you?"

The heat in his face spread to his ears.

She smiled. "In some of the stories—Little Mouse and Bosome— the gods inspire great passions in their creations. We are like grass in the wind before them."

Bosome, the goddess of the moon, who had entranced the sculptor Little Mouse and carried him away into the sky to nestle him within her crescent. Clay tried to keep from stammering, but his tongue betrayed him. "Were—were Doto female, I might—"

"Oh, nonsense, boy. Do you take me for a fool? You've never shown interest in the girls around the village, even when your brothers were panting after them like jackals. Do you think I never saw where your eyes strayed?"

His stomach lurched. "You knew? But why not report me? Have me cast out?"

"It wasn't like you're the first boy whose eyes wandered to unexpected places," she said, smiling. "I've seen more than sixty rains, and there have always been boys like you. Some grew out of it. Some grew into it. And as for the gods, let's just say that in some of the stories we don't tell the children, they are less than discriminating."

He stared at her, shaking his head. "I can't believe you knew all this time."

"I suspected," she answered. "Not the same as knowing. So. You and this god interested each other, you say. Please continue your tale."

He tried to tell the rest, but her comments had flustered him, and he stammered out the rest unevenly, mixing up events and correcting himself as he related the truth of the encounter with Jai and Ulo, the encounter with Sarmu in the fire mountain, and finally his excursion with the fire hunters earlier in the day.

She shook her head when he was finished. "It's an incredible story, Clay."

"I know," he admitted.

"Can you prove any of it?" she asked.

He shrugged. "My foot grew back. Isn't that proof enough?"

Pursing her lips, she answered, "I suppose it is. I can see why you didn't want to tell anyone else about this. I think that's wise, for now, especially since no one feels very kindly toward forest gods right now. And Laughing Dog would no doubt use it against you. He's gotten very good at that."

"Or Ogya has," Clay said grimly.

She sighed. "Yes. That is a worrying thought. Worse than a demon. What are we to do, hated by one god and manipulated by another? And if he persuades the King to turn our fires against the forest… None of us would survive a war between gods. Whatever we do, we must not let that happen."

"But what actions could we take?"

Cloud opened her mouth as if to speak and then looked down at her dress, rubbing it gently between her fingers. Her next words she spoke very low and quiet. "Great Ram is a drunkard and a fool. He doesn't know how to make decisions and in one irrational moment might side with your brother. He has already ordered Ant With a Leaf to marry Laughing Dog against her will. He is dangerous and not fit to lead the people. He cannot be King. Clay, you must do it."

He blinked at her bluntness. "What? No, Cloud, I can't do that. Take the rule from my brother? I would be wronging him. And no one here would accept it."

"They all know he drinks too much," she said, her eyes lowering. "They've seen him staggering about the village or shouting his half-thought-out edicts from his tent. No one wants him as King. But he is, by birthright. That's the law. You could challenge him for it though. People would accept that." She grimaced. "I know you don't like the idea of confronting your brother over this, Clay, but your father was King, and these are your people. Your responsibility. They need you."

Responsibility. His father had spoken of that long ago, saying that Clay needed to be prepared. That if something happened to Great Ram before he had an heir, it would be up to Clay to lead the people. It would be a difficult task, his father had said. Not pleasant, not desirable. Being King was a duty, not a privilege. It meant sacrificing yourself for your people. Clay had tried not to worry much about that. Great Ram was healthy and strong, and he was sure to have many sons. Clay had always expected to spend most of his young life as a hunter, and perhaps a leather crafter when he was older. But his father had always reminded him that one day, the choice of how he spent his life might be taken away from him.

Now, unexpected, that possibility had returned. He sat unspeaking before his old friend, who called him to his responsibility. He felt the weight of his father's hand on his shoulder again, the burden in his eyes, the reverence with which a King spoke of duty. But what of Doto? Even a King could not disappear into the forest for trysts with the god he loved. At least, not easily. He imagined a life like that, one of hiding and sneaking around, of trying to keep his passion concealed when all eyes were on him, and any hint of the truth could be his downfall. Becoming King would mean giving up Doto. He wasn't sure that he could do that. Nor was he sure he wouldn't be decried as a demon if people ever saw what happened to him when he set foot into the forest. Or what would happen when Doto came to the village looking for him. No, he was sure this was not his duty. Not anymore. There were other responsibilities than birthright, and he owed his to a god.

"Even if people would accept a challenge to rule, they wouldn't accept me," he pointed out. "No one will approach me anymore. They distrust me. Fear me. Why would they accept me as King over my brother?"

"Distrust you?" Cloud said in surprise. "Is that what you think? Clay, except perhaps for Laughing Dog and his fire hunters, they are in awe of you. You disappeared from us with a missing foot and returned whole, touched by the gods. You've spoken to them. What would make for a higher claim than that?"

"That's a strange thing to hear," he confessed. "But listen, my brother is still King. He may be a drunk, but you don't depose a King just because he drinks. Or even if he makes bad decisions. If Ram knew what a threat Ogya is and what's happening with the forest, maybe he would listen."

"And if he stopped drinking palm wine," Cloud reminded him.

"Yes, but even if he did, he wouldn't listen to me. He never has. I doubt claiming I've spoken to the gods will win him over either. It might have escaped you, but I've a reputation for…sanctimony."

"Laughing Dog claims to have spoken with a god, and he's had your brother's ear for far longer," Cloud said. "He's poisoned Ram's mind against the forest along with anyone who disagrees with him or challenges him. I'm not sure the King can be convinced anymore."

Clay rubbed his chin, thinking. "But Ram still worships and follows the gods, or the people would never obey him. Would the Teller help us?"

"The Teller?" Cloud pondered a moment. "It's hard to say. He does as he sees fit. He might tell a pointedly timed story here and there, but he limits himself to the tales he knows. He wouldn't speak outside of them."

"But there are stories he doesn't know," Clay said.

"That's true. If the Teller heard your tale and what you learned from Sarmu, he might be very interested. And if he told all the people about the treachery of Ogya, it could be very difficult for anyone to command that the forest be burned." Cloud got to her feet and walked back and forth across the tent. "I spoke to him before, but then we didn't have the stories you've brought back with you. Yes, yes. You should go to him. Tell him what you told me."

"Can I trust him?" Clay hated asking, but the Teller had always been strange. As Cloud said, he acted according to his own reasons, and Clay couldn't assume those would be good for him.

"Clay, there are only two people I can count on absolutely in this whole village," Cloud said, putting a hand on his shoulder. "Ant With a Leaf is one. The Teller is the other. He may not do what we wish, but for a teller of tales, he knows how to keep a secret. You can trust him absolutely."

Thanking her for both the advice and the blankets, Clay rose and left to find the Teller. Burning Star stood waiting a respectful distance nearby and followed him as he walked down the rise toward the Teller's tent. He didn't get in Clay's way or threaten him, but neither did he let Clay go unwatched for even a moment. It was a persistent reminder that he was under guard. It was only when Clay reached the bottom of the hill that he realized Cloud had not included him in the list of those she trusted. He glanced over at Burning Star, who gazed back impassively. No one in the village really trusted him anymore. It was fair, he supposed. He wasn't entirely sure he trusted himself.

⌢⌢⌢

"Clay, come in, come in." The Teller welcomed him into his tent with wide arms that tended to plumpness even in times of privation.

Clay stooped as he entered and sat down on a stool the Teller waved toward. He hadn't been inside the Teller's tent since he was a boy, and then they had been ever on the move, always traveling light in case they needed to pack up and travel again the next season. Homes then had had few decorations, the Teller's included. Now, a startling assortment of curiosities decorated the tent: many stones and pebbles, brightly colored and oddly shaped; dried flowers and twisted bits of wood; bones and skulls from various animals daubed together with clay to form skeletons; brightly colored arrangements of feathers to be woven into costumes for stories; and along one wall of the tent, scraped goat hides charcoal-stained with a seemingly random series of odd squiggles and shapes. Clay wondered how the Teller had managed to collect all these in the few seasons since the people had settled near the forest.

The Teller saw him staring at the decorated hides and nodded. "Part of the telling of tales is the finding of them. How are you, Clay, son of First Claw? Even I had lost hope of seeing you again, and wonders are my business."

Very well, Clay nearly said, and then stopped himself. No point in hiding the truth from the Teller. "It was not the homecoming I expected," he confessed. "This isn't the village I left. My father. My brothers."

"Yes." The Teller spread his hands. "There are few tales older than that of the boy who leaves his home, and the man who returns to find it small. But even among those tales, few have returned to find a home this much smaller. Your father will be missed."

"I miss my brothers, too."

"And they you, no doubt," the Teller said wryly. "None of us are who we were." He smiled and extended his stick to poke at Clay's left foot. "You do me a great cruelty, Clay. You have brought me a story untold. All wonder at you and speak of it. Most believe the gods healed you as a reward for some task you performed for them. Some say it was witchcraft. Some think you a demon disguised as Clay. Everyone yearns to know the story, but none, I think, have greater longing than mine. It is my charge to remember and pass on the stories of our people. Would you make me derelict in that duty?"

"No, of course not." The warmth and humor in the Teller's voice was comforting and familiar, and Clay found himself both relaxed and eager to share his tale. That had always been the Teller's charm: he never seemed judgmental, only curious. He was a man people liked to make happy, and the way to make him happy was to tell him their stories. People would confess things to the Teller that they wouldn't tell their spouses, their parents, or their friends, and would later be shocked that they had said anything at all. But the Teller never gossiped, never shared stories from person to person. Once in a while, you might hear the things you'd told him appear in a story, but they would always be disguised in such a way that you never felt your secret had been betrayed.

So Clay told his own story, his voice low so he wouldn't be overheard by Burning Star outside, and he found to his astonishment that he related even the parts he had intended to keep secret—namely, those that involved his intimacy with Doto. The Teller nodded and gave attentive smiles, but never made any other reaction until Clay recounted his meeting with Sarmu, and then his brow grew troubled, though still he remained silent until Clay finished his tale.

"The Sarmu tales," the Teller said, rubbing at his bald head. "Then those are the accounts we lost: the devastation of Kwaee, the betrayal of Ogya, the birth of the savanna. How could we have forgotten them, even after a thousand rains? It is a grievous error."

"This is why I've come to you. If Laughing Dog convinces Great Ram to begin burning the forest…"

"Then we fail to learn from our ancestors," the Teller finished. "And we may doom ourselves to suffer their fate. Yes. I will think about what must be done. I must find the story in the words you have spoken."

"What do you mean?" Clay asked, surprised. "I've told you what happened."

"Oh yes. But what happened is not the story. Events are but drops of water. The story is the river." The Teller looked up at Clay. "You, for instance. You have a story." He lifted his walking stick and pointed at the wall of the tent. "The river of your story has met a hill. Will it go left?" He swung his stick. "Or will it go right? I can know every drop of water in your story and still not know the way your river will go. That is for you to decide."

Clay followed the sway of his stick back and forth, crossing an invisible wall between two fates. "I don't know what you mean."

"Ah, yes," the Teller said. He got to his feet and leaned on his stick. "It's always easier, at first, to tell ourselves we don't know. But it makes our choices crueler when they come. Good night, Clay of gods and kings. May your sleep bring you peace."

<center>~~~</center>

Sleep did not bring Clay peace; nor, in fact, could he get any of it. He sprawled and rolled across the hides that Cloud had left for him, but could find no comfort. They were no substitute for the firm but yielding forest floor, and much less for the warm, sturdy comfort of Doto's arms. The tent felt alien and smothering rather than sheltering and safe.

Questions hung like the fragments of a stone tongue or the ruins of a lost city, at any moment ready to fall and plunge him into an abyss, or to topple and crush him. Why had Doto not returned yet? What had happened with his meeting with Kwaee? Supposing the great forest god had hurt or imprisoned him in some way? The thought frightened him as soon as it occurred to him. Doto might not be able to get away. How long might he stay captive? A moon? A rain? A hundred rains? Sarmu had been trapped for a thousand. It wasn't likely, Clay tried to assure himself, but it was possible, at least, that he might never see Doto again. And lying alone in his tent in a village full of strangers, the fear grew within him until it seemed terrifyingly real. But what else could he do? He would simply have to be patient.

He forced himself to lie still, to quiet his mind, recounting in his head the names of his relatives and ancestors, going back as far as he could remember. But why had Doto not come? A heavier answer came to him: perhaps Doto had not returned because he thought Clay didn't want him anymore. Clay had promised to dance for him in the forest, but he had not been able to get away. The guard followed him everywhere, and one step into Kwaee's domain would give him away.

He thought of Doto waiting in the forest, listening for his worshiper's adoration and love, and day after day not hearing it. Perhaps Doto thought Clay had forsaken him. Perhaps even now he was waiting, despondent and alone.

Clay sat up. No wonder he couldn't sleep. Doto had gone into the forest to risk Kwaee's wrath for Clay and his people, and Clay wouldn't even dare venture outside of the village. Shame burned the tips of his ears. On all fours, moving as quietly as he could, he crept to his tent opening, lifted the flap a hand's breadth, and peeked out.

Torchlight made him flinch. Ogya's eyes. Thankfully, none of the torches had been planted very close to his tent. He blinked their glare from his vision and scanned the area. Burning Star sat nearby, his spear resting across his folded legs. His shoulders rose and fell steadily, his chin on his chest. Asleep, then. But he was a hunter, his ears trained, and he would wake at the slightest sound. If Clay was going to do this, he would have to be cautious.

Moving so slowly that the muscles in his arms and legs ached, Clay peeled back the hide covering the opening of his tent and slid through, replacing it just as carefully. Once, when he was a boy, he had crept through a herd of sleeping eland without waking a one. This was far easier by compare. He stayed on all fours, keeping low to the ground so he would not be seen, and so there would be no chance of losing his balance and making a skidding step, or crunching gravel or leaves in the dark. Moving one limb at a time, he crept around the side of his tent and out of the light of the torches.

It would be no good making for the village gate; that would be well-lit and guarded. But he and Laughing Dog had built at least a quarter of the fence that surrounded the village, and not all of the posts were secure. There was one spot where the ground had been so wet, and a puddle so deep, that they had not been able to secure the branches easily, and had relied on the bindings to keep the wall intact. Below that was a gap—a narrow one, true, but one that could be widened.

Clay continued past the tents behind his. Most of these belonged to elders, and they would sleep soundly enough. He reached the wall and followed it around. When he came to the gap, he found that it had been filled in, but a little digging proved the earth very soft and easily scraped away. In a relatively short time, he dug a hole large enough to admit him. He squirmed through it and out into the open air behind the village.

He took a deep breath, already feeling better. He had no torches, but there was a little moonlight, and he knew once he passed beyond the forest boundary, Doto's magic would help him to see well enough, so he followed the village wall, trailing his fingers along it, until he found the new section of the fence, built after the forest had destroyed the old. Again he dropped down to all fours so that he could pick his way forward, crawling over the splintered wreckage of the old wall.

The edge of the forest hummed before his nose. He checked with one hand to make sure the fetish still hung around his neck—though he never removed it, he still sometimes had nightmares about great trees lifting him into the air. Reassured by its solid presence, he pushed through. The grass and trees rimmed with silver moonlight, growing distinct in his vision, as the scents of wet wood and crawling insects and fermenting fruit filled his nose. His ears hummed with a song of flies and wind and a choir of night birds, and he wondered how the forest could have seemed so quiet only a moment before.

He stood, now easily able to make out the part of the forest that he had danced to Doto. The masses of destroyed clayfruit lumped the ground and buzzed with flies. He flexed his feline toes. Now that he was inside the forest, he could move swiftly and silently, so he padded deeper into the small part of it that was Doto's, finding the spot farthest from the village—now that he could see clearly in the night, he felt vulnerable, as though anyone might see him just as easily, so he retreated until he was sheltered from view of the village walls by several large trees. Here he felt relaxed and at peace, the troubles in the village seeming distant and nearly irrelevant. He could almost feel Doto's arms around him. But that only made him miss his god more.

"Doto?" he called, in as loud a voice as he dared. He wasn't close enough to the village that anyone ought to hear him, but there was no need to go shouting either. "Doto, please come back. Things aren't what I expected. I'm sorry I couldn't come before. They've had me under guard. Ogya is here, or some part of him, I think. My brother says he has him under his control, but it's made him terrible and crazy. And I can't tell anyone about you, or even risk going into the forest, because…well…" He didn't want to tell Doto that his people might think him a demon rather than a god, nor that it was the very man he'd convinced Doto to let free that had put the idea in their heads.

"It just hasn't gone well," he said. He gazed into the black depths of the forest. Was Doto in there, somewhere, watching him? Could he even hear him?

His voice broke. "Doto, please come back. I miss you so much." He took a deep breath. "I love you."

And then he danced, his voice ringing lightly over the songs of the frogs and crickets as he hymned his longing for his lost forest god, his Doto, his love. But if the forest heard him, it did not answer.

Flagror Non Consumor

Laughing Dog hunched in his darkened tent, cracking bones with his teeth to suck out the marrow. A sharp pain wrenched his jaw as the bone twisted and cracked a tooth. He cursed and threw it at the side of his tent, where it clattered into a pile of bones already licked clean. He rummaged around for a fresh bone as the god-magic inside him healed the fractured tooth, sealing it back together.

"Your traitorous brother Clay has ruined your plans," Ogya told him. "He is allied with the enemy. You know it. You saw the charm he bore. You ought to kill him."

"I know what you think," Laughing Dog said. "But the people love him. If something happened to him now, just when he's returned and touched by the gods, they might be harder to convince. Besides, he's my brother. And he's good with words. If he sees things from our side, he could help us."

"He will not. I have seen him from my flickers. He talks to the forest gods as though they were friends. He journeyed with one to a far land. He will destroy you. He will find your weakness and use it against you. You should kill him now. I will tell you ways."

"Be silent," Laughing Dog ordered, but the voice of the fire god was never silent. Always it nattered and gnawed at the edges of Laughing Dog's thoughts, and often he could not tell whether he heard it with his mind or with his ears. It had learned to imitate the voices of others, tricking him into thinking those around him had spoken to him, and mocking him when he answered. He drank continually to keep the voice still and small, but if the water still had an effect, he could not tell. He wondered sometimes if it had ever worked at all, or if Ogya had simply been deceiving him. But no. He couldn't doubt himself now. He had had mastery over the god ever since that day at Deraji-Wem, the oasis where he quenched Ogya's fire, and he had it still. Even if that mastery was exhausting.

It took focus throughout the day to keep the voice's suggestions separate from his own thoughts. When he forgot which belonged to him, he began to do mad things. Sleep was never sound, but it helped a little. In the mornings, he was clearest and most coherent. By the time night fell, it was all he could do to keep the insanity at bay. At night, he fed his hunger and fell prey to Ogya's most cruel and useless suggestions.

He didn't understand why Ogya wished to torment him so. They both worked, at least for now, toward the same purpose: convincing the people of the village to join him in his fight against the evil god Kwaee, who ruled the forest and wished to destroy them all. Few openly agreed with him. Whatever virtues he possessed, winning the love and support of the common people was not among them. He could see the way they looked at him: hating him, despising him for his defiance against their subservient ways, for what they perceived as his gluttony. True, he ate almost as often as he drank, but that was only because the god's power inspired such terrible hunger in him. If he gorged, then for a time, the pangs would subside to a tolerable level, but as long as there was food to be had, he hungered. He hardly recognized his own body, the way his thighs rubbed raw when he walked, the painful stretch of his skin and bounce of his belly, the sweaty reddened patches under his arms. He was as heavy as the richest man ever to have lived, but he hungered like the poorest.

"You see?" Ogya would mutter to him. "This is but a fraction of my hunger, and I have felt it for hundreds of rains, never easing, always raking at me. I must eat. You must feed me, and then your own hunger will be eased."

"What am I supposed to feed you?" Laughing Dog had asked him.

"A god." Ogya had groaned the words with anticipation and longing. "Feed me a god, and then at last my hunger will be quelled."

Laughing Dog knew which god he meant, of course. And he knew, too, that if he could give the god of the forest over to Ogya, and Ogya was satisfied, the forest would at last be his. No gods to deny them the bounties of the rich jungle, no laws to say where they could not go or what they could not take. He and the People of the Savanna would own the forest and shape it as they saw fit, and no one would stop them. It would be glorious.

But no one else could see his vision, and he could not make them see it. If only they trusted him, he could have killed Great Ram and become King. But Ogya whispered to him, no. They despise you. They loathe you. They will not listen. He knew it was true. It had always been so. And so he had labored to win their support, little by little, while side-stepping the interferences of people like Two Broken Hands and Cloud. Two Broken

Hands had conveniently been killed by some forest beast, but Cloud had proven a more obstinate threat. He'd found no simple way to kill her without arousing suspicion. She was continually wary and slept with one eye open. It would take just one open mistake to turn the people against him and thwart his aims forever.

He had tried to poison her tea with a toxin Ogya had showed him how to make. He took acacia pods and squeezed them in his hands, until he felt Ogya's magic channeling through them, searing the skin of his fingers and melting the pods into a thick, black liquid. But he had made a mistake; whatever he had poisoned was not her tea, and people started to get sick and die. He had turned that to his advantage for a time, claiming it was the forest working through her medicine that had poisoned everyone. But he'd never meant for anyone else to die from it, and though Ogya screamed and railed against his decision, he'd persuaded Great Ram to force Cloud to throw out the poisoned medicine, blaming her for the plague.

And still people trusted her more than him, even his own promised! He didn't know what it would take to win them over. He'd brought them food with his fire hunters, all who'd been sworn to secrecy before he would show them the new power he wielded. And he loved to wield it. As terrible as his hunger was, when the flames flowed from his fingertips, it was almost joy. It was like a dance, a personal dance that only he knew, in celebration of his own power and strength: he, Laughing Dog, god of fire. His men were devoted to him, partly out of awe, partly out of fear at his magic. They'd seen animals scream in flames that ate them like oil. None of them wanted to die like that. And he didn't want them to either.

What he told none of them was that, when his fires burned something, he felt it. Its energy, its spirit, surged through him in an ecstatic thrill and went to Ogya. The antelope or eland that the flames consumed sent him into a bestial, bloodthirsty glee. He could taste its essence on his tongue. He never wanted to know what it felt like to kill a man that way. Ogya had urged him to try it. He had refused, though at night, when he was exhausted and scarcely knew himself, the temptation was severe.

His plans had been proceeding slowly, too slowly for Ogya. That, no doubt, was why the god tormented him and urged him to acts of such deep irrationality. Ogya's hunger made him impatient. Left to his own designs, he would surely burn the village up in a flash of greedy consumption and then have no followers to help him blaze a path through the forest to the god Kwaee, the great divine meal that would finally assuage his hunger. Ogya screamed and railed for everything to be given to him immediately, for the forest to be immolated today. But Laughing Dog had ignored his voice as much as he could, instead focusing on guiding the winds of political favor toward him. And now, finally, he had Great Ram's ear, he had the council disposed to listen to him, and, thanks to his fire hunters, the gratitude of the people for feeding them. He had been so close to taking charge. One more act of terror from the forest, and the people would have been ready to listen to him. Then he would have had no more need of Great Ram. He could have killed him, become the new King, and led the People of the Savanna in a savage strike against the forest that would have brought Kwaee to his knees. Victory had been so near that he could feel its beating heart in his jaws.

And then, out of death and legend, Clay had returned, and all his hopes had been dashed—Clay, not he, would inherit the rule of the people if Great Ram died. And his brother had returned not merely whole and cheerful, but touched and guarded by the forest gods, even healed by them. All spoke in wonder of the miracle that had restored Clay's foot. The people would follow him, certainly, if he became King. And just as certainly, Clay would brook no war against the forest. Not his dear, sweet, respectful brother Clay, who was eager to bend a knee in subservience to any who would command him. A servile King. The thought of it sickened Laughing Dog. Clay would never truly lead, never take a bold stance. He would order his people to cower and surrender before the forces that wished to destroy them.

If he were to save the people, he would need a new tactic—though none immediately presented itself. Even Ogya floundered in his designs. Great Ram's death would have been suspect. If both brothers died, suspicion would become outright condemnation. The people would never follow him then. And if Laughing Dog could not get rid of both Clay and Great Ram soon, then Ram's heir would be born and one day inherit the rule, leaving him with nothing. Not an insurmountable problem, but one he would like to avoid. He tried to sort out his obstacles, think of a new way to motivate the people, but the day had already grown long, and Ogya's voice was more difficult to ignore. Laughing Dog's focus and self-control were already waning. He took a deep drink from his water skin, but it did not ease the clamor in his mind.

"Laughing Dog." A voice from outside his tent—Great Ram's, if indeed it was a real voice, and not one of Ogya's torments. "Are you in there?"

No, surely that was real. He rubbed at his temples, wondering if he would manage to control himself this time. He would try. "Yes, just a minute."

He breathed deep a few times, trying to calm his mind. He rose and exited the tent. Great Ram stood just outside, the brightness of his royal finery in torchlight contrasting the grave expression on his face. He looked sober. Laughing Dog had been plying him with palm wine for moons now, finding that his brother drunk was far easier to persuade than sober, but lately Ram's drunkenness had guided him down erratic and unpredictable paths, so Laughing Dog had stopped supplying the wine as readily. "What can I do for you, my King?" He looked from Ram's face to the two guards behind him, his own fire hunters, but they were expressionless. Behind them stood Left Rabbit, craning his neck and shifting from foot to foot like a small boy needing to urinate. Laughing Dog turned a questioning gaze back to Great Ram.

"It's about Ant With a Leaf," Ram said, looking rueful. Laughing Dog clenched his teeth. "I know you looked forward to your wedding four days from now, but she came to me. She told me that she changed her mind. She is rejecting your proposal."

"I told you," crowed Ogya from over his shoulder. "I told you she would turn against you. You should have taken her that night outside the village as I bade you. It would have broken her. She would have had no choice."

"She would have killed me," Laughing Dog hissed under his breath.

"What is that?" Great Ram asked, peering at him.

"I said it kills me," Laughing Dog said. "That she would do this. Not just to me, but to you. To throw your own edicts back in your face in such a way. To flout your rule. It seems she's not who we all thought she was." He gave a long sigh and tried to make it sound sad and resigned. "I suppose it's just lucky for me that we learned of her selfishness now, rather than after I married. That she has such little concern for you, or me, or even her own self, to open her parents up to punishment like that...I can scarcely believe it."

"Then you would see me punish her as I threatened?" Great Ram asked. "Banishment for her and her parents? It's a harsh penalty."

"Don't forget that she was plotting to overthrow you," Laughing Dog reminded him. "Her marriage was a sign of good faith, and she's broken it. We can't trust her." But, he considered, if Ant With a Leaf's family were banished with her, then she might see no reason not to tell everyone about that night outside the village and what he had done. With a few words, she might set his plans so far back that he could never complete them. And what would Ogya do then?

"Devour you," Ogya's voice crackled as though he were burning the tent behind Laughing Dog. "All your strength and power come from me. I will take it away, and you will be nothing. You will die horribly."

"Ogya?" Great Ram asked, sounding perplexed. "What are you talking about, Laughing Dog? You've been stranger than usual lately."

He had said something out loud and hadn't known it? It was too late in the day, and he was too tired for this conversation. "A—a prayer. Apologies. No. If I might counsel, show mercy, King Great Ram. Leave Ant With a Leaf's parents alone. But she must be arrested. I am not certain we can trust her to banishment. She may be angry and seek revenge. She may return in the night. We will have to determine what to do with her."

"Kill her. Kill her. Burn her alive and give her soul to me."

Great Ram nodded. "I'm pleased to hear you speak of mercy, Laughing Dog. I think Father would have approved."

"If only the forest had granted him that mercy."

"Oh, not this again, Laughing Dog," Great Ram said with a groan. "I've told you many times, we cannot go burning the forest. It serves no purpose."

"No purpose?" Laughing Dog demanded. "What purpose does justice need, Ram? What purpose does vengeance require other than its own sake? The forest killed our father. It has killed so many of us. You know that."

"Burn it burn it burn it all to ash and cinder. Feed the trees and grass and animals into all my hungry mouths."

Great Ram's face darkened. "You shame me, brother. Did you not hear Clay's tale? The forest gods believe us their enemies. It's burning the forest that has turned them against us to begin with. We're only lucky I didn't listen to you from the start. Listen to me: I'll have no more talk of that sort from you again. You are never to speak to me nor anyone else in this village of attacking the forest or defying its gods. Not once. Do you understand me?"

"I will give you the power now. Burn him and his guards where they stand."

"Look," Laughing Dog said, trying to calm himself. All his efforts were imperiled. He had to do something. "You're getting a lot of different stories right now, but you can't shut me out. You're in danger—we're all in danger. Why should you believe Clay and not me? He's been in the forest. You know that! He may have been corrupted, turned against us. What if the prisoner's story is true? Then he's a danger!"

Ram folded his arms across his chest. "That may be, Dog, and I will be sure to keep watch over him. But he urges caution and patience where you advise violence and destruction. I know which of those courses Father would have taken."

"You're not half the King that Father was," Laughing Dog heard himself sneer. The words were ill-advised, but he was too weary to stop them. They had been building over moons and moons of steady arguing and appealing to a King who was erratic and indecisive. He was sick to death of this. Ram wasn't a brother anymore. He was just an obstacle, one Laughing Dog desired nothing more than to flatten. "Father wasn't a drunk and a layabout. He had his own mind and made decisions for himself. You'll never be like him. And even if you were, you'd still be making the same mistakes he did—sitting back and watching while people die of starvation and drought instead of taking action. He was a fool, and you're a bigger fool. You'll doom all of us if you don't listen to me, and when the people finally decide they've had enough of you, I won't speak against it."

He stopped himself finally—too late. His words hung in the still night air. Great Ram was silent. He kept his face calm, but his fingers pinched at his folded arms. The guards looked at each other uneasily. But beyond all that, even Ogya was quiet. No hissing, mocking jibes came from the fire god.

Great Ram puffed through his nostrils, strangling for a moment on his own words. Then he jutted a shaking finger under Laughing Dog's nose. "You think you're allowed to speak to me like that because we are brothers. But I am the King now, and you have spoken treason. So now I say to you: you are no longer my brother. I want you gone from my sight. You will not come to me in my tent. You will not offer me a single word of advice or counsel, by order of the King. You are dismissed from my favor and my family. Do you understand me?"

"Wait—" Laughing Dog reached out to Great Ram. It had all gone wrong just now. He hadn't said those things. Ram hadn't replied in that way. "Wait, Ram, please, I—"

"I said do you understand me?" His brother's voice was as smooth and deadly as a lion's tooth.

It took every ounce of self-control remaining for Laughing Dog to dip his head low, to keep his frightened voice steady as he answered, "Yes, my King."

Great Ram's lips twitched as if with further invectives he wished to let fly, but he simply spun on his heel and marched away, and behind him, their spears at the ready, the fire hunters—*Laughing Dog's* fire hunters—followed.

"Well, what do you think I should do now?" he demanded of Ogya.

The fire god said nothing. Without the incessant muttering and threats, Laughing Dog felt suddenly alone, his head as hollow as a calabash.

But he was not alone. "Um, I don't know." It was the voice of Left Rabbit, who stood to one side, so still that Laughing Dog had forgotten he was there. "But I believe you."

"Believe me?" Laughing Dog said. "Believe me about what?"

"About Clay." The man shuffled forward, not meeting Laughing Dog's gaze. "If—if I saw something, then that would mean I did good, right? It'd mean I had good eyes and was alert. You need good eyes to join the fire hunters. And it would mean I'm loyal to you. Prince Laughing Dog," he added, daring finally to meet his prince's gaze. "So maybe you could let me run with your fire hunters?"

"I might. That depends on what you saw, doesn't it?" In truth, Laughing Dog had no intention of letting Left Rabbit join his hunters. The man was an idiot and an annoyance, always following about at his heels, simpering and begging for attention like a tamed jackal pup begging for scraps. Loyalty was to be valued, of course, but servility was not loyalty. It was merely weakness, and Laughing Dog had no place for that among his hunters.

Left Rabbit crept closer, his face wide and earnest. "I heard noises when I was on guard last night. From the forest. So I went to see what they were. And when I followed them…I heard singing. I couldn't see anybody, but it was Clay's voice, Prince Laughing Dog. He was somewhere inside the forest. Past where it was supposed to be safe. And singing."

Laughing Dog's pulse quickened. This was important; he knew it. "Listen to me. You heard him singing. What were the words?"

"I don't remember most of it. He was singing something to someone named Doto."

That was the name that Ogya had whispered to him, the son of the forest god, their enemy. He seized Laughing Dog by the shoulders, pulling him close. "Doto, you say? Are you certain of this? You are sure it was the name Doto?"

Left Rabbit nodded emphatically. "Yes. He called him Doto the Mighty. And asked him to come back. He said he missed him. But I still haven't told you the strangest thing. I hid behind a bit of the old wall and watched him as he left. It was his foot, Prince Laughing Dog. At first I thought it was just the shadows and the moonlight, but he came close to me, so close I was afraid he might see me. He sniffed the air, like he could—like he could smell me. I didn't look any more, because I didn't want to get caught, but I know what I saw. His foot—it was a cat's foot. I know you probably won't believe me, but I swear that his foot was a cat's. Like a lion's, or a leopard's. He walked on it all strange."

Laughter. The air was full of crackling, popping laughter. It was Ogya. He roared with glee. "A leopard's foot. The boy has a leopard's foot! Incredible. The foolish little godling has piled up kindling before his own forest for us. I can tell you how to light it, my prince. You will use my fire to take the whole forest and all its gods' might for yourself."

Laughing Dog listened to his captive god and smiled. The hollowness was gone. He had stepped back just from the edge of disaster. The people would be his. The forest would be his.

"Did I do right to tell you?" Left Rabbit asked, observing Laughing Dog's smile. "I wasn't sure it was the right thing. I thought about it all night and day."

"Yes," Laughing Dog assured him. "It was right to tell me."

"Then—you will let me join your fire hunters?"

The man's eyes were wide and hopeful. Laughing Dog frowned, for a moment considering, but the hunter must have taken it as a sign of rejection, for he got down on both knees and took Laughing Dog's hand in his, looking up at him with eyes wide with hope. "Please, my prince. Please give me this position of honor at your side. I swear to you I will earn it. I will do everything you command."

A wave of disgust washed through him. This groveling was pathetic. He pulled his hand away from Left Rabbit's, stepping back in revulsion. "Honor isn't given. It's taken. Look at you, squirming in front of me like a worm. My fire hunters are men. You could never be one of them."

"But Prince, you promised—" Tears welled in Left Rabbit's eyes, and that only made Laughing Dog despise him even more.

"I promised nothing. If you had come to me and demanded that I include you, I might have considered it. But instead you drop to your knees and cry like a young girl. Get out of here."

With a stricken expression, Left Rabbit stood. He turned, shoulders slumped.

Ogya's voice hissed in his ear. "The boy will tell others. He will ruin our plans."

Now why had he not thought of that himself? But of course, his thoughts were hazed with hunger and exhaustion. Still, the fact that Ogya considered this when he had not bothered him. "Wait. Rabbit, wait."

When Left Rabbit looked back, there was a shining streak down one cheek. Laughing Dog fought back a frown of disgust. "Forgive me. I spoke hastily. It's the other hunters, you see. They don't think you're ready, and

I'm not so good at convincing them. But you are right. You're devoted, true, and you've proven yourself a capable hunter. You deserve a place among my fire hunters, and when they learn how you have aided our people, they will think differently. But they must see it for themselves. Speak nothing of this to anyone for now. I will need time to prepare, and to lay up defenses against the evil the forest god works against us. If we show our arms too early, it will all be for nothing. Do you understand?"

Left Rabbit's face shone. He wiped at his cheek with the back of a hand. "Yes, Prince Laughing Dog. I understand. And I will be a fire hunter, too?"

"My own men will demand it when they learn what you have done."

Laughing Dog waved off Rabbit's bowing and babblings of gratitude, finally escaping them by retreat into his tent. There, he settled back onto his bed and closed his eyes. He felt more at peace now than he had since he could remember. Ogya was not silent, but he neither seethed nor nattered. Instead he crackled with satisfaction.

Little threads of pleasure washed through Laughing Dog, and he knew they came from the fire god. Perhaps they were a deliberate reward for his labors finally forging a path to their goal; perhaps they were only glimpses of the glee Ogya felt and could not contain. Whichever, they bloomed with warm pleasure in his mind, spread down his body, made his hips twist.

"Do you enjoy that, my host?" Ogya whispered over him.

"It is nice."

"It is but a wisp of smoke compared to the joy of my inferno. Look."

Images resolved in Laughing Dog's mind, more real than imagining, more real even than the visions of a dream. He closed his eyes and sank into the scene.

He was roaring through a forest, mighty, invincible. Nothing could stand before him. He consumed it all. Trees dwindled into ash within his body. He closed fiery claws around a group of slavering antelope. They leapt in desperation, but were far too slow to escape. He felt them scream and smoke and char in his grasp as he ate them. Rivers could not stay him; they erupted into hot, hissing clouds beneath his toes. He glided across bodies of water larger than any pond or oasis he had ever seen, and they boiled against him, paining his flesh as they shrank, but not enough to diminish him. He ate and ate, and as he ate, he grew. He swelled in size and power, so mighty that his fingers reached from great water to great water. It was the thrill he felt in the hunt when his flames caught an animal and burned it alive, but this was that thrill magnified over and over and over. Ecstasy beyond his comprehension speared through his being, obliterating any thought other than to consume and grow until he was the earth itself, until he was all there was.

That was what had once been. That was what would be again, but it would be his power this time, not Ogya's. It would be he, Laughing Dog, with the full power of divinity within his hands. Then no god could demand anything of him ever again, nor of any who followed him. Any who did not—any too foolish to prize strength over servitude, the will of man over the will of their domineering gods—well, they deserved to be consumed.

He could almost taste them.

The Face of Ogya

At long last, Doto reigned, god of the forest, at Kwaee's side. He sprawled in the throne of his young moabi and set his mind away from all he had lost. He sent it into the forest, along the channels of power that radiated outward from his father's temple like the roots of a giant tree. For the first time, he could see all of the forest at once, from the oceans in the south and west to the mountains in the east, and north to the edge of the savanna. Beyond the edges of the forest, he could see nothing, but within its boundaries teemed uncountable life, all of it sprouting and devouring and mating and suffering. It was all a dance to Kwaee, to the forest, to life, to itself.

Doto cast his omniscient gaze across the many quiet troubles of the forest, staring out into a world his father had all but forgotten. Here, small fires flickered—nothing to worry about, no true intrusion of Ogya. There, a blight struck the roots of trees and withered them. A diseased hippopotamus died in a large pool. Its flesh would poison any who drank from it. To the south, two armies of chimpanzees waged screeching war against each other. In the southeast, a flower budded with a change that gave its color a new brilliance, one that would attract bees from greater distances. Its sprouts would thrive more easily.

He could see everything at once. Trillions of lives blinked into existence, starved and foraged, scratched for food, fluttered for mates, weakened, and died. And so it went. The forest continued as it should. None of the individual lives meant anything to Doto; nor could they. He could no more care for any individual life than he could care for any individual blade of grass that covered a particularly beautiful meadow. The forest was so full, and yet it was so empty.

A voice said something, spoke his name, but it was lost in the whirl of life all around him, and he ignored it. It spoke again, and this time he gave it more attention, seeking its source. He traced it through the forest, tuning his vision to it as he might follow a single gnat in a swarm, and found that it came from a leopard standing beside a still and staring body that, after a moment, he distantly recognized as his own.

The voice was his father's. He drew himself out of the roots of power that spread from the temple, shrinking back into himself, his mind retreating from the visions witnessed by trillions of eyes into those of a single pair: his own. He slid down in his throne, suddenly aware of the hardness of the bark beneath his rump, the thick heat of the air. He breathed deep, like he had forgotten how. He reminded himself how to focus his eyes.

Kwaee stood next to him, arms folded across his chest. "You watch the forest, then? Even knowing that you might see the fire bearers and face their sorcery?" Suspicion sprouted in his eyes. "Or perhaps you are hoping for it."

Doto's sat up, a cub-like sense of guilt burning his cheeks. "I only wanted to see what it was like. I've never known what a…what a true god sees when he looks out over his realm." Half-god. The distinction still shamed him, even now, with a seat at his father's side.

Kwaee sighed, uncrossing his arms, his shoulders relaxing. "Yes. It can be entrancing. At times I would lose myself for days, years, or longer, doing nothing but watching the forest. Now I dare not look."

"I do not know if I like it," Doto said. "I feel far away from everything."

"You should say far above it, son. You *are* far above everything else."

Doto leaned back into his throne. "What was it you said to me when I was watching? Your words were lost in the noise."

Kwaee grunted. "I said that I was proud of you. You have surprised me, proved yourself wise and strong, the way that you have thrown off the fire bearer's spell on you. I know that it was difficult."

There was no good answer to that. Kwaee knew far more about the magics of the world than Doto ever would, but the fire bearer's hold on him did not feel like a spell. If watching the forest with the eyes of a god was to see it from so far away that all else became irrelevant, then the magic of his attachment to Clay came from seeing him not at distance, but close—so very close that when he thought of Clay, everything else disappeared, and he and Clay became a part of each other.

How could Doto admit that that hold was far from gone? In separation, it had only intensified. He found it difficult to think of anything but Clay. In every moment, he yearned to climb down from his throne and rush back to his fire bearer's side. The urge frightened him.

"It hurts," he said, lacking any other response.

"It will for a while." Kwaee's voice was gentle. His sympathy sounded odd—false, even—to Doto's ears. Perhaps it was simply unfamiliar. "Listen. The years will be difficult at first. You will feel this pain inside you, like a gall in the wood of a tree. But like a tree, you will grow, and the gall will not, and soon you will forget the pain, as though it were not even there. It will be such a small part of you that you will no longer notice it."

"I will not forget him," Doto declared.

"No. But he will forget you. It is the way of their people. Do you believe your mother was the first fire bearer with whom I dallied? The only one ever to ensnare me so, true, but not the only one I knew. The others, they were enthralled with me for a time, and I enjoyed them, but when I left, they forgot me. Your fire bearer will find other mates and other interests. He will grow old as quickly as day turning to night, and then he will die. It is better not to see that. That would hurt far more. But you have stepped away in time. His spell over you will weaken, and you will be wise. You will never be tempted by another fire bearer again."

"Then let us calm the forest," Doto urged. "If I will not be tempted, and you will not, then what reason is there to kill the fire bearers?"

Kwaee's eyes flashed in anger. With a growl, he turned on Doto, leaping into his own throne and crouching in it as though about to pounce. "And what further reason should I require? They burned me at Ogya's bidding, lest you forget. And they have done it again recently. Oh yes," he added, noting Doto's surprise. "One of your precious little captive's nestlings sent flames into my body. Ogya will use them to attack again."

"Only because you provoke them! They depend on the forest for food. If you calmed it, then they would leave you alone. Sarmu told me—"

"Sarmu knows nothing." Kwaee snarled, digging his claws into the bark of his moabi. "Indolent, ungrateful. He was only a lesser god before I sacrificed my body to create his great savanna, and now he thinks he knows my errors? It doesn't matter what I did to the fire bearers or why. I am a god, and they beasts. To rise up against me at all was the only proof I needed of their treachery."

"But if you *could* stop them from attacking again—" Doto began.

"Enough!" His father shouted. His voice shook with hints of petulant anger that were all too familiar. "I will hear nothing more of leniency toward those creatures. They are violations of the natural law, and they must be destroyed."

There was no use pressing things any further. Kwaee had only just begun to show him kindness, and Doto would not dare throw that away so quickly. He huffed through his nose, leaned back in his throne and tried to push his thoughts away.

He considered sending his mind out into the forest once more to let the hum of life lull him into forgetfulness, but some little part of him recoiled at the thought, finding the submersion of his awareness distasteful. Drowning. That was what it was. It was alluring, true, but frightening.

And besides, there was a tiny section of the forest he could not see when immersed in the roots of his father's power: his own temple, and those little patches of forest, here and there, where Clay had danced for him. Those were not his father's, but his, and his senses of them were drowned out utterly by the vastness of Kwaee's domain.

He sent his mind to these, listening to each in turn, and found the longing for his mate soothed. There, in the grove of ebony trees, he found the spot where Clay had danced for him the first time and given him his first taste of worship. There the feather had sprouted from his forehead. And again, two more forest circles that were his, tracing their journey to the great Asubonten. And another, on the other side of the river, not far from Abansin, the ruined city. There Clay had been so weak, suffering with blood poisoning from his wounded leg. Then, the dances in Doto's temple and on the edge of the forest. More than dancing had gone on there, and Doto felt his loins pulse with the memory. Each of the circles was a reminder of his time with Clay. He could even feel, far more distantly, the tiny pepperings of forest extending out into the savanna, all the way to the base of Ogya-Bepow.

The last place he and Clay had shared each other was near the village of the fire bearers, a great stretch of land stolen from his father for the two of them. Doto sent his mind to that. He could not see into the village through it; all beyond its edges were walled to his senses, but within it the scent and memory of Clay was fresh, and he drifted to that, feeling his worshiper's footprints still in the earth and broken grasses. He tasted Clay's memory with the feet of ants, and scented it with the questing noses of mice. It comforted him.

His mind basked in the memories, and he scarcely noticed when Kwaee said something to him. When he finally opened his eyes, the day had turned to night, and his father was gone, wandered off into the forest somewhere. Doto didn't care; after immersion in the memory of his bearer, the empty forest temple only intensified his longing, so he rejected it, closed his eyes, and listened through his forest circles once more.

Fingers pressed down on his grasses, and then toes. They were Clay's. He knew them intimately and perfectly. He held his breath, savoring every touch of his mate. He rejoiced to feel it.

It was wrong to listen, however right it might feel. He ought to close his senses now. It would be better to draw his mind back, to shut out the forest circle so that Clay could not tempt him away. His father had warned him of this.

But Doto could not draw back. To shut out his senses and bar himself from Clay was nearly unthinkable. This was his worshiper, his mate, his love. He had to listen, and he had to embrace Clay with everything that he was. The intensity of the feeling frightened him. And so he listened and could not stop listening.

His mate was calling for him. His mate was lonely and afraid. His mate needed him.

His mate danced.

∧∧∧

Doto tossed restlessly in his throne. Clay's pleading the night before had torn at him. He felt as though the fire bearer had wrapped claws around his heart and lungs and now pulled at him, tearing deep and grievous holes as he dragged Doto against his will toward the fire bearer's nest.

Kwaee noted this restlessness and commented again that the longing would hurt for a while, and then ease, but that above all else, Doto must not go to Clay, must try to put him out of mind.

As well try to stop a river by holding up a paw.

The day passed so slowly that Doto felt almost certain he *had* been ensorcelled in some way. Why else would the sun crawl like a dying ant ever more feebly across the sky? Perhaps it would stop altogether, leaving Doto trapped eternally in one endless, empty noon. Despite himself, he yearned to feel Clay return to his forest and dance again, even though it would surely worsen Doto's mood. He waited for the night, but the sun faltered above him and would not move.

When the night finally returned, so did Clay, calling for Doto again, his voice shaking with loneliness and misery. How could Doto hear it and not help? How could he not go to him?

He hopped down from his throne, ignoring his father's curious inquiries. He had to go to Clay now. But at the edge of the temple, he paused.

There was something awful inside him, something that had felt pleasure at killing Ulo, the fire bearer, that had enjoyed feeling Jai's eye crush in the grip of his roots. That was his nature, his father's nature, deep within him. No matter where he went, nor what he did, he could not escape it. Clay had seen it once, and when he did, that bright and hopeful light in his eyes had gone out. True, after a time, he had cheered again, and been close to Doto once more, but now Doto knew his own nature. One day he would again do something terrible. He would break his promise, and then Clay's eyes would be sad always. The cruelty of Kwaee was a part of him, part of the magic that he was made of. *Something is wrong with the gods*, Clay had said. He had believed it. And was not Doto a god? Whatever was wrong with the gods was wrong with him, too.

Adanko the hare had tried to warn him. *We can't fight our natures, can we? We are who we are, and nothing we do can ever change that.*

It was inescapable. He was his father's son. "Goodbye, Clay." He mouthed the words so that not even his father would hear them. With one long look outside the temple, he returned to his throne. He would dull the pain, send his mind into the numbing power of the forest. This was his inheritance, his birthright, his kingdom. He just needed to close his eyes, shut the outside world away. Eventually all these miserable feelings would fade into the past.

One last look, he resolved. One last look into the little fringes of forest near the fire bearers' village, and then he would look away forever. He sent his mind to it for the last time in his life.

A pair of feet, belonging to a fire bearer he did not recognize, stood in his grasses. A voice spoke, and so Doto listened to it with the ears of grass-hoppers and birds and shrews.

"Lord Doto?"

He did not know the voice.

"Lord Doto, if you can hear me, you must come quickly. Clay doesn't know it, but he is in terrible danger. We all are. If you don't come soon, Clay will die."

⁀⁀⁀

Night deepened the sky outside the fire bearers' village. Doto crouched in the brush, his spotted pelt shifting in the fading light, hiding him from view of any unwelcome eyes. He shouldn't be here, but even the distraction of being an entire forest had not been enough to keep his thoughts silent. Clay was in trouble. Clay would die. And a trillion teeming voices could not drown out that single terrifying thought.

He shouldn't be here. He was dangerous. He had a monster inside him. He would kill.

And yet here he was. Perhaps, he thought, he could resolve things. Save Clay from whatever threatened him and then speak with him one last time. Then he could explain, somehow, with words he had not yet found, why a mortal and a god could not be with each other. He would order Clay out of the forest forever. Clay would protest, would weep perhaps, but he was obedient. He would comply, and then he and Doto would never see each other again. It would be difficult to such issue a command—so difficult that to imagine doing it made Doto feel feeble, as though he stood

outside the forest, with no power at all. But that weakness made him certain of the order's necessity. The fire bearer's hold over him was already too great.

And besides, it would be a relief to see Clay one last time, to hold him in his arms, nuzzle an ear, feel the fire bearer's embrace about his waist. It would be a kindness to Clay too, for him not to have to wonder what had happened to his god.

So Doto crouched and waited in the twilight for the owner of the voice that had pleaded for him to return.

The twilight deepened into night. The fire bearers chattered in their village. The stink of their waste and their charred food plucked at Doto's nose. He could smell fear among them as well, tracks of it winding through the odors of their consumption and sweat and desires. The glows of their little fires stained the trees with orange light and made shadows flicker.

They sang a little and beat the Cry of the Dead, and then, after a time, their noises subsided. If Clay's voice had sung out among theirs, Doto had not been able to distinguish it. Their village darkened as most of the fires were put out. Then all was stillness.

Doto waited. Perhaps nothing was wrong at all. Perhaps the fire bearer who summoned him had been lying. Crickets and birds sung the pulse of the night.

After a time, a figure appeared from around the side of the village. It was not Clay; Doto could tell that at once. This fire bearer was taller and much fatter. It carried a torch as it walked, making its way toward him purposefully, as though it knew he were there. It picked its way along the wall of the village, and then turned and stepped into his part of the forest. Its eyes fixed exactly on the spot where he crouched, as though his camouflage had faltered.

Doto did not like the look of it. Its face was sagging and drawn; a haunted expression twisted its eyes. It looked to him like a maddened beast: dangerous and tormented.

"What am I looking for?" it asked. It spoke with the voice that had called him the night before.

He stared at it, perplexed. Was it speaking to him? Could it see him? No, that was impossible. His magic concealed him perfectly from any mortal creature.

"No," the fire bearer said, as if in answer to an unasked question. "I don't—" Its voice broke off, and its eyes bulged out in shock. Its tongue protruded from its lips. A strangled, choking sound guttered in its throat. Then, stiff as though manipulated by a giant hand, it tottered back and forth on its legs, turning, step by ungainly step, until it faced away from Doto.

Uneasily, Doto crouched lower in the brush, his ears flattening.

Something was moving on the back of the fire bearer's head. Like Clay, it had twisted the black mane that all fire bearers grew into long, dangling braids, but these now shifted about as though the flesh stirred behind them. Then a furred muzzle pushed aside the braids, extending and growing outward, capped by a black nose. It growled low as it protruded. It snapped white teeth. The muzzle grew out into a face—that of a snarling hyena, and when it was fully extended, it opened eyes that had neither irises nor pupils, but blazed with yellow flame.

Fear like none Doto had ever felt bound him where he stood.

The creature staggered toward him with backward steps, its eyes of fire glaring into his own. "Little Doto," it named him, and its voice was the crackle and roar of burning trees. "I know you are there. A god can always find another god. There is no sense in hiding."

Doto forced himself to stand, letting the concealment fall away from him. "Ogya."

The god laughed from a slavering muzzle. "At last we meet. I'm pleased to see that you answered my summons."

Through his fear, Doto felt for the forest beneath him, sending his will into vines and brambles. He could tear this thing apart now and be done with it. "If a god can sense another god, why can I not sense you?" Hopefully the question would distract Ogya while the forest did his bidding.

"Because I am not truly here. This is but a fraction of my power I have granted to this foolish boy. I speak to him in a voice loud and a voice silent, so he struggles against the loud and unthinkingly obeys the silent. And thinks he possesses me."

Doto nodded, and then frowned, trying to appear puzzled. "But why would you do that?" With thorny brambles, he reached out toward Ogya's throat.

"Ah-ah," Ogya cautioned him, shaking his head. His reversed arms bent upward, popping sounds coming from the fire bearer's unnaturally twisted shoulders, and then fire shot from his palms, bright orange coils of it. They licked at the forest floor and caught, spreading to form a thin wall that encircled the possessed fire bearer.

Doto hissed and crouched. He could feel the flames burning his forest, consuming it, taking it away from him, lessening him bit by bit and granting the land to Ogya.

"It's the first time you've felt that, isn't it, little godling? So young, to never have your body taken from you by a fire bearer and given to another. But you've been stealing your share, haven't you? Bits of your father's forest, little spots of the savanna. If Kwaee had only known you'd grow up to be such a little thief."

Doto crept back from the flames, not liking the flush of their heat on his face. "I am no thief," he declared. "All the savanna was once my father's, and all that is my father's I share."

Ogya licked his jaws. "So I noticed. I have watched you and your little pet from many of my glows."

"Clay," Doto growled low. "Where is he? What have you done with him?"

"He is unharmed. He has more to fear from you than from me."

Doto clenched his fists in fury, his claws pricking into his palms. "He should fear you most of all. You killed nearly all the fire bearers."

"True," Ogya answered, his eyes blazing brighter, "but there were not so many left to kill. Not after your father finished with them."

"You rallied them against the forest!" Doto shouted. "You would have burned it all if you could have."

"Do not presume to lay the guilt for this on me, *boy*." Ogya spat the last word, a plume of fire erupting from his jaws and scorching the ground at Doto's feet. "The war started with you. Everything that has happened since that day happened because you were born."

Doto flattened his ears. "That's not my fault."

"I saw it. You must know that. Abansin was filled with torches. I watched through many eyes. All the fire bearers knew that your mother was to give birth to a god. But you were too strong for her. Too much of a monster. She lay twisting on their altar to Kwaee. Then she screamed. She screamed and screamed as you tore your way out of her with tooth and claw. Do you understand that, godling? The first thing you ever did was murder your own mother, fill your father's heart with hate, and start the war between the fire bearers and the forest. You were born in blood. The slaughter of the fire bearers, the burning of the forest, your father's thousand years of silence—these all happened because of you."

Doto put his paws to his face, shaking his head. All around him, the forest lashed in a reflection of his agony. Vines flailed, striking at him, some curling through the walls of fire and igniting like fiery snakes, like the plumes of flame that had arced from the top of Ogya-Bepow. Trees groaned, bent, and split open. "You're lying. It's not my fault. You were the one who convinced the fire bearers to turn against the forest."

"Convinced them?" Ogya laughed. "You think they needed any persuasion from me? No, they begged me. They pleaded with me for vengeance. And of course I aided them. I pitied them. They deserved justice against your father for what he had done to them. Then your father and Sarmu conspired to turn them against me, to teach them lies about how I had injured them, about how it was I, and not Kwaee, who had betrayed them all. For hundreds of years, my name was spoken in hatred. For hundreds of years, not one fire bearer worshiped me."

His blazing eyes burned more brightly. "And what ecstasy their worship is. It is wondrous. I know you have felt it." He pointed at the feather growing from Doto's forehead. "And now, just when they have forgotten, when they have begun to sing my praises and worship me once more, your little pet wishes to turn them all against me again. He tells them that I'm an enemy, a betrayer, just as Sarmu and Kwaee would have them believe. He would have me starved for worship once more. I will not accept it."

Doto's thoughts whirled. Once he would have decried Ogya as a liar immediately, and thought nothing more of it, but had Kwaee not lied to him, over and over again? The truth was as impossible to catch as starlight. "What do you want?" he groaned.

Ogya lolled his tongue. "Why, for you to tell everyone the truth, godling. Tell them what your father did to them. Tell them how he murdered their ancestors and why he turns the forest against them now. You will come to the edge of the forest at the moment of the third dawn. By then I will have all the village here to witness. You will tell them of Kwaee's treachery, and of my innocence. You will tell them all to worship me."

"And—and why should I do that?"

Ogya grinned—or perhaps he only bared his fangs. "Because if you do not appear and make your confession, I will kill your precious Clay. And if I sense your presence in or near the village before that time, I will kill him for that, and you will be weak, and there will be nothing you can do to stop it. I will kill him slowly. Perhaps I will eat his hands first, or his feet, searing him with my fire to stop the bleeding, to ensure he does not die too slowly. And all the time, I will whisper into his ear that this suffering is because of you, because you would not save him. And that too, godling, will be your fault."

A Cry in the Dark

Cloud paused outside the entrance to Laughing Dog's tent. The smell that hovered around it was foul and rotten. A sickly buzzing came from inside: black flies. She stifled a shudder of fear and looked back at Clay. "You're sure he's gone?"

Tilting his head as if listening, Clay paused and answered, "He and all his fire hunters. He's promised to bring back a great feast for tonight."

Cloud snorted. "Only Laughing Dog would have his promised imprisoned and then proceed with the marriage feast."

"Not the Laughing Dog I remember." The boy looked out over the village below, wrinkled his nose, and then turned his gaze to the forest, staring at the green canopy that hovered beyond the wall.

Cloud wondered if he could see how he himself had changed: the way he walked with a different gait, both graceful and precise; the way he focused on people's faces when they spoke, his eyes unblinking and unshifting, watching them as though they were curious creatures he had never seen before. He was familiar to her still, and yet a stranger. And he was always watching the forest.

"You miss him, don't you?" Cloud asked.

"Laughing Dog? I suppose I miss...who he used to be. My brother."

"No. Him. Your forest god."

Clay frowned. "I do miss him. I keep calling for him, but he hasn't come. I don't know why he wouldn't, unless something has happened to him." He shifted from foot to foot, bouncing on the balls of his toes as though about to spring away or pounce on something.

The god's absence troubled him—that much was plain. Cloud wished she knew what to say to him, but what could she know of longing for an absent love, especially when that love was for intimacy with a god? Like Laughing Dog, Clay had left his home and come back changed.

When he had first returned, it had seemed like the turn of the seasons, cause for great hope. In the moments before, Cloud had been prepared, finally, to challenge the King for rule of the people, to compel him to surrender that rule to the council. There was little chance that such a challenge would have been successful. Far more likely would have been exile for her, or even execution, leaving the people without an experienced healer. But at the last, glad moment, Clay's return had taken that terrible choice out of her hands. He was perhaps the only person remaining who might demand rule from the capricious hands of Great Ram and not be called usurper by the people.

But Clay had come back older—and wilder, touched by gods. Cloud didn't fear him as she did Laughing Dog; despite his changes, he was still Clay, still gentle and kind, still a dreamer. But his heart was someplace else, and she wondered now if he could ever be persuaded to take up his brother's rule.

His gaze drifted back toward the forest, and she followed it. Was there truly a god there now, perhaps pacing the borders, watching them with merciless eyes? "You want to go to him."

He coughed a laugh. "Every minute. But the forest is—no. No, Cloud. My place is here. My people are here."

A man might say he had no food to eat and sound happier about it than Clay. He must have noticed her concern, for he relaxed his shoulders and smiled. "You should hurry up into that tent if you still want to poke around. The fire hunters are gone, but someone else might see us and wonder what we're doing skulking around here."

The buzzing from within the tent pressed back into her thoughts. "You're right." She took a deep breath. "Whistle if you see anyone coming." Before she allowed herself another pause, another endless hesitation, she steeled her resolve and pushed open the flap of Laughing Dog's tent. She stepped inside.

The dark bowels of the prince's tent made her gasp. Animal bones were littered everywhere, and they clustered with flies. Cloud had always had a horror of flies, ever since she was a young girl. It wasn't unnatural; any sensible healer would avoid them. Flies and disease were always found together. Swarms of them would disgust anyone. But even isolated, wandering flies gave her a sense of uneasiness. Here, where they clustered in great, hungry clumps, their glossy wings flittering, their wretched black tongues swabbing down over gristle and rot, her fear was almost unbearable. She would have asked Clay to take this task for her, but Clay would not have known what she was looking for.

She propped open the roof flap to admit a little light. The masses of flies stirred in annoyance. Flinching away from a few that hummed past her, she peered around. The hides of Laughing Dog's bed were caked with grey ash that had surely rubbed from his skin. Taking care to avoid the littered bones and the insects that crawled and feasted upon them, she reached down and probed with her fingers at the pelt of Laughing Dog's bed and then into the flattened straw that cushioned it. Nothing. She rummaged through the trophies and tools that hung from the wall. She poked through the heaped piles of beaded bracelets and leathers and necklaces and cloths that comprised Laughing Dog's garments and attire. Nothing there either.

That meant searching through the bones. Her hands shaking, she stepped closer, extended her walking stick, and nudged at a large black mass of them. The end of the stick struck a bone and sent the pile clattering into a collapsed mess. With an angry buzz, a swarm of black flies rose up, disturbing the others. They filled the air in a whirling, droning cloud. She dropped her stick in fright and covered her face with her arms and robe, hunching down. Their tiny bodies beat against her limbs and the cloth of her robe. They wriggled as they trapped themselves in her hair. The tickle of them crawled along her scalp. She would cut off her hair, she resolved. She would cut it all off as soon as she was out of there.

Several flies lit on her arms, and another on her neck, squirming as they climbed along her flesh. The one at the base of her neck gave a sample nip, tasting her. It didn't hurt, but she could take no more—she shrieked and flailed at them with both arms, beating at her neck, her hair, her dress, sending the wretched things careening away to find tent walls upon which to settle.

"Cloud?" came Clay's voice from outside. "Are you all right? I saw a lot of bugs fly out the top opening."

Shaking, she crouched down to take her fallen stick and knocked it against the ground to startle a couple of flies from it. "I'm—I'm fine," she called. "Just gave me a fright, that's all."

The whirring exodus of the nasty little things had not improved the rank odor of the tent, but they had cleared away from the bones somewhat, enough that Cloud could poke around without causing them to swarm again. She prodded a few piles with her stick, lifting the bones to look beneath them. A small clump of flies had not roused with the others. On closer inspection, she saw that they were not even moving. Why had they not stirred when the others had? She poked at them, and their bodies crunched beneath the end of her stick, falling away and littering the ground. Another nudge and more dropped, motionless. They were all dead.

Something solid lay beneath them: a thin crescent of something not like bone poking out of the black mass. With the end of her stick, Cloud pushed the thing out of the pile of dead flies, rolling it toward her. It was a little clay bowl. She knelt down and, with trembling fingers, picked it up, tilting out the remainder of the flies. The hollow of the bowl was dark, so she lifted it into the bright shaft of sunlight beaming through the tent opening.

The inside of the bowl was coated with a shiny, black substance, one she had seen only once before. She scratched at the hard, smooth surface with a thumbnail, lifted it to her face, and sniffed.

Bad eggs and burnt spice.

Anger and grief so powerful she almost couldn't breathe flooded her. She had thought she might find this, even hoped it, but now that she had confirmation…

She stumbled out of the tent, the bowl clutched in one hand.

"Cloud?" Clay sat crouched, keeping a patient gaze on the village below, but turned when he heard her. "What did you find?"

"Proof." She leaned on her stick, relieved to be out of that terrible tent and back in the sunlight.

He came closer, peered at the bowl, then looked at her with inquisitive, worried eyes. "What kind of proof? Is it what you were looking for?"

She pitied him for what he was about to learn, but he had to know. "The stuff in this bowl was used to poison my willow bark. It's what killed Red Moth and Whistling Thorn."

He wrinkled his brow. "But you found that in Laughing Dog's tent. That would mean that he—that he is—"

"A murderer." She spoke the ugly word so that he wouldn't have to.

He stared at her as though she had spoken a nonsense word for a moment, struggling to keep his expression even. His ears twitched. Finally the effort proved too much, and he turned around. She knew it was so she would not see him weep, but she could tell from the bow of his head, his ragged breaths, the shudder of his sides. She put a hand on his back. "Clay, I'm sorry."

"He's my little brother." His voice cracked with grief. "He's just my little brother. It's not his fault. We didn't take care of him. I didn't take care of him. I should have been here. I should have stopped Father from sending him away."

"Don't you speak that way. Laughing Dog made his own choices. You were always a good brother to him. I know it better than most. Your father did too."

He turned to her, his eyes puffy, cheeks streaked dark. "We can still reach him. It's Ogya that's done this, not him." His eyes pleaded with her.

But Laughing Dog had murdered an injured woman and a small boy, and neither of them in crimes of passion nor accident. He had let them die over days. He had known their suffering and done nothing to stop it. These were crimes Cloud could not forgive. They were the kind of crime a man could not come back from. She could not give Clay that untruth, even as a kindness. So she said nothing.

Clay rubbed at his eyes. "What are you going to do?"

"The Teller is going to give his new tale tonight. I expect it will make Laughing Dog angry. He may challenge the Teller or even the King. When he does, I will bring out the proof in front of everyone." She sighed. "I never wanted this. I tried to convince Great Ram before, but he would not listen. There, in front of everyone, he will have to listen. The people will be angry."

"And if he doesn't?"

"He will. Many report that he's disowned Laughing Dog. He's very angry with him already. Now is the moment to act." Cloud gripped Clay's arm and spoke as earnestly as she was able. "But if he is drunk or capricious and doesn't listen, then we all have a King who would let a murderer free among his people. We can't have that, Clay. If that happens, then you have a responsibility. You must know that."

He looked back at her, his face full of grief and fear, and this time, it was he who said nothing.

∧∧∧

Though fueled by no more wood than usual, the council fire burned as high and bright as Cloud had ever seen it, its flames licking above the fences surrounding the village, roaring with intensity, blazing like a beacon. Few villagers danced around the flames tonight; most sat with their loved ones, stretching their fingers over strained bellies. The fire hunters had brought back a great feast of antelope and buffalo, and everyone had eaten and drunk their fill. Now they sat with full, contented bellies around the fire and leaned on each other, chatting. Someone played the drums and another sang, but most sat in a satisfied torpor and waited for the Teller to speak. He had slyly let slip to a loose-tongued few that there might be a brand new tale tonight, and the ensuing conversation had stirred the village into excitement. The Teller's stories rang from the past, so a new one was a rare occurrence.

Cloud sat cross-legged near the back of the circle, her robe folded over her knees. Beneath it, she kept the tainted clay bowl. She scanned the crowd for Laughing Dog, but couldn't see find him among the people. He was not seated with the fire hunters, who clustered together in a group, talking only amongst themselves except when they teased the children. Boys and girls alike, unslowed by the feast, played and laughed near the fire, daring each other to venture close, and tossing rocks or twigs or dirt into it and shrieking with delight when the embers sparked and puffed. Laughing Dog was not near the King, of course, though Clay was, sitting at Great Ram's right hand—a promising sign. The King was so drunk, however, that he could not sit straight, and weaved from side to side like a lazy cobra. That was less hopeful.

Ant With a Leaf was not present. She had been bound and placed in a newly constructed wooden cage with Jai the interloper. That construction alone was an unprecedented disgrace to the village. Other peoples of the world were reputed to put their transgressors in cages, but it had been a point of pride among the People of the Savanna that they had never done so. Now they had two imprisoned at once. Well, it was less cruel than binding them both to the wall, Cloud supposed. She had earlier crept off to carry sizable portions of the feast to both Jai and Ant.

The King's wife, Hibiscus, was also absent from the feast, but that was no surprise. The woman seldom ventured down the hill these days, preferring the shade and comfort of her tent.

But as far as Cloud could see, all others were present—all but Laughing Dog. She wondered what he was up to. It wasn't like him to miss a meal, much less a feast. If he didn't show up to face Cloud's planned challenge, she wasn't sure what she would do. There might be other opportunities, but likely, none as well-timed as this. Not that she had found undeniable evidence of the poisoning, she could hardly keep quiet about it. Even if Laughing Dog planned no further mischief, sooner or later, he would notice the missing bowl, realize it had been taken, and cover his tracks with another clever lie.

Perhaps that's where he was now, Cloud worried. Perhaps he'd already noticed that someone had gone rummaging around in his tent and was looking for the absent evidence of his treason. There was no time to wait. Whether Laughing Dog was there to answer her accusations or not, tonight would have to be the night.

She caught Clay's gaze from across the crowd and nodded to him. He grimaced and looked away. She wondered whether the frown was due to the memory of his brother's crimes or the burden that lay before him. He didn't want rule of the people any more than she did. But it was his birthright. He would have to take it. The people would demand it if Great Ram failed to punish Laughing Dog for poisoning them.

From beyond the fire circle, the Teller came forward, draped in cloths of red and green, yellow beads strung about his neck, the colors faint in the orange light of the bonfire. The crowd settled their chatter as he approached. The drummers' beats died away. The few who had the energy to dance settled to the ground, crossing their legs beneath them. Parents called their children close. Even the King straightened and watched with less of an inebriated sway.

The Teller raised both arms. "Friends," he called. "People of the Savanna. I know you all have been told that you will hear a new story tonight. This is both truth and lie, for all stories that can be told have been told already, and the tale I bring to you tonight is nearly as old as any. It is not as old as the tale of Fam, Earth Mother, who three times made her people out of clay and baked them in the oven of the earth. It is not as old as the tale of Wem, Sky Father, who spat the entire world out of his mouth and found it beautiful. But it is older than the tales of the Firelands, and older than the tales of the savanna and sahil, older than the stories of the trickster Adanko, or the devastation of Mpo, or the great cities of the east. And yet this tale is new, for none of you have heard it before. Would you hear this old tale?"

"We would hear it." Cloud spoke the words along with her people and, for a moment, was united with them again, felt a part of something besides herself.

"Then answer me this: how many of the gods do we need?"

The crowd murmured amongst themselves, but no one answered.

"Could we lose a god or two?" the Teller asked. "Many people are angry with Kwaee, god of the forest. Perhaps we do not need Kwaee anymore. Maybe we, the people of the savanna, could do with one less god."

The murmuring around the circle grew louder, with more than a few tentative calls of agreement, especially from the group of fire hunters.

"But what about Atekye, goddess of the swamp? What has she done for us? Or Mpo, who rules the great water? Do we truly need to worship those goddesses as well? Perhaps we should not follow them either, since we cannot see their designs in the world around us. We are the People of the Savanna, are we not?"

"We are!" the crowd called. Some got to their feet. Some cheered.

"Then what gods do we really need but Sarmu, the god of our land; Wem, the Sky Father; and Fam, the Earth Mother?"

People grew quieter again, their agreement less enthusiastic, more uncomfortable. A Teller wasn't supposed to trick you into agreeing with something that was wrong.

"And all those gods obey Wem, do they not?" the Teller spread his arms wide, his grand robes blowing in the evening wind, his body framed by sparks from the fire. "Then why not serve only Wem ourselves? Why not follow just one god?"

No one spoke now.

"Or perhaps no gods," the Teller suggested.

"No!" someone cried, and others echoed him.

"We need all the gods," someone else said loudly—No Rocks, Cloud thought. Mother of the dead child, Whistling Thorn.

The crowd, most of it anyway, repeated the words in unison: "We need all the gods."

The Teller lowered his arms. "All the gods, yes. But the people of this world did not always believe so. Tonight I will tell you of that time." He made his way around the fire, letting the people quiver for his words. Cloud smiled despite her growing worry. Basket had always loved blowing the crowd before him like leaves on a gust of wind.

"Once, long ago, the forest covered all the land, and the people lived within it, and were happy, and loved all the gods, and the gods loved them.

"But no one loved the people more than did the god Kwaee, and he favored them above all the beasts that crawl on the earth, and above all the birds that fly through the air, and above all that grows from the ground or burrows beneath. He loved the people so much that he would walk among them and speak to them, just as you and I speak to each other. Indeed, there was one whom he loved as man loves wife, and he sang to her the songs of the trees, and he gave to her gifts of the forest, and made her a Queen among the people."

Some of this was not in the report that Clay had given Cloud, and she suspected the Teller of embellishing the story. But as the Teller was fond of saying, there is what happened, and then there is the truth, and they are very often not the same.

"But one night a terrible thing happened."

"What happened?" someone called.

The Teller was silent for a moment, letting the question boil in people's minds before he gave his answer, and they leaned forward with their bodies tense, ready to hear.

He never had a chance to answer.

As he took a deep breath, a woman's scream tore a gash in the silence, shrill and ragged and full of pain and terror. It came from the hilltop at the edge of the village.

People rose from where they seated or crouched, the orange firelight illuminating expressions of shock, fear, and confusion. Had they truly heard it? Was this some strange, new part of the story?

Cloud knew she'd heard it and wasted no time, gathering her robe in her fingers and picking her way past people toward the hill. That was the scream of someone who had been terribly injured. She wracked her memory for who it could be. Who had not come to the feast? Ant With a Leaf, she thought, and her breath went heavy in her lungs. Laughing Dog was not here either. He had done something to her.

Another scream, and this one was deeper, and quieter, and ended in a strangled yelp.

Great Ram leapt to his feet. "Hibiscus!" he shouted. "That is my wife!" He ran forward, but his drunkenness betrayed him, and he tripped over his feet and went sprawling to the ground.

Cloud felt a momentary surge of relief at the thought that the scream might not belong to Ant With a Leaf and then was immediately ashamed. The crowd rose around her, pressing forward. "Out of my way!" she shouted. "Whoever it is will need a healer! Out of my way!"

But the people were too upset to listen. They pushed past her, most of them head and shoulders taller than she, their feet thumping her shins, hips shoving at her sides as the crowd jostled around her. One nearly knocked her to the ground, but she caught herself by grabbing at his arm. In a frightened, chattering group, the people moved up the hill, and if the woman screamed again, Cloud could not hear it over the clamor.

At the top of the hill, the crowd spread out, weaving around the tents toward the one where Hibiscus slept. A man's horrified cry barked above the noise of the crowd. Another. A woman's thin and uncontrolled scream. Another moan. Then the people ahead began to wail and cry.

"What is it?" Cloud called above the noise. She pushed at the heavy bodies in front of her, her thin arms unable to shove past them. "Let me through. I am the healer, by Wem's eyes, let me through!" Still they would not move, so she lifted her walking stick and gave the men in front of her a couple of good whacks to the shoulders. "I said let me through!"

Finally, they seemed to hear her and shuffled aside, one by one. She wriggled past them, giving an extra knock or two with her staff if they didn't move quickly enough. Up near the front of the crowd, men bowed prostrate, their elbows on the ground. Women knelt, their faces turned away, weeping into their hands.

Cloud had seen many bad things in her life. She had seen bones broken through the skin. She had seen disease that puffed people up black and yellow and seeped through their skin. She had seen a man trampled on the head by an elephant, and another gored. She had seen men savaged by lions or hyenas, trying to hold their insides together with both hands. But what she saw now was more terrible than any of these, so horrific that for a moment, her mind refused to accept what her eyes told her.

Hibiscus lay on her back before her tent door, her head toward them, eyes staring into Cloud's, arms spread as though to embrace the heavens. She gasped for breath, blood spattering from her mouth. Something had attacked her, probably inside her tent. Her right leg was bloody and torn below the knee. Cloud guessed that that injury had provoked the first scream. Whatever had gone after her leg had not stopped. There was a hollow where Hibiscus's belly should be, a gaping crescent between ribs and hips. Her blood streamed out into the earth. There was no sign of the infant that had been inside her. Devoured, Cloud thought grimly. Something ate the baby right out of her.

She had been prepared to send someone for herbs and poultices, but there was no helping Hibiscus now. The woman's eyes rolled in fear and pain. Cloud came closer, kneeling down to take her head in her hands. Hibiscus choked for breath and Cloud brushed lightly at her cheek.

"It's okay," Cloud said. "It's gone. It's not going to hurt you again."

"Baby." Hibiscus gasped the word.

For once, she knew what to say. "Your baby will be all right. It's all right."

Hibiscus's struggles eased. The tautness went out of her shoulders and neck.

"What did this, Hibiscus? What attacked you? Was it man or beast?"

Hibiscus looked up at her, her eyes wide. She worked her lips, struggling to form the words. When she finally managed it, she spat the answer more than spoke it, her blood misting the air. "Beast." And then, "Man."

Then Cloud felt her die. It was as though the body became heavier without the spirit to hold it up. Her head sagged, the muscles of her neck limp. Her empty eyes stared up toward Wem, and Cloud closed them with her thumbs.

The crowd behind her was silent, but for weeping. Then Great Ram's voice called out, "What is it? Move aside, curse you, and let me see." Swearing and stumbling with drunkenness, the King shoved his way through the people.

"Go back, Ram," Cloud called, summoning her sharpest voice. "You don't want to see this. It will do you no good. Go back!" She knew the warning was useless. Nothing would keep him away.

"What has happened?" Great Ram said, pushing his way forward. "What have you—" He broke free of the crowd and halted, his demands dying in his throat. He stared at the ravaged corpse of his wife and the hole in her belly. He shook, rubbed at his eyes, and stared again. Then a great, hoarse cry came from him as though torn out of his chest, wordless, almost inhuman. He dropped to his knees and crawled toward Hibiscus, taking her lifeless body and cradling it in his arms, sobbing long, raw howls of despair. The bare white jut of his wife's ribs left streaks of blood on his side.

Cloud got to her feet and turned away, sparing her King the dignity of his grief. The faces of those around her were stricken with grief and fear. Clay stood not far away, and she gave him a questioning look. Had he seen anything like this before? Could his journeys among the gods explain it? He gave a slow shake of his head, his eyes cast low.

"Come on," she said to the crowd. "Come on, let's go. It does no one good to watch now. We will have respect for the dead."

The people listened to her for once, turning to shuffle back down the hill, but then, behind her, the King's voice, harsh and commanding, rasped, "Wait! Who did this? *What* did it? What killed my wife and took my son?" His braids were in his face, his eyes wild, his lips pulled back from his teeth.

The people murmured, but no one spoke up.

"Well?" Great Ram screamed at them. "Well? Someone must have seen something! Who was it? Who saw?"

A man's voice came from the back of the crowd, clear and confident. "I saw it."

The crowd turned, parting to reveal the speaker, though Cloud did not need to see him to know who had spoken. It was Laughing Dog. In that moment, she was absolutely certain that somehow he, or the fire god inside him, was responsible for this, though she had no idea how. And she was just as certain that everything was about to get much worse.

"Where have you been?" the King demanded. "You weren't at the fire tonight."

Laughing Dog moved forward through the crowd, carrying his spear, his great girth supported by a powerful, confident stride. "I was watching the gate. I wanted to ensure all my hunters had the chance to attend the feast," he said. He his eyes lit on Hibiscus, and Cloud saw a flash of shock and dismay cross his face. Could it be possible he didn't know what had happened? He put a hand to his head. "Oh, Ram, this is terrible. Terrible. Now I wish even more that I had caught it."

"Caught it? Caught what?" The whites showed around Great Ram's bulging eyes.

"I was watching the gate, listening to the sounds of the feast up on the hill and feeling hungry. No one had brought me any food. Then, as I turned my head, a shape went by, so quickly that I thought I imagined it. It was only a blur, a movement in the darkness. I assumed it was the wind blowing at the torches and twisting the shadows, but then I heard the screams from inside. Of course, I ran to see what was wrong, but as I did, a beast came out of the shadows. No. Not a beast. Half-beast, half-man. Its jaws and claws were stained with blood. It growled at me, and I thought for certain it would attack, so I held my spear at the ready, but it then it just ran by me. I was certain that it had attacked one of us, so I ran after it as quick as I could, but it was quicker. I pursued it through the village, out of the gate, but then it ran into the forest, and I dared not follow." He glanced at Hibiscus again. "Had I known what a terrible thing it had done, I fear I might have chased it into that dread forest anyway. Now I think surely it must be the same monster that savaged Two Broken hands and killed our father." His fingers tightened around his spear shaft.

Ram stumbled forward, his hands shaking as he reached out to grip Laughing Dog's shoulders. "This monster—what was it? What did it look like?"

Laughing Dog shook his head. "King Great Ram, I should not say. It would be better for all if you didn't know."

"Curse you, Dog," Ram snarled, baring his teeth, "if you saw it, then tell me. Tell me what it was. That is a command from your King!"

The prince looked down. "Then…it was a leopard, King Great Ram. A great leopard that walked upright as a man."

"You—you're a liar!" The voice was Clay's, and everyone turned to look at him.

Cloud's heart sank. No, Clay. What have you done?

"And just how would you know that?" Laughing Dog asked. A triumphant light flashed in his eye.

Clay looked about in panic, clutching at the pendant around his neck. "I—I just—"

"Did *you* see the thing that attacked Hibiscus? From all the way down at the fire circle?"

"No, of course not, but I—"

"Then why do you call me a liar?"

People in the crowd muttered suspiciously. Cloud tightened her fingers on the bowl. She had to do something now.

Clay backed up against the tent behind him, looking frightened. "Because…because—"

Cloud filled her voice with all the righteous anger she could muster. "Because you *are* a liar, Laughing Dog. You want to foul your brother's good name, but you can't even come up with your own story. So you borrow an outsider's."

Laughing Dog bared his teeth at her. "What?"

"We've all heard this nonsense before, from the mouth of the interloper, Jai. Haven't we?" She asked this last of the crowd and was rewarded with a few shouts of agreement. "Something about a leopard that walks upright and murders men, wasn't it? Does that sound like the truth to anyone here?"

"No!" the people cried.

"No, but this mad outsider claims that our Prince Clay travels with an imaginary beast and kills people, and so it's a very convenient story for you, isn't it?"

"And why would it be convenient for me?" Laughing Dog demanded. "Why would I ever want to hurt my dear older brother?"

Cloud hesitated at that. She couldn't very well accuse him of being possessed by Ogya, compelled by a desire to burn the forest to the ground. No one would believe that. She stared at him, then at Great Ram, then at Hibiscus on the ground. What reason would there be besides the mere fact of Clay's inconvenience?

"Well?" Great Ram asked. The hollow, disconnected tones of loss were beginning to flatten his voice. "Do you have an answer, Cloud?"

She looked at the great hole in Hibiscus's belly, then back up at Great Ram. "You have no heir," she whispered.

The King gave her a dull, confused stare, and then he widened his eyes. His expression cracked like slate, and all that was behind it was despair.

"If something happens to Clay, and you die, Laughing Dog becomes King. That's why he wants Clay gone. He's planning to usurp you."

The crowd began muttering again. Laughing Dog looked back and forth at their staring, suspicious faces. His shoulders tensed—and then relaxed. He shook his head and laughed. "Oh, Cloud, you old adder. You've never liked me, but I never thought you could crawl this low to the ground. How can you possibly think I would turn my back on my own family? Next you'll accuse me of calling animals out of the woods to murder Hibiscus myself, I suppose? What will you say next, that I killed my own father?"

She pressed her lips together. "I have not ruled out that possibility."

"You know, I think you might actually mean that. Cloud, no one will be quicker than I to acknowledge all the good you've done for your people, but, well, you're not that young anymore. Do you think you might be getting a little confused?" He feigned sympathy for the crowd, but behind it was a trace of that confident, arrogant smirk. He thought he had won.

"I am sharper than you have ever been, boy."

"We all know you were once wise and quick-witted," Laughing Dog said, nodding to the crowd, "but Cloud, you did poison all those people."

"I thought you might mention that," she said and produced the clay bowl from within her robe. "But you likely didn't know I found this in your tent." She held it high above her head, so at least those standing nearby or tall enough to see over the heads of their fellow villagers could get a look at it. Laughing Dog, at least, recognized it—he gave it a perplexed stare. His eyes widened. So, you hadn't planned for that, had you, she thought in satisfaction.

"What is it, Cloud?" Great Ram asked.

She held it out to him. "King Great Ram, I told you I found poison dripped onto my willow bark, the poison that sickened the people and killed Red Moth and young Whistling Thorn. It looked like hardened black sap and smelled like bad eggs." She glanced out toward the crowd and saw Whistling Thorn's father, Firefly. His mouth was agape, his thick brow low over attentive eyes. "This bowl contains the remains of that same poison. I found it concealed beneath a pile of bones in Laughing Dog's tent. It is difficult to come to any conclusion other than that he deliberately tainted my medicine to discredit me and my counsel."

Laughing Dog stepped backward. "You didn't take that from my tent. You can't prove it."

"Oh, I did. And it was a foul place in there, full of bones and decay and flies. No place for a sane man. No place for a prince. Clay is my witness that I found it within."

"You—you can't believe him! He's the one who's been calling this madness down on us from the forest. It's not even my bowl."

Great Ram lifted his head, his brow furrowing. "It *is* your bowl. I remember when you made it. You pressed that pattern around the rim with a lion's tooth."

Laughing Dog took another step back. Both smirk and false sympathy had vanished from his face now. "Well, even if it were my bowl, that could be anything in there. It's not poison."

"Then convince us," Cloud said. She held the bowl out to him with both hands. "Taste it."

He gaped at her. "I—I'm not going to put that in my mouth. It's disgusting. I—" He faltered, looking at the expressions of suspicion and anger in the crowd, then back to the bowl. Then he reached out and struck it from Cloud's hands, dashing it to the ground.

"You venomous toad!" That was Firefly, pushing his way through the people as though they were river reeds. He pulled his knife from his belt and lunged at Laughing Dog. "You murdered my son!"

The fire hunter Mirage flung himself at Firefly's back and grappled him, pulling him away with both arms as the older man sliced the air with frenzied, desperate strokes.

Laughing Dog scrambled backward, out of his reach, and clutched at his head with both hands, muttering, "No… no…" as if to himself. It was Ogya he was talking to, Cloud had little doubt.

"Let me free!" Firefly bellowed. "I will have justice for my son!" And the crowd shouted its angry assent behind him, pressing forward to converge on Laughing Dog.

"Silence!" Great Ram's voice shouted above them all. Two guards— fire hunters, both of them—stepped to his side and lowered their spears.

The crowd went silent. Laughing Dog hurried to stand behind the guards, next to the King. All were quiet but for Firefly, who had fallen to his knees and now wept moaning sobs into his hands.

"You demand justice?" Great Ram thundered. "You all squabble among yourselves like children while my own wife lies—lies ravaged at your own feet? I will have vengeance for her before all else." He glared at all of them.

After a moment of quiet, he turned to Cloud. "Have you any other proof behind your accusations?"

"Not beyond the discovery of the poison itself, King Great Ram," she answered quietly.

He nodded, and addressed Laughing Dog. "And you. Do you have any proof that this monster you claim to have seen exists?"

Laughing Dog straightened his leathers and took a deep breath, his eyes closed. "We have seen the beast's devastation three times now. I had hoped that that would be enough for you. But yes, since you ask, I do have proof."

"Well?" Great Ram asked, when Laughing Dog said nothing more. "Where is it? Show us this proof!"

"Are you certain you want to see it, my King?"

"Yes, curse you!" Ram snapped. "Of course I want to see it!"

"Then follow me." Laughing Dog turned and lifted a torch from a stand. "And bring Clay." Without another word, he pushed his way through the crowd of people and strode down the hill, the light of his torch blazing above his head like a beacon.

"Wait just a minute," Great Ram called after him, but Laughing Dog did not stop, and the curious crowd began to mill after him.

Two fire hunters clasped Clay's shoulders and propelled him roughly behind the crowd. "You're in for it now," one of them—Scorpion, grinning nastily—whispered in his ear, though loud enough that Cloud could easily hear it. She wondered what he knew.

The King stared after them with a stricken expression. "What has happened, Father?" he asked the stars. "I tried to do right, and now everything has fallen apart."

"It's never too late to do right," Cloud told him. He twitched his head toward her as though he had forgotten she was there, and when she reached out to put a comforting hand on his arm, he pulled away.

"It's too late for everything," he slurred. Even shock and grief had not been able to cleanse the palm wine from his tongue. "One way or another, my family ends tonight." He bent in the direction of his wife, but did not look at her. "It has already ended." Then he followed the crowd down the hill toward whatever terrible surprise Laughing Dog had waiting.

Cloud paused by the body of Hibiscus, her belly open to the moon and wind. It wasn't right, leaving her here like this, unattended. Her body should be cleaned, the wound bound, her skin treated with palm oil, her hair with incense. She was dead, and now left lying in the dirt. It was the healer's job to take care of these things. But it couldn't be helped. Clay needed Cloud. "I'm sorry, Hibiscus," she said. She made her way down the hill, letting her walking stick bear her and the deepening heaviness in her bones.

⁓

When finally she caught up to the crowd, they were moving single file against the outside wall, flattening themselves against it, shrinking away from the threat of the deadly forest that bordered it to the south. The ground was littered with the wreckage of tents and the remains of the smashed fence. No one looked very happy to be here, this close to the threat of the murderous woods, but they followed Laughing Dog nonetheless.

Cloud had some difficulty picking her way through the branches and poles that sprawled across her path or jutted up irregularly, and had to depend on the scant light of the torches ahead to illuminate her way. She balanced uneasily on a log too large to step over, and her stick slid on the soft, wet wood. She felt herself tipping, teetering. A strong arm caught her, hefted her up with a squeeze, and set her safely down on the ground. She looked up to see Left Rabbit, and thanked him, but he just nodded and moved ahead.

The people gathered, pushing and jostling each other, just outside the little section of the forest where a large patch of strange fruits had grown and been smashed by Laughing Dog and his fire hunters. Though the area was reportedly safe to stand in, no one dared venture inside. It might be a trap. The forest might turn at any moment. In the midst of the crowd, at the edge of the destruction, stood Laughing Dog, already speaking, the King at his side. Each of the two fire hunters had Clay's arms gripped firmly in their hands. He must have struggled against them before, for his face was dark and puffy, and he now sagged between them with a defeated expression.

"And it was here that I saw Clay," Laughing Dog cried, his voice ringing out in the night air, "outside of the village without the guard King Great Ram assigned to him. What could he be doing out here in the forest, I wondered. I hid myself in the bushes so he would not see me. He was dancing a strange dance that I have never seen before, and he prayed to someone he named 'Lord Doto.' It was just as the outsider Jai told us. Clay said in his prayer of anger that someone he named 'unworthy' had taken his Father's reign, and called for this demon to which he prayed—or god," he added in response to the restless murmurs from the crowd, "or whatever it may be, to deliver the rule to him. He thanked it for all that it had done so far and prayed that it would return on the morning of the fourth day hence to receive his offering."

Rapt faces flickered in the twilight—some suspicious, others angry, but most just frightened, flinching at the flicker of shadows in the night. Cloud watched them out of the corner of one eye, gauging who nodded approval at Laughing Dog's words and who frowned in disbelief. Then she caught Left Rabbit's expression. He was staring not at Laughing Dog, but out into the darkness of the forest. His brow was furrowed, and he muttered something to himself. She couldn't hear his voice, but his tongue curled around the words: *Lies. Lies. Lies.*

Great Ram scowled, the torchlight warping his features into a parody of his father's. Even from a distance, Cloud could see the way grief tortured his expressions, and she recalled the old King after losing his wife. "If all this were true, then why did you not come to me at once? Why did you keep it to yourself?"

Laughing Dog smiled, and his eyes flashed as they caught the light. "Because, brother, you ordered me not to. Remember? What did you say, exactly? 'You will not offer me a single word of advice or counsel, by order of the King,' I think. What could I do?"

Great Ram glowered at him, but could offer no argument, surrounded by his subjects. "Well, it's all a frightening story, but where is your proof, Laughing Dog? You said you had it. Now my wife's body cools and my grief beats at my eyes, and all I hear from you are demon tales."

"But I haven't even told you the most frightening part," Laughing Dog said. "Clay told us the gods healed his foot. And maybe they did. But there, dancing in the forest, he had a *leopard's* foot. If this is indeed our brother Clay, he is not human anymore."

Cloud knew now what Laughing Dog intended to do, and there was no way to stop it, but she pushed her way forward anyhow, daring to step inside the forest if only to move more quickly around the crowd. She called the king's name, but her voice was joined by the gasps and cries of the people.

"This is madness!" the King shouted above the din. "Do you expect any of us to believe this? A leopard's foot? Why should I trust you now?"

Laughing Dog smiled. "You do not have to. You can trust your own eyes."

The pain in her knees and ankles protested, but Cloud forced herself to the front of the group. "King Great Ram, no. Please, you must not listen to him. If ever you trusted me in anything, trust me now. Your brother deceives you."

"You've conspired against your King long enough, Cloud," Laughing Dog said. "It ends tonight."

There was movement behind her. Strong hands gripped her shoulders and held her in place. She did not have to look to know they would be ash-painted. There was no point in struggling. She tried to think of what to say. She never knew what to say.

Laughing Dog nodded to the hunters holding Clay.

Gripping his arms, they dragged him up to the very edge of the forest. He squirmed and thrashed in their grasp, but could not escape. His eyes locked with Cloud's, frightened, pleading. She reached out toward him and the hands on her shoulders tightened in warning.

The two hunters holding Clay exchanged glances. They stepped forward, their forearms bulging hard with their grip, and dragged him beyond the edge of destruction, into the forest.

Clay's chest swelled with a deep, gasping breath, the look on his face almost one of pleasure. Then his foot and leg changed, warping too quickly for the eye to follow into something bestial, powerful and clawed. Fur wrapped his leg from his toes, all the way up his leg past the knee.

People screamed, and nearly the whole crowd pressed backward, up against the wall, those who could not see what had happened responding to the fear from those who had. Cloud could not fault their reaction. Even though she had known what to expect, the sight was inherently frightening. If a leg was human one minute, it was supposed to be human the next. To see it change, distort, become something else—it hurt something in her mind, something that needed the world to be stable and understandable. It scared her. She had always believed in the old stories, but stories were supposed to be told around fires or sung to the stars, the pictures only in your head. Now they shouted themselves to the world.

Now gods and monsters were stepping out of the tales, reminding them all that tales were once actions, events, witnessed by real people in the real world. Stories were not just part of all their pasts. They bared their teeth in the present, they howled down a wild and unknowable future.

Clay had regained some of his fight with his change, tugging and pulling at his arms. He wrenched like a beast, his body writhing, and as the muscles in his new leg strained, the fire hunters had more difficulty keeping hold of him. "Please," he begged. "Please let me go. I will try to explain what I can, I promise! If you love the gods, let me go!"

His pleas went unacknowledged. The King stood aghast, his mouth slackened, eyes wide. Even he had taken a step back. But not Laughing Dog. Laughing Dog stood straight and confident. He knew he had won. "Look, brother. Would you ever have believed me before?"

"I would not." Ram whispered the words, never tearing his eyes from Clay. His face bulged with fury.

"And it is not just the leg. Look at the forest. See how it moves around him? See the grass sway? See the roots and vines?" He pointed.

Cloud leaned forward in the grip of the fire hunter behind her, straining to see. At first she thought it a trick of the flickering firelight, but no— the grass was moving, pulling backward in the same direction that Clay tugged, and when he shifted direction, so did the grass. Around the feet of the fire hunters, roots and tendrils from nearby plants plucked at their toes and ankles, some of the smaller, lengthier vines curling all the way about.

"You see?" Laughing Dog said. "It is not just the thing's leg. It might once have been our brother, but now it is a creature of the forest. The wood itself moves to free the beast. This is what called down the leopard demon that killed your wife. I am certain of it."

A low, inarticulate moan rose from Great Ram's throat. He fumbled at his belt for his knife and then lunged at Clay, knocking him to the ground. Clay cried out as he fell. Ram crouched over him, his knife raised.

Cloud had seen many deaths. The sight was never welcome. But she could not bear to see this boy die. She looked away.

"Brother, wait!" Laughing Dog's voice rose above the shrieks of the crowd.

The King shuddered at the cry. He looked over his shoulder, eyes wild, streaming with furious tears. "What?"

"Do you not want vengeance?"

"Of course I do! I'll kill him for what he did to Hibiscus! To my child. Gods, my child!"

"But what of the demon, Doto, that killed her for him? Suppose it killed Two Broken Hands, and father as well? Do you not want vengeance?"

"I swear my most terrible vengeance on the demon *and* on the miserable traitor who called it," Great Ram vowed through bared teeth.

"Then we must keep Clay alive a little while longer. Remember? The beast intended to return for him the morning after next. It may not come if its ally has been slain. Stay your vengeance, brother, and we can catch both at once."

Great Ram stared at him. The hand holding the knife shook.

"Only a day and a night more," Laughing Dog said, his voice calm and soothing. "At the moment of that dawn, you will be avenged. Hold onto your wrath until then. And think how you would torment yourself if you allowed your tender heart any doubts, if you did not give yourself this final, certain proof. Wait until the demon shows. The instant he does, Clay dies."

The King turned back gripped his knife more tightly, and then flung it aside. He collapsed into a huddle on the forest floor, his back shaking with weeping.

Laughing Dog pointed at the two fire hunters standing over Clay. "Pick him up. Take him back to the village and confine him. Make certain he is securely bound and guarded. We cannot have him escape, nor risk that the beast may come and attempt to free him before we are ready."

They dipped their heads. "Yes, Prince Laughing Dog."

He turned to the guard holding Cloud. "And you. See that she is confined as well. She has colluded with him to usurp rule of the People of the Savanna, along with Ant With a Leaf and the Teller."

The people cried out in shock at this last claim.

"They must all be imprisoned. The King will decide their fates later."

The fire hunter guided her back to the gate, heavy hand never releasing her shoulder, though the notion that she might actually escape him was unthinkable. She obeyed his nudging directions in a haze.

What had happened? In the span of less than a year, everything had gone wrong. Clay would be killed. She could see no way around it. And she and Ant and the Teller would all suffer. But worse than all of that, she had failed her friend, First Claw, who had asked her to guide his people and look after his sons after he was gone. She had sworn to do so. But now his sons were maddened, possessed, or…something else, and his people were in the grip of a malevolent god. Maybe she could have done something. She should have done something. She should have challenged Great Ram for right to rule, given it back to the council.

But it was too late. Whatever Laughing Dog and Ogya had planned, she could see no way to stop it now.

The City Time Forgot

What could the life of one little fire bearer mean, compared to the unfathomable breadth of the forest? Seated on his throne, lost in the flow of the forest, Doto could almost forget Clay. He immersed himself in his father's domain. He let it sprout from his eyes and set roots through his toes. He filled his mind with the roar of all life so that the voice of his sole worshiper might be drowned out. He needed to forget.

He drifted on the wind and floated in swamp water. He nestled in the wings of birds and rode the feet of ants on their winding patterns. He hid in the living blood carried in the belly of a fat mosquito. The forest was infinite, and it could hide him from those things he couldn't bear to see.

Then he followed the snuffling of a forest pig and found the scent of Clay in the leaves. In that instant, all his forgetfulness shattered. He sought to cast his mind someplace, but it was impossible. There were reminders of Clay all throughout the forest, little imprints of him in the soil, traces of the oil of his fingers on the bark of a tree, the scattered trails of waste and scent that every living being leaves behind. And now that he considered them, they prodded at the edges of his mind. He circled his awareness around one of these spots. A footprint, still in the mud. A rut, where Clay's wooden paw had slid and scarred the earth, tearing grass, gashing a root.

On an impulse, Doto moved the gashed root, sliding it under the earth, plucking it away from its bush. He stirred the earth smooth with the roots of other trees, and sent deer to eat the torn grass. There. Now no trace of Clay remained in that spot. Doto had erased the forest's memory of him there. That place would never again remind him that Clay had existed. Erasing it created a kind of deep, hollow pain inside him, but also a sense of satisfaction.

He found another spot and cleared that,too, stirring the earth and shifting the leaves. That hollowness deepened, and he was pleased. He deserved the pain. He was a forest god, not a beast, and yet he had loved and mated and fought like one. He had ignored his father's warnings. Following the trail through the forest, he began purging every sign that Clay had ever been there.

Then he reached the little circle of flowers, deep in the forest, where Clay had first danced for him—the very first time he had felt the love and worship of a fire bearer, where the song to him had been composed, where the feather that marked him as adored by the fire bearers had sprouted from his forehead. There, he had felt his first taste of joy. It was holy ground. It belonged to him and Clay. And it would forever be an unwelcome reminder of his lost love, unless he removed it.

With a bitter thrill, he sent his will into the circle and wilted the flowers. They shriveled, curled, and fell into the reeds, brown and dry. The vines cracked and died, the grass thinned, and the sprouting saplings went still and hard. Then he surrendered the territory, ceding that small, stolen parcel of land back to his father. The forest circle was Kwaee's once again.

Step by step, he followed the trail to the next circle. That would have to go as well. All of them would have to go. And his own temple—he would have to erase any signs of Clay's visit there. It would be the only way he could go on once Clay was... He could not make himself finish the thought, so tore his mind away from it and set to the task of erasing the second forest circle.

But as he worked at killing off all the new life that had grown there, his connection to the forest was suddenly severed. He found himself in the air, spinning upside down. He twisted his body as he fell, landing in a crouch. He was still in his father's temple. "What happened?" he demanded, looking around, his hackles prickling.

Kwaee stood near their thrones, ears back. "Why would you not answer me?" he demanded, echoes of familiar anger and fear barking in his voice.

Doto stood, brushing his fur back into place. "I didn't hear you speaking."

"What were you doing? I had to wrest you from the throne to stop you!"

"I was tending the forest. That's all. What has upset you so?"

"You cannot be so oblivious as that." Kwaee gestured toward the edges of his temple. "Look. *Listen.*"

Doto pricked his ears, and then was astonished he had not heard it before. A sound like that of a heavy rain whispered from the forest. It was as though a great storm had descended on the trees, but there was no rain and no wind. He looked up. The leaves were falling from the trees, letting go their branches and cascading to the ground in green curtains. "No," he whispered. He sent his awareness up to the bird above the treetops. Everywhere, as far as their eyes could see, the leaves fell.

"What did you do?" Kwaee demanded. "Do you have any idea how much time and effort it will take me to repair the damage you caused?"

"I didn't know it was happening! I was only trying to remove the traces of…of…"

Kwaee's voice softened with sympathy. "Your little fire bearer? You still have not let go of it? Son, you know you cannot touch the forest with these emotions in you. A god cannot afford that. See how your attachment hurts our domain? When you are unhappy, the forest is unhappy. But I cannot think what you might have been doing that would kill the forest like this. You must control these feelings."

"How am I supposed to do that?" Doto asked. "Clay's going to die, Father. He's going to be killed by—by *Ogya*. And there's a chance I could save him."

"You can't save this creature. You know that. Even if you could rescue it for a day, or a year, or a hundred years, it would die. And the longer you spent with it, the more attached you would become. The pain would be that much greater. It is better to let it go now."

"Even if I love him?"

Kwaee sighed and came forward, putting a warm but rough paw on Doto's shoulder. "Son. You know so little of love. Yours is young. All you understand is its infant breaths and its kittenish energy. It is enthralling, I know. You feel that you cannot get enough. But I have watched many fire bearers within my forest and have seen their affections and their bonds, and what happens after. What you do not know about love is that it *always* ends in pain. Always. It is part of the natural law. Love dies, or lovers die, and those are the only ways it can end. The longer and stronger the love, the more terrible when it's over. Look at how you are now, so twisted and tormented you began to kill the whole forest. How would you be if that love burrowed deep into you? What would pain like that, like you cannot even comprehend, destroy? I know you wish to save your fire bearer, but for your own sake and for the sake of the whole forest, you must let it die."

"Couldn't I just save him and leave after that?" Doto pleaded miserably.

"No!" His father gripped his shoulder tighter. "Listen to me. Whatever you do, stay away from their nest, and especially stay away from Ogya. In a day's time, this will all be over. Understand?" He fixed Doto with a steady gaze.

"I understand."

"Good." His father released his shoulder and looked out into the forest. "I had better start undoing the damage you caused. If you did this to my own forest, I cannot imagine what your own temple must look like."

Doto cringed. "My temple…" Without looking, he knew what had happened to it, but he couldn't bear to consider it from afar. He had to see it with his own eyes. "I'm sorry, Father. I have to go."

Without waiting for acknowledgement or permission, he bolted from the temple. At his top speed, he tore through the forest, a golden streak, moving too quickly to pay much attention to the world around him. He knew that there was a chance now that he might trip, or that a bush or liana might not move out of his way in time, but he didn't care. He would just get up and keep running.

Even at this speed, he could tell that the havoc he had wrought in the forest was severe; in places, he ran through piles of freshly fallen leaves that nearly reached his waist. Birds blinked, perplexed, from their perches on bared branches, their nests exposed. He had never in his life done something so terrible and far-reaching before, nor could he have on his own, but in the seat of the forest, connected to all that power, he had harmed the world without even thinking of it. But even now he could see his father's restorative magic at work, forming fresh green buds at the end of each twig. In a few days, or a moon perhaps, the forest would be restored.

He raced up the side of the mountain that cradled his temple, and even before he reached it, he could see the damage. The stream that ran through it was dammed up, clogged with fallen trees and leaves. It spread across the meadow below his temple in a growing pool.

The trees guarding the only opening to his temple were bare as old bones. He paused at the entrance, panting, though whether in exhaustion or shock he wasn't certain. He stepped inside. Everywhere there was death. All his flowers and vines had wilted. The mushrooms had shriveled and turned brown. Fruit had gone soft and fallen off the vine, lying in sagging, pungent pillows below their stalks and branches. The soft, mossy bed where he had mated Clay was now grey and brittle, crunching under his paws. The strings of nude willow branches hung from dying trees and swayed in the wind. There was no color or life anywhere, except in the poison brambles. These he had felt growing long ago, when he first left the temple with Clay on their journey to the savanna. He had felt them sprout from his soil and grow thick, wicked thorns. Now the brambles filled his temple, their coils as thick around as his arms, lined with dark red, tooth-like barbs that glistened wetly in the moonlight. All along the brambles, dark purple fruits had sprouted, fat and heavy. Doto knew without trying them that they would be bitter, and deadly poisonous.

This was what love had made of him. It had gone wrong. Everything had gone wrong. This was what he was now. And Clay would die.

Doto sat in the middle of his temple, next to the stream that floated with fallen leaves and dead flowers, and wept.

In the middle of the night, an awareness plucked his senses. He looked up. Something was wrong, something missing from the world. He got to his feet and ventured outside his temple. The trees outside were tipped with baby leaves, tiny and yellow-green. His father had made great progress in repairing the forest. Doto looked around, sending his senses out. Something was certainly awry. Then he realized: he could not feel Kwaee. Just as it had been the day when Doto had first returned to the forest and his father's temple, Kwaee was gone. The ripples of power that should have been emanating from the forest god's location were still and silent.

The feeling was familiar, though only now, in his temple, did his father's absence stir old memories. There had been times before this, many times, when the ebb and flow of divine magic in the forest had faded. He had never paid it much mind; it was no more remarkable than the errant twinkle of a star, and indeed, often he had always wished to avoid his father, so an absence was welcome rather than concerning. But surely this meant that his father was not in his temple, nor indeed in the forest at all, but someplace where his magic could not touch it.

The mystery stirred Doto from his grief. Why should he not be able to tell where his father was? Could he actually have left the forest? For a hopeful moment, Doto considered that perhaps his father had gone to save Clay himself. He almost laughed at the thought. Kwaee would not even dare look out into the rest of the forest, much less venture outside of its borders. He would never approach the fire bearers, especially not if Ogya walked among them. So if not outside the forest, where could he be, that Doto could not detect him?

Surely no place in all the forest could still a god's magic so. But no. There was one place after all, and Doto had been there with Clay: the lost city where Kwaee had killed all the fire bearers. Where Doto's mother had died. The place no god's power touched. Abansin. But why would his father have gone there? And why would he have been there before?

Doto had to know. He looked back at his desolated temple, sick and poisonous. It hurt to look upon. But he could not spare the time to think about healing it now.

He ran. With long strides, he streaked through the forest, knowing that at any moment, Kwaee might return to his temple and leave this mystery unanswered again. He moved silent in the night, determination pushing aside any weakness or unsureness in his step, his divine strength with him.

Perched atop the cascades of the mighty Asubonten where the broken stone tongue stretched out over the waters, the eerie ruins blotted out the starlight. The shadow of the great artificial mountain jutted up into the sky like a broken ear, rough-hewn buildings squatted below it along the root-shattered stone path that led into the center.

Doto stalked back and forth outside. His tail switched. This was not a place he was meant to enter. Raw fear seemed to crawl out of its warped configurations, to linger in its darkened doorways and eroded bones and plants. The city was wrong, outside the laws of nature. Perhaps his father was not here. It would be better to look somewhere else first.

A sound made his ears prick—deep, muttered words echoing off of stone walls. The strangeness of the place warped the words so that he could not make them out, but he recognized the accents and intonation of god-tongue. Then his father was here after all. He crept inside, and the strangeness enveloped him, folding and flowing around his skin as he moved, like a river of cold mud.

Everything about Abansin was wrong. The air drooped flat and lifeless, and a breath drawn from it felt like suffocation. Sounds did not carry as they should, but warped high and thin, or rumbling and syrupy. A footstep might sound like an earthquake or be completely inaudible. Even the light bent oddly; the edges of everything looked too crisp and angular. Doto had had dreams, when out on the savanna, and Abansin reminded him of those. It was a place badly remembered, somewhere between reality and thought.

As he moved through the city, grass and flowers sprouted in his footsteps, his divine presence restoring natural law to the land, if only for a short time. Strangely, he could see no trace of his previous trip through Abansin. He had left footprints of grass then, with flowers sprouting in them, his paws restoring divine magic wherever he'd set them, but those had been erased clean.

The sound of the mutterings echoed along the path into the city, and he followed them, keeping his eyes forward and trained away from the gaping maws of buildings that hid bones of dead occupants, their walls clutched by twisting tree trunks and gnarling branches as though they were in the grasp of giant, green spiders.

"I'm sorry. I'm sorry," the words came bounced off of the stone walls in slow echoes. The voice was unmistakably Kwaee's. Beneath it were rattling sounds, as though someone rummaged through branches or stones.

Doto crouched lower. He could feel no emanations of power coming from ahead, but if there were some way for a god to mask his presence, Doto did not know it. Perhaps it was simply the atmosphere of this place that suppressed it. When he reached the large, open square near the base of the crafted mountain, filled with the bones of hundreds of fire bearers, he crept even more quietly, letting his rosettes mask him from the light—an instinct only, and one he doubted would deceive his father. He sidled up to one of the stone buildings and peered around.

Kwaee crouched in the middle of the square, his tail limp, his ears flattened to either side, plumage lowered. He picked through a pile of bones, one that Doto was suddenly certain he'd rummaged through many times before. Finding a skull, he lifted it in one huge paw and turned it over and over, inspecting it.

"Was this you? I think…I think maybe…?" He tilted his head one direction, then the other, and then replaced the skull with surprising delicacy. "Or maybe this?" He plucked up another. "Yes, this. This was you."

Doto could not discern any markings that distinguished this skull from any other. All fire bearer bones looked alike.

With both arms, Kwaee hugged the skull to his chest. "Are you with Wem now? I've asked him where your spirits go when you die, but he doesn't answer us. He never has. He put us here and gave us power and told us nothing." He sighed. "I miss you, Oko. A thousand years, and you haven't let me go. Why will you not let me go? I tried to stop it. I came back. You know I came back. I tried to stop everything but it was too late. I stopped what I could." He sat and buried his face in his paws. "I tried to stop it."

Doto stood from his crouch, his fur prickling. Oko? Was that his mother's name? Could that be her skull in his father's arms? He leaned closer, watching intently, but his father only sat, his face hidden, body motionless but for the shaking of his shoulders. As if in a dream, Doto stepped forward. "Father?"

Kwaee started, looking up with wide eyes. Anger replaced surprise on his face. "What are you doing here?" he snarled. "I told you never to come here."

"What are *you* doing here?" Doto switched his tail. "Picking through old bones, talking to them? Are you mad?"

Kwaee did not meet his son's gaze. "That is none of your concern. This is my forest. I am the god here. I will go where I choose."

Doto took several careful steps forward, keeping his voice calm, reasonable. "But this place is wrong. It's abandoned by the gods. How can it be like this if you—"

"What are you doing?" Kwaee shouted at him, pointing at the ground. "Look what you've done!"

Doto followed his finger to the line of grass footprints he'd left through the city. "I'm not *doing* anything. It just happens," he tried to explain, but Kwaee rushed forward, pushing past him.

"You can't bring plants in here! You'll ruin it! Everything has to stay. Stay as it was." The great leopard knelt and put one paw to the ground, closing his eyes. The paw prints of grass and flowers shriveled and retreated, stems dwindling and shrinking back into the earth as though they'd never been, footprint after footprint erased from the city. Again Doto's fur prickled. These actions of his father were deranged—but less than a day ago, Doto himself had been wiping away Clay's footprints from the forest.

"This place isn't like this because you forgot it," Doto said in dawning understanding. "You've been *keeping* it like this. Keeping the plants and the bones from growing, or aging, or rotting away."

Kwaee opened his eyes and scowled, but he shifted from side to side like a cornered animal. "So what if I am?"

"But that's mad! How long have you been doing this? A thousand years?"

"What concern is it of yours? It is not your forest, nor your city, and it is not your fire bearer."

"That's my mother, isn't it?" Doto demanded, and as soon as he saw the look on Kwaee's face, he knew he was right. "You didn't forget her. You didn't grow past it. You've been—been keeping her here like this. You told me I should let Clay go, that it would hurt for a while, but I would get better. But you never did!"

Kwaee backed away. "That is different."

"No, it isn't." Doto stepped toward him, getting even closer than before. He was aware now how much his father towered over him, nearly twice his height, and yet in this moment, Doto felt taller, surer, stronger.

"It just is. You won't feel what I did. You'll heal."

"How can you say that?" Doto shouted. "How can you say that I won't hurt like you did? Do you know what I did today? Do you know what my temple looks like? Do you have any idea how much it hurts already?"

"But you'll get over it. You can forget."

"And why can I forget? How am I different? How do you know you're not turning me into a—a—" He lifted his arms toward the eroded city, frozen in a moment in time from a thousand years ago, never aging, never dying, and yet more dead and empty and old than anything else in the world. "—A mad fool like you? How am I different, Father?"

"Because you don't have to watch yours die!" Kwaee roared, and at the moment of his bellow, the ground around his feet erupted in black thorns. The ancient green of the frayed grass turned grey and dead in a circle, spreading outward. The blades disintegrated into dust, hovering in the air about his toes. "Oh no," he gasped. He dropped to all fours, and as he did so, the skull tumbled from the crook of his arm and broke on the ground. The eye sockets sagged as the bone crumbled.

"No!" he cried. "Look what you've done! Look what you made me do! No!" He crawled around on all fours, scooping up fragments of the skull in his fingers, trying to seam them back together with his magic, but they turned to dust in his paws. "I tried to stop it, Oko," he moaned. "I tried to stop it, but I was too late."

The city shuddered as though waking, and the still air stirred. The dust streamed from between Kwaee's fingers.

Doto stared at him. "You watched her die. You were there." Realization prickled down his spine. "You haven't been hiding from the forest this whole time. You've been hiding from yourself. Because you could have stopped it. You could have done something, and you did nothing!"

"Done something, done something," Kwaee repeated, watching the dirt sift through his paws. "What could I have done?"

"You could have saved her!" Doto wanted to shake him. "You had the power! You could have healed her!"

"Healed her." Kwaee shook his head. "You think I should have healed her. The cost. The cost was far too high."

"Higher than this?" Doto waved again at the ruined city, at his father wallowing like an animal in a circle of decay.

His father laughed bitterly. "Higher than this. You have no idea what healing costs."

"Yes, I do," Doto said quietly.

"What?" Kwaee sounded distantly puzzled. He looked up, fear glowing in his eyes. "What do you mean?"

"I know what it takes to heal. Clay's foot. I healed it. He was dying, remember? He would never have lived if I hadn't saved him."

"But—but that means you lost—"

"Some of my power, yes," Doto said. "And he gained it. And I would do it again. And again if I had to. I told you. I love him."

Kwaee said nothing to that.

"Look at you. You've been doing this for a thousand years because you wouldn't save her." Doto clenched his fingers into fists. "And you were going to make me do the same. You were trying to stop me from saving Clay!"

Kwaee looked away, at the great pile of bones in the middle of Abansin, the branches and vines that wound throughout them. "I thought...I thought if you didn't see... Look what I did when I saw it! Just look, son! Are you willing to risk that? Are you willing to risk what you'll do if you have to watch him die? You are a god! You won't be able to control your power. You'll do terrible things, son! Terrible!"

"Not saving the person you love, that's a terrible thing," Doto said. "You were too late for yours. But I won't be."

As if in answer to his vow, an eagle screamed above. Its cry was answered by the calls of forest birds, hundreds of them, waking. Doto turned to look. The pale promise of the approaching dawn lit the eastern sky.

A Line of Fire

None of the people came to visit Clay on his last day in the village. He had been securely tied, wrists and ankles, and deposited in his tent, a fire hunter posted outside his door to be sure he didn't somehow get free and escape—or maybe to ensure that nothing came in after him to set him free. With his arms tied behind his back, he could find no comfortable position to lie down, so he rested on one side on his pallet. His shoulder and arm dug into his side, and in the heat of the day, his sweat streamed down his side and face and soaked the hides, but he scarcely noticed. He tried to understand how he had ended up here, his father dead, his brothers turned against him. Even the gods had stopped answering him.

Waiting was all he could do now. If there had been some task he was supposed to have performed, some prayer he had failed to utter that would have prevented all this, it was too late. Laughing Dog and Ogya had all but seized control of the village. He entertained thoughts of waiting until night and somehow scratching through the coarse palm fiber cords that cinched his ankles. He could steal through the village until he found a knife, then try to free Cloud, Ant With a Leaf, and the Teller. But then what? Escape into the wilderness? There would be nowhere for them to go.

And they had no remaining allies in the village. Clay had hoped a few might have remained loyal among his friends and extended family. But no one came to visit. They had believed Laughing Dog, whose lies were so close to the truth that they were almost uncontestable. That, or they were under orders not to approach Clay or speak to him, which was likely.

Still, on his last day to live, he would have liked to have seen somebody. He would have liked to hear a comforting voice, someone to tell him he'd done all right. Instead he had only his hot tent and fingers and toes that tingled as they fell asleep. Several times during the day, the tent opened to admit three fire hunters who held him at spearpoint as they placed a bowl of water and a little meat and fruit next to his bed. They snatched their hands away quickly, as though he were a mad jackal, and would not respond to his pleas for information, nor his insistence on seeing Great Ram again. Their faces were drawn, their lips tight, and they said no words to him. He'd known them all since he was a boy.

The day seemed shorter than a day should be. He had expected it to crawl by interminably, but the daylight turned low and orange long before it should have. He felt cheated to have this final day of life rush past him. Perhaps it was the certainty of death that took it from him.

Still, he had the night remaining to him. Then, before dawn, his brothers—his own family—would drag him out of his tent, past the whole village, to the edge of the forest. Then they would wait for Doto. But, of course, Doto would not come. Clay would not call him.

He wasn't sure why Laughing Dog had made the claim that the forest god would appear tomorrow morning. He must expect that Clay would call to him, pray to him, and beg him to come. But why wait a full day? Why not that same morning? Maybe he wanted to give Clay time to grow afraid of death, to be sure that he would beg and plead with Doto to come. Then Ogya would use some trap—lure Doto out of the forest, perhaps, and imprison him in fire as he had the god Sarmu.

But if that was Laughing Dog's plan, why promise to kill Clay when Doto appeared? It didn't make sense, and the more Clay considered it, the more puzzled he grew. But he would not call out to Doto, no matter what happened. And even if he did, Doto would not come. The god had not answered his prayers for days. Perhaps he didn't hear Clay's prayers. Maybe he was trapped by Kwaee and could not come. Maybe he had changed his mind about Clay and would not. That thought pained more than anything else, and a distant part of him marveled at the pain. Everyone in his old life either hated and feared him or had been imprisoned, but the one thing that sent him truly dizzy with grief was the thought that his god had abandoned him.

He had no illusions that he would survive the next day. Doto would not appear, and then Laughing Dog and Great Ram would be disappointed, but they would not spare him. They would have him standing there in the forest while they waited. It would be easy for Great Ram to kill him there, where his foot would curl into a leopard's paw, where they could all see the inhuman thing that he'd become. Tomorrow morning, his soul would rise up to Father Wem.

If that were true, he reminded himself bitterly. He had never asked any of the gods what happened to souls when people died. It had never occurred to him before now that his people's tales about that might be just as false as their tales about how they were given fire. Maybe souls perished at death. Or maybe, he considered with a rising horror, every time the people burned a body, they gave it over to Ogya. Yes, wasn't that what Doto had said? That everything burned became Ogya's territory? Clay thought of the fire god owning dominion over his dead flesh, and hoped with a sudden fervor that his people would refuse to honor his body and would not burn it, but leave it in the forest to rot and be taken by animals. There, in some small way, he could be with Doto forever. Or at least until Ogya burned the forest down, he reminded himself.

His thoughts grew bleaker as the night deepened, his misery flattening into a dull despair, and his worries into a fear that shook at his bones. He longed for just one person to come and talk to him, even an angry person. It would be better than this. But still no one came, nor could he hear voices around his tent. And so he did the only thing he could still do: he prayed. Not to Doto—even if his prayers could be heard by a half-god at such a distance, he dared not risk that Doto might learn of his plight and come to save him. But he prayed to Kwaee, asking that the god of the forest see how the people worshiped him and how they needed the forest. He asked Kwaee to forgive the people and let his wrath towards them go. And he asked that Kwaee learn the goodness of his son, to be a father to him once again.

He prayed to Sarmu, urging him to rise up from his prison, to break free and help the people of the savanna, whom he loved but had abandoned. He prayed to Asubonten and Atekye and Mpo, reminding them all that the people loved them and worshiped them. He even prayed to Adanko, god of hares, and all the other minor gods he could name. He prayed to Ogya, asking that his insatiable hunger be quenched at last, that his greed no longer consume him, and that he turn back, satisfied with the power he had taken already.

And last, he prayed to Father Wem and Mother Fam, asking them to remember the people they created, reminding them that the people suffered but loved them still. He begged them not to forget their creations now, when it seemed like the whole world would be swallowed in fire.

Then there was no one left to pray to, so he lay in the dark and tried not to fall asleep and waste the precious time that remained to him.

"It was a nice prayer," said a woman's voice near his ear. He was so exhausted and frightened that he thought at first he had imagined or dreamed it. "But prayers are often nice when people are in trouble. One gets the sense that the words are truly meant. Yes?"

In confusion, Clay rolled onto his back, blinking in the darkness, but he could see no one. "Who's there? Who are you?"

"Quiet, now," the woman's voice answered. It was a rich, deep voice, full and honeyed, unhurried and unafraid. It sounded familiar, a voice from a long time ago, one remembered by bones and flesh, not his mind. "You don't want to bother that man outside, do you?"

"No."

"Don't look for me now. I can't give you a face to see. Not here."

"But who are you?" Clay asked again.

"Don't ask me that. The question stops you remembering. You know me. All children of the earth know me."

He would have argued, but her voice wrapped him up, held him against her bosom, rocked him until he was comforted. "Mother Fam," he whispered.

"Clay," the goddess said fondly.

"Thank you for coming."

"I came for you. You were lonely."

"Am I going to die?" he asked her.

"Not even Father Wem knows which way the winds will blow the next day. Do you wish to die?"

"No. Are you going to help me?"

The voice was quiet for a moment, so long that Clay feared perhaps she had gone away. "All I can do is speak with you. What humans shape, a god's magic cannot unshape."

"Then go to Doto," he urged her. "Warn him to stay away."

"I am forbidden to enter the forest." Her voice filled with sadness. "It has been that way for a very long time."

"Oh." He wasn't sure what to say to that. "I'm sorry."

"Do not be sorry, Clay. You have come along and changed everything. The forest gods are waking up."

"It doesn't seem like I've done anything at all. Except make Lord Kwaee angry and my people afraid."

"Clay." Mother Fam's voice was gently reproachful when she spoke his name. "It is time to grow up."

Dismayed at being chided by the goddess of all the earth, he turned his face toward his pallet. "What do you mean?"

"You humans. You all make the same mistake. You believe yourselves weak. You think you are like the animals. You think the things you do cannot change the world."

"Well, I—I know that all of us can change things, but—"

"Not all of you. *Each* of you. You have such terrible power, and you behave as though you did not. You too, Clay. Look what you have done.

You have taken the heart of a forest god in your hands, and you toy with it. Do you think it does not matter what you do with it?"

"I—" He faltered. The people were so much less than the gods. How could they ever be so arrogant as to think they were important to them?

"You are strong, Clay. So strong. And those who are strong but do not understand it will hurt others without meaning to. Nor will they know how to offer that strength when they can."

"Laughing Dog thought he was strong, too. He always talked about challenging the gods. And now look at him. Ogya controls him. I never wanted to make the same mistakes he did. We're supposed to be humble before the gods." Clay hesitated, realizing that he was arguing with Mother Fam, and lamely added, "…aren't we?"

"Poor Laughing Dog," the voice said sadly. "Even he did not know his strength, not well enough to understand the pain he could cause others. He does not understand how dangerous that strength can be when wielded by a god."

"Is there any hope for him?" Clay asked, fearing the answer.

"There is always hope."

"Even for me?"

"Still you don't accept your strength. What will you do with it?"

"What can I do?" he asked, tugging at his bonds. He tried not to sound frustrated.

"You still hold a god's heart. But you left him."

"To help my people!" he protested.

"But you did not lead them."

"They would never have accepted me."

"So wise to see the direction the winds of tomorrow blow."

He sighed. He felt lost and confused now, the comfort of her voice gone. It was no good being visited by a goddess when you couldn't shake the feeling you'd deeply disappointed her.

She spoke more gently, as though sensing his dismay. "Take the strength that you have and use it to save what is in your own heart."

"And if I don't know what that is?"

"You know."

"And if I can't decide what I choose?"

"Dear Clay, you have already decided."

"But if I've already decided, then why did you come?"

The voice laughed, a deep, earth-shaking belly laugh. "I told you. Because you were lonely and needed comfort."

"There are a lot of people who need comfort besides me," he pointed out.

"True. But gods don't talk to most humans. It's not good for you. It tends to make you go mad."

"It does?" He wondered what it would be like if Father Wem's face appeared in the sky and told everyone in his village what to do. It would change everything in their lives. He couldn't even imagine it. "Well, why didn't I go mad?"

"I told you. You are strong."

"Oh." He paused. "You keep calling me a human, not a fire bearer."

"Many of the gods know you as fire bearers, but your people have many names. Humans, fire bearers, world-dancers, the children of a thousand, the god-kin."

The list astonished him. The names hinted at old stories that he had never heard, at wondrous secrets long forgotten. "What do all those mean?"

"If you see my Doto again," Mother Fam said, "tell him that I miss him. Tell him to come and find me in the mountains, and I will tell you everything."

"Couldn't you have told him before?"

She sighed. "Alas, I was forbidden to do so. Besides, Doto had secrets he needed to learn on his own. The best that I could do was help him on his way. I did what I could. Little things, like sending a friend to guide your way or opening a path into a fire mountain."

"So that was you. Thank you for helping us."

"You are welcome, Clay. But I have to go now. There are men coming."

"Already?" he asked in dismay. It did not seem like the sky was lightening yet, but then his tent faced west. The night must have passed more quickly than the day. "Can't you tell me anything more? Can't you tell me what I'm supposed to do?"

Her voice was fond when she spoke again. "Not even a goddess can guide another's heart, Clay. You decide for yourself what you want. That's the only way it works."

From outside, the crunch of footsteps approached the tent. It sounded like more than a few people.

"Farewell, Clay," the voice said. "I will be watching you. I hope to see you again."

He squinted toward the voice in the darkness, but could see nothing. "Thank you, Mother Fam. I'll tell Doto about you, if I can." No answer came back to him. "Mother Fam?" The only sound was the approaching footsteps.

Torchlight glowed orange around the edges of his tent flap.

"Has he been still?" That voice was Great Ram's.

"Yes, mostly." That was Burning Star, the fire hunter assigned to guard him. "He's been talking to himself for a little while. Muttering, like."

"No doubt praying for this Doto creature to come and save it," Laughing Dog said. "Well, we'll all see soon enough. Bring it out."

One meaty hand yanked the flap aside. Burning Star stooped into the tent, having to turn so his broad frame would fit through the entry. "Come on, you. Your time's up." He grabbed the cords binding Clay's ankles and dragged him out of the tent.

Clay winced at the dirt and rocks scraping at his skin. The visages looking down at him were illuminated by torches and the pale twilight of the approaching dawn. There was Laughing Dog, a triumphant half-smile twisting his face. And Great Ram, haggard and drawn, his eyes puffy. He looked as though he had not slept since the previous night. Around them stood the fire hunters, all twelve, and Left Rabbit, and many of the other hunters from the village. The elders Bad Water and Okra Bush hovered nearby, rubbing sleep from their eyes.

"Cut its feet free," Laughing Dog ordered. "It will need to walk."

Scorpion bent down, flint knife in one hand, and sawed at the bonds. Clay shuddered and pulled away, but Burning Star planted one heavy foot on his chest.

"Enough squirming, big brother," Laughing Dog's voice hissed in his ear. Clay twisted to see him crouched near his head, dark braids hanging down and brushing against his cheek. They twisted and shifted in the firelight as though something moved beneath them.

"You won't be needing *this* anymore, big brother," Laughing Dog murmured, and he lifted the bramble loop with the wooden leopard from about Clay's neck.

It was all Clay had left of Doto, his only proof that a god had loved him, had listened to him, that for a little while at least, his life had mattered. "No! That's mine! You can't have it! Give it back!" He twisted, rolling back and forth in the dirt, but his efforts were useless. Burning Star grunted and pushed down harder with his foot. Something deep in Clay's side broke, like the cracking of a knuckle, and then warm pain stretched up around his lung. Each breath made it spread a little farther, stab a little deeper.

Laughing Dog gathered his braids with one hand, pulling them aside, and dropped the fetish about his own neck. The wooden leopard—Doto's leopard—settled between the thick mounds of fat and muscle on his chest. "You want it, don't you? Of course you do. But did you really think we would let you try to protect yourself using that murderous creature's magics?" He rubbed one fleshy finger along the edges of the carved cat. "You see, my King? It's only more proof that this thing we once called our brother is now allied with the evil forest god."

Tears beaded the corners of Great Ram's eyes. "Let's get this over with."

To the fire hunters, Laughing Dog said, "You heard your King. Get the prisoner to its feet. And gag its mouth. We don't want it calling out to the demon in the forest and warning it away."

Burning Star hoisted Clay roughly to his feet, making the pain in his side roar. Another fire hunter grabbed either side of his jaw, squeezing. As soon as his mouth opened, thick fingers shoved a dirty wad of straw into his mouth, tying it there with a length of the cord that had been used to bind his legs. Stiff fibers of it jabbed into the roof of his mouth and poked at the back of his throat. It was all he could do not to choke. So that was it. There would be no pleading for mercy, no entreaty to his people, no more prayers. What could Mother Fam expect him to do now? Still, it was a comfort to remember her visit. Out of the many silent and sullen gods, he knew now that at least one of them was watching what happened and cared. He would have liked to have been able to see Cloud once more, to tell her and share that comfort.

"Let's go," Great Ram said. He shuffled forward, his shoulders slumped. Burning Star shoved Clay from behind, forcing him to take several running steps to avoid a tumble, as having his hands tied behind his back made keeping his balance difficult.

Laughing Dog approached the edge of the slope leading down into the main village and put his hands to his mouth. "People of the Savanna," he called. His voice cut through the morning quiet and set birds chattering in the fields. "Dawn approaches. If you would see the monster that has threatened your lives and murdered your King and infant prince, rise up now. Follow us to the edge of the forest and see the truth about its gods. Rise now!"

In the village below, sleepy people emerged from their tents, stretching stiff limbs and rubbing their eyes. Clay wondered why Laughing Dog would want them all to follow. Surely there was nothing to gain from it; he would get everything he wanted now.

One hope remained: perhaps Doto would not come. He had not answered any of Clay's previous entreaties; why would he come now? And if he did not appear, Laughing Dog would look like a fool or a liar. Great Ram would surely grow uncertain about killing Clay then. Maybe there would be a way out. He tried to think of ways he could explain his leopard's foot—the gods had cursed him with it, for his insolence perhaps, and he had been praying to them to restore it. Or perhaps he could tell the truth: it was an artifact of the forest magic that had healed him, and had nothing to do with any beast that had been attacking their people. Yes. There was no reason to think Doto would come. It was a chance, at least.

But the chance was slim, and as he was marched through the village, he found himself gazing with the eyes of a man who would never see home again. Cloud's tent, the tanning racks, the fire circle, the work area, the hunters' tents—he took in every detail with a profound sense of loss. As the troop progressed through the village, his people gathered behind him, following in the hopes of seeing a monster, following to watch their prince die. Clay had been afraid they would shout curses and insults at him, but all were silent and grave. Their faces were sorrowful. He longed to say goodbye to them, but could not. The straw in his mouth jutted into his throat and made him gag. Saliva ran down his chin, adding to his indignity.

He passed through the gate to his village for what would surely be the last time, and Firefly, who stood on watch, turned and joined them. Nearly the whole village followed behind, now. Clay looked to the faces of the fire hunters on either side of him, hoping for some expression of mercy or a comforting smile, but their features were stony and serious, and they did not look back.

They followed the southern wall of the village, moving to the patch that Clay had danced to Doto days before, keeping clear of the edge of the forest. Without the magic of the fetish to protect him, Clay knew that if he ventured too close to it, the vines and brambles would ensnare him and drag him into its shadowy depths, where he would be torn apart. He shrank closer to the village wall at the thought, and Burning Star gave him a warning push from behind. "Keep moving."

Clay almost did not realize when they reached Doto's part of the forest. Without the wooden leopard around his neck, he couldn't feel the invisible wall humming before him. Laughing Dog certainly could, however—the flesh on the back of his neck and arms pimpled like a plucked guineafowl. When he stepped into the forest, he gasped, his eyes going wide, and he staggered in place. Great Ram turned to him, asking if everything was all right. Laughing Dog just nodded and turned back to stare at Clay, clutching at the fetish about his neck.

A rising fury wiped away all Clay's fear for a moment. That magic was his, not Laughing Dog's. It had been a gift from Doto to Clay. It was precious. Laughing Dog did not deserve to see the wonders and beauty of the forest through the fetish's magic. If in that moment Clay could have snapped his bonds and tackled his brother to wrest the fetish away, he would have.

But it was no use. He forced his anger back down and stepped into the forest after Laughing Dog, wincing as he felt nothing but the twisting of bone and flesh in his left foot. The people behind him drew sharp breaths and cried out anew at seeing the transformation. Clay supposed it looked different—more real, perhaps—in the crisp early morning twilight than at night, twisted by shadows and dark fears. He curled his feline toes against the ground, feeling the curved claws flex. He wondered if he could some-how slash at Laughing Dog with them and run away. But where would he go? The forest would destroy him, and the only other place to run was the savanna. Runners and trackers would chase him down eventually.

They stopped just inside Doto's patch of forest. "Well?" Great Ram asked. "Where is the demon-god you promised, Laughing Dog?"

"Patience, King," Laughing Dog said, dipping his head. "It is not yet dawn. But you will want to be ready."

"Ready?" Ram looked weary and confused.

"Your knife, brother. Put it to your captive's throat. You must be ready to take your vengeance at a moment's notice. You would not risk the demon-god setting the murderer of your wife and child free, would you?"

Ram set his teeth. "No." He stepped behind Clay and put one arm about his neck, pushing him forward. The hard flesh of his chest was clam-my against Clay's back. His limbs trembled. His breath stank of palm wine. He fumbled with his other arm, and then the keenly sharpened edge of his knife pressed up under Clay's chin. Clay swallowed, and the knife bit into his throat.

Laughing Dog ordered his fire hunters back up against the wall, be-yond the edge of the forest and instructed them to hold their spears and bows at the ready. When he was satisfied, he returned and stood at Great Ram's side.

The woods were dark and still. The calls of waking birds hooted and chirped and croaked from within, but Clay could see no movement. He wondered bitterly how much more Laughing Dog could see now, if his brother was already learning to decipher the birdsong and hear the words implied in the calls. They were all a mystery to Clay now. He tried to hold as still as he could, but with every breath, the edge of his brother's knife chewed at his neck. A tickle of blood crawled down his chest.

They waited, and the morning light grew brighter, pale twilight filtering through the trees. Now Clay saw that the branches of the trees were partially denuded, stripped of their leaves as though blown by a mighty storm. Fallen foliage was strewn across the forest floor, and new, pale green buds had already formed at the tips of the branches. Something must have distressed Kwaee to cause this kind of destruction. Perhaps he and Doto had fought? Maybe that was why Doto had not come. The thought was comforting in its way. Now, surrounded by enemies, he needed more than anything else to believe in someone. He needed faith.

Brighter the morning grew, and still no noise from the forest. Behind him, the clearing of throats and quiet muttering suggested the people were growing restless. The sun was taking forever to rise, but Clay savored every moment, enjoying the dampness of the air against his skin, the moist earth and the tickle of grass underneath his feet, the rustle of a gentle breeze in his fur.

"Why won't the blasted sun rise?" Ram swore, his voice loud in Clay's ear.

For a moment, Clay wondered if perhaps Doto or the other gods had worked some kind of miracle and held back the sunrise to save him. That would be a tale worth telling for all ages. It would not be impossible. Not for gods. A surge of hope lifted him.

Then the sun's rays broke above the horizon to the east, pale yellow light filtering through the trees and grass. Dawn had come. Clay watched its clear illumination climb down the trunks of trees as the sun rose. Birds flocked up from the treetops. The light crept lower and lower until it lit up his face and pierced his eyes.

Everyone looked back to the forest. Still there was no sound from it but the call of birds. Clay searched the forest floor, but could see no sign of Doto, though that didn't mean he wasn't there. Great Ram's arm relaxed slightly about his chest. "Well, Laughing Dog?" the King said. "You said the beast would arrive to prove your story. Here it is, dawn, and nothing has come. Where is your proof now?"

"Patience, brother," Laughing Dog said, but Clay could tell from the tone of his voice that he was worried. He stepped forward, peering into the forest, and paced back and forth several times. "It will come."

"This has been a waste of time," Great Ram growled. "Proof indeed! All it proves to me is that you would have your own brother killed for a crime he cannot possibly have committed."

"If I wanted that, I would have let you kill him two nights ago," Laughing Dog said. "Just wait a little longer."

Ram took his knife from Clay's throat. "I have waited enough. It is time to be done with this."

Then came a loud sound, like a sturdy gust of wind shuddering against a well-staked tent. Doto stood before them, his toes amid the decaying shards of broken clayfruit. His brow was lowered, his ears back, and fur bristled all down his shoulders, back, and tail. He let out a low, threatening growl. And though it surely meant his death, Clay had never been so happy to see anyone in his whole life.

Many of the people behind him screamed; others gasped or shouted, and Clay heard the sound of more than one pair of footsteps as several of them fled outright, crashing through the underbrush to escape.

"It cannot be," Great Ram murmured in his ear and pressed the edge of the knife to his throat again.

"Let him go now," Doto thundered, and the forest resonated with his voice, a great, ethereal boom, and Clay loved him. "Let him go if you want to live."

Laughing Dog stepped closer to Great Ram. "You have your proof, my King. Kill him now. You must do it now, before it's too late!"

"No!" a voice shouted. Left Rabbit rushed into the forest to stand before them, reaching out to Great Ram. "King Great Ram, listen to me. Laughing Dog lied to you. It was not he who saw Clay dancing in the forest, but me. I—"

"You lying snake!" Laughing Dog roared, and lunged forward. With a wild swing, his fist crunched into Left Rabbit's face. Rabbit stumbled backward, clutching at his nose with both hands, blood running out between his fingers. "How long have you been allied with him, you traitor?"

"Be quiet!" Doto's voice roared above them all, full of bestial fury. "Let him go. Now."

Left Rabbit stumbled away, back out of the forest. Laughing Dog shrank back to Great Ram's side. "My King, you have to kill him now," he muttered. "Quickly, now, before it's too late."

Clay ignored all of this. He couldn't tear his gaze away from Doto, his forest god, come to save him at last, full of might and righteous fury. He tried to smile, but the straw jammed in his mouth prevented it.

The hand holding the knife against Clay's throat shook. "Is it true?" Great Ram muttered. "Can it be a lie, even now?" He let go with his other hand, and fumbled at the knots tying Clay's gag in place, pulling it free.

Clay let the soggy wad of straw drop from his mouth, and spat stray stalks of it, working his dried tongue and sore jaw.

"Brother, what are you doing?" Laughing Dog asked in rising alarm.

Great Ram spoke low into Clay's ear. "Listen to me. Deny it now, and I swear I will believe you. Tell it to go away. Just say you had nothing to do with it. I'll believe you. I swear I'll believe you."

Clay swallowed against the knife. He looked out across the brush toward Doto, whose divine ears would surely have heard every word. His god looked suddenly fearful, as though standing alone before an approaching river of fire that would burn him away. Clay's heart filled with so much love that he thought he would split apart. Mother Fam was right. He had made his decision long ago. There had only ever been one decision. *I will always choose you.*

He took a deep breath, wishing his arms were free so that he could reach out, and called, "Doto!"

Great Ram's fingers tightened on his shoulders. "No!" he whispered hoarsely. "No!" He drew a line of fire across Clay's throat.

The pain blazed, sharper than any Clay had ever felt. He stumbled forward, wanting to clutch at his neck. He sucked in a breath and felt his lungs fill with fluid. Wet heat ran down his chest and belly. He tried again to breathe, but could get no air. Doto stared at him with a stricken expression, jaw slack.

He was dizzy. The world spun around him, and his vision dimmed. He took another step, and then fell. It took a very, very long time to hit the ground. Doto spread his arms wide. Clay wished he could tell him that it was all right. He tried to say that he loved him, but his tongue wouldn't work. Behind Doto, the forest melted and twisted. Trees wrenched their trunks in half, reaching their branches forward as they fell. Thick, thorny vines erupted from the soil like lunging cobras. The earth boiled with twisting roots. Then the light dimmed. The edges of everything blurred. By the time Clay felt himself hit the ground, he could see nothing at all. Then he knew nothing.

The Sins of the Father

Doto could not move. His feet were rooted to the spot. His arms would not reach out. Clay's blood ran into the earth, and Doto had been too shocked to catch him, to do anything. He felt Clay's heart thump once against the ground, then again, weaker, and then no more. His mate, his worshiper, his love was dead, just as his father had warned.

An overwhelming surge of profound and unimaginable loss wracked him, almost throwing him from his feet. He heard himself roar, not a wordless cry of anger or grief, but predatory, like an animal. Around him, his forest thrashed with his shock and fury. He felt his trees tear themselves in two and fling themselves to the ground. He was so furious he could barely see. He would murder the fire bearers who had done this, every single one of them.

His vines surged forward, snapping and twisting in the air, but the fire bearers were already fleeing, pushing and stumbling over each other in their rush to escape his wrath. He could not reach them outside the forest; beyond the wall that separated forest from savanna, his plants fell limp and motionless. Answering his fury, stems and roots coiled around one of the fallen tree trunks and hefted into the air—a massive bombax, its limbs shattered from its fall—and hurled it of their own accord toward the fleeing fire bearers. Many of the fire bearers screamed and flattened themselves against the ground, but the trunk was flung too high to hit any of them. It sailed over their heads and crashed into their nest. Their feeble wall protecting it splintered as though constructed of nothing more than dry straw, dead branches and poles knocked free or snapped in half. The trunk smashed their little round tents where it landed, and then began to roll down the slope of their village, flattening anything in its path. The remaining fire bearers fled to either side of the hole in their nest, some running as fast as they were able, others staying behind only long enough to assist those who had fallen or to carry their cubs.

Only two now remained within Doto's reach. One was the bearer possessed by Ogya, grinning with mad delight. None of Doto's weapons touched him; they coiled and flailed to either side, but would not attack. Thorns avoided his skin, and tree branches could not grasp at him. By some magic, he was safe from the forest's attack.

But he was not Doto's primary target. That was the one who had dared slit his mate's throat, the tall, important-looking one covered in bright colors. He had been foolish enough to stand within the forest, and now he could not get away; roots had tugged his feet into the earth and chewed on them, and lianas coiled about his arms and chest. He screamed for his people to come and help him, but no one came, nor did the one possessed by Ogya make any attempt to assist him.

With a rage that shook his back and pulsed in his head with such intensity he could barely see, Doto strode toward his mate's assassin, stepping past Clay's body and lifting his arms to summon thick brambles from the ground, barbed with wicked thorns. He coiled them all about the fire bearer's body, up legs and back and belly, lashing around the arms and the throat. He kept them loose, only scratching the wretched thing when it wriggled or tried to get free. This one had killed Clay, and Doto could take his vengeance only once. He did not want it to be over quickly. It would need to last for an eternity. He held out his paws, claws bared, fingers extended, and then closed them ever so slightly. The thorns constricted, hundreds of points piercing the bearer's flesh, the scent of his fresh blood mingling with that of Clay's. It smelled the same.

"Please!" the fire bearer screamed. "Please, Lord Doto, don't kill me! You've already killed my father, my wife, my child. Isn't that enough?"

"You killed my mate!" Doto roared back at him. He ignored the other petty accusations. They were irrelevant. "In front of me! You must have wished to die."

"Your—your what?" the bearer stammered. His gaze dropped down to the body on the ground. A look of horrified understanding spread across his face. "No, please! I didn't know! I didn't know demons took mates."

"Demon?" Doto clenched his paws tighter, sliding his thorns under the bearer's skin, feeling its sinew and tendons jump with pain. "Insolent creature. *I am a god.*" With that, he extended one of the lianas around the fire bearer's chest until it coiled around his neck.

"A god?" The fire bearer sputtered his words, gagging as the vine tightened. "No! I swear I didn't know! I repent, Lord—Lord Doto! I repent all my sins against you, just let me g—" His words were cut off as the liana cinched tighter, making him wheeze for breath.

Doto watched in calm fury as the fire bearer struggled, waiting to feel something, some sense of satisfaction, as there had been when he'd torn apart that brute, Ulo.

Ulo. Clay had almost been unable to forgive Doto for what he'd done to that fire bearer, and for the way he'd tormented Jai. Like Jai, this fire bearer now struggled and repented and pleaded for his life. And it was Clay who had stopped Doto, Clay who had made him promise never to kill or harm another needlessly again. But Clay was dead, and murder was in Doto's nature. His father had loved a fire bearer, and so had he. His father had killed them all, and so would he.

He watched his captive gag and twitch and bloody his own arms against the thorns in feeble attempts to clutch at the choking vines.

We can't fight our natures, can we? We are who we are, and nothing we do can ever change that. The hare god had said it to him days ago. But the hare god was a liar.

The fire bearer's tongue stuck out as he gagged. He would die in another minute or two. And then what? Doto looked over to the other fire bearer, the one possessed by Ogya. He was watching raptly, eyes shining as he watched his kinsman die. This was what he wanted. This was what Ogya wanted. Not what Clay would have wanted.

Clay, who had made a promise to Doto that he would always choose him. He had kept that promise even though it meant his death. Shame made Doto falter, the liana relaxing. The fire bearer took deep, gasping breaths, blinking tears out of his eyes.

Doto had promised too: never to kill or harm another fire bearer without need. How could he abandon that now? Killing this pathetic creature might be satisfying, but it would be a betrayal. That meant more than his anger, more than his grief. He let the liana slide away, withdrew his thorns.

"What are you doing?" the Ogya-possessed one demanded. "He killed your worshiper, your mate! You must hate him for what he's done! Destroy him!"

Doto stared at the other, at the hatred and misery that twisted his face, the murder that blazed in his eyes. So like Kwaee. "No." With the word, his fury fell away from him like water out of his fur. All around, the creaking trees ceased their movements, the vines stilled their whipping, the grass lay flat and still. One tree, leaning at an angle too heavy for it, creaked and uprooted itself, crashing to the ground in the forest behind him.

The one who had killed Clay dropped to the ground, drawing in deep, hoarse breaths.

The possessed fire bearer bared his teeth, spittle flying from his mouth as he hissed. His voice was the cracking and popping of fire. "You have to kill him! You must! You are a god! Vengeance is yours!"

"I am not my father," Doto said, and as he spoke the words, he knew their truth. He would never hide himself away in the forest, filled with self-hatred and regret. He *had* changed his nature. He had changed it by stepping outside of his world, by questioning all the stories he had been told, by looking for truth even when it was ugly. He had changed it by loving Clay and by healing him.

His fur prickled. Healing him. Maybe it was not too late.

He turned and stooped, lifting Clay's body. It was limp and oddly heavy in his arms. Blood pattered across the ground as he lifted it.

"No," the possessed one shouted. "No! Come back here! Finish what you started!"

The other still gasped for breath, picking brambles away, pulling thorns out of his flesh. "Laughing Dog, you traitor," he croaked.

"Oh yes, I'm a traitor." Laughing Dog approached the other, taking up a vine in both hands. "But you're a bad brother and a worse King. I'll rally our people and burn this forest to the ground."

"They'll never follow you," the other said. "I'll see you executed for treason."

Laughing Dog grimaced. "Did I say our people? I meant *my* people."

Doto ignored them, their words catching at his ears as he streaked off into the forest with Clay's body in his arms. The last sound he heard was that of a fire bearer being strangled.

Once he was a safe distance into the trees, farther than any fire bearer could see from beyond the wall, he set Clay down on the ground. Clay's eyes were still open, staring up past Doto into the treetops. He did not move. Doto combed claws backward through short, curly hair that had loosened around the ends of the black braids.

Death was permanent, but it was not immediate. After the heart stopped beating, life still flickered through the tissues of the body, struggling to hold on, clinging, as all life did, to every precious instant. It might not be too late.

There would be a cost. It didn't matter. With both paws, he clasped Clay's cheeks and neck, lifting his head upward. The ugly red gash in Clay's neck gaped open, baring white folds of tissue.

Doto took a deep breath, bracing for whatever would happen next, and summoned his power, sending it into the fire bearer. Like before, when he'd healed Clay's foot, the magic started with an electricity in the air, a hum and potency that tugged at every strand of his fur. Curved arcs snapped in his whiskers. A flurry of sparks crackled up a nearby tree trunk. The air began to crackle. Tiny bolts of lightning buzzed and snapped, jumping from leaf to blade of grass to ground to insect to strand of fur to trunk to bough to leaf.

The wind rose, at first only a shift in the breeze, a breath, and then a gust that circled around them, scattering fallen leaves. It rapidly increased in speed and force, whirling into a zephyr, spinning the leaves high into the air, a vortex of brown and green. The wind sped to a gale, rattling the branches of the trees, tearing their leaves away, forks of electricity grasping like skeletal fingers at limb and branch. Trunks creaked as they swayed. More fallen leaves and brush lifted from the ground, whirling around them in a rising cylinder that whipped at Doto's fur, flattening it backward. With ripping sounds, whole branches and strips of bark tore from the trees and joined the gale. The cyclone gouged dirt and stones from the ground, bared the roots of the trees. All around them was a roaring wall that stretched all the way up to Wem.

Something deep began to pull free of Doto, out of his lungs and stomach and muscles and eyes. Then brilliant light, as bright as the sun, beamed from his paws and fingers, soaking into Clay's skin. It was so bright that Doto could see nothing but the light. The forest and the cyclone melted into dazzling white radiance.

"Take what is mine." He heard himself speak the words distantly, clear above the howl of the storm. Just hearing them was not enough. He had to mean them. He willed their meaning. He felt the power inside him pulling free, felt his body and spirit clutching at it, trying to hold onto it at all costs. But he would not hold onto it. He forced himself to let it go freely, unquestioningly. It would be gone forever, he imagined Kwaee warning him. The cost was too high. He thought of his father's temple, a prison; of Abansin, a ruined shrine to loss and pain. What cost could be higher than that? Of all beings that ever lived, only Clay had chosen him. Clay had given his own life to prove it. There could be no cost too high to save him. Doto spoke the words and meant them with all his power.

"Out, out, into flesh and bone, into blood and scar, into mind and heart, into lung and limb, into body and spirit, take what is mine. Take what is mine. Take what is mine."

Insurrection

Cloud sat, bound, inside the cage—the actual *cage*—her own people had built. The Teller, and Ant With a Leaf sat to either side of her. No one felt like saying anything. A little while ago, while the sky was still dark, Great Ram and Laughing Dog had led Clay out of the village with nearly all the people following behind. That had been some time ago. Whatever had been happening since then, it couldn't be good.

None of them could sleep. The Teller stared down at his toes, his shoulders slumped. He had said nothing since being arrested, not even when Ant had asked him about the new story he had planned to tell. Cloud had never seen him look so defeated, not even in that time long ago when, after her husband had died, she had quietly sat next to him and explained that they could never be with each other again.

While the Teller barely moved, Ant with a Leaf could not sit still. She leaned against the walls of their prison. Sometimes she would pry hard at the wooden rails or deliver powerful kicks to them with her feet, but the cage was built sturdily enough to hold, at least for now. Cloud supposed with enough time they could escape, but there would not be enough time.

Jai lay on the ground, his wrists and ankles bound, and responded to little. He was thin, his ribs jutting through his skin. Bruises mottled his sides. He must have been badly treated since being captured. Cloud cursed herself for not noticing long ago. Once, an outsider, even a hostile one, would have been treated with great courtesy and respect. Certainly he ought to have been fed and sheltered properly. But those were the customs of another people, a people who humbly served the gods, who trusted each other. Those were not the sorts of people who built cages.

Cloud set her jaw. It was her fault, true, but not only hers. The blame belonged to all the people. They had let themselves be swayed by fear and mistrust. They had willfully followed a bad King. They had held onto their past so tightly, they had choked it. But then, who had helped them do otherwise?

Screams rose from the southeast, beyond the village wall, a great chorus of shrieks. Cloud felt a moment of dread—were people being injured or killed? But these screams sounded more of fear and shock than pain. Then, following them, a loud, rumbling boom, like a voice and thunder all at once, but if it contained any words, they were undiscernible.

"Do you think he's all right?" Ant asked, and Cloud had no idea who she meant—Laughing Dog, Clay, or the King.

"I don't think anything's all right."

They waited in silence for a moment more, staring out through the bars of the cage. Soon came a loud, bestial roar, followed by screams. With dread in her heart, Cloud turned her gaze above the walls of the village to see the treetops shaking as if in a powerful storm. There was a rush, like that of wind. Creaks and cracks groaned from the forest.

"By all the gods," Cloud murmured, and then the village wall exploded, shards of broken wood blasting inn all directions before the bulk of a massive tree trunk crashing through the fence. Cloud knew the tree; it was a bombax, so large, with overhanging branches, that the guards had worried forest apes or other invaders might use it to surmount the village wall, but none could devise a way to fell the titan, so the tree had stayed. Now it flew through the air as though no more than a flung twig. It plowed through the upper landing of the village, smashing several tents into ruins, and half-bounded, half-rolled down the hill flattening everything—tents, racks, torch stands, *everything*—in its path. Cloud whispered a blessing to the gods for keeping their prison out of the path of the trunk, but the words faltered on her lips as she watched it twist on one end and obliterate her own tent in an instant, rolling over it and finally rocking to a stop, one end in the fire circle.

Everything she had was gone. If she had time, she might be able to pick through and salvage herbs and seeds from the rubble, but a little rain would surely drown everything in mud. Some of the supplies were virtually unrecoverable: saved from their old homeland lost to drought; or passed down to her by her grandmother, who had brought them from Bogana. They were all gone now. She dearly hoped that no one outside was seriously injured, as she would have little resources to aid them, but the sounds of screams left her scant promise that was so.

"By all the gods," Ant With a Leaf echoed, "what is happening?"

Cloud gripped at the wooden bars of the cage. "I don't know. But it isn't good. I'm afraid our King may have awakened something terrible."

"He is not my King."

"He may not be anybody's."

The Teller rubbed at his balding head. "I pray he is unharmed, but if Kwaee has come to us at last—"

"I don't think it's Kwaee," Cloud said. "I think it's Doto."

There was nothing further they could see up the hill, but someone was shouting something.

"Cloud!" a voice shouted. It was Left Rabbit, running up the hill, his eyes wide with panic.

"What's happened?" Cloud could see the blood running down his mouth and chin even from a distance. "Are you hurt? Is Clay all right?"

Left Rabbit shook his head as he approached. When he reached the and bit into his lip. "He's dead. Clay is dead. The King—Ram killed him. He cut his throat."

Cloud's knees refused to hold her up, and she clung to the bars of the cage to keep from collapsing. "It can't be." Through the corner of one eye, she saw clouds swirling over the forest, dark at first, then lit from within by a brilliant light. She wondered if she were imagining it at first, but then saw the Teller and Ant With a Leaf staring at it too. There was no understanding anything anymore.

"The forest went mad." Left Rabbit took his knife from his belt. He began sawing through the mixture of cord and hard, red ochre putty that bound the cage closed. "That leopard thing attacked just like Laughing Dog said. Everyone ran, except for Laughing Dog and the King, but I'm not sure either of them could. No one was going to wait to find out."

"Did they live?" Ant With a Leaf asked.

"I don't know!" Left Rabbit swore as he twisted his knife in the solid putty and dropped it. "I don't know how they *could* be alive. Everything's gone wrong." He crouched to pick up his knife, but also to hide the tears his choking voice betrayed. "He lied, Cloud. Laughing Dog lied. It was me who told him about Clay's leopard foot. I saw it, not him. I thought he would—he would let me hunt with him. This is all my fault. I knew he was lying. I was too scared to say anything. And I thought—I thought he knew what he was doing. He was always so smart."

Cloud nearly shouted at him. If he'd spoken up sooner, he might have saved Clay, saved them all. A burst of curses and insults built up inside her, and she had to force herself to remember that the poor boy hadn't known what he was doing. He was suffering enough now. And besides, she thought, how many times had she had the chance to stand against Great Ram? How many times had she told herself she was just a healer, not a ruler, to impose her will on others? She had let this happen too. "Listen," she said. "What's happening would have happened anyway, you understand? You are not to blame for this."

"I'm still sorry," he cried. "I'm so sorry." He stood and hacked away at the ochre with his knife.

"I know," Cloud told him, and reached through the bars to pat his arm. "I'm sorry too. You know that you don't have to let us out. If Laughing Dog finds out, he might be very angry."

Left Rabbit wiped at his eyes with the back of one hand and set his jaw. "It doesn't matter. You shouldn't be in here. I have to do what's right."

Cloud looked down at the ruined tents in the village below. "Yes. You're right. We all do."

∧∧∧

A few people returned to the village, mainly looking for children or spouses who had stayed behind. They gave Cloud and the others frightened looks but said nothing, even when Ant With a Leaf demanded to know what had happened.

Cloud picked through the remains of her tent as well as she could, but it was no good; the wreckage had been flattened into the soft earth and could not be moved. Whatever supplies had survived the damage were trapped beneath the hide and bone of her tent.

Left Rabbit recovered his spear, and Ant With a Leaf her bow. The Teller ran to inquire after his daughter, Baobab, only to find her gone. "She must have gone outside with the others," he said with a worried expression. "I pray to the gods she's all right."

As they passed through the gate, they saw their people clustered around Gamewatch Rise. Few spoke. Parents clutched their children near, and husbands, their wives. To Cloud's relief, none appeared to be injured. She searched through their faces, trying to count everyone, naming everyone she could remember and seeking them out in the crowd, though she knew the effort to be useless. At the top of the hill, Laughing Dog's twelve fire hunters stood tall, their strong bodies striped and spotted with ash, their expressions stony. They held bow and spear at their sides.

The Teller and Ant With a Leaf hurried toward the crowd, calling for their kin, but Cloud stood a little distance away, holding onto Left Rabbit's arm to keep him from leaving. People trusted him. They believed him. If she were to succeed now, she would need his confession. She hoped she would not need him for more than that, but noted with approval that his fingers were white-knuckled around his spear.

"People!" Laughing Dog's voice rang out over the crowd. He stepped from behind the fire hunters. Unlike them, he was not ash-smeared, and the morning sun made him seem to glow bronze. He wore his brother's finery, the white and gold sash draped over his fleshy shoulders and pushed apart around his great, round belly. The sash was spattered red with fresh blood. At his chest hung two necklaces—the first, Clay's odd circle of thorns with the carved leopard pendant. The other was the King's lion tooth necklace. If Laughing Dog had that, then Great Ram was surely dead. Cloud gripped Left Rabbit's arm more tightly.

Laughing Dog lifted his own thick arms. "People of the Savanna, I am so grateful to see, and hear from my guards, that you are all, each of you, unharmed after the terrible attack from the forest god. However, it is with great sadness that I must deliver these dread tidings: both of my brothers are dead." He paused as if waiting for gasps, but no one seemed shocked by this news. He cleared his throat. "Both died in the attack this morning, and I can scarcely grieve their loss. It is so fresh in my mind.

"I never desired to stand before you as King, but King I am today. We all must surely know now that that which we first imagined to be a demon, the thing called Doto, is no demon at all, but another god of the forest. Yes, a god! And no ordinary god. Not a god who shelters and watches over us and treasures our praise and prayers. No. We have all seen that *this* god is an evil being, one who deceived and corrupted our dear prince Clay to his own purposes, one we now know must be responsible for the death of my father, that of Two Broken Hands, those who were lost in the forest, and perhaps even dear little Whistling Thorn, poisoned by forest magics.

"My brother Great Ram, may Wem hold him forever in his bosom, sought to save you from this evil and, through the embrace of death, to release Clay from its perverse sorcery. For this heroic act, the malicious god Doto slew him most brutally, strangling him with the vines of the forest." He put one hand to his face as if in grief. "His body lies among the trees now, untouchable, as any who might seek to retrieve it would surely be slaughtered. This is how we may know with no further doubt. The forest gods are our enemies! They seek to deny us our right to burn our own and send them to Wem. They spit in the eye of the Sky Father!"

He stared out over the crowd. "But we will not let them do this! We will not stand by as our homes and our lives are taken without concern or care by this foul god. Nor will we abandon the body of our King. If the gods of the forest will not surrender their bounties to us, then we will *take* them by force and by fire—yes, fire! It is the strength of Ogya we will use to defend ourselves. We will give Doto and Kwaee such a reckoning that all the gods of the world will listen. The heavens themselves will tremble at the mention of the People of the Savanna!"

Muttering rose from those gathered, and Laughing Dog smiled. It was the wrong thing to do. The people were in shock, grieving over the loss of their King and prince and homes. And if there was one thing Cloud knew, it was grief. Grief could take a lot of shapes. It could wear a lot of faces. But it never looked like the expression on their King's face right now. It never wore smirking ambition. And everyone there knew it.

Laughing Dog scanned the crowd, easy, comfortable, confidant. But he halted when he noticed Cloud. He stared at her, frowned, and leaned to Mirage next to him, whispering a word or two. Mirage nodded and put both hands on his bow.

The usurping King faltered when he spoke again. "Now—now I know that my brother Great Ram was a good King and well-loved, but there is one area where I think we can all see he made a mistake, and that is in his insistence on reverence to the gods of the forest."

Well, he had already seen her. No point in keeping silent any longer. Cloud let go of Left Rabbit's arm. "That's nonsense and you know it!" she called, as loud as she could. She ignored the people who turned to stare at her. "Stopping you from burning down those damned woods was the only sensible thing your brother ever did!"

"Cloud." Laughing Dog's voice strained with forced amusement. "Now, what traitor went and let you out, I wonder?" He stared at Left Rabbit, who began to tremble.

Cloud tried to stand taller. "You are the only traitor here, Laughing Dog."

"That's *King* Laughing Dog. You forget your place, Cloud."

"It is you who has forgotten *my* place. I am *Elder* Cloud. And I depose you by right of council." The crowd went completely silent, watching her. She looked away from the self-appointed King and sought out the bright blue robes of Teller in the crowd. She found him to one side, with Baobab in his arms. He nodded to her, and she remembered him again, his eyes young, full of compassion and rebellion, lying with her in that tall grass. Her nose tingled with the familiar scent of spice and musk.

The self-made King chuckled, but Cloud thought he sounded uneasy. "Depose me? There is no such thing."

"So quick a King, and already you think you know all about it. There were not always Kings, boy. Once there was only the council. The council appointed the first King, and the council can *un*appoint." She felt tall now, full of strength and purpose. It was as though the gods themselves tugged the words from her throat. This was so late. Too late. She should have done it long ago, but there was no time now for regret. "And so I do unappoint. I call on the other council members to uphold my judgment. Laughing Dog, you have defied the gods and your King. You have poisoned your people. You have threatened and assaulted your own promised. You have laid false charges against your brother, charges that resulted, as you intended, in his death."

Laughing Dog gave a slow shake of his head. "We have all heard these accusations before, Cloud. Do you expect to surprise us with them again? You will recall you were arrested for them before."

"It's convenient that everyone who speaks against you is a traitor, isn't it? How long until we are all traitors? You claim you saw Clay call on the forest god, Doto, to make him King. You say you witnessed it yourself. Isn't that true?"

The confident smile faded from his face at last. "It serves none of us to listen to your nonsense anymore. Two of you, take her away and tie her up again. And see she doesn't get free this time."

Two fire hunters—Burning Star and Mother's Tree, she thought—lifted their spears and moved down Gamewatch Rise toward her, but she ignored them. "Go on, Left Rabbit," she said loud enough so all could hear. "Tell everyone the truth."

The crowd went silent again, and even the fire hunters paused on the hill. Laughing Dog took a step back and turned to Mirage. "Kill him," he said.

In one fluid motion, Mirage lifted his bow, nocked an arrow, and loosed it. There was a hiss. A thud.

With a puzzled expression, Left Rabbit blinked down at the arrow shaft buried in his chest, still vibrating from its flight. He toppled backward into the grass and landed with a thump. His fingers pawed at his chest. He worked his jaws, and his final breath escaped his lungs, spraying his lips with red. He blinked twice, and then never again.

Cloud stared down at him in disbelief. She'd known that *she* was in danger, but she'd never thought Laughing Dog would dare kill Left Rabbit there, in front of everyone. The crowd shared her shock. Many gasped. Some cried out in outrage. Even the fire hunters drew back from Mirage, who stared down at his own bow as though it had betrayed him.

There was a death on Cloud's hands once more—not because her healing had been insufficient, but because she'd tried to be something else. She'd left her incense and cooking pot behind. She'd faced leadership, and someone had died. Now she felt the old urge to surrender, to hide away. All she wanted was to stop the confrontation, to beg forgiveness, to be a healer. But that wasn't what the people needed. They needed a leader.

All I want to do is help our people, she'd told the Teller. All true. All a lie. She crouched down and closed Left Rabbit's eyes, and wondered if she would be shot next. She stood.

"What King murders a man rather than let him speak the truth?" she called to the crowd. "Not a King we need. And so I depose you, Laughing Dog, by right of council. Will the other council members stand with me?"

She looked out over the crowd, not daring to glance at the fire hunters again. She feared that if she saw another bow or spear pointed in her direction, she would run.

"I will," the Teller said, his voice loud and clear. He had set Baobab down and come to stand next to Cloud.

"Well, of course you will," Laughing Dog sneered. "You're a traitor just like she is."

"I will stand with her too." Bad Water emerged from the crowd, his small, bent frame shaking with age.

"And I." Okra Bush followed closely behind him.

Okra Bush was joined by Long Neck, and Long Neck by Twig, and then Broken Calabash, and then the whole council—save Wasp and Half Moon, the fire hunters recently appointed—stood behind Cloud. She glanced at the troop of armed hunters up on the hill and half-wished the council members were standing in *front* of her instead.

"We are in agreement then, Laughing Dog," she called up to him. "You are no longer King."

Laughing Dog's face had gone purple, swollen as a boiled root. "You think this means anything? Look at you. A bunch of tired old men and women. I have all the hunters at my side. Strong men, who can provide food and fight. What difference do you think your decision makes?"

"They're our elders!" That was Firefly, shouting in disbelief. "Who do you think you are?"

"I am King!" Laughing Dog roared.

No Rocks answered him, calm, assured. "No King of mine would so callously throw aside the wisdom of the people. Nor kill a good man rather than let him speak." And she clasped Firefly's hand in her own and went to stand with Cloud.

Then, one by one, people followed, straying out of the crowd to join her, the group growing in number behind her.

"Fools!" the would-be King shouted at them. "You're all fools. Listen to me. There is a great battle coming. I have seen it. If I have done terrible things, it is only because I wish to save you—all of you—from the cataclysm ahead. Who will protect you from the savagery of the forest gods? The elders, who would bow and submit to any injustice committed against us? Or someone strong? Someone who dares to stand up for his people? Someone who wields for himself the power of the mighty Ogya?"

And then Laughing Dog lifted his hands toward the skies and burst forth blazing fire from his fingertips. The crowd shrunk back in shock as columns of flame wreathed his wrists and forearms, spiraling up to the sky with a terrible roar. Cloud's knees buckled and she dropped to the ground, covering her eyes with one forearm, the light of divine fire too brilliant to look upon. Only the fire hunters stood still and impassive. Only they had seen this power wielded before.

Cloud had heard Clay's stories of the possessed prince using his magic for hunting, but seeing it with her own eyes beggared her imagination. Those around her wailed; those who had not joined dropped to their knees. Could Laughing Dog have turned this magic against them at any time? Why had he not simply revealed it to them early on? But no, she decided. He might have been hunted as a demon. Few had trusted him, not with the memory of their lost King fresh in their minds and a legitimate, if drunken, heir to guide them. But in this new world of gods and monsters, real power could have a terrible allure.

"This is what awaits the enemies of the People of the Savanna," Laughing Dog howled above the thunder of flame and the cries of the people. He turned his hands toward the broad-limbed acacia that crowned the hill and engulfed it in greedy, red fire. The tree cracked and popped as it burned, sending showers of sparks and embers raining down toward those gathered below, who scampered out of the way. The air filled with heat and the smell of char, a drifting pillar of black smoke rising up from the tree. Even the fire hunters leapt out of the way as one huge limb came crashing down toward them and broke on the ground, spitting its blazing yellow blood into the grass.

Laughing Dog stood slightly bent, his arms swallowed up to the shoulder in serpents of flame. Barely visible through the light, his face was contorted in a rictus of pleasure, his eyes bulging manically, mouth stretched wide as though in laughter. His hips twitched as though seized by erotic passion. In mere moments, the tree was gone, nothing remaining of it but a twisted, black finger bone jutting toward the sky.

All around stared up at their self-pronounced King in awe and terror. He stood in a cloud of smoke and drifting embers, a dark and nebulous shape. "People of the Savanna," he cried out, and now, in the aftermath of the show of power, in the echo of the billowing fire, his own voice seemed thin and small, as though he choked on the air. "Can any of you truly still wish to follow Cloud now? Stay with me. Fight for your place in this world at my side, and you will have a god's power to protect you—to *serve* you. Leave now, and you will be counted among the enemies of this tribe. You will be exiled. Is it truly worth it to you? To any of you?"

Exile was as good as a death sentence. Laughing Dog had twelve strong, capable men at his side, the bulk of the hunters for the village. They had proven especially capable of providing food in this hostile land with an even more hostile forest. Without them, people would go hungry. And they all knew it. And now that the village's wall had been destroyed, if additional beasts emerged from the forest to attack them, they would need those hunters' protection. Cloud hunched against her stick, bowing her head so that when the people moved back into the larger group, as surely they must, she would not have to see them and remember their faces.

But Ant With a Leaf stood tall, her braids blown back by the wind, ash flecking it. "A murderer with magic is still a murderer," she cried back. She stared at Mirage defiantly as though daring him to lift his bow and fell her as he had Left Rabbit. "We do not need the protection of madmen and bullies. I can hunt, and so can Firefly, and Beetle. And Twig and Long Neck, age may have taken your strength, but it has not taken your craftiness. We will use your help to set snares and traps for our food." She came and stood at Cloud's right side, putting a hand on her shoulder so firmly that Cloud nearly buckled.

Again the people moved toward Cloud's group, but there were fewer of them now, and they moved more hesitantly. Above them, Laughing Dog folded his arms and scowled furiously. When at last the movement stopped, Cloud turned and surveyed her accomplices in treason—far more had joined her than she had dared hope, but still perhaps only a third, and many of these were older, men and women who had turned to less physically demanding work, who were used to shade and stillness. The young— strong and quick, too brash and confident to understand the benefits of long experience—had largely stayed behind. Those young men and women who had joined Cloud had followed family members. She wondered how many others had stayed behind solely to protect their own kin.

"Well," Laughing Dog said, "it seems that our people have grown stronger today. We say farewell to the old and the weak. We will defend ourselves better without having to protect them. We will fight the forest more fiercely without their dithering and second-guesses. Those of you who choose treason against your King, you must leave now. Today. Never return here, not even to beg forgiveness. You will not be trusted. Today you are no longer the People of the Savanna. You are nomads. Do not return to the village. Do not collect your possessions. You are all exiled. Go."

His words were not received as he expected. Cloud well remembered the night Laughing Dog was sent to the wilderness. He had stalked away from the council fire carrying nothing, full of pride and righteous anger.

Perhaps he saw this as his retribution. But Laughing Dog had never understood the people. They did not march away angrily, nor did they slink away in shame and defeat.

Instead, the people, who had been paralyzed by fear and mistrust; the people who Cloud had despaired of, had thought devoid of all sense and compassion, now at last remembered themselves. Both those who had chosen to stay and those ordered to leave rushed into each other's arms. They hugged. They wept. They said goodbyes and made promises. From those who were staying, runners were sent to the village to collect things for the exiled: clothes, knives, spears, and water skins. Food and precious heirlooms exchanged hands.

Many came to Cloud and clasped her shoulders, wishing her well, or expressing admiration for the way she had stood against the King. Some confessed a secret desire to accompany her and gave her wistful apologies for not standing with her. More than one gift of food or medicinal herbs or spices were pressed into her fingers.

The sun climbed in the sky, and still people lingered, telling stories and clasping each other, as Laughing Dog sat up on Gamewatch Rise, looking furious and bewildered.

The fire hunters tried to stand tall around him, but the thick smoke invaded their throats, and they coughed frequently. Once or twice, one of their mothers or uncles or siblings climbed the hill to urge them down. Questioning looks toward their tyrant for permission were answered only with narrow-eyed scowls.

Finally, Laughing Dog must have had enough. He drew himself up tall and shouted for those who had committed treason to leave immediately, reminding those who lingered with them that they were traitors, and those who commiserated with the enemy might be banished as well.

At last the group of exiled formed behind Cloud, many with tears on their faces, none of them joyful. Ant With a Leaf and Firefly carried the body of Left Rabbit between them. Cloud had resolved to find a place to build a pyre and send him to Wem tonight. She didn't trust him to Laughing Dog. She only wished that she still had her oils and incenses so that she could give him the honor he deserved, but that was impossible now.

She surveyed her people, all watching her, all ready to follow her away from their homes and lives. This wasn't what she had wanted. But they were a strong people. They had left their homes before and survived. They could do it again. After a moment or two, she found the Teller and stood by him, looking out into the open savanna. She reached for his hand and took a step, and then another. The people followed behind.

"Well," she said, "I've done it at last. And now I pray I haven't doomed a third of us."

"Why make such a sad prayer?" he asked. He squeezed her hand. "Have I made you so accustomed to regret? Pray instead that you may save the other two thirds."

She smiled. "Yes. It's a good prayer. We must try to do it, try to save the rest. And we must stop Laughing Dog. There's something terrible in him, Basket. He will burn the whole forest if he can. And now there is no one left willing to tell him no. You have to tell everyone the true story of what happened. You have to make them understand."

"I see you give me the easy job. And where will you lead us all, Cloud?"

"That's up to the council," she reminded him. "But if they agree... west."

"West? Why west? What do you have in mind?"

"West is Bogana, where my grandmother lived. Perhaps I yet have family there. And surely they are dependent on the forest as well. If we can find people there who are willing to return with us and fight, then maybe we can still stop Laughing Dog."

"The Great Water. What tales they must have there! And what tales we will bring back once we have seen it!" He smiled at her.

"I hope no tales at all. Tales mean trouble, Basket, and you know it. You remember why my family left it to begin with."

"Yes." His voice was graver. "The plague."

She drew a deep breath, and confessed. "I don't want to go there. The things my mother saw...what happened to my aunt... I'm afraid."

"And when you are afraid," he said, "you will come and tell me. And I will tell you some half-true story that doesn't help at all."

"Yes," she agreed. "Your stories are very useless. I've changed my mind. I do hope you get some new ones on this trip."

He laughed, and though she was tired and sad, she also felt strangely young. There were dark days to come, but she didn't have a tent to hide in anymore. It had been flattened by a giant tree. So there was nothing for it but to stand out here with her people and try to find a way forward.

A man came hurrying up to her—Buffalo Tail. She was glad to see he had come; he was an excellent cook. "Cloud," he said, panting. He was clutching one arm. Red seeped out from between his fingers.

"Yes, Buffalo Tail, what is it? Are you hurt?"

"A little," he said, and lifted his hand. There was a nasty slash down the length of his forearm. The edges of the wound were ragged, with dark clots, as though it had been bleeding for a while. "I thought it would be okay, but it won't stop bleeding."

She stopped and frowned, examining the wound. It wasn't a severe injury, but the flow of blood wasn't good. "We need to bandage this." She looked around. Nothing suitable in sight, and of course, they dared not venture into the forest. She wished she could have recovered some of her supplies, but even the runners sent into town had not been able to pick anything out of her flattened tent.

"Can you do something?" he asked. "Please?" The blood ran down his arm.

"Well, we will have to make do with what we have," she said. She leaned down and with both hands tore a long strip of green cloth from her dress.

The Cost

Clay lay in hard soil and fallen leaves and didn't move. No part of his body would stir when he wished it, nor could he remember how to make it do so. His flesh was only a container, a solid, unmoving thing that held him. He was only the light that filled it. And not just he—everything was light. Everything. He wondered that he had never seen it before. The trees were light. The rocks were light. The grass, the air, the sky and sun, everything was brilliant white light, many motes of it, impossibly small, whirling and swimming and joining and melding and breaking away. Doto was light too—powerfully bright, so much so that it dazzled Clay to look at him. Doto's light was a brilliant gold-green, mingled with points of white that shone and sparkled through him.

Inside Clay were tiny wisps of that brilliant, golden-green light, but other colors as well: blood red and brilliant blue, deep violet and radiant orange, and pink and pale green and the color of stars and morning skies and dew and even rich black that somehow shone with a light all its own. None of these colors held predominance within him—most of his light was the same white as everything else—but they all swirled around inside him with a glittering iridescence. He might have wept at his own beauty had he known how to make the shell that held him weep.

But there was a hole in the shell, and his light was escaping, pouring out into the world and floating away. He could feel less and less of himself each moment. Each moment he understood a little less what a self was; surely it was just an illusion, an agreement between many points of light that had collected together for a while. But now the lights would go away back into the world. Maybe some of the Claylights would soak into the soil, or coalesce in a seed, or an ant egg, or a fawn. He found himself increasingly unconcerned with the question as the lights spilled out of him—as *he* spilled out of his shell—in a funnel that rose up toward the skylights.

Then the gold-green blaze of Doto neared him. Its shell touched his. Doto's light flowed into him. It filled him. It became him. And his own light fled his shell and entered Doto's. It filled Doto. It became Doto. He had so much less light to give that his own contribution was like a trickle of water. Doto's light was a torrent that flooded him, until nearly all his light was golden-green, so bright and overwhelming that he could almost forget he was filled with lights of many colors. They coalesced inside him, joined, ran together.

But this was wrong. He was not lights. He was the shell.

The shell.

The body.

He was the body. The body needed eyes to see, a mind to understand what it experienced. There was no way he could see lights inside himself with no eyes. That had been only a dream, a trick of his mind. And his mind was unconscious. Unconscious minds could not remember the lights.

He opened his eyes and took a deep, gasping breath. Above him were the branches of trees, and when he breathed in, they bent toward him. A wind gusted over him, filling his lungs with cool forest air. He tasted acacia and khaya and acidic earth. Duikers. Pottos. Stem and flower, pollen and pulp, chip of rock, dust from the legs of spiders. He tasted the sun on the leaves, changing exhale to inhale.

He allowed himself to breathe more slowly and watched the branches bend toward him and away from him again. He smelled Doto. He smelled a leopard's fear and grief. He smelled his own village somewhere to the northwest and smelled the fire bearers in it, their odors pungent and sour.

The earth rippled strangely below his spine, or did his spine ripple strangely against the earth? He twitched his ears, listening to the sounds of the forest around him. Termites crawled in fallen and soft wood, chewing with hungry fervor. Birds argued with each other about whose tree was whose, or made wildly exaggerated sexual claims.

Clay's heart beat steadily, a calm and persistent drum. He was alive somehow. He was alive. And he felt good. Strong. Energetic. But surely his throat had been cut. He struggled to remember what had happened, but could not. He recalled the pain at his throat, seeing Doto angry, the forest moving, and then...nothing. He grasped at his neck with one hand, and felt fur with his fingers, which themselves felt strange. Different. He lifted his hands.

They were not hands. They were paws. The fingers were shorter, stubbier, covered with fur and capped with claws. The fur down his arms was golden and white, patterned with dark black rings. The arms themselves looked thicker, more powerful.

His heart beat faster, and all around him, he felt the forest bristle. He decided to get to his feet and bounded upright so easily that he nearly launched himself into the air. He felt his spine whip behind him, fur tugged by the breeze. A tail. He had a tail. He staggered to one side, and of its own accord the ground lifted itself beneath his toes, rising into a hump that pressed up under his foot, steadying him.

Looking down at his own body, he saw a white-furred chest and belly and strong limbs, golden and spotted. He lifted his fingers to his face and prodded it, feeling a snout and long jaw, pointed ears that twitched away from his touch. Now that he was aware, he could feel his tongue in his mouth: longer, settled between predatory fangs.

He was a leopard. Doto had turned him into a leopard. It couldn't be. He couldn't be this. This couldn't be his life. He was dead. He was dreaming. He was dreaming while dead. That had to be it.

Doto. He looked around and saw the forest god lying on the ground, eyes closed. Clay realized he could feel something emanating from the great cat, a kind of energy, a ripple in the air. There were other ripples too, coming from far away—many of them, some of them far more powerful than those that radiated from Doto. He knew without knowing how he knew: the ripples were made by gods. He could sense them out there, massive powers moving and shifting through the world, altering it and shaping it just by existing.

How can you know that, he asked himself, and his mind shied away from the answer. Better not to think of that.

He crouched, perching easily on his toes, and felt the muscles in his legs compress like bent bamboo, felt his tail sway behind him, tugging at his lower back as it caught his balance. He put his hands at Doto's sides and lifted. The cat was astonishingly light. Clay felt he could easily have hoisted him into the air and even tossed him up into the treetops. Again he pushed his mind away from considering what that meant.

"Wake up, Doto!" His voice sounded different. Deeper, perhaps. There was a growl in it, like in Doto's voice. He had no difficulty shaping the words, but his tongue curled strangely between his fangs. He shook his mate a little. "Wake up! Wake up!" Doto just flopped limply in his arms.

His heart beat faster and faster, and as it did, the trees began to rattle all around him, clattering their limbs together, straining at their trunks. He was hurting them. He could feel it. He closed his eyes and lay down, pushing his face into Doto's chest, trying to slow his own breathing, trying not to panic. He shut out the sight of the rest of the world. But it was no good. Even with his eyes closed, he could still hear fresh buds growing in the branches on the trees, bit by bit. He could smell their new greenness, could taste it on his tongue, or somewhere just above it, in some new organ between tongue and nose. He could feel wind in his fur, and the pulse of the gods roaming the world all around. It was too much. It was overwhelming. He tried to go to sleep. He *willed* it—and collapsed into Doto's side.

∧∧∧

Something terrible was happening, something worse than anything Doto had ever experienced. It was like a mite crawling under his skin, burrowing into muscle, gnawing at him. He lay for a moment, his eyes closed. When had he gone to sleep? An uncomfortable feeling had settled in his bones, a weakness. His connection to the forest had diminished; he could sense that easily. The link was still there, and the power still flowed through him. But not as much. Of course. He had given it to Clay. He felt the world around him, and was relieved to find it still thrumming and flowing through his senses, not utterly muted as it had been when he left the savanna. He could still feel the gods here and there, moving about the world.

There was one right on top of him, in fact.

He opened his eyes. A leopard's head rested against his chest, one arm around his waist. Its body pulsed with divine power.

Doto gently lifted it off of him and got to his feet. He looked the god up and down. It was handsome, strong, and, though feline, still unmistakably Clay. It had his wide eyes and narrow jaw. Its brows arched in the same way, and its mouth quirked as Clay's did while sleeping. And it was alive.

"Clay," he said, nudging its leg with his toes. "Wake up now." He felt again that terrible sensation of something under his skin, eating away at him. There was a scent on the air, sharp and awful. He ignored it. "Clay!"

"What?" Clay opened his eyes, and though they now shone golden-green like Doto's, they were still Clay's—wide, startled. "Doto!" He grinned, and then the grin faded. "What…what happened?"

"I saved you." A surge of some emotion he didn't know rattled through him. It made him want to leap and scream and shake branches from the trees. He loved it. "You are alive! And you—you *chose* me." He could not resist; he dropped and pressed his muzzle to Clay's in a fervent kiss. Clay's mouth was stiff and unresponsive beneath his, but that was probably just that he was not used to being a leopard yet, Doto decided. "You chose me, Clay. And you died. So I gave you some of my magic, like before. I healed you, and it changed you. But do not worry. You are just as handsome as before." He paused, considering. "Possibly more."

"Changed me?" Clay rolled to his feet in an easy motion. He looked down at his paws, at his belly and toes, and his ears went back. "I thought— I thought I dreamed it. I'm a—a—"

Why was Clay looking so frightened and panicked? Doto had saved him, saved his life, and given…more than he could afford. "A god."

"A *god?*" He began panting and bouncing from foot to foot, making the grass around his feet fray, the bushes start tearing themselves in consternation at their inability to please him.

"Yes, now calm down," Doto said, a bit cross and a bit more worried. "You're upsetting the forest. Look."

Clay looked about, his ears flicking up and down and right and left independently of each other. Doto supposed he hadn't learned how to control them yet. He bent over, bracing his paws on his knees, and took in deep, long breaths. He paused. "Ugh! What is that awful smell?"

"Which awful smell? There are many."

"You know, the—the dead—and the foul—*that* smell!" Clay looked around, testing the air, sniffing, and then looked at his own body. His nose wrinkled. "Feeugh!" He plucked at the bits of dead animal that hung around his middle. "It's my leathers!" He gave them a tug and tore them away from his body, holding them out at arm's length. "Oh, they're terrible! Why didn't you tell me?"

"Yes," Doto agreed. "They are horrible. I always wondered why you wore them. I thought perhaps liking awful smells was something fire bearers did. Why else would you make your nest smell like that?"

Clay dropped the nasty bits of dead animal on the ground, standing naked, which Doto decided he much approved of. "My nest," he repeated. "Oh no, Doto! My village! My brothers! What happened?"

"I didn't kill them!" Doto announced proudly. "I almost did, you know, like Kwaee, when you died. I was so angry. But then I didn't. I saved you. But the fire bearer with Ogya in it was very angry, too. I think he killed another one. I'm not sure."

Clay gasped. "What? No! Doto, we have to go to them now! We have to save them!" He turned, his ears perked, sniffing the air.

The bad feeling crawled under Doto's skin. He knew what it was. He knew what the smell was. He just didn't *want* to know. "Wait, Clay, no!" he shouted, but he was too late. Clay raced away from him, a golden blur, leaves rising in a flurry behind him.

Doto sighed. He didn't need to run that fast. It wasn't that far away. He was going to have to teach Clay a lot about being a god. He sped after Clay, toward the direction the bad feeling came from.

It took no time at all to get there. Clay was on his knees, gaping before an inferno. The forest burned, blazing with red and orange flames that rolled to the tops of the trees, blown higher and hotter by wind. The feeling of it was terrible, a gnawing at Doto's bones, a sense of being eaten alive. Doto realized that he could actually feel the wall of the forest moving, being pushed back bit by bit by the advancing flames

"It hurts," Clay groaned to him, arching his back. "It hurts, Doto. Why does it hurt?"

Doto strode toward him, the hot, dry winds of the flames blowing his fur back. He put an arm around Clay's shoulders. "You are a god. You are part of the forest, and the forest is part of you. When it hurts, you feel it."

"It hurts too much!" Clay raked at his own arms, his claws tearing bloody gashes in his flesh that healed instantly.

"Then shut it out. Find the part of the forest that hurts and take yourself out of it."

"I don't know how!"

"Focus. Find yourself in your body, and will yourself out. Go into the forest. Feel its life. Feel where it burns. Do you feel it?"

Clay concentrated, baring pointed fangs, his ears flat against his skull. "Yes."

"Now pull yourself out of it. Surrender it. You say to yourself: you will not watch this part of the forest anymore. You will forget it. Do you understand?"

"I think so."

"Good." Doto waited. The tensed muscles of Clay's shoulders relaxed under his fingers. Clay's heartbeat slowed. "Better?"

"Yes." Clay stood, gazing into the blazing forest. "But it's terrible to see."

"We can do nothing to stop it," Doto told him. "We will hope that Father Wem sends rain."

"Wait." Clay twitched his ears toward the forest. "There's something else there. Something's coming."

Doto felt it too, the approach of one of those great ripples of power. Kwaee. He winced inwardly. He would not relish this confrontation.

In a blur and a powerful rustle of wind, his father appeared, standing near the edge of the conflagration, twice Doto's height, his plumage raised, the muscles beneath his fur bunching with rage. If he noticed Doto and Clay, he did not look at either of them. "Ogya!" he roared. His voice was as loud as Doto had ever heard it, so loud as to damage the ears of anything not a god. "Ogya, show yourself!"

Clay clutched at Doto's sides, smelling of fear. Doto wrinkled his nose in disapproval, but reminded himself that Clay was yet new—just a kitten by a god's terms—and had not yet learned how to be a god. Besides, he realized, some of that odor was coming from him.

He wasn't sure what his father was expecting. Surely that little fire bearer with the shard of Ogya inside it would not be so foolish as to venture into the flames. But then he felt the pulse of another approaching god, and as it grew closer, it grew more powerful, the intensity increasing more and more until it began to terrify him. Not since he was a kitten and had been looked after by Mother Fam had he ever felt a god with such power. The earth shook beneath his toes, and the flames twisted and boiled into a cyclone.

"I think we should go," Clay keened into his ear.

Doto inwardly agreed with him but forced himself to stand steady, grasping his mate's furred shoulder with one paw. "Not yet. We need to see this."

At Doto's words, Kwaee's ears twitched. He turned and looked sharply in their direction. His jaws gaped. If he had anything to say, though, he was cut off.

The cyclone of flame twisted and bent, blazing with red light higher and higher, reaching far above the trees. It rippled, melted, and transformed into the shape of an enormous scorpion, standing upright in the manner of the gods. Its eyes were fountains of white fire, its gaping mouth flanked by enormous pincers that snapped above the tops of the trees, igniting their fresh leaves, sending sparks spraying into the sky. It spread four clawed arms and bore itself on four hideously jointed, segmented legs. Held aloft over its head was a massive, barbed tail that dripped molten fire. "Kwaee," it hissed in a roar of flame. Fire belched from its mouth as it spoke.

Doto shrank back from it despite himself, his fur bushing. "I have never seen Ogya before," he muttered to Clay, "I was expecting a hyena."

"You dare encroach on my realm again?" Kwaee bellowed. "What do you want now, Ogya?"

The great scorpion clattered its pincers. Its flaming eyes winked, and following them, eight more spots down either side of its neck winked in rippling emulation. The many eyes of Ogya. "I want everything. I want to feel the whole world slide down my gullet and die."

Kwaee curled his lips in a defiant snarl. "I stopped you before, and I will stop you again. I will find some way to take back everything you have stolen."

"You? The old fool who hides in his temple to nurse his precious feelings? You've had a thousand years, Kwaee, and it's all you'll get. You don't have a savanna god to save you this time. Inch by inch, year by year, I am going to eat every piece of your forest." Ogya chittered, his limbs rubbing against his segmented sides. "But I could make you a deal."

Kwaee's eyes narrowed. "And what deal is that?"

"A thousand years more," Ogya hissed. "A thousand years to grow your forest, to prepare, to plan, to think of ways you might stop me."

"And what would a glutton and a thief like you want in exchange for those thousand years?"

Ogya tilted his broad, flat head. Like wings, the massive pincers that grew from his face banked, one crashing into the forest canopy and lighting the floor with a shower of embers. "I've tasted many things as I've eaten the world. Forest and savanna, earth and sky. Secret caves under the ocean. The heart of the world. All so delicious. None satisfying. But never in all my existence have I tasted a god." His great bulk skittered forward with the advance of the flames, and he lowered his massive head toward Kwaee, who despite all his power and pride, stepped back from the advance of the inferno. "Give me your son, forest god. Open a path to his temple. Let me taste the sweet flesh of divinity. Let me scorch him alive. I hunger so. It aches at me, gnaws at my belly. For thousands of years, it has chewed at me. I know the taste of a god would satisfy me. And I vow it: you will have one thousand years before I visit you again."

Doto flattened himself to the ground in terror. His father would be able to give him over to Ogya in an instant. Doto's temple was fixed in one spot. He had no territory large enough to move it to. If Ogya were permitted into it, if Kwaee bent his forest out of the way to open a path to Doto's secret heart, then nothing could stop Ogya. The fire god would devour the temple, and Doto would be consumed. He braced, grateful to have Clay with him now, grateful to have had the moments with him. He would run, but there was no place to run.

But Clay broke free of his grip, pulled away from him. His once-fire-bearer stepped out and stood between Doto and the conflagration, raising his arms. His claws were out, his fangs bared in a snarl.

Doto almost smiled. Clay was trying to protect him. He thought in some way he could stand in the way of the wrath of gods like Ogya and Kwaee. It was foolish, but Doto loved him for it all the more.

"Think of it, Kwaee," Ogya said. "You will know when I am coming. And all it would cost you is this weak excuse for a godling. We all know what his birth did to you, what he meant to you, how you raged so fiercely that the god-kin turned on you. You must despise him for what he's done. So why not be rid of him? Feed him to me. What do you see when you look at him but hatred and pain?"

Kwaee turned his plumed head. Doto crouched before him, half his power gone, uselessly defended by the fire bearer he'd given it to. He knew what his father would see. He was weak. Stupid. Barely a god at all. In his father's eyes, below contempt, someone who had given away half his god-hood to a dying animal for no other reason than feeble, foolish sentiment.

Kwaee stared at Doto a long time, his eyes unreadable. Then he turned his regard to Clay, who still stood before Doto, arching his back in the manner of a frightened cat, puffing himself up to look more threatening before the oncoming might of two of the great gods of the world.

Clay had always bowed and prayed to the gods, had always been reverential. He had prostrated himself before the mighty Asubonten, had pleaded in obedient tones for Kwaee's protection, had pressed the hot stone of Ogya-Bepow against his sensitive skin when confronted with the shifting bulk of Sarmu.

"You can't have him," Clay cried back to the two gods. His voice was thick and harsh with a leopardine roar. "I won't let you take him. I love him. He brought me back from death. I owe everything I have to him."

The love that coursed through Doto now was so powerful, so intense, he wondered that it did not tear him in two.

Kwaee, the great god of the forest, stared at them a moment longer, then turned back to the massive scorpion of flame.

"Give him to me," Ogya urged. "Now." His pincers spread wider, drooling greedy fire. "Or I will never be stopped. I will chew my way through your forest day by day until it is nothing but smoke and cinder."

Kwaee's plumage spread wide. He put back his shoulders and bared his teeth. His answer cut through the roar of immolation and blinding smoke. "No."

About the Author

Ryan Campbell was raised in Arkansas in a family of nine, but eventually escaped to California to seek his fortune. Instead, he found a job at a university. In 2008, he married his husband David, and they live happily together in the San Francisco Bay Area. There, he tries to write the kinds of books that kept him both sane and strange growing up. He is the author of *Smiley and the Hero*, the *Fire Bearers* series, and numerous short stories.

About the Artist

Zhivago is a freelance fantasy artist born and raised in southern California, where she still lives with her boyfriend and two cats: Tequatchi and Kumatora. The oldest of five equally artistically-inclined sisters, she works in a wide variety of mediums and styles and is always on the prowl for new creative challenges. You can find more about her art and design work, including a schedule of upcoming conventions, at *www.fandomfashions.com*.

About the Publisher

Sofawolf Press was founded in 1999 to provide a venue to showcase great anthropomorphic storytelling and promote the genre to a wider audience.

Since the debut of their first publication, the short-story anthology *Anthrolations*, they have produced over 75 publications including: novels, shared-world and thematic anthologies, short story collections, graphic novels, artists' sketch books, and some things that defy categorization.

Their publications, and the talent featured within them, have been the recipients of numerous nominations and awards, including: 23 Annual Anthropomorphic Literature & Arts awards, one Russ Manning Promising Newcomer nomination for Teagan Gavet's work on the graphic novel *Nordguard: Across Thin Ice*, and both the 2012 Hugo Award for Best Graphic Story and the 2013 Mythopoeic Society Adult Literature award for Ursula Vernon's fantasy graphic novel *Digger*.

Visit their website at *www.sofawolf.com* for more information about their titles, submission guidelines, and upcoming events and releases.

www.ingramcontent.com/pod-product-compliance
Lightning Source LLC
Chambersburg PA
CBHW071158020726
47502CB00002B/459

* 9 7 8 1 9 3 6 6 8 9 4 9 1 *